Challenge to
Musical Tradition

Da Capo Press Music Reprint Series

GENERAL EDITOR

FREDERICK FREEDMAN

VASSAR COLLEGE

Challenge to
Musical Tradition

A NEW CONCEPT
OF TONALITY

BY

ADELE T. KATZ

DA CAPO PRESS • NEW YORK • 1972

Library of Congress Cataloging in Publication Data

Katz, Adele T
    Challenge to musical tradition.
    (Da Capo Press music reprint series)
    "The underlying approach is based on the method used by
Heinrich Schenker."
    Bibliography: p.
    1. Music—Theory. 2. Harmony. 3. Schenker, Heinrich, 1863-
    1935. I. Title.
MT40.K3   1972   781.2'2   79-180046
ISBN 0-306-70428-5

This Da Capo Press edition of *Challenge to Musical Tradition*
is an unabridged republication of the first edition published
in New York in 1945. It is reprinted by special arrangement
with Alfred A. Knopf, Inc.

Published by Da Capo Press, Inc.
A Subsidiary of Plenum Publishing Corporation
227 W. 17th St., New York, New York 10011

Challenge
To Musical Tradition

Challenge
To
Musical Tradition

A NEW CONCEPT
OF TONALITY

ADELE T. KATZ

NEW YORK
ALFRED A. KNOPF
1945

To HANS WEISSE *whose inspiration as a musician and encouragement as a friend made this book possible.*

Acknowledgments

I SHOULD like to thank the following publishers for the use of music illustrations quoted from copyright works: The Associated Music Publishers, Inc., New York, representatives of Breitkopf & Hartel, Leipzig, Germany, and Universal-Edition, Vienna, Austria; Elkan-Vogel Company, Philadelphia, representative of Durand & Cie. and Jean Jobert, Paris, France; Galaxy Music Corporation, New York, representative of J. & W. Chester, Ltd., London, England; Edition Russe de Musique, Paris, France; Russische Musik Verlag, Berlin, Germany; and Clayton F. Summy Co., Chicago, representative of Peters Edition, Leipzig, Germany. I am indebted to the Theodore Presser Co., Philadelphia, for permission to use a musical analysis from Donald Tweedy's *Manual of Harmonic Technic*, and to W. W. Norton & Co., Inc., New York, for the use of an analysis from Walter Piston's *Harmony*.

To Dr. Felix Salzer I am especially grateful for the warm and unflagging interest he has shown from the inception of this book through its final phases, and for his provocative point of view which evoked so many stimulating discussions of problems dealt with in this book.

I would like also to thank Ernst Oster for his careful examination and checking of the graphs throughout the book. My thanks also go to Laura Abbott Dale and Julietta B. Kahn for their invaluable help in proofreading the manuscript and the graphs, and to Antoinette Leger, not only for her careful typing but for her interest.

Contents

INTRODUCTION   xxi

Purpose of book: to demonstrate difference between customary conception of tonality derived from textbooks and Schenker's conception
evolved from music. | Tradition defined. Tradition versus principles. |
Challenge within tonal concept. Challenge to tonal concept. | Discrep-
ancies to which accepted theoretical approach leads. | Practical value
of Schenker's approach. | Choice of composers explained. Reasons for
including Debussy, Stravinsky, Schönberg in discussion of tonal techniques.

CHAPTER I. THE CONCEPT OF TONALITY   1

Schenker's conception of tonality. | Customary conception defined by
contemporary composers. | "Pivot" and "fence" chords as modulating
agents. Effect on tonal coherence. | Present-day methods of harmonic
analysis. Analyses by Tweedy (Example 1), Piston (Example 2). |
Chord grammar or syntax versus chord significance or function (Ex-
ample 3). | Fundamental distinction between harmony and counter-
point. Diverse roles they enact. Fifth association as source of harmonic impulse. Origin. Expression, tonic-dominant relationship.
Fundamental I—V—I progression (Example 4). | Harmonic progres-
sions. Difference from customary modulating cadences. | Distinction
between chords. Harmonic versus contrapuntal. Origin (Example
5). | Contrasting functions; structural, prolonging (Example 6). | Me-
lodic prolongations. Structural top voice. Difference from melody.
Types of prolonging motions (Examples 7–9). | Horizontalization or
chord-arpeggiation as applied to outside voices. | Basic structure
defined (Example 10). | Harmonic prolongations. | Relation of basic
harmonic progressions to primordial structure (Example 11). | Funda-
mental distinctions between chord prolongation and modulation. | To-
nality as structural coherence. | Types of harmonic prolongation. (1)
Expansion of member of basic harmonic progression (Example 12).
(2) Applied dominant. Preceding tonic (Example 13). Following
tonic (Example 14). (3) Incomplete harmonic progression (Example
15). Use in presto, Beethoven's Opus 59, No. 2. (4) Chords of har-
monic emphasis (Example 15). | Function of structural, prolonging
techniques in structural organism.

CHAPTER II. JOHANN SEBASTIAN BACH   39

Nature of Bach's art. | Basic innovations. (1) Symbolic treatment of
text. (2) Stress on chromatic passing tones. (3) Use of dissonance. |

ix

Contents

Chorales. *Association of word and tone (Example 16). New tendencies in prolonging techniques. Cruger's and Bach's settings of same melody (Examples 17, 18, 19).* | Chorale-prelude. *New treatment of form. Discussion of Pachelbel's, Buxtehude's, and Bach's versions of Durch Adams Fall (Examples 20, 20A, 20B). Bach's symbolic treatment. Origin and function of leap of seventh (Example 20C).* | Fugue. *Polythematic replaced by monothematic fugue. Tonal unity of monothematic fugue.* | Innovations in treatment. *(1) Single organic structure. Use of horizontalization in C minor fugue* (Well-tempered Clavichord, *Book I*). *Introduction of augmentation, inversion, stretto. Role in prolongations.* | *(2) Emotional quality. Eb minor fugue (Book I). Elasticity of prolonging motions. Dramatic value.* | *Effect of Bach's concepts on fugue.* | Innovations in form. *New dimensional outlines. F major fugue (Book I). Use of double exposition, development; role of stretto.* | *C major concerto. Adaptation of form to two solo claviers. Extension and stability of tonal outline. Differentiations in treatment.* | *Eb minor fugue for organ. Introduction of free improvisation. New character of prolongations. Imagination of conception.* | *Factors in re-creation of fugue.* | *General discussion of Bach's use of dissonance. Explanations by* Casella *(Example 21), by* Schönberg *(Example 22). Analysis of points of view. Origin and function of dissonances in question.* | *Summing up of Bach's innovations. Far-reaching effects on development of music.*

CHAPTER III. PHILIPP EMANUEL BACH   66

Challenge to preceding age. | New stylistic trends. *Subordination of horizontal to vertical tendency. Use of contrapuntal techniques. Challenge to contrapuntal style.* | *Experimentation along new structural lines. Organic conception of form.* | *Innovations in treatment, Prussian and Württemberg Sonatas.* | Emphasis on vertical *style. Stress of melody. Use of recitative style. Effect of rests. New character of subject matter. Originality of melodic and structural prolongations (Examples 23 to 26).* | Emphasis on horizontal *style (Example 27). Contrapuntal treatment. Use of imitation. Character of melodic figure. Prolonging techniques.* | *Concrete contribution to classical sonata.* | *Discussion of structural outline of* exposition, Prussian *and Württemberg* Sonatas. *Irregularities cited.* | *Bach's main contribution to form.* Development section. *(1) Prussian Sonatas. Contrasts in technique.* | *Vagueness of motion, first and third sonatas (Examples 28, 29).* | *Originality, clarity of prolongations, second sonata. Use of technique by successors.* | *Overlapping of development and recapitulation (Example 30).* | *Expansion of dominant chord (fifth and sixth sonatas). (2) Württemberg Sonatas. Four of six developments regular.* | *Discussion of irregularities in A minor sonata (Example 31), Bb*

Contents

major sonata (Example 32). | *Influence of Bach on classical sonata.* | Recapitulation. *Grasp of essential outline. Interweaving of recapitulation and development (Example 33).* | *Shift of contrasting section to tonic chord. Comparisons, treatment of exposition, recapitulation. Melodic ingenuity (Examples 34, 35).* | *Sonata form as structural coherence.* | Use of dissonance. *Origin, function.* | *Conflict between altered and unaltered tones (Example 36).* | *Effect of motive and suspensions (Example 37).* | *Factors creating dissonance. Effect on structural motion.* | *Summing up of innovations.* | *Expansion of tonal framework.* | *Reaffirmation of principles of tonality.*

CHAPTER IV. JOSEF HAYDN   99

Significance of contribution. | *Vague, elastic forms of pre-Haydn quartet, symphony.* | *Summary of innovations in material, technique, style, form.* | *Discussion of sonatas limited to first thirty-two.* | Sonata form. *New elements in treatment. Difference between Bach's and Haydn's outlines of form.* | Development section, *vital point. Detailed analysis of new tendencies in structural, prolonging techniques.* (1) *Sonatas. Early Bb, D major sonatas. Use of neighbor-passing chord (Example 38), neighbor-note chord (Example 39). Inconsistencies in prolonging motions. Parallelisms in melodic outline. New tendencies in treatment.* | *Later stylistic trends.* | *C, E, F major sonatas. Breadth of conception. Elasticity of form. New character of melodic material. Boldness of prolonging techniques. Stability of structural framework (Examples 40, 41, 42).* | *Influence of melodic figure on prolongations. New trends in growth of form (Example 43).* | *Single instance of vagueness in structural outline. Similarity to treatment in early Bach sonatas (Example 44).* | (2) Quartets. *Transition from pre-Haydn to classical quartet.* | *Haydn's first eighteen quartets, cassations. Qualities found in later works.* | *Haydn's innovations in treatment of form. Opus 9, No. 2. Boldness of prolonging technique.* | *Opus 9, No. 3. Expanded dominant, structural outline in development section. Intensity, richness, prolongations (Example 45).* | *Opus 17, No. 1. Importance of viola, cello. Dramatic use of tonic chord at start of development. Origin, function. Melodic parallelisms (Example 46).* | *Opus 17, No. 2. Contrasting use of tonic chord.* | *Comparison with treatment in Opus 17, No. 1 (Example 47).* | *Opus 17, No. 4. Outstanding quartet. Role of melodic figure. Influence on prolongations. Unique expansion, III– V–I progression. Motive prolonging factor in V–I progression. Remarkable demonstration of organic unity (Examples 48, 48A, 48B).* | *Opus 20, No. 5. Customary treatment of III–V progression. Originality of prolonging techniques. Usual explanation of Db major chord. Role in motion.* | *Technique of interruption; its form-making function (Example 49).* | *Comparison of expanding techniques, Opus 17, No. 4,*

xi

Contents

and Opus 20, No. 5. | Effect of new stylistic tendencies in early quartets on development of form. | (3) Symphonies. | Character of pre-Haydn symphony. | Haydn's debt to transition composers. | Early symphonies of Haydn. | First movement. Clear definition of structural outline. Varied techniques, symphonies in D, C, A major. | Significance of neighbor note, development section, Le Matin, Le Midi, Le Soir. | Comparison with treatment in early sonatas. | Richness, intensity, prolongations, Le Matin (Example 50). | New tendencies in instrumentation. | Slow movement in general. Greater significance. New character of material. Melodic simplicity. Emotional quality of prolongations. Introduction of theme and variations. | Minuet and trio. New character. Robust folk-song quality. Use of irregular accents, phrases. Contrast between minuet and trio. Vital element in classical form. | Presto. Contrast to character of allegro. New tendencies in treatment. Use of rondo form. Introduction of fugal style. Effect on later composers. | Summary of innovations. | Impact of technique, style, on later trends. | Growth of form. | Possibilities inherent in tonal concept.

CHAPTER V. BEETHOVEN   144

New tendencies. | Customary explanations discussed. | Lenz's "three styles." Fallacy of theory. Same techniques characteristic of early and late works. | Use of emotional intensity. Individualistic aspects of treatment. Analysis, Opus 13, grave (Example 51). Simplicity of melodic figure. Importance of rhythm, suspensions, retardations, transfer of register. Unusual character of prolongations. Ingenious use of neighbor-note technique. Effect of tension. | "Eroica" Symphony, funeral march theme (Example 52). Chord-like nature of melody. Significance of rhythmic figure. Instrumentation. Use of horizontalization. | Comparison with Wagner's technique, Götterdämmerung. | Opus 57, allegro assai, exposition. Contrasting elements of theme. Intensification of melodic impulse. Importance of neighbor-note figure. Use in prolonging, structural motions (Example 53). | Major-minor mixture. Richness of expansions. New dimensions of structural framework (Example 53A). | Impact of new tendencies on development section. | Comparison with Haydn's treatment. | Innovations. | Analysis, Opus 57, allegro assai, development. Wide expansion, III–V progression. Function of E major chord. Customary explanation. New tendencies in expanding techniques. Heightened tension in prolongations. | Imprint of Beethoven's personality on section (Example 53B). | Unique conception of form. Opus 57, andante. Extraordinary use of neighbor note as link with allegro non troppo (Example 53C). | Summing up. | New tendencies in technique, style. Effect on form. | Growth of introduction. | Purpose, function in general. | In works of Haydn, Mozart. |

Contents

Increased significance and enlarged function in Beethoven's works. New melodic, structural stimulus. Tension, emotional suspense of prolongations. Effect on allegro. | Extraordinary use in development section. | Opus 13, allegro. Role of grave in structural motion (Example 54). New tendencies in prolonging techniques. Thematic importance of passing chords. Organic nature of conception. Daring use of material. | Introduction as emotional suspense. First Symphony (Example 55). Striking use of dissonance. Origin, function, opening seventh chord. Significance of melodic figure in prolongations. Unconventional versus conventional techniques (Example 56A). | Later development of technique. Opus 59, No. 3, andante con moto (Example 57). Explanations of Marx, Abraham. Challenge of opening seventh chord. Function. Tonal ambiguity versus tonal stability. Diverse interpretations. Daring treatment of prolongations (Example 57A). Effect of suspensions on voice leadings. Effect of tension on allegro. | Innovations in conception of treatment. | New character of introduction. | The coda. Origin. Function in suite and variation forms. Treatment by Haydn, Mozart. New status under Beethoven. | Study of three stylistic periods. "First period." Opus 10, No. 3, largo e mesto (Example 58). Emotional quality of treatment. Role of melodic figure in prolongations. Intense chromaticism of prolonging chords. Metrical grouping. New aspects of prolonging techniques. | "Second period." Opus 53, allegro (Example 59). Close integration into movement. Different opinions as to start. Thematic importance, Db major chord. Origin, function. Chromatic passing chords. Boldness of melodic treatment, prolonging techniques. | "Last period." Opus 127, finale. Use of different rhythm, tempo, key signature. Comparison with "Farewell" Symphony presto (Example 60). Unusual aspects of Haydn's treatment. Impression of coda as independent organism. | Impact of Beethoven's techniques (Example 61). De Marliave's explanation. Tonal implications of "unprepared modulation." Status and function of C major chord. Revolutionary tendencies in technique. Adaptation of melodic figures (Example 61A). | Summing up techniques. Theory of "three styles" negated. Innovations within tonal concept. Effect on form.

CHAPTER VI. RICHARD WAGNER   194
Diverse opinions of impact of style on tonality. | Wagner's reactions to music. Influence on treatment. | Importance of text. Effect on structural, prolonging motions. | Leitmotiv as characteristic factor. Origin, development. | Use in Ring. (1) Psychological. Association of motives. Similarities in melodic outline (Example 62). (2) Symbolic, Valhalla (Example 63). Effect on prolongations. (3) Realistic, Wanderer (Example 64). Intense chromaticism. Vagueness in technique.

Contents

Two interpretations. New trends in horizontalization. Function of motive (Example 65). (4) Impressionistic, Magic Sleep (Example 66). Conflicting analyses of Hull, Kurth. Use and purpose of enharmonic exchange. Unique aspects of treatment. Implications of technique. | *Analysis of preceding measures (Example 67).* | *Connection with Magic Sleep (Example 68). Function of motive in expanded I–III–V–I progression. Boldness of conception. Mystic quality of motive. Intensification of prolonging techniques.* | *Summary of innovations.* | *Influence of text.* | Motive in prelude. | *Study of techniques. (1) Prelude,* Parsifal. *Psychological aspects of treatment.* | *Faith (Example 69). Conflicting aspects of technique. Vagueness of structural, prolonging motions. Two interpretations. Impact of structural top voice. Significant role of neighbor note. Symbolic treatment of motive. (2) Prelude,* Die Meistersinger, *Act III. Psychological implications of motives.* | *Wagner's intentions discussed by Newman.* | *Structural motion test of success, failure.* | *Interweaving of chorale theme, Cobbler's Song (Example 70). Three-part form. Amazing use of prolongation. Richness of voice leadings. Originality of expanding techniques. Psychological significance. Possibilities for individualistic expression of tonal concept. (3) Prelude to* Tristan. *Controversy aroused. Diverse opinions on tonality.* | *New tendencies in treatment (Example 71). Chromatic nature of motives. Abnormal use of rhythmic stress. Intensity of prolonging motions. Extraordinary use of submediant chord (Example 72).* | *Musical and psychological significance. Subtle implications of technique. Suspense dominant factor in prolonging motion. Unique structural framework.* | *Summing up of treatment of motive in prelude.* | *Comparison with motive used in connection with text.* | Wagner's use of chromaticism. *Contrasting effects on tonality. (1) Tristan the Hero.* Kurth's explanation *(Example 73). Explanation through different approach (Example 73, graphs A, B). Conflicting interpretations of techniques, tonal implications. Function of motive.* | *Analysis of succeeding measures (Example 74).* | *Results of harmonic analysis negated.* | *Use of prolonging fifths. Lack of structural outline. (2) Prelude, Act III (Example 75). Alteration of Love motive. Effect of dissonance. New tendencies in prolonging tonic chord. Dramatic conflict in voice leadings. Extraordinary use of horizontalization (Example 76).* | *Unique treatment of neighbor note to intensify melodic conflict. Stability of structural framework (Example 76A).* | *Innovations in prolonging techniques.* | *Summary. Fidelity of music to text, action. Varied effect on prolongations. Growing significance of chromatics. Melodic, rhythmic distortions.* | *Use of music as emotional, dramatic agent. Expansion of range of expression. Narrowing of function as self-sufficient force.* | *Impact of* Tristan *on Wagner's successors. Unconscious contribution to breakdown of tonality.*

Contents

CHAPTER VII. DEBUSSY   248

Debussy, Wagner. Origin of stylistic differences. | Effect of sensory
impressions on Debussy's style, technique. | Extension of established
techniques. (1) Horizontalization. Use of seventh in arpeggiated
chord (Examples 77, 78). | Ninth, unresolved suspension. Character-
istic succession of fifths. Seventh as neighbor note (Example 79).
Diverse opinions of origin, function. (2) Neighbor note. "Girl with
the Flaxen Hair." | "Cadential formula" (Example 80). | Role of neigh-
bor note in melodic figuration, prolongations (Example 81). New treatment of neighbor note, neighbor chord. Characteristic tendencies in
voice leading. Mlle Boulanger's explanation. | Origin of seventh chords
(Example 81A). Function in motion. Originality of prolonging techniques. Clarity of structural framework. (3) Passing chords. Unconvincing use in I–V–I progression. Effect on structural outline (Ex-
ample 82). | Convincing use (Example 83). Clear-cut function. New
treatment of horizontalized chord. Enharmonic exchange as prolonging
factor. Bold innovations in expansion of V–I progression. New trends
within tonal concept. (4) Harmonic prolongations. (a) Expansion
of member of structural progression. Characteristic tendencies in treatment. Imprint of personality on technique (Example 84). (b) Prolonging fifths. Expansion of I–V progression. Elasticity of prolonging
techniques. Use of horizontalization, neighbor note, transfer of reg-
ister, chromatic passing tones, prolonging fifths (Example 85). | Sum-
ming up of new tendencies in use of old technique. | Wider deviations
in treatment. | Growing trend toward experimentation. | Present-day
interpretations. Results of purely descriptive method. (1) Marion
Bauer. Explanation of Minstrels discussed. Contrasting analysis offered (Example 86). (2) Miller. Debussy's use of dominant eleventh
chord. Chord grammar versus chord significance (Example 87). |
Dyson. Succession of ninth chords cited. Explanation as "side-slip"
technique. As elision. Origin of technique. Vagueness of motion (Ex-
ample 88). | Lenormand. Passage quoted as use of whole-tone scale.
Contrasting point of view. Function of whole-tone chords defined. |
Origin of technique demonstrated (Example 89). | Discussion, analysis
of Sarabande. Use of horizontalization, contrapuntal passing chords,
neighbor note as prolonging techniques. Contrapuntal origin versus
vertical emphasis. New tendencies in treatment (Example 90). | Frag-
mentary nature of examples cited by present-day authorities. | Descrip-
tive method used, not explanation. Knowledge of function necessary,
whether triad or thirteenth. | Summing up of innovations within tonal
concept. | Experimentation along new lines. | Tendency toward atonal-
ity. Adaptation of old techniques to new medium. (1) Chord prolongation. New types of space-filling motion. Extension of Wagner's
treatment. Incoherence of passing motion. Effect on tonal stability

Contents

(*Examples 91, 92*). (*2*) *Horizontalization applied to augmented chord. Discussion, analysis,* Voiles (*Example 93*). *Use of whole-tone scale. New type of problem involved. Contrasting results of new and old technique. Motion versus immobility. Prolongations replaced by repetitions, chord outline. Structural coherence replaced by structural design. Principles of tonality negated. Significance as new medium.* (*3*) *Third as dominant factor,* Les tierces alternées (*Example 94*). *Third as symbol of tonal technique. Melodic pattern sole consideration. New aspects of treatment. Inconsistencies in technique. Sacrifice of tonal stability for melodic interest. New tendencies not explained by descriptive method. Chord grammar, scales, not sufficient. Problems raised not solved by structure, prolongation.* | *Necessity for new method derived from new techniques.* | *Summing up Debussy's innovations. Extension of techniques within tonal concept. Challenge to tonality through new techniques.*

CHAPTER VIII. STRAVINSKY   294

Difference between polytonal, atonal systems. | *Challenge to principles of tonality.* | *Inquiry into principles of new systems.* | *Stravinsky's works in two categories. No division into periods. Later tendencies intensification of early trends.* | Extension of older techniques. (*1*) *Harmonic progression.* L'Oiseau de Feu, *Lullaby* (*Example 95*). *Expansion of I–V–I progression. Predominance of motivic figure. Effect on voice leadings. Vagueness of passing chords. Impact on structural motion.* (*2*) *Neighbor-note technique.* Petrouchka, *Easter Song* (*Example 96*). *Adaptation of characteristic figure. Combination of diverse triads. Customary interpretation versus explanation as neighbor motion of chords. Daring aspects of treatment.* (*3*) *Horizontalization.* (*a*) Russian Dance (*Example 97*). *Applied to chord of ninth. New tendencies in chord prolongation. Ingenious use of neighbor note. Mechanical effect of dissonance. New possibilities of old technique. Boldness within tonal concept.* (*b*) Sérénade en La, *Finala* (*Example 98*). *Use of horizontalization. Linear technique. Stravinsky's explanation of title. Primitive nature of counterpoint. Exchange of melodic for harmonic impulse. Dissonant effects.* | *Comparison of Bach's treatment of similar dissonances. Daring use of altered and unaltered forms of same tone* (*Examples 99 to 102*). *Difference in treatment, difference in conception.* | *New tendencies in Stravinsky's use of older techniques.* | *Possibilities of development.* | New technique. *Examples of so-called "bitonality."* (*1*) *Passage from* Petrouchka (*Example 103*). *Use of* F# *major, C major chords. Psychological implications. Structural, tonal definition lacking. What principles underlie bitonal concept?* (*2*) *Further use of conflicting chords,* Petrouchka (*Example 104*). *Growing intensity in struggle. Imaginative treatment of suspense in entire scene.*

xvi

Contents

Bold conception of structural implications. New aspects of technique. Daring experiment in chord conflict. (3) Sacre du Printemps, introduction (Example 105). Simplicity of melodic figure. Repetition prolonging third. A minor-major chord versus C♯ minor chord. Purpose of conflict undefined. Contrast to use in preceding example. Customary explanation as "polytonal harmony." No clarification of motions or technique. No definition of structural principle. (4) Sacre, "Dance of the Adolescents" (Example 106). E♭ seventh versus F minor chord. Three possible interpretations. No solution of problems by contemporary theorists. Sacre, Jeu de Rapt (Example 107). Nature of conflict. Origin of technique unclear. Explanation of chords as rhythmic agents without tonal implications. | Sacre, Jeux des Cités Rivales (Example 108). | Explanation by Fleischer quoted. His "principle of harmonic coupling" discussed. Statement of tonality challenged. Misleading implications of association with past. New aspects indicative of new concept. | Sacre, Rondes Printanières (Example 109). Use of E♭ minor key signature. Definition of E♭ minor chord by outside voices, B♭ major by middle. | Comparison with passage in "Eroica" Symphony. | Difference in conception, treatment. Ambiguity of Stravinsky's techniques. Discussion of Les Noces, opening scene (Example 110). Melodic outline of F♯ minor chord. Conflicting nature of instrumental lines. Belaiev's explanation discussed. | Divorce of new treatment from old (Example 111). Conflicting melodic patterns. Diverse planes. No definition of status, function. Uncharacteristic aspects of treatment as counterpoint. Sacrifice of melodic to rhythmic impulse. | Inability of harmonic analysis or Schenker's approach to clarify techniques. New system required. | Ambiguity of technique (Example 112). | Conventional treatment of upper voices. Anomalous character of bass. Rhythmic displacement as possible explanation. | Tonal versus so-called "bitonal" techniques. Bitonality as outgrowth of tonality disputed. Contradictory opinions of Dyson, Schloezer. | Result of Schloezer's conception of tonality. Necessity to differentiate between tonal and so-called "bitonal" techniques. | Stravinsky as symbol of present. | Extraordinary use of rhythm. | Variations in meter in Sacré, Les Noces. Constant change in time signature. Arbitrary use of rhythm. Comparison of treatment, Bach, Beethoven, Brahms. | Loss of inherent function. Sacrifice of melodic, contrapuntal, harmonic functions. Incessant pulsation versus rhythm. | Linear technique. Definition. | "Back to Bach" slogan challenged. | Octuor for Wind Instruments (Example 113). Essential factors. Problems in voice leading. Use of ostinato. Contradictions in motions. No evidence of constructive principle. Function of voice leadings not defined. | Discussion of interval. Its role in works of pre-Bach composers. | Piano sonata (Example 114). Diverse opinions regarding type and

Contents

period it represents, nature of technique, Mlle Boulanger, Blitzstein, White. | Comparison with Bach's preludes, fugues, and French and English Suites challenged. | Discussion of Bach's and Stravinsky's counterpoint. Superficial resemblance versus fundamental distinction in conception, treatment, effect. Injustice of comparison. | Necessity of evaluating Stravinsky's music on own merits. | Innovations challenge to principle of structural coherence. | New constructive principle not defined. | Is organic unity necessary factor in new system?

CHAPTER IX. SCHÖNBERG   350

Challenge to tonality. | Evolution of twelve-tone system. Contributing factors. | Conception of tonality. Recognition of inconsistency in modulatory principle. Reaction. | Approach to harmony, counterpoint. Explanation of functions. Difference from Schenker's point of view. | Statement regarding foreign tones discussed. Far-reaching implications. Effect on contrapuntal function. | Application of Schönberg's theories. Analysis. (1) Bach chorale (Example 115). Result of theories on tonality. | Explanation in terms of structure, prolongation. | Contrasting interpretations of "foreign tones." Effect on techniques, motion, structural outline. (2) Beethoven's Opus 59, No. 2, presto (Example 116). Emphasis on prolonged C major chord in key of E minor cited as unconvincing use of tonality. Daring innovation. Challenge to tradition, not to tonal concept. Unique use of prolongation. | Inadequacy of customary conception of tonality. | Difference between Schönberg's and Schenker's interpretations. (3) Eighth Symphony, allegretto (Example 117). Cited as unconvincing use of tonality. Stress on E♭ chord disturbing factor. Analysis of passage. Function of E♭ and B♭ chords clearly defined. | Summing up of Schönberg's approach to problems of musical structure. Effects of his conception of tonality on interpretations of Bach, Beethoven. Bitonal implications. | Conception as revealed in own works. | Early works. Verklärte Nacht (Example 118). Clear definition of structural motion. Use of transfer of register, chromatic passing tones, neighbor note, passing chords, embellishing motions to prolong supertonic. Use of "foreign tones." Function as passing chords versus status as chord tones. New aspects of prolonging technique. | Conception of tonality in practice, theory. | Verklärte Nacht, cantilina (Example 119). Use of two harmonic progressions in structural motion. Technique of unfolding. Space-outlining, space-filling motions. Significance of neighbor note. Use of suspensions, passing tones. Distinction between harmonic, contrapuntal functions. New tendencies in treatment. | Demonstration of tonality contradicts theories in interpretation of Bach, Beethoven. | Gurrelieder. Influence of Wagner. Intense use of chromaticism. | Du wunderliche Tove (Example 120). Remarkable prolongation of dominant seventh

Contents

chord. *Expanded neighbor-chord motion. Stress on chromatic passing tones. Vague tendencies in prolongations. New elements in treatment.* | D minor quartet *(Examples 121, 122). Germs of later technique. Growing importance of chromatics. Wide leaps in melodic lines.* | *Independent voice parts. Lack of tonal implication.* | *Comparison of treatment in pre-Bach era and with* Tristan *technique.* | *Atonal tendencies versus tonal stability, preceding examples.* | Kammersymphonie. *Experimentation along new lines. Unusual character of opening theme. Prominence throughout work. Significant role of interval of fourth. Use in later techniques. Fourths and fifths versus triad. Lack of tonal definition.* | *F minor quartet, opening theme (Example 123). Contrast to treatment in* Kammersymphonie. *Outlined I–V harmonic progression. Use of horizontalization, passing chords, enharmonic exchange, neighbor note, and transfer of register in prolonging motions. Vague status of A minor chord. Interesting use of neighbor chord. Originality of expansions. Effect on tonal outline.* | *Difference in treatment of third and fourth movements. Growing significance of chromatics. New status. Inclusion as chord tones. Impact on tonality. Contrast with use in first movement. New stage in Schönberg's development. Forerunner of twelve-tone system (Example 124).* | *Twelve-tone system. Period of experimentation. Explanation of system, status of tones. New types of chord structure, new techniques, values.* | *Discussion of first of* "Three Piano Pieces," *Opus 11.* | *Basic distinctions between tonal, atonal techniques.* | *Twelve-tone row. Period of organization. First systematized approach to new theory of composition. Definition of principles. Series as "tone-complex."* | *Illustration of techniques,* Suite for Piano, *Opus 25 (Example 125). New conception of unity versus principle of structural coherence.* | *Problems of form. Evolution of suite, sonata, concerto out of tonal concept. Use in new systems incongruous. Necessity for evolution of new forms indigenous to new systems.* | *Arguments for and against twelve-tone technique.* | *Steps leading to atonal system.* | Tonality versus atonality. *Conception of tonality as symbol of artistic unity. Function of structural, prolonging motions. Active structural principle demonstrated.* | *Evolution of twelve tones as series.* "Motif relationships" *as unifying agent. Contrast to tonal principle of unity. Difference in origin, function, conception. No functional relations. Arbitrary arrangement of the twelve tones. Necessity for "functional mode."* Growing supremacy of dissonance. | *Use of consonance, dissonance, in tonal system. Differentiated functions. Fundamental law of variation. Origin and use by pre-Bach composers. Bach's use of dissonance as emotional intensity. Adherence to principles of voice leading.* | *Treatment in series explained by Krenek. Degree of tension only consideration.* | *No functional principle formulated.* | *Inherent weakness discussed.* | *Possibilities of development.* | *Past and present. Ne-*

xix

Contents

cessity for true understanding of tonal techniques. Tonality as present-day medium of expression. | Divorce of new systems from old. Need for new methods of analysis to explain new techniques. | Challenge to tradition.

SOURCES CONSULTED   398

Introduction

TRADITION AND LAW *in music. Principles versus rules as demonstrated in the concept of tonality. The basis on which the composers under discussion have been selected.*

THIS book is neither a history of music nor a biographical study of the lives of great composers. Nor should the reader be misled into believing that it contains any short cuts on how to listen to music. It is, frankly, a book on music; and as such it deals primarily with the life of music. It shows by means of concrete examples various changes in style, technique, and form that have taken place from the latter part of the seventeenth century to the present day.

To cover so vast a period, it was necessary to make a basic decision: whether to discuss briefly the many composers who have shared in the development of music during the past two hundred and fifty years or to dwell at length on a small group and examine their works in detail. The latter method has been chosen, because a book dealing with problems of technique and form should offer to musicians the same evidence for the author's conclusions as is demanded of the scientist in other fields. A statement should be accepted, not on its face value, but only if it has been proved to the satisfaction of the reader. This requires a number of illustrations from the works of each composer, with a detailed discussion and analysis of each illustration. It is obvious that it would be impracticable to pursue this method with a large number of composers.

The reader should not assume that the small group included is intended to represent the only challengers to tradition or that the composers selected have necessarily made the greatest contributions to the development of music. On the contrary, they have not been chosen on the basis of their relative merits, their status in musical history, or their popularity among present-day musicians. They have come under discussion because their works are diverse in character and style and cover a wide spread of time. These works reveal not only the various factors that were responsible for the growth of the tonal concept, but also those elements that led to its decline. Thus, because of the individuality and originality of their techniques, these composers offer a well-rounded picture of the possibili-

Introduction

ties afforded by the tonal system, as well as an introduction to the techniques of the polytonal and atonal systems. Furthermore, the composers considered in the following chapters are "challengers" not only because they rejected in their artistic maturity certain restrictions and limitations in technique and style that had been accepted by their predecessors, but because they either evolved new forms or introduced such dynamic innovations in forms already established that they contributed an entirely fresh impulse to musical expression.

We must recognize, however, that these challengers fall into two distinct groups: (1) those who defied tradition within the framework of tonality and (2) those who attacked tonality in order to defy tradition.

To avoid any possible confusion, let me define the word "tradition" as it is used in the following pages. In the generally accepted meaning, tradition implies a custom or usage that has functioned for so long a time that it has become a precedent, an unwritten law. This interpretation can be applied to music. Many traditions have come to be accepted in the various branches of music, but those in which we are primarily interested here concern composition. Some composers have accepted traditions regarding certain techniques, styles, or forms as static and fixed; others have rejected traditions, but have acknowledged the musical principles on which they were based and have molded them to their own needs.

Bach, for example, used the contrapuntal forms that for the most part had been established by his predecessors. But who would claim that in his symbolic treatment of the text in both the chorale and cantata, in his use of the recitative, in his contrapuntal daring in the chorales and chorale-preludes, and in his technical changes in the fugue he was following the traditions set down by Crüger, Pachelbel, Böhm, and Buxtehude? Again, who would deny the influence of Philipp Emanuel Bach's experimentations in technique and form on the sonatas of Haydn? Yet who would say that Haydn had accepted the younger Bach's sonatas as more than models on which to build the configurations of his own imagination? In like manner, the structural outlines of the sonata, quartet, and symphony had been permanently established when Beethoven appeared on the musical scene. Yet who would deny the technical and architectural innovations by which he transformed the earlier concept into a flaming demonstration of his own aesthetic inventiveness?

The term "tradition" also applies to the practices enunciated in harmony textbooks as the basic rules of composition. These rules concern the

Introduction

classification of chords and chord inversions. Although Zarlino in the sixteenth century, was the first to recognize the inversion of intervals and Werckmeister in 1687, the first to deal with fundamental chords and chord inversions, it was Rameau in his *Traité de l'Harmonie* in the eighteenth century who established the system of chords and chord inversions on which the present-day teaching of harmony is based. It is often pointed out, however, that the compositions of the masters do not adhere to the practices outlined in the textbooks. In fact, various authorities have cited specific instances in which composers not only have violated traditions in regard to style, but the rules that theorists have established as the foundation of the harmonic system. As a result, questions frequently arise as to why certain rules for the use of chords and chord progressions which the student of harmony is taught to observe as supposedly inviolate, are transgressed by the very composers whose works are held up as models. Why is there this divergence between the techniques used by Bach, Haydn, Beethoven, and numerous other composers and the rules that surround the use of these techniques as stated in the textbooks? We must assume either that the practice of harmony as taught in the majority of textbooks is not applicable to composition or that the compositions of the masters do not serve as practical models for the student of harmony.

Although the distinction between the practical and theoretical approach evidences itself in various ways, the basic difference lies in the concept of tonality revealed in the music and the concept to which its analysis gives rise.

Tonality is customarily defined as the establishment of one key center within a work. But the term "key center" in itself is elastic, since it permits modulations to other tonalities on the basis of their relationships. Here is a contradiction that has given rise to much confusion. Does tonality mean the use of one key for the beginning and conclusion of a work, with numerous modulations to other keys between? Are such explanations of the masterworks by the analysts adequate interpretations of the music? Did Johann Sebastian Bach, Philipp Emanuel Bach, Haydn, Beethoven, and Wagner hold and demonstrate this idea of the tonal function, or did they recognize tonal stability as the expression of one and only one key? The answer to these questions, we believe, can be found in the chapters that follow. The meaning of tonality, its function, and the principles of unity to which its techniques give rise constitute the major subject of our discussion.

Introduction

Throughout the book, the underlying approach is based on the method used by Heinrich Schenker in his *Tonville, Neue Musikdlische Theorien und Fantasien, Das Meisterwerk in der Musik,* and *Der Freie Satz.* In a study of hundreds of examples from the works of numerous composers, Schenker evolved a concept of tonality that is based on the principles revealed in the music rather than on a textbook definition. He demonstrates that tonality, contrary to the customary belief, is the expression of one and only one key; there are no modulations outside the key, as these so-called modulatory excursions lie within the tonal orbit.

Since the first chapter is given over to a full explanation of this conception of tonality, it is unnecessary at this point to go into further details. It is enough to state that the Schenker method is not a theoretical approach to music, but a practical means of expressing what we hear in the music if we are guided by our aural perceptions rather than by a purely harmonic training. It demands more than an elementary knowledge of chord grammar. In addition to defining the status of a chord as a tonic, supertonic, or subdominant, it is concerned with the function a chord demonstrates in a specific passage, since, as we shall see, the same chord can serve various different functions in the same phrase. For this reason, this method is of as much importance to the student of composition as it is to the student of analysis, since it develops a way of hearing that is essential to the true understanding of music. Furthermore, it demonstrates that tonality is the expression of a single key and rejects the customary theory that to begin and conclude a work in the fundamental key with modulations to various different keys in the intervening sections, is an expression of tonal coherence. The customary definition of tonality in contrast to atonality and bitonality, is the use of one key. The Schenker method adheres to the letter as well as to the spirit of this conception of tonality and explains the various techniques that create and maintain the artistic principle of organic unity.

None of Heinrich Schenker's books, now under the Nazi ban, has been translated into English. His distinguished colleague, the late Hans Weisse, who introduced his teachings in this country and carried them to a further development, aroused a tremendous response through the inspiration of his creative approach. The rapidly increasing number of students and musicians who recognize the advantages of this way of hearing makes it essential that the far-reaching implications and consequences of Schenker's conception of structural coherence on the understanding and inter-

Introduction

pretation of music be revealed to a wider public. It is hoped that this book will fill this need, which is its *raison d'être*.

I should like to make it clear that the musical selections cited have been chosen completely on my own responsibility and that their analysis and the solution of the problems they contain are entirely the result of my own findings. It is also necessary to point out that these examples do not represent a comprehensive investigation of every aspect of a composer's work. For example, in the discussion of Bach, the illustrations are limited more or less to his chorale technique, since it is possible in a few measures to show specific tendencies that are equally characteristic of his treatment of the fugue, the suite, and the various other forms in which he found expression. In citing examples from the works of Haydn and Beethoven, no structural outline of a symphony is given, since such an analysis would take up a large part of the chapter; it seemed wiser to quote various examples from sonatas and quartets, inasmuch as the techniques revealed in these smaller works are equally indicative of the treatment of the larger form.

In general, the examples have been selected for their fitness to demonstrate certain techniques and also because of their compactness. At no time, however, has there been any intention of providing a full study of the various forms that any one composer uses. Where possible, these examples, for practical purposes, have been chosen from works for the piano, so that the reader may easily hear the music as he follows the discussion. Inasmuch as Johann Sebastian Bach was the first composer to set forth the possibilities of the diatonic system (in his *Well-tempered Clavichord*), and since in so doing he enunciated the principles of structural unity that evolved through the system, I have analyzed various examples from his works as evidential material on which to build the foundation for Schenker's definition of tonality. I have then applied the same method to the works of Bach's successors, so that the reader may judge exactly what these principles are and how long they have prevailed.

When so small a group of composers is being considered, a question inevitably arises as to why this composer was included and that one omitted. Such queries spring from the reader's special preferences, his historical prejudices, or his musical convictions. He will ask: "Why include Johann Sebastian Bach and omit Handel? Why discuss Philipp Emanuel Bach or Haydn and ignore Mozart? Why Wagner instead of Brahms?" These are all legitimate questions, which must be answered. First of all,

Introduction

wherever selection is necessary, personal preference, whether conscious or unconscious, has a voice. However, the composers treated in these chapters have been chosen, not out of personal preference alone, but because as a whole they represent diverse technical and stylistic periods within a span of over two hundred years and because their innovations still affect us.

Various elements in Bach's music have had a far-reaching effect on the whole development of music. For example, although the major and minor systems already were established before Bach came on the musical scene, his wider exploration of their possibilities in connection with the concept of tonality was a vital factor in determining the future trend of music. It is equally true that he used many of the same forms as his forerunners, yet he invested them with a new mastery of contrapuntal technique, a new sense of tonal security, a fresh comprehension of the structural problems, as well as with a nobility of spirit and an emotional fervor that are characteristic of him only. It is Bach's music rather than Handel's to which the present-day composer turns for his models of counterpoint. Bach is closer to the artistic spirit of our age than any other composer, in spite of the changes that have come into our music.

In like manner Haydn is more important to the development of instrumental forms than Mozart, although Mozart's contributions to the opera cannot be overestimated. Haydn sensed the importance of Philipp Emanuel Bach's new variations in technique, style, and form. He ventured still further; he not only brought about the stabilization of sonata form, but definitely established the sonata, trio, quartet, and symphony. No one would deny Mozart's development of these forms or the individuality with which he invested them, but it was Haydn who provided the tonal and structural outlines for Mozart's use.

Wagner has been chosen rather than Brahms, not because he is a greater artist, but because his use of the leitmotiv, his psychological treatment of a text, and his bold chromatic technique have greatly influenced the works of twentieth-century composers. Furthermore, the music-drama was an individual form of expression. Because of the close association of word and tone that Wagner established, it is necessary to find out whether the same principles of tonality that govern the forms of absolute music have survived in his treatment of the music-drama or whether the principles of structural unity have been sacrificed on the altar of the leitmotiv.

There may be a difference of opinion as to why Debussy, Schönberg,

Introduction

and Stravinsky have been included. Whether or not their contributions earn them a place among the great masters is not the subject under discussion. What is of vital importance is that these men began their careers as followers of the romantic tradition, then broke with the past and experimented with the tools of music, at times also with its form, in terms that rejected both the traditions and principles of the past.

Debussy represents the first challenge to the bulwark of tonality. Therefore his works, whether or not they survive permanently, are important to us because they opened the way for later invasions of the tonal citadel.

Since Schönberg and Stravinsky are recognized as representatives of the new order in music, it is as necessary to understand the principles that underlie their works as it is to recognize those on which the music of their predecessors is based. Only in this way can we evaluate their contribution and judge their works from a musical rather than a prejudicial point of view. Contrary to Schönberg's belief that the assimilative capacity of the ear is the determining factor, I believe that a more fundamental critique is required; for the artistic principle of unity, however expressed, is still the essential element in all art.

Stravinsky and Schönberg are important because their respective systems have exercised a powerful influence on present-day composers. Each has found an original means of expressing his rejection of the so-called romantic traditions of a preceding age — one in what he regards as an extension of the tonal boundaries, the other in a negation of them. However, since both systems, irrespective of their differences, repudiate the tonal concept embodied in the principle of coherence as it is explained in the following chapter, we must determine what new principles they demonstrate to replace the old.

The music of the eighteenth and nineteenth centuries shows constant changes in technique, style, and form. It also reveals that to achieve the full power of their imagination, composers of one period often destroyed the fetishes and traditions of a preceding age. Yet in spite of the changes in the manner of expression and the new traditions these changes demanded, the structural principle remained intact. Thus, although the challengers broke innumerable traditions that might have frustrated the tremendous impulse their creative needs gave to the development of music, they preserved the law of unity represented by tonality.

The purpose of this book is: (1) to interpret that law and show how it has functioned for over two hundred years; (2) to clarify the difference

Introduction

between its practical application and the theoretical explanation of its function; (3) to point out the various factors, both in the music and in the method of analysis, that have led to its decline; (4) to demonstrate various instances of mistaken identity, which contemporary composers cite as containing the germ plasms of the atonal and polytonal systems; and (5) to investigate these systems, to find the new concept of unity they express.

Challenge
To Musical Tradition

CHAPTER I

The Concept of Tonality

AN EXPLANATION of the individual and combined functions of harmony and counterpoint as applied to free composition.

THE BASIC factor that differentiates Heinrich Schenker's approach from the customary method of analysis is his conception of tonality as structural coherence.

Although there are some musicians, such as Krenek,[1] who regard tonality simply as the key in which a composition is written, the majority agree with Schönberg's statement [2] that it is "the art of combining tones in such successions and such harmonies or successions of harmonies, that the relation of all events to a fundamental tone is made possible."

As an explanation of how this relation is maintained, Douglas Moore says,[3] "In every piece or group of pieces, there is a central tonality, a key to be used as a point of departure and conclusion. . . . Whenever we change key, we begin relating the notes to a new tonic, a new tonal allegiance is established and this gives a feeling of variety and progress useful to sustain interest in an extended design. When eventually we come back to our original key, there is an unconscious recognition of our return and a consequent contribution to the sense of unity of the whole work."

In this statement, we find a clear-cut definition of tonality as the term is generally understood. It is a central key in which a work opens and closes, but which serves as the point from which to modulate to various other keys. Each of these keys in turn becomes a tonal unit through the use of its fundamental as the tonic of a new tonality.

According to this point of view, tonality does not define the boundary of a single key but embraces the territory outlined by numerous different keys. In fact, we need only turn to Walter Piston's statement for a confirmation of this conclusion. He says: [4] "Composers appear to have been in

---

[1] *Music Here and Now* (W. W. Norton & Co., 1939), p. 143.
[2] *Schoenberg*, edited by Merle Armitage (G. Schirmer, 1937), p. 280.
[3] *Listening to Music* (W. W. Norton & Co., 1932), p. 132.
[4] *Harmony* (W. W. Norton & Co., 1941), p. 77.

1

constant agreement that to remain in one key throughout a piece of any length is aesthetically undesirable."

How can we reconcile such a conception of tonality, which is based primarily on the necessity for modulation, with Schönberg's dictum "that the relation of all events to a fundamental tone is made possible"? In other words, how can a succession of new keys, each of which defines its own tonal center, at the same time demonstrate its connection with the fundamental of the key in which a work opens and concludes?

Let us turn to the textbooks for our answer.

Piston says,[5] "Any chord, or any group of tones, can be interpreted in any key. This is but another way of saying that a relationship can be found between any given chord and any one of the twelve tones chosen as a tonal center or keynote." From this fact, Piston points out that any chord common to two keys can serve as a "pivot" or link by means of which to approach the new key. In short, the chord of G major can be regarded both as the I of G and the IV of D, the new tonal center. The establishment of the new key, however, demands the presence of a cadence that, according to Hindemith,[6] "in its shortest form consists of three chords of a tonality, the last of which is always the tonic triad."

The application of this use of a pivot chord and its result upon the tonal clarity of a work is demonstrated in the analysis of a Bach chorale,[7] *Valet will ich dir geben,* by Donald Tweedy, as given below.

EXAMPLE 1

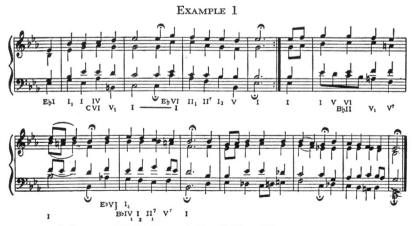

5 *Harmony* (W. W. Norton & Co., 1941), p. 77.
6 *Traditional Harmony* (Associated Music Publishers, 1943), p. 99.
7 J. S. Bach's *389 Choral-gesänge* No. 315 (Breitkopf and Härtel).

The Concept of Tonality

In his explanation of the analysis, Tweedy says: [8] "Let us next consider the chorale from the standpoint of modulation.

"In the first phrase there is a modulation from E♭ to C; the 'fence-chord' which may be considered to be in both keys is A♭–C–E♭ which is IV of E♭ but is VI in C. . . . The second phrase, considered alone, would be entirely in E♭, but the first chord happens to be identical with the tonic triad of the old key [C minor]. The third and fourth phrases are repetitions of the first and second. The fifth phrase modulates to B♭ through the chord C–E♭–G which is VI in the old key and II in the new. At the beginning of the sixth phrase, there is a transient modulation to E♭ through the chord B♭–D–F–A♭ in third inversion. The gate into E♭ is opened but Bach takes one step on the other side by following the chord whose root is B♭ by one whose root is E♭, though both are in inversion. But he now turns back; the second chord in E♭, the I being equivalent to the IV in B♭, in which key he continues and concludes the phrase."

Although this does not conclude the analysis, it is sufficient to illustrate the role that the pivot or 'fence' chord plays in leading to a cadence in the new key. In addition, it offers a concrete example of the devastating effect of such an aural approach on the music.

Let us begin with the first four measures. What does Tweedy gain by modulating through the 'fence' chord of A♭ major to the key of C minor when he immediately returns to the fundamental key of E♭ major? How does this temporary excursion into the key of C minor give greater clarification to the music than if we hear the C minor chord as the submediant of the basic tonality? In the fifth phrase, the C minor chord is shown as a 'fence' chord which leads to a cadence in the key of B♭ major although this B♭ chord is the dominant of the E♭ major which follows. Most remarkable of all, however, is the explanation of this fundamental E♭ chord of the tonality as a "transient modulation to E♭"! Again, although Tweedy admits that the inverted B♭ major chord (measure 6) moves to the E♭ chord, he hears this E♭ chord as the subdominant of a cadence within the key of B♭ major!

Since the value of any analysis is its help in clarifying what we actually hear in the music, the sole factor by which we can judge Tweedy's interpretation is its representation of our aural impressions.

In listening to the first four measures, do we hear a modulation from the key of E♭ to the key of C minor and back to E♭ major, or do we

[8] *Manual of Harmonic Technic* (C. H. Ditson & Co., 1928), p. 28.

3

hear the passage as a motion within a single key of E♭ major? Undoubtedly the presence of a G major before a C minor chord has led Tweedy to hear the C minor chord as the tonic of a new key rather than as the submediant of the fundamental tonality. This implies that any chord preceded by its dominant automatically becomes the fundamental of a new tonal unit. But is this true?

The reader will find in the numerous examples throughout the book countless instances in which a chord, irrespective of its position in the key, or its use as a neighbor-note or passing chord, is preceded by its dominant. This dominant serves one purpose only — to enrich and strengthen the chord that follows by the harmonic emphasis of its fifth relationship. Since such a dominant can be applied to any type of chord whatsoever without changing its status or position in relation to the fundamental key, it will be referred to as an *applied dominant* to differentiate its function from that of a dominant that appears in a harmonic progression. The function of the applied dominant in relation to the succeeding chord can be compared with the use of an adjective before a noun. The adjective intensifies but does not change the meaning or alter the syntax of the word it modifies. In a similar manner, the applied dominant neither changes the status of the chord it stresses nor converts it into a tonic of a new key. On the contrary, it reinforces the original position of this chord in the basic tonality. The difference between the functions of an applied dominant and a dominant of a harmonic progression will be discussed in detail later in the chapter.

Since in the analysis Tweedy immediately shifts from the key of C minor to the original key of E♭ major, is it not more consistent with the music to hear the C minor chord as the submediant of E♭, with the G major chord as its applied dominant, rather than as the tonic of its own key?

In a similar manner, why modulate through the C minor chord (measure 5) to the key of B♭ major, if we regard the inverted B♭ major chord which follows (measure 6) as a dominant of the succeeding E♭ major chord? If this is a modulation to B♭ major, then the new key is retained through the B♭ chord in measure 8, in which E♭ should be labeled not as a tonic, but only as a subdominant of B♭. On the other hand, if we understand the inverted B♭ chord (measure 6) as a dominant of E♭, then we must recognize the motion from this E♭ chord (measure 7) to the B♭ chord (measure 8) as a I–II₇–V progression in the key of E♭ major, not as

4

a second modulation to B♭ major. Either we hear this passage as a modulation to B♭ major or we hear the B♭ chord as a dominant of the fundamental key, but we cannot have it serve both functions and give a consistent explanation of the music.

It would seem as though such an approach, based on a constant shift of tonal center, tended to destroy a natural aural impression of tonal unity by breaking it up into a group of separate tonal entities. Furthermore, instead of clarifying the music by showing how it demonstrates the tonality indicated in the key signature, it complicates it by converting the basic impression of a single organic phrase into a series of fragmentary modulations that both the music and our ears belie.

However, since the reader may claim that this type of analysis is not used in all textbooks, let us turn to an example from a textbook by Walter Piston to see if a different analytical approach is used.

In connection with a five-measure phrase from Weber's Overture to

EXAMPLE 2

5

Challenge to Musical Tradition

Der Freischütz, Piston says,[9] "When the temporary tonics are themselves unsatisfactory chords of the main tonality, the impression of modulation is given, although in many cases these modulations are so fleeting that even a farfetched explanation of the relationship of the chord to the main key is preferable. In the following example two analyses are offered. The first is non-modulating, but necessitates reference to the minor triad on the dominant and the triad on the lowered seventh degree as tonics. The second, on the other hand, shows four changes of tonal center in as many measures of rapid tempo, only to return to the original key of C."

Let us first consider the non-modulative reading indicated by the numerals directly under the music.

Piston's objection to this interpretation is that it "necessitates a reference to the minor triad on the dominant (measure 3) and the triad on the lowered seventh degree (measure 4) as tonics." This is a most confusing and inconsistent statement since, if the passage is non-modulating, the only chord that can function as a tonic is the fundamental C minor chord. Is it possible that the presence of the D and F seventh chords that appear respectively before the chords of G minor (measure 3), and B♭ major (measure 4), has led Piston to regard these latter chords as tonics? If so, it is extraordinary in view of the space he devotes to non-dominant or secondary seventh chords in Chapter XX of his book.

Again, it is necessary to point out that the E♭ major, G minor and B♭ major chords are enriched and intensified by their respective applied dominants, but that these dominants in nowise alter the status or the position of these chords as they occur within the basic C minor tonality.

The second reading, in terms of modulating sequences, in which there are four different tonal centers in five measures, is indeed farfetched. If it is possible to modulate to a new key in every measure, what tonality does such a phrase demonstrate? How can we reconcile such an explanation with the definition of tonality that relates all that occurs in a work to a fundamental tone?

It is difficult to believe that anyone listening to this passage would be aware of the four changes in tonal center that the analysis indicates. In fact we hear these measures, not as a succession of fleeting modulations, but as a motion within a single key — C minor. We have only to turn to the larger section of which these measures are a part, to realize how strongly the characteristics of the basic C minor tonality are defined.

[9] *Harmony* (W. W. Norton & Co., 1941), p. 219.

The Concept of Tonality

As a suggested explanation, Example B shows these five measures as a motion from the opening to the final C minor chord through which the top-voice ascent from E♭ to its octave is effected. In this, the intervening chords of E♭ major, G minor, B♭ major and the diminished seventh on B♮ serve as passing chords. The first three of these passing chords are enriched and colored by their respective applied dominants, but these dominants neither convert the chords they emphasize into tonics of a new key nor alter their status as passing chords within the space outlined by the two C minor chords.

The top voice shows an ascent of an octave. The bass moves upward from C to E♭ but instead of continuing its climb in thirds from E♭ to G and B♭ and on through B♮ to C in a higher register (Example C), it changes its course in a descent of a sixth from E♭ to G, an inversion of the ascending third. This descent, however, brings the final C in the same register as the C of the opening C minor chord. Although, for purposes of register, the ascent by thirds has been halted by the inversion of E♭ to G into a descending sixth, this does not change the character of the underlying technique by means of which the passing chords have been achieved (Example C). In short, it is necessary to differentiate between a basic technique and the manner in which a composer adapts it to meet the requirements of some aspect of the treatment.

According to this point of view, the term "passing chord" has a different meaning from that in which it is generally used. It is not restricted to a single chord but can be applied equally well to a succession of chords, when these chords provide the motion in any clearly outlined space. Passing chords may be diatonic or chromatic; they may be preceded by their applied dominants; they may move stepwise or by thirds, as in the example under discussion. Yet so long as they create motion between any two chords which circumscribe a well-defined space, they will be called passing chords to differentiate their function from that of the chords that demarcate the space. Because of this distinction in the status and function between chords that outline a space and chords that move within a space, the author hears this passage as a motion within a single chord of C minor.

It is possible, however, that the reader may claim that neither of the interpretations offered by Tweedy and Piston represents the customary approach and that these explanations are no more typical of the accepted method of analysis than is the author's.

7

Challenge to Musical Tradition

To overcome any such objection, let us take an example from one of Bach's chorales [10] *Schmücke dich, O liebe Seele*. In this, the progressions are so clear-cut that there is little opportunity for a divergence of opinion as to the character of the chords in their relation to the key.

EXAMPLE 3

I V V₇ VI V₆   I   I₆ V₇   I   V I   IV₆ I   IV   I₆   V   V₇ I

Since this analysis is strictly in keeping with the method advanced in the majority of textbooks, the reader undoubtedly will be in full accord with the status of the chords indicated by the roman numerals. Yet even so, what do we know of the music, other than that Bach has used certain chords that can be identified as belonging to the key of F major? What do the labels we have given these chords tell us about the function these chords demonstrate? We know their names as tonic, dominant or submediant; we know whether they are in root position or inversion; we know when a triad or a seventh chord is indicated. In short, we understand the syntax of each chord, exactly as when we parse a sentence we define the syntax of each word as a noun, pronoun, adjective, verb or adverb. But just as each of these terms denotes the grammatical status of a word in a sentence, so the terms tonic, subdominant or dominant indicate the position of a chord in the key. In the one case, we admit that to parse a sentence correctly does not automatically enable a student to comprehend fully the meaning of a drama by Shakespeare, a poem by Shelley, or an essay by Macaulay; yet, on the other hand, we expect a student who knows only the names of chords, the rules of chord progressions, and certain elements of style and form to analyse and interpret a Bach chorale, a Mozart sonata or a Beethoven symphony.

Is it not more consistent and realistic to grant that just as grammar is a necessary preparation for the more advanced work in oral and written English, so the study of chords and chord structure, which underlies harmonic analysis, is an elementary preparation for a more comprehensive understanding of music? In other words, harmonic analysis provides the

[10] J. S. Bach's *389 Choral-gesänge* No. 304 (Breitkopf and Härtel).

The Concept of Tonality

student with the grammar of music, as the study of word syntax provides the student with the essential elements of sentence structure. Both are a means to an end — but neither is an end in itself.

It is necessary to know what chords Bach used in this chorale, but we also must find out what they mean and what functions they demonstrate in relation to the tonality. To recognize a chord as a tonic, supertonic or dominant does not explain its presence nor show why it, rather than some other chord, is employed. In short, the syntax of chords, that is the grammar of music, is an inevitable first step in the study of music. But instead of regarding it only as a groundwork for the next step in a student's education, it has been made the primary factor in his analytical approach. As a result, the most important aspect of his training — the use of chords according to their varied functions — has been entirely neg-lected.

To know the status of a chord as a tonic, subdominant or any other position of the key is not sufficient. We know only its name, the same as we know the name of a character in a play; yet until we understand the role the character enacts, the name has no significance. The same is true of chords. To label a chord as a tonic every time it appears does not explain its role in the music, as the same tonic chord may occur several times within a phrase, each time in an entirely different character, each time serving a totally different purpose in the music. For instance, every C major chord in the key of C major is labeled a tonic, but every one of these C major chords does not necessarily demonstrate the function of a tonic in a harmonic progression. This leads to an explanation of what we mean by the significance or function of a chord.

To answer this question, we first must clarify the distinction between harmony and counterpoint, the two branches of composition, and differentiate between the individual impulses they impart to music.

The basis of all harmonic activity lies in the relation between a fundamental and its fifth. The proof of this is found in the natural phenomenon of sound, the overtone series, in which the first four harmonics of any fundamental produce its octave, the fifth above the octave, a second octave and the third above it (Example 4A). When contracted into a smaller space, these tones form the major triad (Example 4B).

Because these tones in their relation to the fundamental and to each other represent the simplest mathematical ratio that exists among any group of tones, they manifest a nature-given principle of unity that has

9

Challenge to Musical Tradition

EXAMPLE 4

made the triad the dominating factor in the development of man's harmonic resources. The relationship among these tones is so strong that, whether they appear in combination as a single chord or in succession with each tone serving as the root of its own chord, the inherent unity of their association still prevails (Example 4C).

Furthermore, in the overtone series, the fifth occurs between the first overtone and its octave, a natural division of the space of an octave that Pythagoras in the fifth century B.C. seized upon as a determining factor in his mathematical calculations. The unifying aspect of this relationship of a fundamental, its fifth, and its octave is the essential factor that has converted a natural association into an artistic principle of which the I–V–I progression is the symbol.

HARMONIC PROGRESSIONS

In the numerous examples throughout the book, the reader will find a constant recurrence of this I–V–I progression, either in its elemental form or in its enlarged form as a I–II–V–I, I–III–V–I, I–IV–V–I, or even I–VI–V–I progression. However, regardless of its presentation, the primary harmonic impulse comes from the fundamental-fifth association represented by the tonic and dominant chords. These two chords represent a primordial association from which all further harmonic activity stems. Accordingly, we shall call this I–V–I the *fundamental harmonic progression.*

As we shall see in the following chapters, the three chords that most frequently occur within the I–V–I progression are the *supertonic, mediant,* and *subdominant.*

Of these, the mediant, because of its position in the overtone series and its third relationship with the tonic, is a strong harmonic factor in the I–III–V–I progression. It often plays an important role in the form of a work, generally when the work is in a minor key, but frequently in a major key as well. In binary form, for example, when the composition is in a minor key, the mediant chord, usually regarded as the key of the relative major, often provides the harmonic environment for much of the

10

The Concept of Tonality

second section; while in sonata form, it furnishes the harmonic framework of the contrasting or subsidiary theme. In such cases, the mediant has a form-making function.

Next in harmonic importance is the supertonic because of its fifth association with the dominant in a I–II–V–I (C–D–G–C) harmonic progression. This indicates that its presence in the progression can be accounted for through its harmonic relationship to the dominant. Here the function of the supertonic is to give a stronger impulse to the motion from the tonic to the dominant through its harmonic connection with the dominant.

The subdominant, on the other hand, in the progression I–IV–V–I, provides an interesting conflict between its harmonic origin and its function in the progression. Harmonically, it is related to the tonic as an underfifth in the same connection which the dominant serves as an overfifth. Its function, however, within the progression, is to impel the motion to the dominant. Therefore, though its harmonic connection is with the tonic, its function arises in its proximity to the dominant. Nevertheless, the presence of both the under- and overfifth constitutes a strong harmonic tendency.

Because of their harmonic origin in connection with either the tonic or dominant, these three chords demonstrate a harmonic function when they are associated with the tonic and dominant in the following progressions: I–II–V–I, I–III–V–I, I–IV–V–I. We shall refer to these three progressions as the *basic harmonic progressions,* as they are the only ones with the exception of the fundamental I–V–I in which every chord can be accounted for on the basis of a harmonic relationship.

Another chord that frequently appears with the tonic and dominant is the submediant, in a I–VI–V–I progression. Here, however, in contrast to the II, III, and IV of the three basic progressions, the submediant has no harmonic association with either the tonic or dominant, and consequently imparts a weaker impulse to the progression. Because of this, we shall consider the I–VI–V–I to be a progression of secondary harmonic significance.

According to this point of view, the fundamental I–V–I, the three basic and the one secondary progressions constitute the only harmonic progressions.

It is possible that the reader may assume that these progressions are identical with the cadential formulas described in the harmony textbooks.

11

Challenge to Musical Tradition

Since the essential distinction between the roles that the harmonic progressions and the cadences play in the music can be understood only when the reader is fully aware of the different concepts of tonality out of which they emerge, the explanation and demonstration of their different functions must be postponed until later in the chapter. Therefore, the reader is asked to forego any conclusions until a full and detailed explanation of the function and use of these progressions can be given.

However, there is one point of difference that can be mentioned. The cadences, although not entirely restricted to final phrases, customarily are found at the end of a phrase. They are comprised of only those chords which form one of the successions we know as a perfect, imperfect and interrupted cadence. A harmonic progression, however, can embrace fifteen, twenty or even fifty measures of a work. As a result, we will find many other chords within the space outlined by the members of the harmonic progression. How shall we account for these if we do not accept them as elements of the harmonic progression?

These chords serve a different purpose. Since it is the chords of a harmonic progression that outline the motion from the tonic to the dominant chord, all other chords that occur in this motion are passing chords (chords which fill the space between any two members of the progression) or embellishments of a single member of the progression. Since these chords do not define a harmonic impulse they do not demonstrate a harmonic function. As passing or embellishing chords, however, they do create a horizontal and contrapuntal motion within the harmonic progression. Therefore, to distinguish the function of these chords from that of the members of the progression whose origin and function are harmonic, we shall call this passing and embellishing type *contrapuntal chords.*

CONTRAPUNTAL CHORDS

Contrapuntal chords resulting from motion in the different voice parts also create the motion that may extened a single harmonic progression over a wide span of measures. These chords may be of a diatonic or chromatic nature and they may be consonant or dissonant, so long as they observe the contrapuntal principles that govern the leading of voices.

All chords that support enrichments of the melodic line, such as neighbor-note chords,* chords of embellishment and chords of melodic empha-

---

* There are instances, however, in which a neighbor note is supported by a member of a harmonic progression, at which time the chord assumes a harmonic status.

sis also come under this classification, since their origin is purely contrapuntal. In the numerous examples that follow, there will be countless illustrations of the use of such contrapuntal chords.

According to this distinction between chords, their status depends entirely on the function they exercise in a specific passage. In one phrase, a chord may serve as a member of the harmonic progression; in a following one, the same chord may be used as a neighbor chord or passing chord. In short, in a work in C major, every D minor chord is a supertonic of the key. But it demonstrates the harmonic function of a supertonic only when it appears as a member of the harmonic progression I–II–V–I.

In the usual method of harmonic analysis, no such differentiation is recognized. Practically every combination of tones is considered to be a harmonic entity, and is labeled according to its chord position in the tonality, regardless of the fact that one and the same chord may act in an entirely different capacity in one phrase than it does in another (or even within the same phrase). This recognition of the different functions chords exercise is of vital importance to the understanding of any musical work.

To show the difference between harmonic and contrapuntal chords, let us take two measures from the Bach chorale, *Jesu, Jesu, Du bist mein*.[11]

EXAMPLE 5

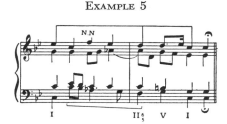

Here, as in all other examples throughout this book, the customary roman numerals have been applied only to those chords which evidence their harmonic function in a harmonic progression. No markings have been given to chords of a contrapuntal nature.

The harmonic impulse is demonstrated by those chords which either define the fundamental tonic-dominant relationship or impel the motion through their harmonic relationship with the tonic or dominant chords. In this case, it is expressed by a I–II–V–I progression. All other chords

[11] J. S. Bach's 389 *Choral-gesänge* No. 191 (Breitkopf and Härtel).

serve the contrapuntal function of creating motion between the tonic and supertonic chords.

The space between these chords is expanded through a bass descent from C to F and by an embellishment of the top-voice motion from E♭ of the tonic to D of the supertonic chord. In this motion, the intervening chords of F minor and A♭ major offer an excellent illustration of the different interpretation the recognition of chord functions brings to a passage.

According to the accepted method of analysis, the F minor and A♭ major chords would be labeled with the roman numerals IV₆ and VI. Consequently, there would be no distinction between their status and that of the chords that comprise the harmonic progression. Now let us look at these chords from a different point of view. They are the subdominant and submediant, respectively, of the key of C minor, but they do not demonstrate a harmonic function: they serve as passing or contrapuntal chords in the space outlined by the tonic and supertonic chords of the harmonic progression. The distinction is between chords that define a space from tonic to supertonic, and chords that create the motion that fills the space. In this instance, the space-outlining motion is circumscribed by two members of the harmonic progression. Instead of appearing in succession as in a cadence, these chords are separated by the introduction of the F minor and A♭ major passing chords. In addition to its function as a passing chord, the F minor chord supplies F as a neighbor of E♭ in the top voice, and thus serves a dual purpose. All passing chords that also define a neighbor-note function will be called *neighbor-passing chords*.

Although this distinction between chords of a harmonic and a contrapuntal origin is essential to an understanding of their individual functions, it does not entirely explain how these functions are co-ordinated to create the conception of tonality we call structural coherence. Thus, in addition to knowing whether a chord is a contrapuntal chord or a member of a harmonic progression, we must also understand the roles these different chords play in maintaining the tonal coherence.

As we have seen in this one of the many examples that illustrate this point, the function of harmonic chords is to outline the harmonic progression upon which the structural framework rests. The function of contrapuntal chords is to expand or prolong the musical content outlined by the harmonic progression.

This brings us to the two basic elements that create unity and coherence — *structure* and *prolongation*.

14

The Concept of Tonality

STRUCTURE AND PROLONGATION

The principle that operates through the harmonic progression has a structural function. The principle demonstrated by the contrapuntal chords serves a non-structural, but an expanding or prolonging, function. In the one case, the harmonic principle provides the structural framework within which the motion of a phrase, a section of a work, or the entire musical organism occurs. In the other, the contrapuntal principle expands the motion within this framework either by filling the space between any two members of the harmonic progression with passing tones, or by enlarging the actitvity of a single member of the progression. In both, the prolonging tendency of these chords is purely contrapuntal.

The following excerpt from the Bach chorale, *Der Tag, der ist so freudenreich*,[12] illustrates the difference between chords of structure and chords of prolongation.

EXAMPLE 6

The chords that comprise the I–IV–V–I progression demonstrate both their harmonic and their structural function since they serve as the structural framework that creates and maintains the tonal stability of these two measures. For this reason, they will be called *harmonic* and *structural* chords. In contrast, the chords that expand the harmonic progression by extending the motion within a structural chord, such as the tonic G major, express a prolonging function. They will be called *contrapuntal* and *prolonging* chords.

This statement necessitates an explanation of what "extending the motion within a structural chord" actually means. How is the motion within a single chord widened through the use of prolongations?

In the graph, instead of labeling the first five chords as I–VI–IV–II–I, which denotes their relative positions in the key of G major, only the open-

[12] J. S. Bach's *389 Choral-gesänge* No. 62 (Breitkopf and Härtel).

15

ing G major chord is given a roman numeral to show its function as a tonic of the progression. This differentiates between the roles of the two G major chords that outline the spaces and the E minor, C major and A minor chords that fill the spaces. That there is a connection between the two G major chords that embrace this motion is evidenced in the top-voice ascent of a third, G–B, and the bass descent of an octave, G–G, each of which represents an interval of the G major chord. Since the G major chords outline the spaces of a third and an octave, the function of the intervening chords is to fill these spaces with a passing motion. Thus they serve the purpose of prolonging the G major chord.

Any chord, irrespective of its origin or function, can be prolonged by horizontalization, that is through the presentation of its tones in succession rather than in combination. In the case of the tonic G major chord, G and B are shown as a top-voice ascent of a third. In combination, they would appear simultaneously as $\frac{B}{G}$. It is the arpeggiation of these tones that converts the vertical interval into a horizontal interval, a space-outlining motion that defines an ascent of a third.

The bass motion from G to G, an interval of an octave, has been horizontalized so that the tones lie apart instead of sounding together. As a result, the space between them has been filled with passing tones that expand the motion from one G major chord to another. In short, instead of showing the G major chords in juxtaposition, in which the top voice leaps from G to B and the bass from G to G, they appear as the beginning and end of the motion in which intervening passing chords transform the leap into stepwise motions.

Thus, when we speak of a motion within a chord, the reader will understand: (1) that the chord has been horizontalized; (2) that the arpeggiated interval forms a space-outlining motion; (3) that the passing chords within this space are of a contrapuntal and prolonging nature, and (4) that the motion as a whole constitutes a prolongation of a single horizontalized chord.

In contrast to this type of expansion, there is the motion between any two members of a harmonic progression, as in the prolonged space between the tonic and supertonic chords in the preceding illustration (Example 5). Consequently, in some instances the contrapuntal chords expand a single arpeggiated chord, while in others they prolong the space between two different chords of a harmonic progression.

The Concept of Tonality

This distinction between the different origins of chords and the diverse functions they demonstrate is an entirely new conception of their use and meaning. It is based on the varied roles they enact in the music and the contrasting characteristics they evidence to create and maintain tonal coherence. Although the conception and the terminology at first may seem strange to those who are accustomed to the more usual method of analysis, the constant reference in every example to the different functions that structural and prolonging chords express will familiarize the reader with the new terminology and clarify the differentiation between harmonic and contrapuntal chords.

Before leaving this chorale, there is a final point of interest that should not be overlooked. This concerns the use of the subdominant of the harmonic progression to support an embellishing tone of the melody.

As already stated, although a neighbor-note or embellishing chord is generally of a contrapuntal origin, there frequently are instances in which the embellishing tone is supported by a member of a harmonic progression. In such cases, though the neighbor note demonstrates a contrapuntal function in embellishing the melodic line, the harmonic function of the chord in the progression is so much stronger that it retains the status of a structural chord. All members of a harmonic progression — e.g., the subdominant C major chord — that sustain an embellishing tone of the melody will come under the classification of *structural chords*.

In this example, C of the C major chord is a neighbor of B of the G major chord. Although C is followed by B, the status of B as a seventh, gives it the function of a passing tone between C, and A of the D major chord. Thus the B that precedes and the B that follows the neighbor note demonstrate two different functions. The one outlines the top-voice descent from B to G; the other occurs as a passing tone between the neighbor note C and A of the descending motion. Here C does not return to B in the form of a completed motion B—C—B, but instead moves to A in the incomplete form, B—C—A, in which the eighth-note B appears as a space filler between C and A. To differentiate between the neighbor note that does return to the embellished tone, the completed motion, and the neighbor note that does not return to the embellished tone, as B—C—A, we shall call this latter type an *incomplete neighbor-note motion*.

This brings us to a discussion of the top voice in which the same differentiation between structure and prolongation is to be found.

Challenge to Musical Tradition

THE STRUCTURAL TOP VOICE

Just as there are *chords* that create the structural framework, and *chords* that expand it, so there are *tones* in the melody that outline a structural motion and *tones* that have a prolonging or an embellishing — and therefore non-structural — function.

Furthermore, as the horizontalization of the fundamental chord provides the spaces outlined by the fundamental harmonic progression I—V—I, so the arpeggiated tones of the fundamental chord create the spaces of an *octave*, a *fifth* and a *third*, within one of which every structural top-voice motion occurs.

In the examples that follow, the reader should understand that the structural top voice is not to be confused with the melody. As the fundamental I—V—I progression represents the primordial harmonic function, so the structural top voice represents the primordial melodic outline. Moreover, as the I—V—I progression is the fundamental harmonic impulse from which all further harmonic activity stems, so the structural top voice is the fundamental melodic impulse out of which all other melodic activity springs. Thus it is a synthesis of the melodic figuration we call the melody.

EXAMPLE 7

Graph A shows a typical structural top-voice descent of a fifth, outlining the tones G—E—C of the C major chord. Graph B discloses the same structural descent, but the entrance of G is delayed by an ascending motion from C. Since this ascent outlines the intervals within the C major chord, it is a space-outlining motion in contrast to the structural descent, a space-filling motion. Although C and E appear in connection with the top voice, they are not shown in half notes as structural tones, since their function is delaying.

It may seem a contradiction to call these tones prolongations of the structural top voice when they precede the tone G on which the structural descent begins. However, the ascending motion from C forestalls the entrance of G and thus expands the top-voice motion as a whole. Because

The Concept of Tonality

of this expanding function, the tones which comprise the ascending motion are prolonging tones. In this instance, the ascent gives the structural tone G a strong melodic impulse as the climax of the upward sweep, and thus intensifies its entrance as the opening tone of the structural descent. In graph 8B, which will be discussed later, we find this situation reversed. Here, the prolongation takes the form of a descending third and derives its melodic impulse from the structural tone. Therefore, in the one case, the ascent imparts the impulse to the structural tone, while in the other, the descent is generated by the impulse of the structural tone. Both, however, serve the purpose of prolonging the structural top-voice motion.

Graph 7C defines the same descent of a fifth that is expanded through a different type of space-outlining motion than the one shown in graph B.

Although the tones that outline the intervals G–C, B–F, C–E, and B–D are indicated in the graph as two separate voice parts, with the structural top voice again represented by half notes, there are many instances where they occur within the figuration of a single melodic line. However, irrespective of the fact they appear within one performing voice, they nevertheless outline an interval that denotes two distinct voice motions. It is evident that G moves through F to E and on through D to C, while C, a middle voice, moves to its under neighbor B returning to C. Thus, though for melodic purposes these tones may be merged to express a certain type of figuration, the motion they outline lies within two different voices. When two or more of these outlining intervals appear in succession, the technique is called *unfolding*, since it is the arpeggiation of the chord that unfolds the intervals horizontally instead of leaving them in vertical position. Illustrations of this technique will be found in Examples 23, 24, 26 and 27, passages from the sonatas of Philipp Emanuel Bach.

EXAMPLE 8

Graph A outlines the same ascending motion from C to G shown in Example 7, graph B. Here, however, the space-outlining motion has been converted into a space-filling motion, through the introduction of the passing tones D and F. This is a prolongation in the form of an ascending motion. The reverse type occurs when a tone of the structural top voice

19

is prolonged by a descent into a middle voice. Graph B discloses two such instances in connection with G and D of the structural line. In the first of these, G descends stepwise to E before passing to F of the structural top voice. Here, instead of G and E appearing in combination in a vertical position, with E as a middle voice, this interval has been horizontalized and outlines a descent of a third. All such motions from a top into a middle voice are prolongations of the structural top voice, since they represent a horizontalization of an interval of the chord.

Although in the motion to E, G may not be retained, it has the effect of being held, since we still hear it above E in the motion to F of the structural line. All such tones of the structural top voice that are prolonged through a motion into a middle voice will be regarded as *retained tones*. The descent from D to B, a middle voice, is a parallel instance of a prolonged structural top-voice tone. This is one of the most frequently used types of prolongation, and numerous examples will be found in passages cited throughout the book.

The third type of motion that the expansion of the top voice reveals is embellishment. This includes every variety of ornamentation that in one way or another elaborates a tone of the structural top voice or a tone of its prolonging motions.

Example 8, graph C is an illustration of one type of embellishing motion. Here the space between G of one chord and G of another, the structural top voice, has been expanded by the descent from C to G. The tones C—B—A are embellishing tones, and the chords that ordinarily would support them are chords of prolongation, since their function is to embellish and emphasize the structural tone G.

The most frequently used embellishment, however, is the neighbor note.

Here, graph A shows a complete neighbor motion G—A—G and graph B two incomplete forms, G—A—F and E—F—D.

EXAMPLE 9

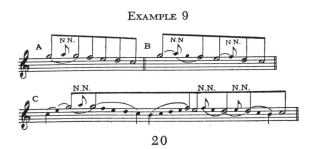

20

Graph C, a purely hypothetical instance, is used to indicate how a space-outlining, space-filling, and embellishing motion can appear within the same melody to effect a wide expansion of a structural top-voice descent of a fifth.

It is not enough, however, to see these top-voice motions function by themselves. It is also necessary to understand how they combine with the bass to prolong the structural motion.

An excellent illustration of the co-operation of the outside voices to extend the motion within the tonic chord is offered in the following passage from the Bach chorale, *Ich danke dir, O Gott.*[13]

EXAMPLE 10

In the graph, the structural top-voice descent from D to G and the I–II–V–I harmonic progression are shown in half notes to differentiate the structural from the prolonging motions.

First of all we see that the structural top-voice motion from D to C is prolonged by a descent from D to G, a middle voice, and by an ascent from A, a middle voice, to C, a top voice. The space of a fifth outlines a motion within the G minor chord, while the ascending third defines an interval within the diminished chord on F♯.

In turning to the bass, we find that just as D of the top voice moves to G of the G minor chord, so G, the root of the chord, moves to B♭, its third. Thus the outside voices outline a space within the horizontalized G minor chord. In the bass, G–D–B♭ are shown as the arpeggiated chord tones

---

[13] J. S. Bach's 389 *Choral-gesänge* No. 180 (Breitkopf and Härtel).

21

that direct the motion. Of these G and B♭ combine with the chord tones D and G in the top-voice descent to define the prolonging motion. Thus they serve a space-outlining function that proves that the motion lies within the arpeggiated G minor chord. The function of the dominant chord in this phrase is entirely different. It supports the passing tone A in the top voice and consequently serves as a passing chord within the outlined space. As a passing chord, it demonstrates a prolonging, not a structural, function; therefore, though it is identical in appearance with the dominant chord of the harmonic progression (measure 3), its role in the music shows that it possesses an absolutely diverse character. The first D major chord is a passing chord in a contrapuntally expanded G minor chord; its origin is contrapuntal and its function is prolonging. The second D major chord demonstrates the harmonic impulse of a dominant in the I–II–V–I progression and supports a tone of the structural top voice; its origin is harmonic and its function is structural. Thus the two dominants serve two fundamentally dissimilar purposes.

We come now to the diminished seventh chord supporting C, a structural tone. This chord is of extreme interest because it shows that a structural tone can be supported by a neighbor chord, since F♯ is a neighbor note of G of the prolonged tonic that precedes it, and of the G minor chord that follows. It is also plain that C, though a structural tone, is at the same time a passing tone between D and B♭ of the G minor chord. Therefore, C has the function of a structural passing tone, since it is a member of the structural top voice.

Just as in a preceding example we saw that the structural function of a subdominant in the harmonic progression was stronger than the contrapuntal and prolonging function of the embellishing tone it supported, so in this instance the structural function of C in the top voice is stronger than the contrapuntal and prolonging function of the neighbor chord that supports it. As a result, this F♯ chord is a structural neighbor-passing chord in contrast to the prolonging neighbor-passing chord that occurs in a prolonging instead of in a structural motion.

In the analysis of these three measures of the chorale, we have seen that the outside voices define a motion outlining the G minor tonality — the structural top voice, through the descent of a fifth, and the bass, through the harmonic progression. Because of the structural function each of these motions demonstrates, they constitute, when combined, the structural framework of these measures in which all further activity in the

The Concept of Tonality

form of prolongations occurs. This fundamental melodic and harmonic framework is the *basic structure* that creates and maintains the tonal stability. Therefore, the term *basic structure* will be applied to the melodic and harmonic framework outlined by the structural top voice and the basic harmonic progression.

However, just as these three measures define a basic structure, it is logical to assume that the measures that follow also will disclose other basic structures, each of which outlines its own structural top-voice motion and its harmonic progression. Although each of these basic structures constitutes an organic unit in itself, a study of the chorale in its entirety would show that these basic structures are themselves prolongations of a single structural top-voice motion and a single harmonic progression that embrace every smaller phrase and section of the work. Without such an integration of the various basic structures into a single all-inclusive melodic and harmonic framework, these basic structures would not be organic parts of an organic whole.

The single all-embracing structural outline is the *primordial structure*, the protoplasm out of which all structural and prolonging motions evolve. As the fundamental source from which all further melodic and harmonic activity springs, it is the synthesis of all other motions that are offshoots of it. The primordial structure is, therefore, the composite outline of all basic structures and prolonging motions that expand it.

Thus far the function of prolongation has been restricted to contrapuntal chords. However, in relating the smaller phrases and sections of a work, that is, the basic structures, to the structural outline of the whole, the primordial structure, it becomes apparent that the basic harmonic progressions are themselves prolongations of the primordial harmonic progression. Therefore, we find that there are harmonic as well as contrapuntal chords of prolongation. To differentiate between them, it is necessary to demonstrate the various types of harmonic prolongation that are used to expand the primordial progression.

HARMONIC PROLONGATIONS

All harmonic progressions other than that which appears in the primordial structure, are *harmonic prolongations*. To illustrate this point, let us turn to the first movement of Haydn's sonata in B minor [14] to see the

[14] *Kritische Gesamtausgabe* No. 32; Breitkopf and Härtel Edition, Vol. IV, No. 38; Peters Edition, Vol. IV, No. 33.

Challenge to Musical Tradition

various harmonic prolongations of the primordial I–III–V–I progression that provide the three sections of sonata form; the exposition, development, and recapitulation.

EXAMPLE 11

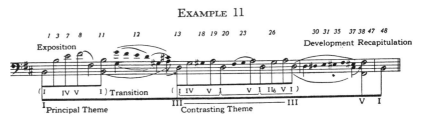

To clarify the distinction between harmonic and contrapuntal chords, we have applied roman numerals only to those chords that demonstrate their harmonic function in a harmonic progression. To differentiate between the primordial progression and prolonging progressions, the prolongations are enclosed in parentheses and marked in smaller numerals. In the case of applied dominants, arrows point to the chords stressed. Other types of harmonic prolongations, such as the incomplete harmonic progression and the II as a chord of harmonic emphasis, are shown in parentheses. All chords that are unidentified are to be considered contrapuntal chords of prolongation.

Here we see that the basic I–IV–V–I progression, the harmonic foundation on which the principal theme rests, outlines a motion within the tonic B minor chord, the fundamental of the tonality. This harmonic progression is an offshoot of the tonic chord of the primordial structure. Although this progression is widened by passing and embellishing chords, they are omitted in the graph so as to emphasize the harmonic prolongation of the opening B minor chord that outlines the essential motion of the first eight measures. A so-called "transition" from the tonic to the mediant D major chord is effected by means of a motion from the B minor through the A major to the D major chord. This A major chord has the function of an applied dominant and thus enriches and intensifies the D major chord; it is a type of harmonic prolongation that will be fully discussed later in the chapter.

The motion from the B minor to the A major chord is also of interest because it illustrates the use of contrapuntal chords of prolongation. Instead of moving directly from the B minor to the A major chord, Haydn has made a detour through the G major chord (measure 11) and the

24

The Concept of Tonality

diminished seventh chord on G♯ (measure 12). In addition, the motion has been further extended by means of a stepwise descent in the middle voice from G in an upper register through F♯, E, and D to C♯ of the A major chord. Thus, in these first twelve measures, we have a clear-cut definition of the difference between a harmonic and a contrapuntal prolongation.

This brings us to the mediant D major chord of the primordial progression, within whose structural outline the contrasting or subsidiary theme appears.

The graph shows three harmonic progressions, each of which denotes a motion within the D major chord. Consequently, these progressions are harmonic prolongations of the D major chord, the mediant of the B minor tonality. From this point of view, the D major chord represents not a modulation to the new key of the relative major, but the expanded mediant of the primordial progression that outlines a motion within a single tonality of B minor.

Since the smaller numerals defining the harmonic progressions show the D major chord as a tonic, the reader might be led to believe that the distinction between a conception of tonality based on modulation and a conception based on prolongation is one of terminology only. This, however, is not the case.

To indicate that these progressions are prolongations of the mediant chord, it is necessary to demonstrate that they outline a motion within the D major chord. Therefore it is logical to identify the D major chord as the tonic of the harmonic prolongations. However, this D major chord is not regarded as the tonic of the key of D major, a new tonal center, but as the fundamental of a prolonging motion that extends the space within the mediant chord of the primordial progression. Thus, there is no motion away from the fundamental key, as in a modulation, but, instead, an expansion of a member of the primordial progression that defines a single tonality.

Turning once more to the graph, we find that the mediant chord that concludes the exposition and opens the development section does not pass directly to the dominant, but moves to the C♯ major chord, the applied dominant of the F♯ minor chord that follows. However, the space between the D and C♯ major chords itself is greatly expanded through an ascending motion from D, the root of the D major chord, to E♯ a middle voice, the third of the C♯ major chord. The exchange of the minor for the major

25

dominant in the succeeding measures further prolongs the motion of the development section.

This ascent from D to E♯ in which F♯ appears as a neighbor note, is a contrapuntal prolongation of the motion from the D to the C♯ major chord. Instead of descending directly to C♯, D ascends chromatically to a middle voice and thus enriches and intensifies the entrance of the C♯ major chord. Moreover, any one of these passing chords could have been expanded by means of its own harmonic prolongation without in any way destroying the coherence of the motion from the D major to the F♯ minor chord.

Here we see how the expansion of the primordial harmonic progression I–III–V–I has provided the essential elements that comprise the structural outline of sonata form. The expansion not only contributes to the richness, color, and variety of the melodic impulse, but at the same time emphasizes the distinctive characteristics and qualities inherent in the tonic, mediant, and dominant chords and thus creates the necessary contrast within the tonal framework. However, the relationship among these chords is so strong, that although they function individually as expanded structural organisms, they also function collectively as a single structural unit to outline a motion within one and the same chord, and, therefore, within one and only one tonality.

It must be apparent, at this point, that modulation and prolongation are by no means synonymous, but that they represent two totally contrasting conceptions of tonality and stem from two diametrically opposed points of view.

The one conception, based on the cadence as a modulating agent, admits the presence of many different tonalities within a work or a movement of a work, so long as the main key is established at the beginning and the end. The other conception, based on the prolongation of a single structural framework, admits of no modulations away from the fundamental key. Here, all phrases and sections of a work or a movement of a work, in spite of the melodic and harmonic contrast they offer, constitute either a harmonic prolongation of a member of the primordial progression, a passing motion between two members of the progression, or a harmonic prolongation of a passing or embellishing chord. Thus, however varied and contrasting is the effect of these expansions, they all come within the boundary of the fundamental tonality, since they are all offshoots of the primordial structure that outlines a motion within a single key.

26

The Concept of Tonality

Here, finally, the distinction between a cadence and a harmonic prolongation, that is the harmonic progression of a basic structure, can be defined.

In the analyses offered by Tweedy and Piston, the cadence serves as a means of establishing the tonal characteristics of the new key. Thus it is a modulating agent that diverts the motion away from the fundamental tonality to a new tonal center that functions as a self-sufficient tonal entity. The harmonic progression, on the other hand, defines a motion that prolongs a member of the primordial progression. As in the case of the D major chord in the example from the Haydn sonata in B minor, the three prolongations do not establish the key of D major as a new tonality or tonal center, but demonstrate their connection with the fundamental tonality of B minor as an expansion of the mediant chord. Thus, instead of appearing as tonal entities, these progressions are organic parts of the primordial structure whose tonal integrity they help to maintain. Therefore, the basic distinction between a cadence and a harmonic progression is that the function of one is to establish new and different tonalities, while the function of the other is to preserve and sustain a single all-embracing motion that defines the one tonality indicated in the key signature.

The possibilities such a single prolonged structure offers are endless, because its own stability permits the use of every type of prolonging and embellishing chord and the richness and contrast these chords contribute without endangering the integrity of the fundamental tonality. The outline of the first movement of the B minor sonata (Example 11) offers a good illustration of this point. Here the passing chords that expand the tonic-mediant and the mediant-dominant progressions inject entirely new and different color values into the primordial I—III—V—I progression and thus intensify and enrich the motion. In like manner, the passing and embellishing chords and embellishing motions that prolong a basic structure may be of a highly chromatic nature and thus give a varied color effect to the motion defined by the basic progression. Although such chromatic prolongations may appear to be so remote from the fundamental key that they usually are regarded as modulations to a new key, the fact that they demonstrate a contrapuntal function nullifies the possibility that they can exert any influence upon the tonal character of the motion outlined by the harmonic progression.

According to this point of view, any type of chord, diatonic or chromatic, consonant or dissonant, can appear as a prolongation of a basic structure without weakening the tonality or moving outside the framework defined by the harmonic progression. Therefore, the passage from *Der Freischütz* (Example 2), which Piston has offered as an illustration of modulation, is, on the contrary, a remarkable instance of the richness and contrast passing chords can provide without impairing the character of the fundamental tonality. To regard these passing chords as new tonal centers, or as modulations away from the established key, when their sole function is to fill the space of an octave within a horizontalized C minor chord, the tonic of the key, imparts to these contrapuntal prolonging chords a harmonic and structural function they do not demonstrate.

However, in explaining tonality as the expansion of a single primordial structure, the author does not intend to suggest that the analytical approach used to interpret the music is the approach used to create the music. To clarify a new and different conception of tonality it was necessary to coin a new terminology to avoid the confusion that might have resulted had terms already used in connection with the accepted method of analysis been given a new and different connotation. Therefore, for purposes of analysis, we have defined the entire structural framework as the primordial structure, its offshoots as basic structures, which in turn may give rise to various other harmonic progressions as further stages of prolongation. Although this breaks down the composition into its smaller phrases and sections, it is not done as a means of dissection, but rather to relate all parts of a work, large and small, to an all-inclusive structural framework. This not only enables us, by differentiating between the various types of chords and the functions they demonstrate, to understand the various techniques the composer used, but also helps us to hear these smaller phrases as integral parts of an organic whole rather than as separate tonal entities. Thus, though this method is of the greatest importance, not only as a means of interpretation, but also for its larger implication as a new aural approach, it would be erroneous to assume that it is meant to apply to the creative process as well.

No one, not even the composer himself, can explain how the creative impulse works; no one can attempt to show the specific fragment of a melody, the part of a motive, or the single rhythmic figure that generates the melodic content of a work or movement of a work. Consequently, when we speak of a primordial structure from which all other motions stem, we do not mean to imply that a composer has a definite type of structural framework in mind from which he constructs the prolongations. If

The Concept of Tonality

this were true, the primordial structure would necessarily be a product of the conscious mind. However, since it originates in the horizontalized chord, an artistic adaptation of a nature-given phenomenon, it may represent an elemental force that lies deeply imbedded in the unconscious.

It is not our concern to consider how much of the creative process is the working of the conscious mind or how much it is influenced by the unconscious. These are problems for the philosopher and psychologist to solve. Our aims lie in a different direction — to understand the artistic and technical principles through which a composer maintains a single tonal organism as the expression of structural coherence.

Although we have seen how the prolongations expand the primordial framework to outline the characteristic elements of sonata form, it is also necessary to know how they function in the smaller phrases of a work, such as the following passage from the Bach chorale, *Auf meinen lieben Gott.*[15]

EXAMPLE 12

These measures show a basic I—III—V—I progression that outlines a motion within the G minor-major tonality. It is the wide expansion of the mediant B♭ major chord that is of primary interest, since it indicates the use of two harmonic prolongations. Although each defines the same harmonic progression, the expanding motions differ. In the first of these (measures 1—2) there is a stepwise descent from B♭ of the tonic to E♭ the third of the supertonic chord, in which the intervening tones are space-

[15] J. S. Bach's *389 Choral-gesänge* No. 28 (Breitkopf and Härtel).

fillers. In the second progression (measures 2–5), there is a descent from B♭ to E♮, the altered third of the supertonic, but here the prolongations are of a different nature.

First of all, the descent is not stepwise but discloses two parallel neighbor motions, A—B♭, F♯—G. The inverted F major chord clearly indicates its function as a neighbor of the B♭ chords between which it enters. The D major chord, on the other hand, although inverted, has the impulse of an applied dominant in stressing the G minor chord that follows. Although the effect of an applied dominant is somewhat weakened when the chord is inverted, this lessening of the harmonic impulse is compensated for, when, as in the D major chord, the third appears as a neighbor of the root of the succeeding chord, and thus assumes the role of a leading tone.

If we compare the function of the G minor chords in the two descents prolonging the motion from the tonic to the supertonic chord (measures 1 and 3), we find that both are passing chords, though the first enters in a stepwise descent and the second is approached through its applied dominant. Although the function is the same, the technique varies through the substitution of F♯ in the D major chord, for the A that appears in the first descent.

Does it not give greater clarity to this entire passage to hear these two progressions as a prolongation of the mediant chord of the basic progression rather than as a modulation to a new tonal center? Does not the differentiation between contrapuntal and harmonic chords, and chords of structure and prolongation, give us a better understanding of the music and the techniques Bach used than to label all chords according to their positions in the keys of G minor and B♭ major?

It again must be pointed out that although the B♭ major chords in the two harmonic progressions are indicated by the roman numeral I, this I does not define their function as tonics of a new key but as tonics in a prolonging motion that extends the influence and sphere of the mediant chord.

The two final measures are of interest because they disclose how the expansion of the mediant-dominant chords engenders two different kinds of motion in the outside voices. In the top voice, the descent from D to A shows a passing motion that is embellished by C, the final quarter of measure 5, as a neighbor of the preceding B♭. Since C does not return to B♭, but passes instead to A of the D major chord, it comes under the type of em-

The Concept of Tonality

bellishment already described as the incomplete neighbor-note motion. The bass also is prolonged by an embellishing motion. Instead of passing directly from B♭ of the mediant to D of the dominant chord, there is an ascent from B♭ to E♭ with a detour through D and C, to D of the D major chord. It is apparent, however, that the embellishments in the bass are engendered by the top-voice descent, since they support the passing tones and incomplete neighbor note in the top-voice motion from D to A. Thus the chords that result from these passing and embellishing tones are passing-embellishing chords of prolongation which enrich the mediant-dominant progression.

This conception of prolongation, both as it concerns the harmonic progressions expanding the mediant B♭ major chord and the passing-embellishing chords prolonging the motion to the dominant leaves the structural organism intact and thus assures the coherence of this passage as a demonstration of a single G minor-major tonality.

Since our discussion of harmonic prolongations has been directed thus far to the harmonic progression, let us turn to another type, the *applied dominant,* to which reference already has been made.

Under this heading come the small V—I progressions in which a chord, regardless of its status in the phrase, is preceded by its dominant. As we saw in the Tweedy and Piston examples (Examples 1 and 2) as well as in the graph of the Haydn sonata in B minor (Example 11), these dominants demonstrate a harmonic but not a structural function, since their sole connection is with the chord that follows. Therefore, since their primary purpose is to emphasize and enrich the chord they precede, they must be differentiated from those dominants that demonstrate a structural function within a harmonic progression. Since this type of dominant can be applied to any chord whatsoever, whether it be a chord of the harmonic progression or a chromatic passing chord, it will be referred to as an *applied dominant* and will be indicated by an arrow pointing to the chord emphasized.

The following measures from Bach's *Christus der du bist der helle Tag* [16] illustrate the use of an applied dominant.

As a whole, the passage defines a I—III—V—I progression, a harmonic prolongation of the primordial progression. The motion from the tonic F minor to the mediant A♭ major chord is not direct but through the E♭ major chord, the applied dominant of the mediant. At first the E♭ chord

---

[16] Orgel, *Band V, Choralvariationen* (Peters Edition).

EXAMPLE 13

appears in inversion, but the G in the bass moves to the root E♭ which lends the A♭ chord the full harmonic impulse of its fifth relationship. This example provides an interesting illustration of the different effects the inverted and root positions of this E♭ chord produce. Had the chord been presented in inversion only, the retention of G in the bass as a passing tone between F and A♭, together with E♭ in the top voice as an embellishment of C, would have given rise to an embellishing-passing chord with a strong contrapuntal tendency. However, the introduction of E♭ in the bass on the second eighth note changes the contrapuntal to a strong harmonic impulse through the fifth association the chord in root position demonstrates with the A♭ major chord that follows. There are instances, however, in which the inverted applied dominant does not appear as a passing chord and consequently does exercise a harmonic function. We have seen this type of applied dominant in the preceding illustration from the chorale, *Auf meinen lieben Gott* (Example 12) in which the inverted D major chord (measure 3) through the leading tone effect of its third, F♯, gives harmonic stress to the succeeding G minor chord.

Accordingly, the applied dominant can demonstrate three different degrees of emphasis. The harmonic impulse is always strongest when the chord is in root position. Next in the harmonic pressure it exerts, is when, in inversion, the third of the chord serves as a neighbor of the root of the succeeding chord in which it has the effect of a leading tone. Its weakest expression of harmonic influence occurs when it appears in inversion as a passing chord, since the contrapuntal function it assumes tends to offset its inherent harmonic impulse.

Another form of this type of applied dominant is the diminished seventh chord which, whether in root position or inversion, as a VII—I, is a substitute for the small V—I relationship.

The Concept of Tonality

A second type of applied dominant is the smaller I—V progression in which the dominant, coming from a tonic, does not return to the tonic, but instead proceeds to another chord in the motion. Its function is not structural but prolonging, since it expands the motion within the tonic chord that precedes it. Although of harmonic origin, it serves the sole purpose of prolongation.

An excellent example of this type of applied dominant is indicated in the Bach chorale, *Hilf Herr Jesu, lass gelingen.*[17]

EXAMPLE 14

The motion as a whole represents a tonic-mediant progression, in which the tonic is prolonged by a I—V—I progression as well as by the applied dominant, the D major chord, that immediately precedes the mediant (measure 4). This passage is of extreme interest because it discloses three D major chords, each of which defines a different function. The first D major chord (measure 2) is shown as a dominant of a I—V—I harmonic progression; the second (measure 3) as a neighbor-passing chord, with C, a passing tone between D and Bb of the G minor chord, and F♯ in the bass, an under neighbor of the G which precedes and follows; the third, as the second type of applied dominant that succeeds the tonic chord it prolongs.

There might be a tendency to assume that the inverted D major chord (measure 3) and the inverted D major chord in the chorale, *Auf meinen lieben Gott* (Example 12, measure 3) are identical and demonstrate the same function. This, however, would be erroneous, since in the earlier example the D major chord exercises the harmonic impulse of an applied dominant while in the example under discussion it defines the contrapuntal function of a neighbor-passing chord within a G minor chord. In short, a chord is an applied dominant only when it emphasizes the entrance of a chord, but not when it already is preceded by the same chord that follows. In such instances, it serves in root position as the dominant

---

[17] J. S. Bach's *389 Choral-gesänge* No. 173 (Breitkopf and Härtel).

of a harmonic prolongation, and, in inversion, as a neighbor or neighbor-passing chord.

We come now to the third D major chord, the applied dominant. There is a descent from D, a top, to A, a middle, voice, with D, a retained tone, emerging as a top voice of the mediant B♭ major chord. The bass shows a I—V—I progression, then a neighbor-note motion around G, after which it descends to D of the dominant chord. This dominant chord does not direct the structural motion to the tonic, but passes instead to the mediant of the basic progression. Consequently, its function is not structural but prolonging, since it expands the tonic chord in a motion to the mediant. Therefore, though it asserts a harmonic impulse in connection with the tonic G minor chord that precedes it, this impulse takes the form of a prolonging rather than a structural function, since to define a structural function it would necessarily move to a tonic chord outlining a I—V—I progression. This type of applied dominant points to the tonic that precedes it, while the small V—I emphasizes the tonic that follows.

The expansion of the mediant chord is of extreme importance because it offers a new and second type of chord prolongation. In connection with a preceding illustration (Example 6) we explained that type of chord prolongation which is created through the horizontalization of a chord. This motion occurs within the chord spaces. The term "horizontalization" also applies if only one of the outside voices defines a motion within a chord space, irrespective of the manner in which the other voice moves. The second type of chord prolongation concerns the motion *around,* rather than *within* a chord. This type will be called *chord embellishment.* It occurs only when neither of the outer voices defines a chord space, but both circle around a chord in an embellishing motion that points to the supremacy of that chord.

In the first two measures of the prolonged mediant chord, we have an illustration of this type of chord prolongation, since the outside voices describe a motion around the B♭ major chord. The top voice reveals E♭ as a neighbor of D in the motion D—E♭—D, with F as an embellishment of E♭. The bass descends from B♭ to G, the third of the E♭ chord supporting E♭ in the top voice, and then ascends to B♭, with A as an intervening passing tone in both motions. It is clear that as the top voice encircles D, so the bass points to B♭ as the start and conclusion of a motion that is purely of an embellishing and prolonging nature in that it consists of two passing tones and a tone supporting the E♭ neighbor note. Since this type

of chord prolongation appears frequently in the examples cited in the following chapters, it is vitally important to recognize that the chords that result from such an embellishing motion have neither a harmonic nor a structural implication. These measures offer a further illustration of the necessity for understanding the role a chord plays in a specific passage in addition to its position in the key. If we had labeled the inverted F major and E♭ major chords in this prolonging motion in the customary manner, as V–IV–V in the key of B♭ major, we would have
$\quad\quad\quad\quad\quad\quad\quad\quad\quad\quad\quad\quad\quad$ 6 $\quad$ 6 $\quad$ 6
$\quad\quad\quad\quad\quad\quad\quad\quad\quad\quad\quad\quad\quad\quad\quad\quad\quad$ 5

denoted their status in the new key of B♭ major, but we would also apply the same numerals to the F major and E♭ major chords that in a different situation, demonstrate a harmonic and a structural, rather than a prolonging, function. Finally, to regard the B♭ major chord the expanded mediant, as the tonic of a new key, when in the measure that follows the passage cited, it moves to the dominant of the structural progression, destroys the organic nature of the I–III–V–I basic progression by breaking it up into two different tonal entities.

The final example, a passage from the Bach chorale *Die Sonn hat sich mit ihrem Glanz* [18] discloses two new types of harmonic prolongation – the *incomplete harmonic progression* and the chord of *harmonic emphasis*. In this instance, the incomplete harmonic progression takes the form of II–V–I but it also can appear as IV–V–I, VI–V–I and V–I, when the V in the V–I progression does not serve as an applied dominant. An incomplete progression generally precedes the structural chord it expands, and thus directs the motion to the entrance of the structural chord. The complete harmonic progression, on the contrary, does not precede but enters simultaneously with the member of the basic progression it prolongs. Thus the incomplete progression is a form of harmonic emphasis.

EXAMPLE 15

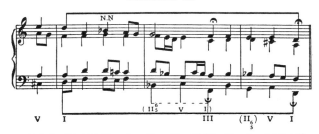

V $\quad$ I $\quad\quad\quad\quad\quad\quad\quad$ (II$_5^6$) $\quad$ V $\quad$ I) $\quad\quad\quad$ III $\quad\quad$ (II$_6$) $\quad$ V $\quad$ I
$\quad\quad\quad\quad\quad\quad\quad\quad\quad\quad\quad\quad\quad\quad\quad\quad\quad\quad\quad\quad\quad\quad$ 5

[18] J. S. Bach's 389 *Choral-gesänge* No. 65 (Breitkopf and Härtel).

Challenge to Musical Tradition

Since these measures occur in the middle of the chorale, the opening A major chord is shown as a structural dominant of the progression in which it appears and not as an incomplete V–I progression, in which capacity it would have served as the beginning of the chorale. Like the complete progressions, incomplete progressions are indicated above the basic motion to denote their prolonging function. On the other hand, chords of harmonic emphasis such as the supertonic (measure 3), appear in connection with the member of the basic progression they stress and are enclosed in parentheses.

These three measures define a motion within the horizontalized D minor chord, the top voice in a descent of an octave, the bass through a I–III–V–I progression. The space between the tonic and mediant chords is widened by an embellishing motion in which B♭ serves as a neighbor of A in the top voice and E as a neighbor of F in the bass. Thus the C major chord, having the harmonic implications of an applied dominant, serves a purely contrapuntal purpose through the embellishing function of the outside voices.

Since the F major chord already enters on the final quarter of this measure, some readers may ask why it is not shown in connection with the II–V–I progression that follows. In other words, why do we regard this as an incomplete II–V–I rather than as a complete I–II–V–I progression? First of all, the F major chord, coming on the last quarter, is extremely weak. This weakness is not offset by an approach through an applied dominant in which the harmonic impulse finds fullest expression, but by that type in which the harmonic impulse is enervated by the contrapuntal function the chord demonstrates. In addition, we hear this F major chord in connection with the preceding D minor chord in which D, a middle voice, is exchanged for C, a passing tone that moves through D to B♭ of the G minor chord. Thus, because of its weakness and its close affinity with the tonic D minor rather than with the G minor chord that follows, we hear this F major chord as a contrapuntal passing chord rather than as the structural tonic of a harmonic progression.

In the customary method of analysis, this II–V–I progression would constitute a cadence establishing the key of F major as a new tonal center. As an incomplete harmonic progression serving as a harmonic prolongation, it emphasizes the motion to the F major chord as the mediant of the fundamental tonality. In the one case, the cadence directs the motion away from the key of D minor; in the other, it accentuates the function of the mediant chord in maintaining the tonal characteristics of the entire phrase. Therefore, the distinction between a cadence and an incomplete harmonic progression is one not of terminology only. It is the difference that results from two opposing conceptions of tonality — the one based on the use of modulation, the other on the principle of structural coherence as the expression of one and only one key.

The seventh chord on E immediately preceding the dominant of the basic progression illustrates a new type of harmonic prolongation, a chord of *harmonic emphasis*. A supertonic assumes this function only when it appears between the mediant and dominant chords of a basic harmonic progression to stress the entrance of the dominant chord. Although as a supertonic it demonstrates its harmonic connection with the dominant, its function is not structural but prolonging, since the structural function already is defined by the chords comprising the I—III—V—I progression. This chord differs from the applied dominant of A major in that the applied dominant would be an E major chord, while the chord of harmonic emphasis has the status if not the function of a supertonic. The B♭ major chord preceding the supertonic is a contrapuntal chord, since its sole function is to support the F in the melody in place of a repeated F major chord. Thus the B♭ major and the supertonic both have a prolonging function in expanding the mediant-dominant progression, though the one is of a contrapuntal and the other of a harmonic origin.

Although in this passage the incomplete harmonic progression indicates a direct motion, there are many instances in which it is widely extended. The variety of colors that such a prolonged motion injects into the tonal character of the primordial progression frequently creates so striking an effect that the prolongation is regarded as a separate tonal entity. A remarkable example of the use of an extended submediant chord in an incomplete VI—V—I progression is the presto from Beethoven's quartet, Opus 59 No. 2. Here the principal theme bears the imprint of an expanded C major chord although the E minor tonality is indicated in the key signature. This unorthodox treatment has led some theorists to believe that the opening theme is actually in the key of C major. In fact, Schönberg points out [19] that the first part of the presto is so strongly indicative of C major that it is possible to hear the subsequent turn to E minor as the third degree of C major rather than as the tonic of the fundamental tonality. However, since this aspect of the work is discussed later

[19] *Schoenberg*, edited by Merle Armitage (G. Schirmer, 1937), p. 279.

in connection with Schönberg's conception of tonality, it is sufficient at this point to cite this movement as an illustration of the prismatic effect of an incomplete harmonic progression on the primordial structure, and the misconceptions to which its interpretation as a modulating cadence gives rise.

This concludes the discussion of the essential techniques that create and maintain the conception of tonality we call structural coherence. Because of space limitations, it has been possible to give only a brief explanation of a new approach and to include only a limited number of illustrations. However, since the entire book is a further demonstration of the techniques defined in this chapter, the reader will find numerous examples to illustrate this new concept of tonality and the various types of prolongation that have evolved within the past two hundred and fifty years.

In presenting a new approach, the author does not mean to imply that the accepted method of analysis is not an essential part of a student's training in teaching him the names and positions of chords within a key and the various types of chord structure with which he must become familiar. The main argument is directed not against harmonic analysis *per se*, but against the use of this elementary system that is concerned only with chord grammar as an adequate preparation for understanding the complicated techniques that compositions of the past and present reveal. To express his own creative ideas as well as to be able to interpret the works of other composers, the student must know not only the names and positions of chords, but the different functions they demonstrate in various situations. Furthermore, the recognition of these differentiated functions leads to a new understanding of what the term "tonality" means — the expression of a single key through the prolongation of a primordial framework instead of the expression of various keys through the techniques of modulation.

To clarify the concept of tonality as organic oneness by showing the many technical and stylistic changes it sustained as well as those which led to its breakdown is the basic purpose of this book. The evidence that the numerous examples offer, leaves the reader free to make his decision as to whether this or the accepted explanation of tonality most accurately interprets and explains the music of the past and the present.

Now let us turn to the music of Johann Sebastian Bach, remembering that it is the music alone that can prove the truth or fallacy of our method of hearing.

CHAPTER II

Johann Sebastian Bach

CHALLENGE TO THE PAST *through his definition of principles of structural unity. New treatment of the chorale and chorale-prelude. Adaptation of form to material — the fugue. Nature of Bach's dissonance, as interpreted by Casella and Schönberg.*

WHAT was the nature of Bach's art? Was Bach an innovator or merely an organizer? In his part writing did he, as Forkel states, "transgress, seemingly at any rate, rules long established and to his contemporaries almost sacred"?[1] Did he, as Casella[2] and Schönberg[3] imply, predestine present-day techniques in his use of dissonance? Unless we can give a decisive answer to these questions, no discussion of Bach's works will be adequate.

Strangely enough, there are still some great admirers of Bach who do not regard him as an innovator. They believe that he caught up the threads that his predecessors had cast aside and wove them together into a fusion of all that had gone before; that his works are a synthesis of what had ·been, rather than the result of a new and daring technical treatment.

Although the chorales alone refute this theory, there is further evidence of Bach's originality in his treatment of the chorale-prelude and fugue, in the emotional intensity of his slow movements, and in the highly dramatic nature of his recitatives. Where in the music of Bach's predecessors can we find the imaginative concept, the technical resources, and the contrapuntal daring that distinguish these works?

That Bach was indebted to the works of earlier composers for his contrapuntal training and his knowledge of the various forms is true. It is equally true, however, that there are creative elements in his music that are the expression of his highly individual artistic personality.

[1] *Bach,* translated by C. S. Terry (Constable & Co. Ltd., 1920), p. 74.
[2] *Musical Quarterly* (April, 1924).
[3] *Harmonielehre* (Universal Edition, 1922), p. 392.

Challenge to Musical Tradition

First of all we must determine if and where Bach violated the established rules. To do this we must understand the principles of harmony and counterpoint, not only as they are defined in the textbooks, but as they actually appear in Bach's works. To grasp exactly what influence Bach had on composers of a later day we must comprehend clearly his use of the harmonic and contrapuntal functions.

There is no better introduction to the art of Johann Sebastian Bach than a study of his chorales. In them are blended the man of faith and the revolutionary artist. Through his chorales Bach is revealed as a composer of deep devotion. They also reflect the vision that enabled the artist to utilize the old chorale melodies in settings whose emotional fervor gave them a new significance.

Each text aroused such an individual response in him that, in examining the more than two hundred four-part chorales in the cantatas, oratorios, Passions, and motets, many built on the same chorale tunes, Terry [4] found only two instances in which the harmonization was duplicated, both deliberate.

Although the term "harmonization" is not defined in textbooks, it usually occurs in those examples in which a student is given a melody to harmonize, that is, to supply the supporting chords. Thus, because of its harmonic implications, it tends to suggest a purely vertical technique. In this sense it would be a contradiction to apply this term to the methods Bach or any other composer has used. For this reason, instead of "harmonization" the term "setting" will be used to define a type of structure in which the harmonic and contrapuntal principles exercise both their individual and their combined functions.

It is well known that Bach composed comparatively few chorale melodies. Instead he utilized those that had been prized possessions of the German people. Yet he invested them with a setting which in contrapuntal richness, depth of feeling, and freedom of treatment was so far removed from the original that the familiar melody often underwent a musical metamorphosis.

Bach made three basic innovations that differentiated his treatment of the chorale from that of his predecessors and contemporaries: (1) the symbolic treatment of the text, (2) the emphasis of chromatic passing chords, and (3) the new use of dissonance as a means of intensifying the prolonging motions.

---

[4] Bach *The Historical Approach* (Oxford University Press, 1930), p. 130.

Johann Sebastian Bach

One of the most inspiring of the chorales, *Es ist genug*,[5] is a typical example of Bach's symbolic treatment of the text through his use of chromatic passing tones.

EXAMPLE 16

Here is a work in A major; yet at the very outset we find the chromatics A♯, B♯, and D♯. In addition, B♯ and D♯ enter on a strong beat and thus bring added emphasis to the alien nature of the chords in which they appear. How are we to regard these chords, and why has Bach introduced them before the tonality has been clearly established?

It is clear that the motion in which these chords occur is from the tonic to the mediant C♯ minor chord. Here the D♯ in the melody has been given a rhythmic stress that belies its function as a passing tone between C♯ and E. In a similar manner, A♯ and B♯ in the bass are revealed as mere passing tones between A♮ and C♯ and serve no other purpose than to intensify the motion between the root and third of the A major chord. Thus the chromatic nature of these inserted chords exerts no harmonic pressure on the main structure; their status is that of space-fillers.

Although it is often stated that Bach transgressed the established rules regarding chord progressions, it is clear, in this instance at least, that the revolutionary aspects of the technique are not of a harmonic but of a rhythmic nature. It is his rhythmic stress of the nonessential passing tones which gives them an importance that their function does not war-

[5] J. S. Bach's *389 Choral-gesänge* No. 91 (Breitkopf and Härtel).

41

rant. We see that Bach, to compensate for this effect, has built a melodic and harmonic structure whose framework demonstrates its allegiance to the key of A major. This is indeed a remarkable instance of Bach's imaginative grasp of the possibilities that lie within the tonal concept. It shows that there are no limitations of key in the prolonging chords, but only in the harmonic progressions that define the structural motion.

There is an interesting feature in the expansion of the tonic-mediant progression. Although the bass moves chromatically from A through A♯ and B♯ to C♯, to give greater emphasis to the chord of C♯ Bach exchanges B♯ for G♯ (measure 2), which has the effect of an applied dominant of the C♯ chord. Thus the primary aspect of the treatment, which is contrapuntal, is given a harmonic flavor through the substitution of G♯ for B♯ in the approach to the mediant chord. This emphasis of the C♯ minor chord is important for two reasons: it stresses a member of the harmonic progression and at the same time it gives greater significance to the word *nimm* (accept) which it accompanies. Here the musical stress adds emotional intensity to the phrase *so nimm, Herr, meinen Geist*. In a similar manner the chromatic character of the G♯ major chord on the first two quarters of measure 2 tends to reflect the meaning of *genug* (enough). It is further emphasized by the use of a fermata. In fact, every element of the treatment conspires to make this passing chord the temporary climax of the motion until it is replaced by the mediant chord.

This is a truly remarkable illustration of the interweaving of the harmonic and contrapuntal principles. The passage shows that any chord may be used in the prolongations to achieve color and intensity without affecting the structural coherence if it lies within the tonal boundaries of the motion. In this instance the use of the F♯ and B♯ major chords as passing chords supplies chromatics that add momentum to the motion, and strengthen the impulse to the C♯ minor chord.

Let us take another example in which the treatment is more conventional, *Herzliebster Jesu*.[6] Here is a clear instance of the difference between Bach's style and that of his predecessors. To perceive this difference, let us first look at the original chorale written by Johann Crüger in 1640 [7] and then discuss two different settings of the same melody by Bach.

It is obvious that Crüger conceived the melody within the G Dorian mode, although the setting has a tonal tendency through the use of the

---

[6] *Ibid.*, No. 168.
[7] Johann Crüger's *Choral Melodien* (Eichler, 1835).

Johann Sebastian Bach

EXAMPLE 17

major dominant. Although the passage shows a prolongation of both the tonic and mediant chords, the expanding motions lack the intensity that the chromatic passing chords in the preceding example produced. In fact, the setting has been conceived entirely from the musical point of view, without the strong reaction to the text so characteristic of Bach.

The top voice outlines an ascent from G to D, at which point the mediant chord enters. Thus the melodic climax is emphasized by the attainment of the structural goal, the B♭ major chord. In the bass the expansion of the G minor chord is the result of two harmonic progressions in which the voice leadings are of a purely diatonic nature. The only variation from the norm is the use of the G major chord as the start of the motion, since it tends to lay undue emphasis on the C minor chord that follows.

Although the motion indicates the G minor tonality, the treatment as a whole lacks the tonal clarity and stability that characterize the technique in the Bach version.

Now let us turn to Bach's setting of the same chorale melody.

First of all we see that the original modal character of the melody has been obliterated through the substitution of F♯ for F♮. This alteration by Bach is unusual, since in most cases he kept the modal nature of the melody intact. For example, in *Aus tiefer Noth*,[8] *Das alte Jahr vergangen ist*,[9] and *Christ, unser Herr, zum Jordan kam* [10] the modal characteristics of the originals have been preserved, not only in the melody, but in the setting as well. Another obvious change is the division of Crüger's one

[8] *389 Choral-gesänge* (Breitkopf and Härtel), No. 31.
[9] *Ibid.,* No. 53.
[10] *Ibid.,* Nos. 44 and 45.

43

EXAMPLE 18

measure of eight whole notes into Bach's three measures of quarter notes. The main distinction, however, lies in the tonal clarity of Bach's technique as revealed in the prolongations.

Graph A shows that the first three measures of the chorale together with the G minor chord in measure 4 outline a I–V–I progression within the tonic G minor chord. This motion itself is expanded by the I–IV–V–I progression that prolongs the opening tonic chord. This latter progression is of extreme interest because it discloses the difference between Bach's and Crüger's treatment of the same type of motion. Crüger used only the four chords of the progression without passing or embellishing chords; Bach, on the contrary, introduced passing chords to enrich the progression and give momentum to the motion. Moreover, there is such a pronounced horizontalization of the tones of the G minor chord, that were it not for the emphasis placed upon the C minor chord (measure 1), we could regard the motion as the result of a contrapuntal rather than of a harmonic impulse. Here the motion from the tonic to the dominant demonstrates a harmonic tendency, while the motion from the dominant to the tonic is strongly contrapuntal. Thus Bach not only achieved a prolongation by means of a harmonic progression, but he intensified this motion through the contrapuntal effect produced by the passing tones.

Although the D major chord of the harmonic prolongation (measure 1) and the D major chord that defines the larger motion (measure 3) are both dominants, there is nevertheless a distinction in their functions that we should observe. The first D major chord occurs within an expanded tonic of the basic I—V—I progression. The second D major chord appears as the dominant of the larger structural organism that embraces the smaller prolongation. Although both are dominants in progressions that extend the G minor chord, their functions are of unequal importance.

The top voice shows an ascent from G to Bb that is prolonged by means of embellishing and passing tones. Here too, there is a distinction between the roles that F♯ in the first D major chord and A in the second, enact. F♯ is clearly a neighbor of G that precedes and follows, while A has the effect of interrupting the ascent momentarily until Bb in the following G minor chord reappears. Although A has the tendency of a neighbor of Bb, its function is entirely different from that of F♯, since in arresting the ascent it gives added intensity to the D major chord as the climax of the structural motion.

Is it not more comprehensible to hear these measures as an expansion of the structural tonic than to give each chord in the passage a label as a harmonic entity, regardless of its function? Is it not more understandable to regard the measures that follow as a motion within the expanded mediant of G minor, than as a modulation to the key of Bb, the relative major?

If, however, we accept this Bb major chord as the prolonged mediant of the tonality, we must also apply this same method of hearing to the larger structures of binary and sonata form in which the expansion of the mediant chord creates a section of the form. The nature of the prolongation may vary; it may or may not be form-making; but the principle underlying any expansion of a member of a primordial harmonic progression is the same, since all prolongations are offshoots of the primordial structure.

Challenge to Musical Tradition

Turning to the melody, we find an ascent from B♭ of the tonic to D of the mediant chord. This is followed by a descending motion within the B♭ major chord in which E♭ appears as a neighbor note and C as a passing tone. Against this the bass outlines the motion B♭–F–B♭, which Bach has expanded by filling the space from B♭ to F with a descending progression of steps and half steps. If we turn once more to the Crüger chorale, we see the bold originality of Bach's counterpoint and the specific means he took to intensify the progression by means of chromatic passing chords.

Crüger has also prolonged the passage within the B♭ major chord, but by ascending diatonically from B♭ to F. Bach, on the other hand, used a descending motion from B♭ to F and moved freely within this space by substituting A♭ for the customary A♮, to lend emphasis to the E♭ chord that supplies the melodic neighbor note E♭, and by inserting the chromatic passing tone G♭ between G♮ and F.

In the difference between Bach's and Crüger's filling of the space from B♭ to F we find the elements of Bach's style that distinguished his work from his contemporaries'. The insertion of such chromatics within the outlined space often gives rise to chords that are striking because of the contrast they offer to the tonal characteristics of the progression. For example, through the introduction of G♭ and A♭ Bach has created chords that bring new color to the motion within the B♭ chord. But because these chords are of a contrapuntal origin, the so-called extra-tonal effects they produce do not affect either the stability of the tonality or the strength of the harmonic progression. Notwithstanding, it is the extensive use of such chromatic chords that has led some theorists to believe that Bach violated the rules governing harmonic progressions as explained in harmony textbooks.

Let us turn now to a second version of *Herzliebster Jesu* [11] by Bach, in which a different text inspired an entirely new setting.

The first chord of this chorale might present an interesting problem were we using the usual method of analysis. In this work, which the signature indicates as B minor, Bach begins with a first inversion of a B seventh chord and follows it with an E minor chord on the first beat of the opening measure. This is a typical textbook dominant-tonic progression and might lead to the supposition that the chorale as a whole is in the key of E minor, with a close on the dominant B major chord. But

---

[11] *Ibid.*, No. 167.

Johann Sebastian Bach

EXAMPLE 19

if we examine the opening phrase more carefully, we realize that such a conclusion is negated by the motion in the bass, which clearly outlines the chord of B major through the tones D♯, F♯, and B. However, when the root of the chord, B, is reached, D♮ appears in the melody, so that at the end of the motion the B major chord has been exchanged for the B minor. These two chords express, not two different tonalities, but a major-minor mixture within the B tonality. Here, as in the preceding version in G minor, the first two measures are concerned with a motion within a single chord. Yet how strikingly different is this type of prolongation from the simpler treatment of the G minor chord, and how varied are the voice leadings that fill the space!

First of all there is the rhythmic and harmonic emphasis of the E minor chord, which tends to confuse the tonality. Next come the chromatic passing tones in the bass, E♯ and G♯, which create chords whose stress and tension bring out the full power of the text and add richness and color to the tonic-dominant progression.

These opening measures provide an excellent example of Bach's technique of prolongation as a means of conveying in the music the growing climax suggested by the words. Although there is no exact English equivalent of the German *wunderbarlich,* it is usually translated as "wondrous" or "awe-inspiring." The literal text is: "How wondrous is this sacrifice." The increasing intensity of the motion supplied by the chromatic nature

47

Challenge to Musical Tradition

of the voice leadings enhances the emotional quality of the text. Notice how the word *Strafe* (sacrifice) is emphasized by its entrance on a neighbor chord. In fact the entire motion of the first two measures serves to intensify the climax on the B minor and F♯ major chords and thus heightens the significance of the words they accompany.

In both versions of this chorale Bach used the same melody and the same structural outline. Yet how different are the two settings in the voice leadings that fill the horizontalized chord! The opening alone is typical of the more complex prolongations of the B minor setting. Due to the profuse use of chromatic passing tones, this version poses many more problems than the simpler one in G minor. This essential individuality of treatment, primarily due to the nature of the text, is indicative of the artistic integrity that Bach brought to each work. That he was able to make this distinction in the music while adhering to the same melody and the same basic structure is additional proof of the tremendous possibilities that lie in the technique of prolongation.

We need only compare the latter version with the original Crüger example to see where Bach's treatment of the chorale differs from his predecessors'. The melody and harmonic outline in both are the same. But what a tremendous growth in contrapuntal technique distinguishes Bach's treatment from Crüger's! Yet it is not only the technique that is responsible for the richness and intensity of the Bach version. There is in addition the emotional aspect of the work. No one can regard this chorale as a mere harmonization of a melody. It is an expression of Bach's response to the spiritual implications of the text; it is a demonstration of the close association of word and tone, not as in Wagner's realistic treatment of the leitmotiv, but in the symbolic form characteristic of Bach.

There are many other instances of such treatment in the chorales. A few such are *Aus tiefer Noth; Ermuntre dich, mein schwacher Geist; Jesu Leiden, Pein, und Tod,* and *Valet will ich dir geben.*[12]

Bach's symbolic treatment of a text is not confined to the chorales. In the chorale-preludes and chorale-fantasies, instrumental forms that have their origin in the chorale, there is equal evidence that the original text has left its imprint on Bach's music. It is true that the chorale-preludes and fantasies of Pachelbel, Böhm, and Buxtehude served as models for Bach. It is equally true that Bach was to become independent of his masters and to produce a type of his own, the chorale-prelude of the *Orgelbüchlein.*

[12] *Ibid.,* Nos. 31, 80, 192 and 194, and 314.

48

Johann Sebastian Bach

Of this, Schweitzer [13] says: "Never before had anyone expressed the texts in pure tone in this way; no one afterwards undertook to do so with such simple means. At the same time the essence of Bach's art comes clearly into view for the first time in this work. He is not satisfied with formal perfection and fullness of sound — otherwise he would have continued to work with the forms and formulae of his teachers in the chorale-prelude. He aims at more than this; he aspires after the plastic expression of ideas, and so creates a tone speech of his own."

How sharply he veered from the prescribed chorale-prelude style is revealed in a comparison of the Bach version of *Durch Adams Fall* with those of Pachelbel and Buxtehude. In the arrangement of the voice leadings, the emphasis of chromatics, and the recognition of the nature of the chorale text, Bach has created a new conception of the prelude, in which the solution of the problems of contrapuntal writing are no longer the main goal, but merely a means to an end. What that end was depended entirely on the initial musical idea and the possibilities it presented to the composer. In this prelude its purpose was to provide a setting for a chorale melody so that the significance of the text would be implied in the music, since the words themselves were lacking.

In the three examples that follow it is obvious that Pachelbel, Buxtehude, and Bach used the same chorale melody as a cantus firmus. The characteristic motive of the counterpoint in all three settings is derived from the cantus, but appears in diminution; that is, in smaller time values.

Even these short illustrations show that however much Buxtehude and Bach may have been influenced by Pachelbel's treatment of the chorale-prelude, neither was a mere imitator of his style. This is especially true of Bach. Using the same cantus and form as Pachelbel and Buxtehude, he was not content to make "formal perfection and fullness of sound" the dominant factor in his music. On the contrary, he injected into the instrumental prelude the essential idea of the chorale text by means of the realistic character of the motivic figure.

Since both the Pachelbel and Bach examples show a structural motion from a prolonged tonic to a mediant chord, it is inevitable that the differentiation in their stylistic treatment lies primarily in the nature of the prolonging techniques.

The Pachelbel version [14] shows a two-part setting in which the contra-

---

[13] *Johann Sebastian Bach* (A. & C. Black, Ltd., 1923), Vol. I, p. 284.
[14] *Alte Meister des Orgelspiels* (Peters Edition), edited by Karl Straube.

EXAMPLE 20

puntal figure A—G—F—E—D is an obvious imitation of the first phrase of
the chorale. Although Buxtehude and Bach also observe this fundamental
principle of the prelude by basing the motive of the counterpoint on the
cantus, they are much freer in their use of chromatics and thus present
a more subtle type of imitation. Furthermore, in the Pachelbel prelude the
counterpoint is dominated by the modal quality of the cantus, while in
the Buxtehude and Bach settings the counterpoint gives a clearer definition of the D minor tonality. The tonal vagueness of Pachelbel's treatment
is especially noticeable in the motion from the tonic to the mediant chord
(measures 4–6).

In the Buxtehude version [15] the technique is more varied and the imitation less obvious. For example, F—E—F—E—F in the alto part is derived
from A—G—A—G—A in the second and third measures of the cantus. In
like manner D—C—B in the tenor (measures 2 and 3) is a diminution of
A—G—F of the chorale melody (measures 3 and 4), while the descent
from A to D in the tenor voice (measures 5 and 6) is an exact imitation
of the opening chorale phrase. Moreover, in spite of Buxtehude's use of
imitation, he achieved a poetic quality and a distinct feeling of rhythmic
symmetry in those measures in which the suspensions form a definite
pattern carried out in the different voice parts. By means of these suspensions Buxtehude created dissonant effects that enrich and intensify the
measures that serve as an interlude.

[15] *Sämmtliche Orgel-Compositionen* (Breitkopf and Härtel Edition), edited by
Spitta.

50

Johann Sebastian Bach

EXAMPLE 20A

The motion is also of interest because it defines a prolonged tonic-dominant progression instead of the tonic-mediant disclosed in the Pachelbel and Bach examples. Here the predominance of the minor over the major dominant (measures 8–10) preserves the modal quality of the melody but does create a tonal vagueness in the motion. Although the treatment throughout is extremely ingenious, it is clear that Buxtehude, as well as Pachelbel, conceived the prelude solely as an abstract contrapuntal problem and in no way injected into the music the dramatic character of the text of the original chorale.

Now let us turn to the Bach [16] prelude.

It is immediately apparent that the cantus is not regarded as a melody divorced from the text. In fact, many feel that the underlying meaning of the text (that is, that Adam's fall is responsible for the debasement of mankind) has been graphically portrayed by the descending leaps of sevenths that occur in the pedal. This, of course, is a debatable question; but there is at least some ground for Spitta's [17] statement that "the pedal

---

[16] *Orgel* (Peters Edition), *Band V.*
[17] *The Life of Bach* (Novello and Company, Ltd., 1899), Vol. I, p. 602.

EXAMPLE 20B

indicates the fall of man by an episode in leaps of sevenths." Whatever the origin, whether premeditated or accidental, the succession of diminished and minor sevenths is remarkable, not only because it suggests a realistic representation of the words of the chorale, but also because of the apparent freedom with which these sevenths enter. Since these sevenths seem to violate the principles that govern contrapuntal writing, they give rise to some vital questions in regard to Bach's technique. In his challenge to tradition did Bach break *laws* (not rules) in his daring use of dissonance? Was his contrapuntal technique a negation of the principles underlying the leading of voices or was it rather a protest against the traditions which militated against the further growth of the contrapuntal style?

First of all let us examine the voice parts to see if there is justification for the contention advanced by some present-day composers that Bach defied the principles that he himself accepted as necessary to the art of contrapuntal writing. We are at once aware of the leap of a seventh in the bass. This interval, whether diminished or minor, was used sparingly in Bach's day and was subject to the contrapuntal rules that applied to all dissonances. As the sevenths appear in this example, they seem to enter freely, without preparation and resolution. Therefore we must look further in order to determine whether Bach actually defied the established rules or whether he upheld them beneath the cloak of apparent freedom.

Below is a strict contrapuntal arrangement of the first four measures of the chorale in which the nonessential tones and ornamentations have been eliminated. The basses that Bach omitted, to give the effect of the falling sevenths, have been supplied within brackets. Although this in no way alters any of the voice leadings, we see an entirely different picture, the difference between what he wrote to create a motivic design and the actual voice leadings of which the figuration is a prolongation.

EXAMPLE 20C

It is evident that the descending leaps of a seventh which are so heavily stressed in the music of Example 20B do not appear when the tones are placed in the registers and the voice parts to which they properly belong. For example, we see that instead of participating in the bass motion in a leap from C to the D♯ below (measure 1), the C actually belongs to the tenor voice as a passing tone between C♯ and B. By omitting the real bass tone A and substituting C in its place, Bach has implied that a connection exists between C in the tenor and D♯ in the bass. In a similar manner, it appears as though E, the actual bass tone on the third quarter, belonged in the tenor. This effect is achieved through the insertion of a rest in the bass.

The emphasis laid on D♯ in the bass is of further interest. Although this chord could be regarded as an altered supertonic in a I—II—V—I harmonic prolongation of the A major chord, its primary function is to intensify the E minor chord that follows. For this reason D has been raised to D♯. Thus its tendency is to embellish the E minor chord rather than to stimulate the motion as a member of a harmonic progression.

53

Challenge to Musical Tradition

An instance that, on a superficial glance, might be cited as proof that Bach ignored the rules of voice leading is the diminished fifth in the bass, from D to G♯ (measure 2). Let us examine this passage carefully to see if Bach did transgress the rules.

The top voice indicates a motion of F—E—D, in which E is shown as a passing tone between the chord tones. The bass defines a motion of D—A—D. Thus the motion as a whole, as defined by the two outside voices, outlines the D minor chord. The E major chord within this motion exerts the same pressure on the chord of A major that B major in the preceding measure exercises on the chord of E minor. Both have the character of applied dominants, but through inversion they give the effect of embellishing chords. As a neighbor of A, G♯ is a nonessential tone in the motion from D to A and in no wise violates the principles of voice leading.

It is also possible to regard the altered seventh chord on E as a supertonic, in which case the motion D—E—A—D constitutes a harmonic prolongation. However, the contrapuntal tendency of the E chord as an embellishment of A major is so much stronger than the harmonic impulse it defines, that it is not indicated as a II in the graph. That interpretation, however, would not change the nature of the voice leadings or the status of G♯ as a neighbor of A in the motion outlined by the tonic and dominant chords.

The difference between Bach's treatment and those of Pachelbel and Buxtehude is marked. It is apparent not only in Bach's clearer definition of the tonality, but in the type of prolonging motions that expand the tonic-mediant progression. In these, the passing and embellishing chords, the incomplete III—V—I harmonic progression, together with the motivic figure, give a dramatic intensity to the motion that is lacking in the other versions.

Here Bach's originality asserts itself, not in an arbitrary defiance of the principles of contrapuntal writing, but in an imaginative adaptation of these principles to emphasize a specific idea. He stresses passing and embellishing tones instead of chord tones and introduces rests to suggest the figure of a descending seventh. We have seen, however, that when the tones that comprise this motive are placed within their proper voice parts, the dissonant leaps no longer exist. In short, although Bach used every technical means to interpret realistically the text of the chorale, be-

54

Johann Sebastian Bach

neath the artistic treatment of the motive there is a strict observance of the fundamental principles that govern voice leading.

Such innovations converted the form Bach inherited into a new and different type of chorale-prelude, which carries the impact of his conception of tonality, the breadth and power of his imagination, and the strength and mastery of his contrapuntal technique. To regard this and other equally dynamic passages as the inevitable results of the contribution of Bach's predecessors is to withhold from Bach a just recognition of his re-creation of the form.

BACH'S FUGUE TECHNIQUE

It was Bach also who was destined to create the fugue form as we know it today, with its possibilities of expansion through the techniques of augmentation, diminution, inversion, and stretto. One must admit his obligation to Froberger, Pachelbel, Böhm, Muffat, and Buxtehude, who had brought the polythematic fugue to a high point of contrapuntal perfection. But however much Bach derived from their technical skill, he was not a mere imitator of their methods. On the contrary, Bach's challenge to the fugue form was in his demonstration of the greater advantages of the *monothematic* over the *polythematic* fugue.

The older form had its origin in the motet and ricercare. It consisted of several different fugues, loosely connected by episodes or interludes interposed between the expositions. In compositions entitled prelude and fugue the latter part was often merely a ricercare composed either of entirely different fugue subjects or of subjects derived from a single theme with the melodic outline and meter varied in each fugue.[18] It was this form that was largely used until Bach concentrated on the monothematic type, although as early as the seventeenth century Frescobaldi had experimented with the monothematic ricercare which had but one exposition.

It is all the more surprising to find that Bach's immediate predecessor Froberger and his contemporary Buxtehude, to name two of the most important, still retained the polythematic form. The monothematic fugue, as the development of a single subject, came into its established position only through Bach, and from his time to the present it has remained the

[18] For illustrations of the ricercare see the fugues in E minor (No. 6), G minor (No. 7), E Major (No. 8), and D minor (No. 10) in Buxtehude's *Sämmtliche Orgel-Compositionen* (Breitkopf and Härtel Edition), edited by Spitta.

accepted form of fugal writing. Bach's grasp of the greater structural unity afforded by the monothematic fugue, together with the artistic variety that such unity permitted, transformed the art of fugal writing into a form that has survived for two hundred years.

The fugue in C minor [19] offers a clear-cut demonstration of the structural possibilities inherent in the horizontalization of a single chord. There are three voice entries in the exposition. The first of these outlines a motion within the prolonged tonic chord, the second a motion within the dominant, and the third a motion within the tonic. Together they define an expanded I–V–I progression, a prolongation of the tonic chord of the primordial structure. The development shows an expansion of the E♭ major and G minor chords, while the final section consists of a prolonged tonic. Thus the entire work is built on the primordial I–III–V–I progression that outlines the C minor chord. In this horizontalization of the fundamental triad, Bach achieved a tonal security that not only stabilized the monothematic fugue form, but gave opportunity for the insertion of the chromatic chords of prolongation that differentiate Bach's style from others' of his day.

For many early musicians the problems inherent in the form were thought of as primarily technical rather than artistic. With Bach, however, the contrapuntal facility that his fugues reveal is always subordinated to the artistic presentation and development of a basic fugue motive. The various techniques of diminution, augmentation, inversion, and stretto, which Bach introduced into so many of his fugues, were not merely technical innovations, but served an artistic purpose as well. They contributed to the dramatic conflict among the different voices and in so doing they injected an emotional intensity into the development section that brought a new impulse to the stylistic treatment of the fugue.

An example of the elasticity Bach injected into the more stereotyped form is found in the fugue in E♭ minor.[20] The quality of the subject at once shows that the motive was conceived, not as a mathematical figure, but as a genuine expression of emotion. The contrapuntal devices by which Bach seeks to bring out the latent possibilities of the motive in the middle section could easily have been made the chief and only goal of this fugue. Instead these techniques serve the additional purpose of creating tension and stress within the voice leadings.

No one who really understands this work could possibly regard it as

[19] *Well-tempered Clavichord*, Book I, No. 2.   [20] *Ibid.*, Book I, No. 8.

Johann Sebastian Bach

merely a demonstration of Bach's contrapuntal prowess. On the other hand, without the contrapuntal equipment Bach could not have brought into play the techniques of augmentation, inversion, and stretto as an essential part of the emotional and structural life of this E♭ minor fugue. Without Bach's dramatic concept of the form, the emotional quality that dominates this fugue would have been submerged by a concentration on problems of technique. It is, in fact, the fine adjustment between technical mastery and creative imagination that has made this composition one of Bach's finest achievements in fugal writing.

There are instances, however, where the innovations in technique create innovations in the form. The fugues that follow are illustrations of this, each one presenting a new and different variety of structural prolongation. Bach's elastic concept of the form permitted him to expand the fugue both to meet the demands of the material and to solve the problems that its specific treatment imposed. He found a solution, not by annihilating the essential impulse out of which the fugue emerged, but by applying the principles of structural coherence to the fugal form. Since a detailed analysis of these fugues would require an entire chapter, the discussion will be directed only to deviations from the customary treatment that demonstrate Bach's contribution.

As a starting point let us take the fugue in F major.[21] Here the innovations arise in a purely technical problem, the use of stretto in the middle section. This is a fugue for three voices; consequently, according to the customary treatment, there should be three entries in the exposition. But here there are six, with an extra entrance of the alto ushering in the stretto technique.

Why did Bach set aside the accepted treatment by introducing a double exposition? If we turn to the second section, we find the explanation. Here the *answer*, which first enters on an A major chord (measure 36), appears three times in succession in stretto, after which the *subject* enters three times in stretto — six entries in all. It is obvious that to introduce this special use of stretto technique Bach required six voice entries instead of the usual three. To make the sections more symmetrical, he therefore employed a double exposition. The additional entry of the alto voice in stretto — most unusual in the exposition — can be accounted for as prophetic of the prominent role the stretto is to play in the following measures. As we have said, it is evident that the technique dictated the

[21] *Ibid.,* Book I, No. 11.

number of voice entries. However, the fluidity of the fugue subject overcomes the purely technical aspects of the work and lends itself to the treatment Bach employed. In fact Bach rightly sensed that only a subject of such simplicity could gain in intensity and richness through the accumulated stress of additional voice entries.

No one can claim that in this fugue Bach's techniques or his treatment of the form are imitative. On the contrary, by adhering to the principles of structural unity Bach felt free to shape the form to permit this highly original use of stretto. It is the elasticity provided by such a recognition of structural unity that enabled him to prolong the two sections of the form without sacrificing the tonal outlines of the basic motion.

A similar adaptation of the form to meet a specific need is found in the last movement of the concerto in C major for two solo claviers, with two violins, two violas, and continuo providing a five-voice tutti.

The last movement in a concerto of this period was ordinarily in a dance form in triple time, as a direct contrast to the more weighty character of the first movement. Bach's first deviation from the norm was to plan this movement as a three-part fugue. But even this innovation is not the most original feature of this work. The problem was to plan the distribution of the material so as to differentiate between the two solo claviers and the string tutti. In its broadest aspects this would logically suggest a fugue for three voices, the *subject* stated by the first clavier, the *answer* by the second, and a repetition of the *subject* by the strings. This, however, Bach avoided. First of all he wished to retain the characteristic lightness of the movement, and secondly he wished to differentiate between the treatment of a fugue for two solo instruments and the more conventional treatment for a single instrument.

That there are eleven instead of three entries in the exposition does not in itself constitute the artistic value of Bach's innovations; this is a result any student could achieve without observing the principles of structural unity. Rather it is that in spite of the prolongations necessary to obtain the additional entries, Bach has never once left the tonal framework nor stepped outside the boundaries of the tonality.

The observance of the basic principles of structure and prolongation permitted Bach to employ the smaller expansions that furnished not only the additional voice entries, but also the contrasting effects between the solo claviers and the accompanying instruments. The increased proportions of the form, the number of prolongations he used, as well as his differentiation of the instrumental parts, prove that for Bach the fugue was not static, its form not prescribed. In other words, each fugue sets new and individual problems whose solution often results in a challenge to the form, but never in a challenge to the structural principles out of which the form evolved.

As a final instance of the effect of Bach's genius on the fugue form, let us turn to the great organ fugue in E minor,[22] which presents an entirely different, although equally interesting, inroad on the form. This fugue was planned in the customary three sections. It is the unorthodox treatment of the middle section with which we are concerned here. In it Bach rejected the usual devices of augmentation, diminution, inversion, and stretto to introduce free improvisation into the heretofore rigid confines of the fugue form. He did not weaken the essential elements of the characteristic structure; instead he seized on the free nature of the episode, for which he substituted equally free improvisation. Although improvisation in itself was a well-established technique as applied to the prelude, its inclusion in the fugue form was entirely new. Moreover, Bach's fine discernment of the fitting place at which to employ the improvisation permitted him to experiment with a new fugal technique and to expand the section to almost grandiose proportions without subjecting the structural outlines of the form to mutation.

These four illustrations are sufficient to show that although Bach accepted the essential elements of the fugue form as defined by his predecessors, he transformed them into a form that was less an adaptation than a re-creation. Rejecting the principle of the polythematic fugue, he introduced those techniques through which the monothematic fugue as a single structural organism was established. Furthermore he gave the form a new concept of tonality. *In toto* we acknowledge that Bach is indebted to his precursors for their establishment of the fugue form and their contrapuntal skill. At the same time we realize that we are indebted to Bach for his stabilization of the monothematic fugue and for the principles of structural unity with which he conceived it, as well as for the vision that changed the conception of the form from a contrapuntal *tour de force* into an exciting drama of emotional conflicts.

Leaving the matter of form, we approach one of the most important problems to which Bach's music gives rise — his extensive use of dissonance.

[22] Bach Gesellschaft Edition, vol. xv.

BACH'S USE OF DISSONANCE

This aspect of Bach's treatment has been the subject of much discussion. It is responsible for many statements regarding his transgression of the rules governing harmonic progressions and the leading of voices. It has frequently led contemporary composers to cite Bach's music as containing the germs of the dissonant chords that figure so prominently in the music of the present day. Our most pertinent questions concern the origin of these dissonances. Are they of a structural or a prolonging nature? Do they occur in the harmonic progressions or in the contrapuntal voice leadings? What is their function, and what effect do they have on tonal coherence?

Before we can answer these questions intelligently, we must first inquire into the origin of the dissonances that are offered as evidence of the relation of Bach's chords to those of the twentieth century. In an article on "Tone Problems of Today," [23] Alfredo Casella points to the modal contrast between the ascending melodic minor scale, with its raised sixth and seventh degrees, and the descending natural minor (without sharps): "The contrapuntal employment of melismata based on these two scales indubitably constitutes the first historical example of the simultaneity of scales and consequently of polytonality, and it was the origin of many bold effects."

To prove his point, Casella cites, among his examples, one by Bach in which F♮ and F♯ appear within the same chord. He regards this chord as an instance in which Bach used two different scales simultaneously.

EXAMPLE 21

Before accepting Casella's theory, let us examine the voice leadings in this passage to see if they explain the presence of F♯ and F♮ within the same chord.

[23] *Musical Quarterly* (April, 1924).

Johann Sebastian Bach

There is an ascent in the bass from E to A against a top-voice descent from E to C, with E embellished by its neighbor F♮. The chords on the first and third quarters of the measure represent two different positions of the E seventh chord, in which the bass and alto ascend a third in tenths, while the tenor descends from D to B (Example 21A). It is evident, therefore, that the intervening chord comprised of three passing tones, F♯–C–A, and a neighbor note F♮, is a neighbor-passing chord. Since the motion in the bass is from E to G♯, as an expression of the E major chord, it automatically accounts for the presence of F♯ as a passing tone. It does not, however, explain the use of F♮ in the top voice.

In the descent from E to D, the seventh of the E major chord, F♮ appears as an incomplete neighbor note. As an intensification of E, it was fitting that Bach employed F♮ instead of F♯. Customarily this F♮ would have appeared as an eighth note in the first quarter of the measure in connection with E of the E major chord to which it belongs (Example 21B). Here, however, it enters on the second quarter, with a group of passing tones to which it bears no relation.

Presumably Bach did not want a metrical pattern of two eights and a half note and therefore transferred the F♮ from the first beat to the second to obtain the more symmetrical design of three quarter notes. Although the grouping together of a neighbor note and three passing tones creates a dissonance, F♯ and F♮ have no connection with each other, and their presence within the same group of tones is due to metrical considerations and not to the use of simultaneous scales.

This is an illustration of the unconventionality of Bach's treatment. It also shows that the complexities of his technique engender problems that can be solved only if we dig beneath the surface of the music to find the origin and function of the tones whose simultaneous presence gives rise to discussion. Here we see that F♯ and F♮ have each been employed for a specific melodic purpose that justifies both, but refutes the contention that their combination is due to the simultaneous use of two different scales.

It is true that this example offers an interesting instance of Bach's daring use of dissonance. Yet it is equally true that to attribute the presence of the F♯ and F♮ within the same passing chord to the simultaneous employment of two scales ignores the status of F♮ as a neighbor note and the function of F♯ as a passing tone. Here we see the results of regarding every chord as being harmonic in origin, since no distinction has been

61

made between the E major chords that outline the motion and the passing chord that fills the motion. In addition the function of F as an embellishment of the top-voice motion has not been taken into consideration in Casella's explanation, since he regards it as a member of the chord in which it appears. Therefore he recognized the space-fillers F♯—A—C with the misplaced neighbor note F♮ as an harmonic entity whose dissonant effect he accounts for in terms of bitonality. The danger of such a conclusion is obvious. Based on a theoretical conception of tonality, it attributes to the music of the eighteenth century tendencies that are characteristic of the twentieth. Thus it is less an explanation of Bach's music than a means of linking present-day techniques to the methods of the past.

A further reference by a contemporary composer to Bach's use of dissonant harmony is made by Arnold Schönberg.[24] In the chapter on *Harmoniefremde Töne,* tones foreign to the harmony, such as passing tones, neighbor notes, changing tones, and so on, Schönberg states [25] that although the older system of harmony accepted the foreign tone as alien to the chord in which it appeared, in reality all tones sounding simultaneously form a chord. Thus every so-called "foreign tone" is a chord tone and an integral part of the chord in which it occurs. A discussion of this point will be found in the chapter on Schönberg.

As proof of his contention that he does not hear these foreign tones as extraneous to the chord, since he regards every vertical combination of tones as a chord entity, Schönberg cites [26] the following illustration from a Bach motet.[27]

EXAMPLE 22

We see in Example A that this entire measure consists of three positions of the chord F—A—C—E♭. This, as a seventh, is itself a chord of motion. The foreign tones D and B♭, to which Schönberg refers as organic chord tones, are in reality passing tones, D between E♭ and C in one voice

---

[24] *Harmonielehre* (Universal Edition, 1922).   [26] *Ibid.,* p. 392.
[25] *Ibid.,* p. 372.   [27] *Motet IV* (Peters Edition).

Johann Sebastian Bach

and B♭ between C and A in another. However, the acceptance of these passing tones as chord tones enables Schönberg to construct the chords F–A–B♭–D–E♭ and A–B♭–D–F–C as indicative of the dissonant element in Bach's harmony (Example 22B).

The recognition of all neighbor notes, passing tones, and embellishments as organic chord tones deprives music of two of its basic principles — motion and coherence. Coherence, as we have seen, is achieved through the outlined space of the chord; motion, by filling the space with passing tones. To believe that these passing tones and all embellishing tones are chord tones eliminates both the fundamental principles of structure and prolongation and any differentiation between the harmonic and contrapuntal functions. This inevitably leads to a conception of tonality that is no longer based on the idea of structural coherence, since all chords, irrespective of their diverse origins, are regarded as of equal importance.

Is not this example clearer if we hear it as a motion outlined by three positions of the F seventh chord than if we give it Schönberg's interpretation? Does it not have greater musical meaning if we recognize the alien tones as passing tones or space-fillers within the motion than if we regard them as organic members of three different chords — especially since such chords have no tonal implications either structurally or as prolongations?

The distinction between chords of melodic and harmonic origin is too rarely stressed, a fact that has led many composers, as well as theorists, to regard all chords as harmonies with a similar functional significance. This emphasis on the harmonic to the exclusion of the melodic element has given rise to the theory that Bach was as original and daring in his use of harmonic dissonance as we have found him in his treatment of voice leadings — a theory that Casella and Schönberg hold, but have not proved. In fact the references of these composers to Bach show that they have attempted to understand his music through their own methods of composition.

The explanations offered by Casella and Schönberg emphasize the need for a new interpretation of Bach's technique. This should be based on a study of what the music reveals rather than on the theoretical approach offered in textbooks. The time has come when the method of analysis that the student is taught should provide a practical explanation of these techniques that the exponents of the present system regard as transgressions. It should be founded on fact instead of theory, on the premise that the system should adhere to the music, not the music to the system. It

63

should not present a set of rules which the student is to observe, but which later, as a composer, he is free to break. On the contrary the preparation should provide a technical background for the student that not only fully equips him to comprehend the works of others, but that can also serve as the foundation of his own creative efforts.

There can be no better model for such a system than the music of Bach, since through its differentiation of the harmonic and contrapuntal functions it demonstrates a conception of tonality which it is essential to understand in order to explain the works that follow.

BACH'S TREATMENT OF EMOTIONAL QUALITIES

A final aspect of Bach's art must be cited, the emotional quality that he brought to the secular forms — the prelude, the fugue, the suite, and the sonata. For example, the prelude in Eb minor [28] is one of many that could be cited [29] as typical illustrations of Bach's ability to use the prelude form to convey a rich and poignant emotional experience.

Similarly there is a depth of emotion in the sarabandes and airs of Bach's suites and in the slow movements of his sonatas that is characteristic of him alone. It is the same penetrating quality that we found in the chorales.

The overtures to the orchestral suites in C major, D major, and B minor furnish further evidence. Because of the mood of sustained emotion that Bach imparted to them, we are aware of the essential difference between the older suite, which was solely an artistic adaptation of the dance forms, and the suite that in its newly-won melodic beauty was the product of Bach's creative genius.

In the slow movements of the Italian Concerto, the concerto in D minor for two violins, the violin and cello sonatas, and the Brandenberg Concertos we find additional proof that the emotional element is significant in Bach's music. This same force is equally typical of the chorale treatment and provides the dramatic intensity that permeates the recitatives, the arias, and the choruses of the Passions and the Mass.

Therefore, although this discussion, for the most part, has centered on various aspects of Bach's technical treatment, it should not be assumed that technique was the sole means by which Bach achieved his dynamic effects. His greatness, on the contrary, lies in the perfect balance he main-

[28] *Well-tempered Clavichord*, Book I, No. 8.
[29] *Ibid.*, Book I: E minor, Bb minor, and B minor; Book II: Eb major, F minor, and G minor.

tains between the intellectual and emotional interests of his material. For this reason Bach's music not only has survived, but is as great an inspiration to us today as it was to the congregation of the Thomaskirche. This is significant in view of the fact that the music of many of the seventeenth- and early eighteenth-century contrapuntists is seldom heard. It tends to confirm the evidence that has been offered to prove that in his technical and stylistic expression and his treatment of the form, Bach was not a mere organizer but an innovator, a great creative artist whose works have influenced the whole trend of musical thought.

By demonstrating the advantages of the tonal over the older modal system, Bach took a step that was to determine the future development of music. Furthermore, in his demonstration of tonality as the principle of unity expressed through the motion within a single horizontalized chord, he defined the interrelationship of the harmonic and contrapuntal functions as a necessary principle of free composition. In addition, in his adaptation and recreation of the prelude, the fugue, the suite, and the old sonata, he expanded these forms to their utmost capacity, so that further development along these lines would have been difficult. Thus, indirectly if not directly, he was responsible for those experiments of Philipp Emanuel Bach in style and form that eventually gave rise to the modern sonata.

It is often stated that the works of Johann Sebastian Bach formed the climax of a great period in musical history, the music of the Reformation. But Bach is more than the end of one period, more even than the beginning of another. He is the foundation of all the music that followed, all that we possess today.

CHAPTER III

Philipp Emanuel Bach

NEW TRENDS *in form and style. Change of emphasis from horizontal to vertical style. Expanded outlines of the sonata within the tonal concept. Adherence to principles of voice leading. A discussion of the Prussian and Württemberg Sonatas.*

HILIPP EMANUEL BACH made two important contributions to the development of music. First, he departed from the contrapuntal emphasis of the preceding age and achieved a lighter and more graceful style, and second, in his experiments with form, he laid down the structural outlines from which the classical sonata was to evolve. Since his own tendencies were against the contrapuntal, or, as he called it, the "strong type of music," it was natural that he should turn from the two- and three-part forms of the prelude, fugue, suite, and the old sonata and concerto, in which the contrapuntal style of his father had attained perfection, to seek a new form of expression that was more in keeping with his own inclinations.

An extra-musical factor, however, influenced the direction his reforms were to take. This was the transfer of musical patronage from the church to the aristocracy. Just as the polyphonic style of the fifteenth and sixteenth centuries emerged out of the Catholic liturgical service and as the contrapuntal style of the chorale, cantata, chorale-prelude, and prelude and fugue became an integral part of the ritual of the Protestant church, so it was equally inevitable that court life should have an influence on the music it fostered. On the other hand, to believe, as is sometimes stated, that the primary impulse for experimentation was due to the interest of the aristocracy is to underestimate the far-reaching results of Johann Sebastian Bach's works. The perfection of his style and technique and his development of form left only two possibilities to his successors — to stagnate in mere imitation or to progress along other and different lines.

In his remarkable book *Versuch über die wahre Art das Clavier zu*

66

Philipp Emanuel Bach

spielen [1] (Essay on the Proper Way of Playing the Piano), Philipp Emanuel Bach discusses the changes that came into music in his time. He says in effect [2] that the four- and more than four-voice setting belongs to the serious type of music, the so-called "heavy" forms, such as counterpoint, fugue, and so on, and is used in those works that are absolute music, in which questions of taste and refinement are not the primary consideration, and that the three- and less than three-voice setting is used to obtain an elegance of style when the taste, interpretation, or effect of a work requires less strict adherence to a given number of voices. Not only do we find the use of the three- and less than three-voice setting in Philipp Emanuel Bach's works, but the accent has been shifted from the horizontal to the vertical through the addition and dropping of extra voices. In fact there is a decided loosening up of the contrapuntal technique.

We should not deduce from these changes that Philipp Emanuel Bach did not hold in great esteem the contrapuntal style in which his father had found expression and in which he himself had been thoroughly trained. Nor should we believe that his stress of the vertical aspect eliminated the contrapuntal. On the contrary, his works reveal that he recognized the interdependence of the horizontal and vertical functions. It was merely a question as to whether the emphasis of the vertical or of the horizontal style was best fitted to express the nature of the musical idea and the specific form the composer wished it to take. His challenge, therefore, was not to counterpoint *per se,* but to the preservation of a style that he believed was ill adapted to express a totally different type of musical idea.

Because Philipp Emanuel Bach retained the primary function of counterpoint as a means of providing motion within the harmonic structure, it is evident that the term "counterpoint" should not be restricted to a single style in which, as in the fugue, chorale-prelude, toccata, and passacaglia, the individual voice parts appear as independent melodic lines. To believe that contrapuntal techniques are confined to these older forms is as erroneous as to believe that harmonic techniques alone are used in a sonata.

We may speak of a vertical or horizontal style in pointing out the more obvious tendencies in the treatment. Yet in the technique itself both the harmonic and contrapuntal principles are present: the harmonic to lay the structural foundations, the contrapuntal to expand them.

Philipp Emanuel Bach challenged the style and forms in which these

[1] C. F. Kahnt (Leipzig, 1925).   [2] *Zweiter Teil, Einleitung,* Nos. 24 and 26.

principles had been demonstrated, but the principles themselves he retained as the primary factor of his artistic credo. In fact it was his use of both the harmonic and contrapuntal techniques that enabled him to expand the structural outlines of the form without destroying its organic unity and to further introduce techniques that had a tremendous influence on the music of his successors.

The link between the sonatas of Johann Sebastian Bach, the *sonata da chiesa* (church sonata) and the *sonata da camera* (suite), and the classical sonatas of Haydn is found in the early Prussian and Württemberg Sonatas of Philipp Emanuel Bach. These sonatas served the young Haydn as a model; both he and Mozart had them in mind when they acknowledged their indebtedness to Philipp Emanuel Bach. Among all the composers of his period, the younger Bach is practically the only one to whom these successors have paid tribute. The point should be noted by those who contend that Scarlatti and, more especially, Johann Stamitz played a more significant role than Bach in the evolution of the classical sonata.

In his outline of the sectional elements of the form Bach was less academic than Stamitz. His three main sections are not sharply divided, nor did he adhere to any set method of integrating these parts into the structural organism. There are some expositions, for example, with no contrasting theme, and others in which the mediant or dominant chord of the primordial harmonic progression is reached only in the final measures. In the development section, at times, the uncertain status of a widely prolonged chord tends to obscure the manner in which the motion from the development to the recapitulation is achieved. The recapitulation also offers inconsistencies by the frequent omission of the principal theme.

Johann Stamitz, on the other hand, is more regular in his equal distribution of the material and in his stronger emphasis on the beginning and end of the individual sections. In his works the theme and contrasting theme, the development and recapitulation, are usually clear-cut and well defined.

With Bach, however, the close interweaving and at times overlapping of the development and recapitulation in his sonatas suggests that he wished to avoid a sharp division of the structural organism into separate and distinct entities, as the growing independence of the sections would ultimately destroy the oneness of the structural whole.

In fact Philipp Emanuel Bach's close interlocking of the various elements points to his awareness of the danger in a clear-cut separation of

Philipp Emanuel Bach

the themes of the exposition and in a too distinct segregation of the development section from the recapitulation. That Haydn, Mozart, and Beethoven — especially in his late works — adhered to this principle was primarily responsible for the fact that the character of the form as a structural organism remained intact. It was only when the rich lyricism of Schubert and Schumann replaced the earlier quality of improvisation and brought about a new independence of the thematic elements that structural cohesion was destroyed. In their period the sonata began to decline, a result that proves the accuracy of Bach's conception of the form.

The study of Bach's innovations and their influence on the classical sonata will be restricted to the early Prussian and Württemberg Sonatas, since they were composed and published before either Haydn or Mozart appeared on the musical scene. There can be no argument as to the influence of these composers on the technique, style, or form of these early works. The structural outlines on which the first and last movements of the Prussian and Württemberg Sonatas were based were a vital factor in the development of the full-fledged sonata form. In general they indicate the thematic contrasts of the exposition, the development section — the major innovation in the form — and the restatement, in which there is a sufficient allusion to the material of the exposition, even if the main theme at times is omitted, to give the feeling of a recapitulation. For the most part this aspect of Bach's contribution and its influence on the music of his successors has been acknowledged. But it has been completely overlooked that these sonatas present an ideal conception of form as a structural organism rather than as a group of segregated and independent parts. Because this conception was adhered to by Bach's successors, his influence penetrated far beyond his innovations in style, technique, and expanded outline to the very heart of music — the growth of form through the elasticity of the tonal concept.

Form, whether in music or any other art, is not a conventional mold into which the composer, painter or sculptor pours his creative ideas, nor is it an arbitrary outward structure that can be superimposed on the material. Form is an integral part of the growth and development of a creative idea; it emerges out of the initial conception and takes its shape from the nature of the material and the character of the treatment. It has no independent existence, but is bound up, in music, with the melodic, contrapuntal, and harmonic elements, both in the germ plasm of the

69

Challenge to Musical Tradition

imagination and in the reality of its fulfillment. It is logical that the nature of the material should affect both technique and form. A fugue subject, for example, demands a different type of treatment from the thematic material of a sonata. But as both the fugue and the sonata form are conceived within a three-part form, the characteristics that determine their individuality arise primarily in the variations of their subject matter, their techniques, and their styles and in the nature of the prolongations.

Since Bach's most conspicuous contribution to the form is the development section, it is understandable that the technical means by which he achieved this innovation was the further prolongation of the basic structure. This is equally true of the exposition, in which the new element, the contrasting theme, emerges from a prolongation of the mediant or dominant chord. Naturally the melodic impulse is equally essential, but the structural aspects are the motivating factors through which the increased melodic activity is made possible.

Bach's new tendencies in style and technique are only one aspect of his contribution to the development of music. He preserved the principles of structural coherence embodied in the concept of tonality while he shaped the outlines of the classical sonata. This was his link to the past and his legacy to the future.

First of all let us examine various passages from these sonatas to see what the new tendencies in Bach's style are and how they are reflected in his treatment of the subject matter and the smaller prolongations.

NEW STYLISTIC TENDENCIES

One of the most interesting of the Prussian Sonatas is the fourth, in C minor.[3] Its distinctly new quality is due only in part to the character of the subject matter, which differs from that of the sonatas and suites of Johann Sebastian Bach and Handel. The main effect, however, is achieved through the technical innovations that are an essential element of Bach's style. Here we see the results of the three- and less than three-voice accompaniment in the pronounced domination of one melodic line, with the two other voices subordinated to give the effect of an accompaniment.

There are other aspects of the treatment, however, that contribute to the fluidity and flexibility of the style. Among these is the frequent use of suspensions and the constant shift of register in the prolongations. The suspensions not only add considerable intensity to the melodic activity

[3] Nagel Edition, 1927.

70

of the opening theme, but are the origin of a most unusual passage in the contrasting section. This affinity of the thematic material in the two sections of the exposition is not limited to this sonata, but is a general characteristic of the treatment. How closely Haydn followed Philipp Emanuel Bach in respect to the organic connection between the subject matter of the main theme and that of the contrasting theme must be apparent to anyone familiar with Haydn's works, in which the similarity of the melodic figures is frequently too obvious to be overlooked.

EXAMPLE 23

The most conspicuous of the techniques used in this passage is the transfer of register as a means of prolonging the structural top-voice motion. This treatment is not confined to these measures, but occurs consistently throughout the entire movement. It appears mainly in the two upper voices and is largely responsible for the expanded motion within the C minor and G major chords.

In the opening phrase there is a shift of G from the top to a middle voice, from which it passes to F, a top voice, in a motion of G—F—E♭ (measure 2). The ascent to F is not direct, however, but is made through the opening up, or unfolding, of two intervals, G—C and B♮—F, each of which represents two different voices. Instead of appearing simultaneously in a vertical position, they are horizontalized. Thus, G and C outline the tonic chord and B and F, the dominant. In this unfolding, however, it is plain that G, transferred from a top to a middle voice, is shifted to F, while C, a real middle voice, moves to B♮ in the same register. Here the unfolding is clearly indicated, but there are instances, as we shall see, in which the technique is more complicated.

Since there is a repetition of the motion G—F—E♭ (measures 2–3) as a descent of a third within the C minor chord, it is evident that G in the first of these motions has the quality of a retained tone of the structural top voice that has been prolonged through a descent to E♭, a middle voice. In the second motion from G to E♭, it is equally clear that G is again retained as a structural top voice that moves to A♭, a neighbor note, while E♭ is shifted to a higher octave.

This interpretation of the top voice as a motion within the outlined C minor chord is borne out by the bass, which also shows an expanded motion within the tonic chord through the use of two harmonic prolongations (measures 1–3). The motion from the C minor to the dominant G major chord is characteristic of the artistry of Bach's prolonging techniques.

First of all we see that G, the structural top voice, has moved to A♭ (measure 3), which in turn descends through G to F♯. This descent, in relation to the G that precedes and follows, constitutes a neighbor-note motion in which A♭ serves as an upper and F♯ as a lower neighbor. Simultaneously the bass moves from C to A♭, which, replacing A♭ in the top voice, acts as a neighbor of the G that follows. Thus the embellishing motion points out the neighbor-note function of A♭ in both voices.

Meanwhile, E♭, a middle voice, shifted above the structural top voice descends through D and C to G of the G major chord. This G is a substi-

Philipp Emanuel Bach

tute for B♮ which is omitted, so that the full emphasis be given to G as a structural top voice. The B♮ is shown in the graph in parentheses to indicate that E♭ descends stepwise to B♮, the third of the G major chord, while the neighbor note A♭ passes to G, the root of the chord. Since there are countless instances of similar substitutions of one tone for another to achieve a specific effect, we are justified in acknowledging the presence of B♮ even though it does not appear in the music. The repetition of the embellishing motions in a lower register brings the passage to a close on the dominant G major chord.

Since these measures show a basic motion from the tonic to the dominant chord, it is evident that the vertical tendencies of Bach's style have not eliminated the horizontal or contrapuntal techniques as a means of prolonging the harmonic progression. We find proof not only in the neighbor-note motion that delays the entrance of the dominant chord, but in the expanded motion within the tonic for which the horizontal character of the melody is primarily responsible. Here the transfer of register, the technique of unfolding, the motion from a tone of the structural top voice to a middle voice, and the embellishing motions are all contrapuntal techniques that expand the basic harmonic progression. They affect the voice leadings and contribute greatly to the interest and character of the passage. However, the dexterity with which Bach has subordinated the contrapuntal to the harmonic tendencies of the treatment should not lead us to assume that counterpoint no longer demonstrates its function of prolongation. On the contrary we should recognize that there is so complete a fusion of the melodic, contrapuntal, and harmonic elements that Bach was able to change the emphasis from the horizontal to the vertical without impairing either the interrelationship of the harmonic and contrapuntal functions or the expression of tonality as structural coherence.

Another instance in which the subtlety of Bach's treatment conceals the strong contrapuntal impulse that provides the prolongations is in the opening measures of the sixth Württemberg Sonata, in B minor.[4] The style here is entirely different from that in the C minor sonata. There is a definite suggestion of the recitative, both in the character of the material and in the rhythmic emphasis, to which the rests in the bass also contribute. The movement as a whole illustrates the distinctive characteristics of Bach's style.

4 *Ibid.*, 1928.

EXAMPLE 24

The adaptation of the recitative style to the sonata is indicative of the unusual nature of the treatment. It is emphasized by the vertical tendency apparent in the accented chords in the second quarter of measures 2, 3, and 4 and by the effect produced by the rests in the bass. Nevertheless, the graph shows that these chords are of contrapuntal origin, since they serve as space-fillers that prolong the motion from the B minor to the F♯ major chord.

In the top and middle voices we find a progression in sixths, while the outside voices proceed by contrary motion. The top voice ascends from D to F♯; the bass descends chromatically from B to F♯. There is a further expansion of the top voice through the introduction of E as a neighbor note (measure 2) and also through the unfolding of the E♯ and F♯ chords (measures 4–7). Since this example of unfolding, which prolongs the structural top-voice motion from E♯ to F♯, is typical of the technique, let us examine these measures as a clue to all other instances of unfolding.

EXAMPLE 25

Example 25A shows the chords in vertical position with a direct motion from the E♯ to the F♯ chord. In example 25B the motion is prolonged through the unfolding of the intervals E♯–B and A♯–F♯. This form of horizontalization delays the entrance of F♯ in the top voice by a middle-voice motion, B–A♯. It also permits the entrance of G♮ as a passing tone in the bass. Example 25C duplicates the unfolding as it occurs in the passage from the B minor sonata, with E♯ and F♯ transferred to a lower voice before the F♯ is reached in the top voice. There is a constant repetition of the motion E♯–F♯, due primarily to the unfolding of the intervals of the F♯ major chord, through which the ascending and descending motions create an exchange of voices.

These three examples demonstrate the same principle of motion from the E♯ to the F♯ chord. The only difference is that in Example 25A the motion has not been prolonged, while in the two other examples the intervals of the chords have been unfolded to achieve an expansion of the top-voice motion. Thus, because it employs the horizontal instead of the vertical position of the chord, the technique of unfolding is a type of prolongation.

Although the treatment throughout tends to accentuate the vertical tendency of the recitative style, it is evident that the beauty of the passage, its color and richness, are due largely to the horizontal aspects of the technique, the chromatic passing chords that extend the tonic-dominant progression.

In the opening movement of the sonata in E minor, the third of the Württemberg group, we find an entirely different type of subject matter,

Challenge to Musical Tradition

which, in its unlikeness to the material of the C and B minor sonatas, shows how varied is the nature of Bach's melodic ideas.

The distinctive character of this sonata is the breadth and sweep of the melodic line, which the vertical arrangement of the accompanying voices tends to emphasize. The constant shift of register is another factor enhancing the effect, which is further intensified by the technique of unfolding.

EXAMPLE 26

The only harmonic functions expressed in this passage are those exercised by the tonic and dominant chords that define the harmonic progression. Every other chord is a passing chord that expands the space between the E minor and B major chords. This is equally true of the B major chord (measure 2), which, although a dominant, serves as a neighbor-passing chord and thus demonstrates a contrapuntal function.

Although the bass descent is clearly defined, the motions of the two upper voices are somewhat clouded by their interweaving in the melodic figuration and also by the constant shift in register. In the first two measures these voices show a descent of a third, moving in sixths. The motion, however, has been prolonged by the unfolding of the intervals B–G, A–F♯, and G–E, of which G–F♯–E represent the top voice and B–A–G the middle. At the end of this motion E appears not in the top voice, but below G, a middle voice. However, an ascent from G through B of the B minor chord to E of the C seventh chord restores E to its proper register. The motion from E to D♯ is. expanded by a descent from E to A,

76

Philipp Emanuel Bach

a middle voice, and by an embellishing motion that duplicates in miniature the top-voice descent from G to E. Such parallelisms reveal the organic nature of Bach's conception and the imagination and artistry with which he manifests it even in the ornamentations. In this as in the preceding examples the vertical aspect is given great emphasis. The addition and dropping of extra voices further contribute to this effect and impart to the style a freedom and fluidity that are characteristic of the new tendencies. Therefore it is all the more remarkable that beneath the outer surface of the treatment there is a strong contrapuntal impulse, whose function of prolongation still remains a vital and necessary element in maintaining the structural coherence.

A final example of the varied tendencies that these early works offer comes from the adagio of the E♭ minor sonata, the fifth of the Württemberg group.

Although in this movement the emphasis is placed on the horizontal rather than the vertical style, Bach has employed some of the same techniques that we found in the preceding examples in which the harmonic tendency predominated. Here, although the nature of the melody, the use of imitation, and the handling of the individual voice parts all combine to bring out the contrapuntal character of the treatment, the function served by the counterpoint is the same as in those passages in which it is subordinated to the harmonic impulse — the function of prolongation.

In our discussion the technical aspects are of primary importance, but we should not overlook the poignant beauty of the melody or the artistry with which Bach intensified its mood by the type of treatment he provided. Its deep and sustained emotion, so well suited to the character of a slow movement, is in many respects reminiscent of the quality that the slow movements of Johann Sebastian Bach reveal.

The passage as a whole shows a harmonic progression of I–V–I. It differs from the preceding examples in that the prolongation is achieved mainly through the expansion of the dominant chord, while in the other instances it was the motion to the dominant that was extended. On the other hand the descent by sixths in the two upper voices, which carries the top voice from G♭ to A♭, is similar to the treatment in the passage from the B minor sonata (Example 24).

By far the most striking element in the technique is the prolongation of the dominant chord. This is achieved both through the harmonic prolongation I–V–I and through the expansion of the ascent from B♭ to D♮

77

EXAMPLE 27

in the bass (measures 6–8) by means of passing tones. In these three measures the extension is due mainly to the prolongation of the top-voice descent from B♭ to A♭ through an embellishing motion in which B♭ ascends to G♭, with a return to A♭ of the structural line. In this ornamentation Bach has delicately outlined the opening motive in augmentation so that the ascent from B♭ to G♭, which might appear to be only an embellishment, also imitates the interval on which the original motive begins. Although the reference to the motivic figure is subtle, the emphasis of G♭, E♭, C♭, B♭, and A♭, outlined in the descent, leaves little doubt as to the underlying meaning of the expansion and the reason for the special form in which it is presented. Here is further evidence of the organic nature of the treatment and the power with which the fundamental melodic impulse is carried over into the prolongations.

Simultaneously with the ascent to G♮ there is a descent from B♭ to E♭, a middle voice, which continues its downward motion until it reaches A♭ in the bass, an under neighbor of the preceding B♭ (measure 6). This A♭ carries the motion upward to C♮, a passing tone between B♭ and D♮ of the B♭ major chord (measures 6–8). The means by which Bach has used this prolongation to repeat the melodic figure of the opening measures not only indicate the ingenuity of his technique, but reveal the breadth and vision of his artistic conception.

Again it must be pointed out that although the emphasis is applied to the horizontal style through the imitation of the motive (measure 4), the arrangement of the voice parts, and the contrapuntal treatment of the voice leadings, the vertical aspect is nevertheless present in its definition of the motion outlined by the tonic-dominant progression. Here the roles that harmony and counterpoint play in the preceding examples are reversed, in that the harmonic impulse is now subordinated to the contrapuntal. Their individual and combined functions, however, remain unchanged. This is the essential point demonstrated by the passage.

The stress of the vertical or the horizontal approach is purely a matter of preference on the part of the composer. It has to do with the special style in which he clothes his musical ideas. But it in no wise affects the functions these factors exercise in defining and prolonging the structure, since, irrespective of the style and regardless of which predominates, both are essential to organic coherence.

Furthermore this passage substantiates the conclusion that could be drawn even from the preceding examples — that Bach did not turn from the "strong or contrapuntal style" because he lacked the necessary contrapuntal equipment. Here we have recognized an essential point in evaluating the results of his experimentation. It proves that Bach's innovations were due, not to an insufficient technique, but to a conscious artistry that found a new medium of expression. In this the contrapuntal element was subordinated to the individual characteristics of his style. It was the departure from the horizontal idiom that led Philipp Emanuel Bach to reject the two- and three-part forms in which the contrapuntal style had achieved its climax and to experiment with a new type of three-part form in which it would serve as a free and unhampered outlet for his art.

Challenge to Musical Tradition

What, then, are the essential elements of the new form, and what is Bach's concrete contribution to the classical sonata? Let us look at the Prussian and Württemberg Sonatas now from the point of view of form. We shall confine ourselves to the opening movements, with a general discussion of the variations in treatment of the exposition, development, and recapitulation.

THE EXPOSITION

1. THE PRUSSIAN SONATAS

The expositions of these six sonatas are regular in that they reveal both the melodic and structural prolongations through which the theme and contrasting theme are defined. In those in a major key the themes demonstrate an expansion of the motion from the tonic to the dominant chord of the basic harmonic progression, while in the sonatas in minor the basic structure is indicated in a motion from the tonic to the mediant chord. In the third sonata, however, in E major, there is a slight deviation from the norm in that the contrasting theme enters on a prolonged F♯ major chord that serves both as the supertonic of the E major and as the applied dominant of the B major chord.

Although in a miniature form, this prolongation of the motion that delays the entrance of the dominant is prophetic of Beethoven's technique in the first movement of the "Pathétique" Sonata, Opus 13. In the latter the motion from the tonic C minor to the mediant E♭ major chord, in which the contrasting theme enters, is expanded through the introduction of a melodic passage within an expanded B♭ chord. We rightfully expect Beethoven to give the melodic aspect of the prolongation a more mature and ingenious treatment. However, Bach's recognition of the dramatic possibilities that the delay of the dominant offers, shown in his third experiment with the form, is proof of his imaginative grasp of the variety provided by the tonal aspects of the form.

2. THE WÜRTTEMBERG SONATAS

In three of these expositions there is an irregularity in form. In the first sonata, in A minor, the character of the contrasting theme is weakened, because it consists primarily of the melodic characteristics of the opening theme, transposed to meet the requirements of the new motion within the dominant E minor chord. There is some new material, but the dominating

80

figure that appears both in the bass and in the top voice is derived from the main theme.

The predominance of one theme throughout the exposition shows how closely interwoven are the melodic as well as the structural elements of the form. It indicates that for Bach the contrasting nature of the material of the exposition was secondary to its fusion into a unified whole. Surely it was not lack of melodic inventiveness that led him to employ the same theme throughout, since he does so in no other of those early sonatas. We can regard it only as a clear definition of his conception of the organic nature of the form. This use of one theme throughout is not confined to Bach's treatment. It can be found also in various works of Haydn, who similarly stressed the nature of the exposition as the flowering of a single melodic idea.

The expositions of the sonatas in E♭ major and B minor reveal a different type of irregularity. In these the attainment of the respective dominant and mediant chords on which the contrasting themes customarily enter comes only at the conclusion of the exposition. Due to this extended prolongation of the motion from the E♭ to the B♭ major chord in one case and from the B minor to the D major in the other, the contrasting themes are lacking. In fact in these two instances the characteristics of the form are more suggestive of the suite than of the exposition of a sonata. Here again Bach has achieved the necessary contrast in the motion that prolongs the harmonic progression, but he has emphasized the nature of the exposition as the expression of a single musical idea.

THE DEVELOPMENT SECTION

This is Bach's unique contribution to form. It should provide the most interesting demonstrations of the technical means by which the coherence of the structural motion is preserved. This aspect of his innovation is of greater importance than the so-called development of the melodic material. The main point of our investigation, therefore, is to find out how the organic nature of the movement has been kept intact and how Bach has welded the three sections of the form into a single structural motion.

1. THE PRUSSIAN SONATAS

The treatment varies greatly in most of the development sections. Consequently, we cannot discuss the techniques as a whole, but will

81

have to concentrate on each of these sections in turn, to point out wherein it differs from that of a preceding work.

In the first sonata, in F major, the development section opens on a dominant C major chord. There is a motion from this C major to a D minor chord, which, after an extensive prolongation, passes directly to the F major chord of the recapitulation.

Example 28

The problem here is the status of the D minor chord, which Bach has not sufficiently clarified.

There is a well defined motion from the dominant C major chord, on which the development starts, to the D minor chord, whose expansion is carried into the final measures of the section shown in the above example. This suggests the use of the D minor as a neighbor chord of the dominant, a customary technique in prolonging the structural motion. However, if it is a neighbor chord, one expects a return motion to the dominant at the close of the development, to lead into the tonic chord that ushers in the recapitulation. Here there is no clearly defined motion to the dominant C major chord, but a stepwise descent from the root of the D minor to the root of the tonic F major chord. In this descent however, the presence of C—B♭—A—G as passing tones suggests a subtle but extremely weak reference to the outlined dominant, to imply a return from the D minor chord. Accordingly, this would explain the D minor as a neighbor chord. The treatment, however, is not altogether convincing. The contrapuntal tendency of the motion from the D minor to the F major chord is so strong that it is difficult to hear the passing tones as indicative of the C major chord. On the other hand, the D minor chord gives evidence of its status as a prolonged neighbor of the dominant chord that opens the development section. Consequently we must accept the technique as representative of the neighbor-chord treatment even though the function of the neighbor chord is not clarified by the presence of a well defined dominant at the close of the section. The vagueness of the motion from the

Philipp Emanuel Bach

D minor to the F major chord not only affects the status of the neighbor chord, but it also weakens the entrance of the tonic chord of the recapitulation and thus tends to obscure the structural outlines of the form. We must regard this example as one of the few instances in these early sonatas in which Bach does not give a clear and convincing demonstration of the neighbor-chord technique as a means of prolonging the structural motion. Even according to the accepted method of harmonic analysis in which the prolonged D minor chord would be regarded as a modulation to the key of D minor, it would be difficult to account for the omission of a dominant chord at the end of the section and for the abrupt transition from the D minor to the F major tonality.

A similar treatment is to be found in the development sections of the first and last movements of the third sonata, in E major. In both, there is a motion from the opening dominant B major chord to an extended chord of C♯ minor, which leads directly to the tonic E major chord of the restatement. The following passage from the first movement is equally typical of the treatment in the last.

EXAMPLE 29

Here the problem is intensified by the fact that there is no connecting motion between the C♯ minor chord on which the development closes and the E major chord that follows. Is C♯ minor a neighbor chord of B major, to which it does not return, or, if not, what is its function in the motion?

This vagueness in the technique might be attributed to Bach's inexperience in dealing with the structural problems of the form, if these two early sonatas were the only instances in which this specific treatment occurs. However, since the same technique is used in a later work, the fourth Württemberg Sonata, in B♭ major, it is evident that it was not the result of inexperience. Moreover, in many of the intervening sonatas the structural techniques are much more complicated but are even more clearly outlined. We can only assume that this specific treatment was

83

motivated either by a desire for a startling effect or by a technical idiosyncrasy.

A fact that substantiates this supposition is the extraordinary treatment Bach used in the development section of the B♭ major sonata, the second of the Prussian group and consequently his second experiment with the form.

The motion begins on a dominant F major chord and passes through the chords of C and A major to the chord of D minor, which is widely extended before it proceeds to the tonic B♭ major chord of the recapitulation. Here there is a motion from the F major through the D minor to the B♭ chord, a descent in thirds which outlines a motion within the horizontalized B♭ chord. In the originality and deftness of the technique with which he binds the development to the recapitulation Bach gives evidence both of his proficiency in handling the form and of the breadth of his imaginative conception. Since, in spite of its more complex treatment, this B♭ major sonata shows a mature grasp of the structural problems of the form, it is impossible to attribute the ambiguity of the neighbor-chord technique in the F and E major sonatas that immediately precede and follow it, either to experimentation or to the lack of technical assurance. It is all the more remarkable that in this, his second sonata, Bach should have demonstrated a type of prolongation that was to serve so many of his successors in the later eighteenth and the nineteenth centuries.

The fourth sonata, in C minor, to which we referred earlier, is of special interest because of the overlapping of the development and the recapitulation. Here the development opens on the mediant E♭ major chord and passes through a prolonged D minor chord to the chord of G minor, on which the main theme is repeated. This suggests a recapitulation. However, only four measures of the theme have been heard when an exchange of the G minor for the G major chord leads most smoothly into the fifth measure of the original theme and into the tonic chord of the recapitulation.

The entrance of the theme, although transposed to the G minor chord, gives the impression that we have reached the recapitulation. This effect is strengthened by the fact that these measures represent the first four measures of the theme, with the fifth measure entering on the tonic C minor chord. Thus, although the melodic material is indicative of the recapitulation, the structural motion shows that this material is still a part of the development section and that the recapitulation is achieved

Philipp Emanuel Bach

only with the entrance of the tonic chord in the fifth measure of the theme. The welding together of the two sections is extraordinary, and it reveals how closely integrated are the sectional elements in Bach's conception of the form. In fusing the first four measures of the theme within the G minor chord to the fifth measure within the tonic, Bach has shown an originality and dexterity of treatment that can be recognized only by comparing these measures with the first five measures of the exposition.

EXAMPLE 30

There are many deviations from the opening theme in the repetition. There is the rhythmic variation caused by the entrance of the theme on the second half of the second quarter instead of the second half of the fourth quarter. This gives the theme a new and different rhythmic character. In addition to the transposition within the G minor chord, there are the alterations occasioned by the fusion with the fifth measure within the

C minor chord. Nevertheless, the absorption of these measures into the structural motion is so complete that there is no break in the melody and little realization that the repetition of the theme is so far in advance of the structural attainment of the recapitulation.

This passage shows not only the remarkable technical dexterity with which Bach fused the development and recapitulation, but also his conception of the form as a single organism whose sections are completely integrated parts of the whole rather than separate entities. It also offers an excellent illustration of the primary distinction between Bach's and Stamitz's treatment of the structural outlines of the form.

The succeeding sonata, in C major, the fifth of the Prussian group, shows a different type of prolongation. Here the expansion of the dominant chord provides the structural motion of the development section. However, the structure as a whole is less clearly defined than in the preceding sonata. This is due mainly to the weakness of the dominant chord on which the development concludes and to the fact that the recapitulation does not start with the opening measures of the main theme, but with a phrase at the end. Thus the entrance of the recapitulation is both vague and ineffective!

On the other hand the development section of the A major sonata, the last in the Prussian group, demonstrates a strongly defined motion within the outlined dominant chord. The only deviation from the customary treatment is the unexpected exchange of the E major for the E minor chord at the close. The reason for this exchange is not indicated in the voice leadings, nor is it due to any demand of the structural motion, since its presence definitely weakens the stronger E major—A major progression through which the development and the recapitulation are bound together. We must assume that the E minor chord was introduced primarily to achieve an unusual and dramatic entrance for the recapitulation.

In both the C and A major sonatas the development section has emerged out of a prolongation of the dominant chord, a technique that was to become a primary factor in the evolution of the classical sonata. Because this technique figures so largely in the works of eighteenth- and nineteenth-century composers, we are likely to take Bach's treatment in these two sonatas for granted. Yet we should remember that it was Bach's intuitive grasp of the possibilities offered by the prolongation of the mediant and dominant chords that provided the new element of the form, the development section. Furthermore Bach's conception of structural coherence enabled him to achieve the larger dimensions of the new form without destroying the inherent unity essential to its future development.

2. THE WÜRTTEMBERG SONATAS

As a whole the development sections in both the first and last movements show a firmer grasp of the melodic and structural elements of the form than in the Prussian group. The form itself is more convincing, the structural outlines more clearly defined, and the techniques reveal greater facility and dexterity. Of the six developments of the opening movements, four demonstrate either a motion from the prolonged mediant to the dominant chord or a motion entirely within the outlined dominant. Although the techniques are different in each case, the treatment of the basic motion is regular and offers no problem as to where the development closes and the recapitulation begins. Nor is there any question as to the nature of the prolongations. We shall confine our discussion to the two sonatas in which prolongations as well as techniques are irregular and therefore of special interest.

In the first sonata, in A minor, the extension of the motion from the E minor chord on which the exposition closes to the E major chord that ushers in the recapitulation is a case in point. The first deviation from the customary treatment occurs when the E minor chord concluding the exposition is followed by a C major chord on which the development begins. The problem to which this motion gives rise is the function of this C major chord which is prolonged for fourteen of the twenty-one measures that make up the development section.

The graph shows that the motion of the development is based on the neighbor-note technique. The chord of F major serves as a neighbor both of the E minor chord concluding the exposition and the E major chord with which the development ends. Thus the F major chord is the essential point to which the motion from the E minor chord is directed.

There are two possible explanations of this motion. One is that the E minor chord approaches the F major neighbor chord through the C major chord, the applied dominant; the second, that the F major chord is reached by a bass motion in thirds, E—C—A—F. Although this latter explanation seems to adhere more closely to the music, it reveals a deviation from the customary technique that should be noted. This is the use of A in the bass as the third of the F major chord rather than as the root of the A minor chord, which the presence of A in the motion would ordinarily represent.

87

EXAMPLE 31

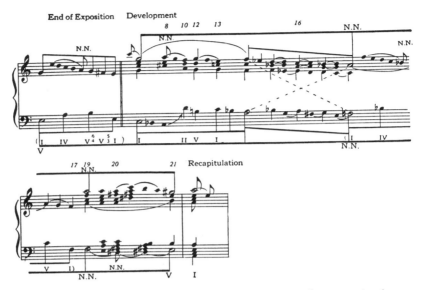

However, the fact that A is combined with F in the top voice is explained by the unfolding of the intervals F and A with a similar unfolding of A and F in the bass, through which an exchange of voices in the outside parts is effected. Thus the type of prolongation that Bach employed is responsible for the unusual element in the bass motion.

Since the motion from the E minor chord clearly outlines a descent by thirds to its neighbor chord, this reading is perhaps more convincing than to regard the C major chord as an applied dominant. Nevertheless, the fact that the first sixteen measures of the development show an expansion of the motion from the C major to the root position of the F major chord speaks strongly for the C major chord in its function as a prolonged applied dominant. Here there are two possibilities, each of which has its strong points and each of which reveals an idiosyncrasy in the technique.

Certain aspects of the treatment again demonstrate the organic nature of the conception. In the prolonged top-voice motion within the C major chord Bach has introduced A as a neighbor note in imitation of the larger structural line. Again, notice how cleverly the expansion of A of the F major chord provides for B♭ as a neighbor (measure 16) with the motion A–G–F, an inversion of the previous unfolding of F to A. In the final

88

Philipp Emanuel Bach

measures (19–21) the motion to the dominant E major chord is intensified by the introduction of D♯ in the bass as an under neighbor of E.

The techniques in general and the nature of the structural prolongations show how broad and elastic was Bach's conception of the form. They are a challenge to the assumption that form is an artificial convention, since they demonstrate that its clarity and coherence result from the special treatment by which every phrase and section is made an integral part of the structural motion.

To appreciate the technical magnitude of this sonata requires a close study of the various elements that went into its making. First of all there are the beauty and strength of the melodic line, the undulating flow of the voice motions, the delicate nuances that contribute to the color effects, the dramatic interest provided by the prolongations, and the exquisite grace and polish of the stylistic treatment. These outward evidences of Bach's innovations have been recognized. We must look deeper to realize how these new tendencies in style and technique are merged with the new structural outline to demonstrate the principle of tonality as it is defined in the organic concept of the form.

The sonata in B♭ major shows an entirely different type of treatment. Here the irregularity originates in the same technical idiosyncrasy that we found in the early F and E major sonatas of the Prussian group. In the development section the motion starts on a dominant F major chord and passes through an expanded D major chord that serves as an applied dominant of the following G minor chord, prolonged to the final measure of the section. The motion to the G minor chord is regular and needs no explanation. It is the motion from the G minor chord to the tonic B♭ major chord of the recapitulation that is unclear.

EXAMPLE 32

What is the status of this G minor chord? Is it a neighbor of the F major chord that opens the section without a return to the F major chord

89

at the close, or is it a prolonged passing chord in the motion F–G–B♭ in which A, the third of the F major chord, is lacking? The parallelism between this treatment and that in the F and E major sonatas of the Prussian group is obvious. It substantiates the belief that in the early works the indefiniteness of these prolongations was not due to Bach's inexperience with the form. The same technique is repeated after the more complicated prolongation of the structural motion in the A minor sonata. This proves conclusively that the cause was not lack of adequate technical resources. However, it is equally true that the type of prolongation is less clear and convincing than Bach's treatment in other sonatas.

On the whole, however, the development sections of the Prussian and Württemberg Sonatas show that Bach has devised a variety of techniques to expand the structural motion. That some of these are more effective than others and make for a stronger and more clearly defined structural foundation is a fact that Bach had to discover through actual practice, since he had no prototypes on which to pattern his treatment of the sonata. We must recognize the amazing aspects of the technique, although it is apparent that the development section is still in its formative stage and is by far the weakest element in the form. Nor should a comparison with this section in the Haydn sonatas lead us to underestimate Bach's achievements. The basic conception of the form expressed in Bach's early works was the dominant influence in the evolution of the classical sonata.

THE RECAPITULATION

The most significant aspect of the third section is the alteration of the material to provide for the entrance of the contrasting theme in the tonic chord. Bach was immediately aware of this necessity. This is already clear in his first sonata in F major, and it should be recognized as inherent in his conception of the form.

In the majority of the Prussian and Württemberg Sonatas the recapitulation starts with a repetition of the theme within the tonic chord, although there are instances, as in the C minor sonata to which we have already referred, when the theme enters before the structural tonic is reached: A similar instance of overlapping can be found in the third movement of the Württemberg Sonata in A♭ major. Here the development section shows a motion within the dominant E♭ major chord. The principal theme enters on the B♭ minor chord three measures before the tonic chord

90

Philipp Emanuel Bach

of the recapitulation appears. The alterations necessitated by the premature entry of the theme within the B♭ minor and E♭ major chords do not
prevent Bach from reaching the fourth measure of the original theme
simultaneously with the tonic A♭ chord.

EXAMPLE 33

In fusing the opening measures of the altered theme with the fourth
measure of the original, Bach shows the same melodic ingenuity that he
demonstrated in the C minor sonata. Again there is no abrupt transition
from the development to the recapitulation, but an unbroken flow of melody, which, together with the strong bass motion, welds the sections into
a closely integrated structure. Here is further evidence of the emphasis
Bach placed on the organic nature of the form through the interweaving
of the development and recapitulation. Another aspect of the treatment
of the third section, of primary importance, is the means by which the
contrasting theme is introduced within the tonic instead of the mediant
or dominant chord as in the exposition.

In many of these sónatas the necessary alterations appear even in the
opening phrase. This limits the exact repetition of the theme to just a few
measures, with the result that the theme is frequently shortened, in some
instances by as much as eight measures. In the third movement of the
Prussian Sonata in B♭ major we already see the deviations in the melodic
line in the opening measure, while in the recapitulation of the last movement of the Württemberg Sonata in A minor seventeen measures of the
principal theme are omitted.

91

Such instances, although unusual, tend to substantiate the trends demonstrated by the treatment in general — namely, the sacrifice of the main theme to assure the entrance of the contrasting theme within the tonic chord. Accordingly the contrasting theme is frequently given greater importance than the opening theme.

Since the transposition of the contrasting theme is the primary characteristic of the recapitulation, let us examine two excerpts from these sonatas to see how it is effected. It must be recognized, however, that to show where the alterations first start, it would be necessary to quote the entire restatement. The following illustrations give only those measures that directly precede the entrance of the contrasting theme in both the exposition (A) and the restatement (B).

The first of these, from the third movement of the Prussian Sonata in A major, shows how cleverly the alterations of the closing measures of the main theme have paved the way for an exact repetition of those measures that lead into the contrasting theme, except for their transposition a fifth below. Here the nature of the voice leadings and the motions they define have been kept intact, as a comparison of these measures reveals.

EXAMPLE 34

In the second example, however, taken from the first movement of the Prussian Sonata in C major, the approach to the contrasting theme has been considerably changed in the recapitulation. Here the original four measures are shortened to three, which in turn are preceded by two addi-

Philipp Emanuel Bach

tional measures of new material. Because of their rhythmic distinction, the added measures greatly enhance the natural intensity of the motion.

EXAMPLE 35

Although Examples A and B show only a fragment of the entire motion of the exposition and restatement, it is clear that one demonstrates a motion from the prolonged tonic to the dominant chord, while the other expresses a motion within the prolonged tonic. In the first the contrasting theme enters when the dominant chord of the basic harmonic progression has been reached; in the second the dominant serves only to expand the motion within the outlined tonic chord. It is by such means that Bach established the character of the recapitulation as a motion within the final tonic chord of the basic harmonic progression, which was expanded through the use of both harmonic and contrapuntal prolongations.

In this discussion of the structural outlines of the Prussian and Württemberg Sonatas we have seen the various techniques Bach used to shape the form into the three sections characteristic of the first movement of a sonata. At the same time we have recognized how each of these techniques has stressed the status of these sections as prolongations of the fundamental structure rather than as independent and self-sufficient entities.

Challenge to Musical Tradition

The result of our study is the realization of the significance that Bach attached to form as a demonstration of structural coherence.

There is a final phase of Bach's treatment that cannot be overlooked — the use of dissonance and its function in the new stylistic tendencies.

BACH'S USE OF DISSONANCE

The first question that naturally arises is what is the nature of these dissonances; that is, is their origin harmonic or contrapuntal? Furthermore, are they employed primarily to achieve an outward effect, a characteristic of the "gallant style," or do they serve a more basic purpose, to provide tension within the prolongations of the structural motion?

Although the later works offer many striking examples of dissonance, we will limit our examination to the early sonatas, which were not affected by the techniques of Haydn and Mozart.

The first passage comes from the adagio of the B♭ major Prussian Sonata. It shows a conflict between G♯ and G♮, F♯ and F♮, and many other dissonant combinations. Since this is the second of Bach's published sonatas, it may be regarded as indicative of this aspect of his treatment.

EXAMPLE 36

These four measures show a prolonged motion within the mediant D minor chord in which the outside voices move in tenths. The top-voice

94

Philipp Emanuel Bach

descent A—G—F has been expanded by the introduction of B♭ as a neighbor note, by the transfer of G to a higher register, and by the ascending and descending motions that result from this shift. The bass is also extended through the presence of G as a neighbor of F of the inverted D minor chord. Although it would be possible to regard this motion as a I—II—V—I harmonic prolongation of the D minor chord, the technique is so strongly contrapuntal in character that it is shown only as a descent in tenths in the outside voices, with the A major chord an applied dominant of D minor.

In trying to determine the reason for the dissonances of G♯ and G♮ and F♯ and F♮, it is clear from graph A that the presence of G♯ and F♯ in the top voice is due to the nature of the motive. This, however, does not explain why G♮ and F♮ have been retained in the bass. It would have been possible to substitute E♮ for G♮ and D for F♮ and thus eliminate the augmented octaves (graph B).

Graph A shows that the embellishing motion on the final quarter of measure 1 is an expansion of the descending third B♭—G♯, in which B♭ serves as an upper and G♯ as a lower neighbor of A. Thus the presence of G♯ is due to its embellishing function. That it enters only on the final thirty-second of the measure is the result both of the rhythm and of the prolonging motion. Its retention on the first eighth of measure 2 emphasizes its neighbor-note character through the motion A—B♭—G♯—A. The graph also reveals that F♯ serves in a similar capacity to G, with E♮ and F♮ in the two last measures offering a parallel connection. This suggests that the neighbor note is an integral part of the melodic figure and a basic element of the motivic idea.

Since G♯ and F♯ are necessary to the pattern of the melody, the reader may inquire why Bach did not avoid this clash by substituting E♮ and D for G♮ and F♮ in the bass. This change is shown in graph B. It leads, however, to a motion entirely different from what Bach indicates. Here, instead of the neighbor-note motion around A, it would be possible to hear an ascent from F in the bass through G to G♯ and A in the top voice, a motion of an ascending third. This changes the character of the motive by robbing it of the parallel uses of the neighbor note that figure so prominently in the melody.

Whether the conflict between the motive and the ascent from the bass into an upper voice was Bach's reason for retaining G♮ and F♮ in the bass can only be conjectured. Nevertheless, the presence of these tones in

95

Challenge to Musical Tradition

the bass defines the melodic figure so clearly and indicates the motion in the outside voices so convincingly that it is logical to assume that he preferred the dissonances to a possible confusion in the voice motions. According to this explanation, G♯ and F♯, the under neighbors of A and G♮ respectively, are embellishing tones that appear simultaneously with G♮ and F♮, the unaltered thirds of the E and D minor chords, for motivic reasons.

The treatment throughout is both daring and unusual. In addition to dissonances occasioned by the melodic embellishments there are some that result from the use of suspensions in the middle voice. It is possible that the effect was a primary factor in the technique. However, it should also be recognized that each of these dissonances can be accounted for on technical grounds. There is nothing arbitrary in the treatment, and no use of dissonances in defiance of the laws that govern the leading of voices. Nor do the conflicting tones represent the simultaneous use of different scales.

The following excerpts from the Württemberg Sonata in E minor offer additional evidence of the originality of Bach's use of dissonance.

EXAMPLE 37

In Example A we see a clear-cut motion from the A to the G minor chord, with the two voices at a distance of an octave and a tenth. The retention of A in the bass in the first half of measure 2 against the entrance of the motive on B♭ creates the minor ninth in question, a dissonance that is immediately resolved when the suspended A gives way to G.

Example B shows a premature entry of D in the bass before the upper voices resolve to F and D of the D minor chord. It also indicates that D in the bass (measure 2) has been retained, while the motive enters on E♭ in the top voice. These dissonances are given added emphasis by forte signs. Here a conventional descent in tenths has been given an entirely new character through the dissonant aspects of the treatment. In both

96

Philipp Emanuel Bach

these passages the dissonances add immeasurably to the interest and intensity of the motion. Their presence is not due to a technical necessity, but to a recognition of the stress they bring to the motivic figure and the dynamic character they impart to the movement as a whole.

Although we have cited only a few of the many passages revealing Bach's use of dissonance, the Prussian and Württemberg Sonatas offer various other instances in which there are equal conflicts among the voice parts. Yet each of these, as in the foregoing examples, shows a distinctly individual treatment, with the techniques similarly varied. The reader will find that at no time does Bach employ dissonance arbitrarily, to create a dramatic effect at the expense of tonal clarity. In fact each of these examples demonstrates that the dissonance is due to the motive, the rhythmic stress, or the treatment of the voice leadings. That it contributes richness and impetus to the melodic figuration and the contrapuntal activity is not the only explanation for its presence. Each of these passages reveals that Bach regarded dissonance, not as an end in itself, but as a means of giving the structural motion greater impetus in achieving a dramatic and arresting climax.

That Bach did use certain means to create a more telling effect is obvious in the various types of ornament found in his works. But even these can hardly be regarded as artificial. Thanks to Bach, the status of the trill, the mordent, the turn and the pralltriller was completely changed. He regarded them no longer as mere embellishments, but as characteristics of the style itself, and he gave each a more clearly defined function by differentiating among the varieties and indicating how each should be performed.

To evaluate the contribution of Philipp Emanuel Bach we must recognize how widespread and far-reaching were his achievements. He adapted the older techniques to the demands of his stylistic tendencies, and he experimented with new ones; he changed the emphasis in style from the horizontal to the vertical; he gave the ornament a new function as an essential element of the treatment; and he defined the structural outlines of sonata form as characteristic of the sonata. These are concrete accomplishments that opened the way to the development of the modern sonata, quartet, and symphony. But equally important for the future trend of music was his concept of tonality, out of which the form was evolved. He demonstrated that the form was a structural organism whose coherence was provided by the motion achieved within a single horizontal-

97

ized chord; he reaffirmed the principles enunciated by Johann Sebastian Bach by showing the distinction between and the interdependence of the harmonic and contrapuntal functions. In so doing he preserved elements from the past that were as essential to the growth of the classical sonata as his innovations.

Philipp Emanuel Bach was the vital link between the periods of Johann Sebastian Bach and Joseph Haydn. His works point in two directions — to the past as well as to the future. He was a daring experimenter and a bold revolutionist who created a new medium of expression within the same tonal concept that had served composers to whose style, treatment, and form his works were a challenge. In short, although he negated the traditions of the past, he retained the principles out of which those traditions had emerged.

When we approach the classical sonatas of Haydn, we are immediately aware of the changes they reveal. In the nature of the melodic material, in its rhythmic treatment, in the more mature handling of the development section, and in the stricter adherence to the opening theme in the recapitulation, Haydn gave his own imprint to the form. But in spite of his many innovations, enriching the melodic content and developing various aspects of the treatment, he nevertheless retained Philipp Emanuel Bach's fundamental conception of the form as an organic structure, the sum of all its component parts.

The value of that heritage and its influence on the future trend in music Haydn disclosed when he said: "He who knows me well must find that I am greatly indebted to Philipp Emanuel Bach since I understand him and have made a serious study of his works." [5]

[5] C. F. Pohl, *Joseph Haydn* (Breitkopf and Härtel, Leipzig, 1878), Vol. I, p. 132.

CHAPTER IV

Josef Haydn

THE PRINCIPLE of structural coherence as defined in the sonata, quartet,

and symphony. Innovations in the structural and prolonging techniques.

Deviations in the melodic and rhythmic treatment.

THE NATURE and scope of Haydn's contribution to the development of the sonata, trio, quartet, and symphony has been somewhat obscured by the more dramatic and resplendent achievements of his contemporary, Mozart. This is due, in part, to Mozart's accomplishments in the operatic as well as in the instrumental field and also to the extraordinary beauty of his melodic invention as well as the perfection and finesse of his style. However, it is not necessary to minimize the unique quality of Mozart's contribution to give Haydn's achievements an equally just evaluation. It should be recognized that it was Haydn, with only the sonatas of Philipp Emanuel Bach as prototypes, who established the full-fledged form of the classical sonata, while Mozart had Haydn's sonatas, trios, quartets, and symphonies to serve him as models.

No one will deny that the span between Philipp Emanuel Bach and Haydn was a much greater gulf to bridge than that between Haydn and Mozart. Nor should we forget that it was Haydn who gave the terms "trio," "quartet," and "symphony" structural significance by converting the vague and elastic forms of the transition period into a concrete form based on the classical sonata. The whole nomenclature of instrumental music was still in a state of flux at the end of the transition period. One of the indications is that Haydn's earliest works for strings and wind instruments are called divertimenti, notturni, or cassations.

The quartet for a group of solo instruments was unknown even in the Bach-Handel period. Music was written either for the orchestra or for a small chamber group. In the middle eighteenth century, however, due to the efforts of Gossec, Stamitz, Monn, and Boccherini, a distinction was gradually made between the traditional orchestral quartet and the quartet for solo instruments. The result was the divertimento, a group of instrumental movements combined into a suite-like form. The final step in its development was the classical quartet of Haydn.

Similarly, the term "symphony" in the same period did not refer to any specialized form, but could be applied to any work written for three or more instruments. Although the transition from this indefinite use of the term to the concrete type of structure it came to designate was the gradual result of experiments by various composers, it was Haydn who imparted to the outlines of the symphony the conception of tonality as the expression of structural coherence.

These are the more obvious results of Haydn's stabilization of the classical sonata. However, many other aspects of his treatment, though less apparent, are also important, particularly for their effect on the music of his successors. The summary of them, however brief, is impressive.

THE ALLEGRO

1. A new and different type of material, in which the thematic impulse is stronger than the motivic.

2. A clearer definition of the contrasting aspects of the exposition through the use of a so-called transition.

3. A stronger development section through the introduction of three basic techniques to prolong the structural motion from the close of the exposition to the start of the recapitulation. In a sonata in a major key the middle section in sonata form is created either by an expanded motion within the dominant chord or by a prolonged neighbor chord of the dominant; in the minor, as in the sonatas of Bach, there is an extension of the mediant-dominant progression.

4. Innovations within the structural outline that permit a development section to begin on a passing chord, a chord of harmonic prolongation, or any type of chord other than the mediant or dominant on which the structural motion actually begins.

5. The use of only a fragment of the theme in this section as a means of prolonging the structural top voice.

6. The conclusion of the development on a dominant chord, to emphasize the structural motion to the tonic of the recapitulation.

7. The start of the recapitulation with a repetition of the theme, instead of a fragment from the end of the main theme or the beginning of the contrasting theme.

8. The introduction of a short coda at the close of the recapitulation.

Josef Haydn

THE SLOW MOVEMENT

1. The simpler and more genuine character of the melody.
2. The introduction of a theme with variations in addition to the customary binary form.

THE MINUET AND TRIO

The addition of the minuet and trio, either as the last of three movements or as the third of four movements.

THE FINALE

1. The new character and mood of the finale, with its heightening effect of contrast to the allegro.
2. The introduction of the rondo form as an additional stylistic treatment of the last movement.

Before considering the generally obvious aspects of Haydn's treatment, the new type of melodic material, the use of irregular phrase-groups, the stress of weak beats through syncopation, and the robust quality of the rhythmic impulse, let us turn to the more subtle and less frequently discussed techniques that had a direct bearing on the form. As in the case of Philipp Emanuel Bach, we shall confine our investigation to early works that can be cited as entirely free of the influence of a younger master — in this case Mozart — which some of the later works reveal. In basing our conclusions on Haydn's early period rather than his full maturity, it is necessary to omit some of his outstanding compositions. This method, nevertheless, avoids any possibility of attributing to him stylistic innovations that might be traced to the influence of Mozart or the later works of Philipp Emanuel Bach.

THE SONATAS

In general the early sonatas consist of three movements. Although Haydn retains the same number of movements that Philipp Emanuel Bach outlined, he does not always adhere to the stylistic form in which these movements were presented. Already this is apparent in the C major sonata listed as No. 1 in the *Kritische Gesamtausgabe,* in which Haydn introduced the minuet and trio to replace the allegro as a third movement. This, however, applies not only to the first sonata, but to the first seventeen, in which the introduction of the minuet either as the third of four movements or as the last of three proves how dominant a role the

101

Challenge to Musical Tradition

minuet and trio played in Haydn's conception of the sonata. In the works that follow, from 1771 through 1776, the close of the early period to which we are confining our investigation, Haydn varies the form. In some the minuet and trio appear as a middle movement between the allegro and the finale, the latter usually in sonata form, while in others they are omitted and Philipp Emanuel Bach's plan of allegro, adagio, and finale is adhered to.

Although the techniques in all these varied movements are of interest and value in a discussion of Haydn's stylistic innovations, it is inevitable that those in the first movement, or, at times, in the finale, will be of greatest significance, since they are responsible for changes within the structural outline that differentiate his treatment of sonata form from that of Philipp Emanuel Bach.

According to the *Kritische Gesamtausgabe,* Haydn composed thirty-two sonatas up to and including the year 1776. Some of these are extremely elementary in structure; yet the majority show that he had already grasped the technical means of strengthening and at the same time of developing the structural tendencies outlined by Philipp Emanuel Bach.

It must be clearly understood that although Haydn is responsible for many new developments in the form, these variations occur within the structural outlines defined by Philipp Emanuel Bach. They in no wise deviate from the concept of tonality embodied in Bach's sonatas, nor do they differ in principle from the type of structural motion out of which the three main sections of the form emerge. It was Philipp Emanuel Bach who drew the blueprint that Haydn, Mozart, and Beethoven used as the basic foundation of the classical form. Each of these composers broadened and enlarged the original plan and contributed to its growth. Each added the impress of his own creative art. All, however, preserved the primary concept of tonal coherence by retaining the essential function of the sectional elements as prolongations of the basic structure of the whole rather than as independent tonal entities.

The entire development of the sonata has been a struggle for stylistic individuality within the bounds – not limitations – of the concept of tonality. This conflict between the necessity of maintaining the tonal clarity of the structural motion and the creative impulse to find expression for new ideas through new techniques and new stylistic tendencies has been a challenge and a driving force motivating every composer. It was not, as is so often believed, a restraint on imagination, but a stimulus to it.

102

Josef Haydn

Since the foundation of the different movements of the classical form comprises one of the basic harmonic progressions, it was inevitable that to achieve distinction of style it was necessary to find an outlet in those techniques that provide the prolongations. Thus the growth of the sonata demonstrates the innumerable possibilities for divergent types of self-expression that the concept of tonality offered to eighteenth- and nineteenth-century composers.

To show how Haydn adapted Bach's ideas to his own needs, let us turn to the first movements of his sonatas.

SONATA FORM

1. THE EXPOSITION

The main distinctions in this section as between the Bach and the Haydn sonatas lie in the character of the thematic material and the more clearly defined contrasting section. However, although Haydn has imparted a greater individuality to the contrasting theme, its melodic contour and structural top-voice motion frequently show a strong similarity to the outline of the principal theme. Some authorities regard this thematic kinship as a weakness in Haydn's treatment. They overlook the important fact that it demonstrates the organic nature of the conception, in which there is but a single melodic idea, whose flowering provides the contrasting theme as an offshoot of the principal theme. In spite of this kinship, Haydn brought out the distinguishing characteristics in each. This is due to his melodic treatment and also to the intensification of the mediant or dominant chord on which the contrasting theme entered. In short, it was his treatment of the so-called "transition" that emphasized the distinctive qualities of the contrasting section.

The term "transition," as generally used, means the motion through which the composer "modulates" from the tonic to the key of the dominant or the relative major. However, if tonality is understood as the expression of one and only one key, there can be no modulation. Instead the transition is a prolongation of the motion from the tonic to the mediant or dominant of the basic structure. It stimulates the harmonic progression by emphasizing the characteristics of the chord to which it is leading. For example, in a progression from an A major to an E major chord, the introduction of an expanded B major chord, an altered supertonic, stresses the structural function of the dominant and differentiates it from preceding

103

E major chords whose function has been to prolong the motion within the tonic. By heightening the individual color characteristics of the harmonies that provide the structural motion Haydn sharpened the sectional aspects of the form while keeping the structural organism intact.

2. THE DEVELOPMENT SECTION

Our examination of Philipp Emanuel Bach's sonatas showed that the development was the weakest element in his outline of the form. Consequently it should be the section in which Haydn's departures from the norm are most clearly revealed.

The function of the development section is twofold. Melodically it is a challenge to the imagination and ingenuity of the composer; structurally it is the link binding the exposition to the recapitulation.

Although in most of the early works the treatment of the melodic material in this section is closely allied to the theme and consequently is not in the proper sense of the word a development, there are instances in which the section does not begin with the theme; in others, it either concentrates immediately on one fragment of the theme or strikes out in a new direction that is only slightly reminiscent of it. These less frequent situations suggest that Haydn had glimpsed the various opportunities that this section offers to the composer's fantasy.

From a structural point of view he stabilized the development section and clarified the various means by which it formed a definite link between the exposition and the recapitulation. He succeeded in doing this primarily by pointing out the three possibilities for expanding the motion of the development section — a prolonged motion within the dominant chord, an expansion of the neighbor chord of the dominant, or, in a work in a minor key, an extension of the motion from the mediant chord on which the exposition closed to the dominant concluding the development. In each of these, the approach to the tonic chord of the recapitulation was preceded by the dominant — a clear-cut and sharply defined motion that stresses the connection of the component parts of the structural whole.

These techniques, as well as the smaller types of prolongation, will be discussed in detail. It is only necessary to point out at this time that by strengthening and tightening the structural motion of the development, Haydn brought to realization the solidarity and coherence that Philipp Emanuel Bach had suggested, but not fully accomplished.

Josef Haydn

3. THE RECAPITULATION

The main distinction between Haydn's treatment of this section and Bach's is that Haydn customarily begins with the opening phrase of the exposition, while Bach frequently starts with a phrase at the end of the principal theme or even with the contrasting theme.

The repetition of the principal theme in the recapitulation brings out the similarity between the opening and closing sections of the movement and creates a feeling of balance and symmetry that formerly was lacking. In addition Haydn preserved a large part of the opening theme before making the changes necessary to the entrance of the contrasting theme within the tonic chord, and the changes themselves are accomplished with greater ease and smoothness. Furthermore, in some instances, Haydn introduced a short coda to conclude the movement.

These, in general, are the principal innovations revealed by a study of Haydn's works of this period. In concrete examples of the techniques he used, we shall give greater attention to his treatment of the development section than to the techniques of the exposition and recapitulation, since it is in the development that the techniques were of vital importance to the growth of sonata form.

Let us begin with the B♭ major,[1] one of the earliest sonatas. It is understandable that this early work should be somewhat reminiscent of Philipp Emanuel Bach. Nevertheless, there are some slight deviations that point in the direction of Haydn's later works.

First of all the opening theme of the exposition shows a metrical freedom that is more characteristic of Haydn than of the composers of the transition period. Consisting of ten measures, the theme is grouped into one four-measure phrase and two phrases of three measures each. This irregularity is emphasized by the five-measure phrase that follows. The contrasting theme is also of interest, because it possesses a character and individuality seldom shown by the contrasting themes in the Bach sonatas.

Interesting as are these evidences of Haydn's individual treatment, the point with which we are primarily concerned is whether there is a greater clarity in the techniques that prolong the basic structure. In short, is the motion through which the development section is achieved more sharply defined as an integral part of the structural organism?

[1] *Kritische Gesamtausgabe,* No. 2; Breitkopf and Härtel Edition, Vol. IV, No. 40.

EXAMPLE 38

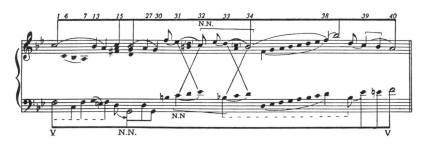

The development shows a motion from the dominant F major chord to its neighbor chord of G minor and back to the F major chord. This is a clear-cut approach to the B♭ major chord of the recapitulation. It is in great contrast to the vague techniques Bach used in the F major, E major, and B♭ major sonatas, in which the neighbor chord moved directly to the tonic chord without a well-indicated return to the dominant. Thus in this second sonata the broad aspects of the structural technique show a firm grasp of the essential elements of the neighbor-note technique. However, it is necessary to find out whether the prolonging techniques are equally clear.

The structural framework of this section shows a top-voice motion of C—B♭—A against a neighbor-note motion of F—G—F in the bass. This has been expanded to forty measures through the prolonging of the F major and G minor chords and by the extended motion from the G minor to the F major chord. The expansion of the F major chord discloses a top-voice motion from C into A, a middle voice, while the bass describes an embellishment of F. The entrance of the G minor chord is stressed through the preceding D seventh chord, an applied dominant, with C in the top voice accentuating the motion to B♭ of the G minor chord.

In the prolongation of the neighbor chord there is also a top-voice descent of a third, from B♭ to G, a middle voice. Since this B♭ is a passing tone between C and A of the structural top voice, the G minor chord serves a double function as a structural neighbor-passing chord. Yet instead of a direct return to the dominant chord, the motion is prolonged through the introduction of the B♭ major chord. The prolongation of this B♭ chord for six measures provides the unusual aspect of the treatment, since its emphasis here weakens its effect as a tonic in the recapitulation, the goal of the entire development section. Furthermore, the fact that it leads to E♭, the third of the C minor chord instead of the root of the E♭ major chord, negates the possibility that it functions as an applied dominant. On the whole the status of this B♭ chord is unclear and its stress tends to confuse the motion from the G minor to the F major chord.

There are, however, many indications of the organic nature of the conception in the smaller details of the treatment. For example, the structural top voice of the whole development shows a motion of a third, C–B♭–A. This same figure emerges out of the prolongation of the F major chord in the opening measures of the section (measures 1–14) and is repeated in the two final measures (39–40), in which C and B♭, embellishments of A, tend to echo the original motion. The interval of a third occurs throughout, both as a descending and as an ascending figure. Notice, too, how strongly the basic neighbor-note technique is imitated in the smaller motions (measures 31–34 and 39). Here the use of C as a neighbor of B♭ in the top voice has the effect of a repetition of the C–B♭ of the structural line, which is accentuated by the duplication of C and B♭ as embellishments of the final A.

Although on the whole the form is in an embryonic stage and the prolonging techniques tend to weaken the structural motion, there are already indications of a clearer definition of the sectional elements than we found in some of the early Philipp Emanuel Bach sonatas. How quickly Haydn strengthened the gaps in the outlined motion is revealed in his treatment of the development sections of the G major sonata, composed in 1766, and the D major,[2] composed in 1767. In both of these the function of the neighbor chord is clearly defined and the techniques are more convincing than in the preceding example. However, since the sonata in D major is more interesting from both a melodic and a structural point of view and offers a better illustration of the neighbor-note technique, we shall concentrate on the later work.

The principal theme of the exposition has a melodic and rhythmic vitality characteristic of Haydn. The improvisatory nature of the contrasting theme, on the other hand, is strongly reminiscent of the treatment of Philipp Emanuel Bach. The material of these themes is not outstanding, nor does the treatment show the technical facility that the development section discloses. In the exposition the motion consists of a prolonged

---

[2] *Kritische Gesamtausgabe*, Nos. 6 and 10; Breitkopf and Härtel Edition, Vol. IV, No. 36, and Vol. II, No. 15; Peters Edition, Vol. IV, No. 31, and Vol. II, No. 14.

D major chord that moves through the altered supertonic E major to the dominant A major chord. Here the substitution of the E major for the E minor chord intensifies the entrance of the dominant chord and stresses its function as a structural force.

EXAMPLE 39

Josef Haydn

Turning to the development section, we find a motion from the A major to the B minor chord, with a return to the A major chord, on which the section closes. Since Haydn again uses the neighbor-note technique, let us examine the various prolongations to determine where the treatment differs from that in the preceding B♭ major sonata.

The opening measures show an expansion of the dominant A major chord, which is effected chiefly by the horizontalization of the chord in the outside voices and by an embellishing motion within the B minor chord (measure 3). The E major chord that follows is of interest, since it is an illustration of the type of dominant that does not proceed to its tonic, but passes indirectly to the B minor chord; therefore its function is that of an applied dominant, which we defined in Chapter I under the head of harmonic prolongations. The diminished seventh chord on A♯, which leads directly to the neighbor chord, brings G in the top voice as a neighbor of F♯, with A♯ in a middle voice stimulating the motion to B. In the expansion of the B minor chord, the techniques are clearly outlined through a motion in tenths in the outside voices. On the other hand the motion from this neighbor chord to the dominant is more complicated and offers problems that must be discussed. This complexity is due primarily to the introduction of the syncopated figure of the contrasting section, which, though of rhythmic interest, tends to obscure the nature of the prolonging techniques.

It is apparent that the B minor chord passes to the chord of A major through the chord of D major (measure 37) instead of by way of the applied dominant, the chord of E major. The function of this D major chord is twofold. It not only retains the neighbor note F♯, and thus serves a melodic purpose, but in conjunction with its own neighbor chord of E minor, it serves the contrapuntal function of prolonging the motion from the B minor to the A major chord. However, it is the motion to this D major chord that presents the difficulties.

Graph A indicates a shift of B from a middle to the top voice, where it descends to G of the E minor chord (measure 32). This E minor chord is expanded by a descent in tenths in which the top voice drops to B, a middle voice, which ascends through C♯ to D of the D major chord. The bass meanwhile descends an octave. The status of the E minor chord is that of a neighbor of D major, with G an embellishment of F♯, E in the bass a neighbor of D, and C♯ in the middle voice a passing tone between B of the E minor and D of the D major chord. Thus the basic neighbor-

109

Challenge to Musical Tradition

note technique is repeated as a means of prolonging the motion to the D major chord. The D major chord is also expanded by an embellishing motion in which the top voice descends from B to F♯ and the bass from G to D. Since these descents are a duplication of the embellishments of the E minor chord, they suggest that the motions arrested to provide the E minor neighbor chord, have been completed and have attained the D major chord as their ultimate goal.

The section as a whole reveals a remarkable grasp of the structural techniques that provide the tonal coherence, as well as those of a prolonging nature that create the smaller expanding motions. Therefore this sonata is significant for us, because as an early work it not only shows the difference between Haydn's and Bach's techniques, but it offers a basis of comparison with later works of this same period. It reveals those tendencies in the treatment that are indicative of Haydn's originality but that are brought to fruition only with the growth of his technical resources.

If we turn to the year 1773, we find three sonatas, each of which presents a distinctly individual treatment not only showing how varied was Haydn's manner of expression, but emphasizing the differentiation between the early and later stylistic trends. These are the sonatas in C, E, and F major.

First of all each of these works reveals a marked progress in the development of the form. We recognize this either in the more elastic conception and the bolder techniques it permits or in the character of the thematic material and the originality with which Haydn adapts it to his needs in the development section. In all of these sonatas the nature of the melodic invention, the greater clarity of the techniques, and the more colorful and richer prolongations are proof of the growth and expansion of Haydn's treatment of the form.

The opening theme of the sonata in C major [3] illustrates the new tendencies of this period. Its melodic and rhythmic vitality is emphasized by the improvisatory nature of the contrasting theme. In both themes, however, the introduction of chromatics enriches the melodic interest and intensifies the function of the prolongations. This is especially true of the contrasting section, in which the momentary exchange of the G minor for the G major chord and the substitution of the diminished seventh chord on F♯ for the D major chord are most effective. In fact this entire

[3] *Kritische Gesamtausgabe*, No. 21; Breitkopf and Härtel Edition, Vol. II, No. 16; Peters Edition, Vol. II, No. 15.

section shows that Haydn has attained a technical surety that gives full expression to his powers of creation.

The same characteristics are found in the treatment of the development section. This consists of a prolonged motion to and from the A minor chord, as well as an expansion of the neighbor chord itself. The technique is so definite and the conception of the whole so imaginative in the many parallelisms within the top voice that there can be little question as to Haydn's mastery of the form.

EXAMPLE 40

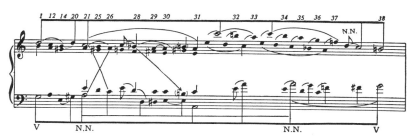

There is a prolonged motion to the A minor chord, with G♯ replacing G♮ in the bass to give emphasis to the neighbor chord that follows. Within this expansion the descent from D in the top voice to B, a middle voice, discloses a duplication of the structural top-voice motion through the entire section. How strongly the interval of a third dominates the prolonging motions may be seen in the extension of the A minor chord. Not only do the first eleven measures of the expansion consist of a third, C–B–A, but this interval is found in the smaller motions, C–B–A and B♭–A–G♯ (measures 21–26 and 28–31). In addition the inversion of the third into a sixth, figures prominently in the relation of the two upper voices when shifted to a higher register (measures 31–37).

Another interesting feature of the melodic treatment is the artistry with which Haydn has suggested the melodic figure of the principal theme in the top-voice descent from the A minor to the G major chord (measures 33–38). This augmentation of the theme in the return motion is not merely a demonstration of technical ingenuity, but an imaginative expression of the structural link between the development and the recapitulation. It indicates an entirely new tendency in the treatment and reveals a fuller recognition of the possibilities that the melodic material offers in unfolding the organic conception of the whole.

111

Challenge to Musical Tradition

The bass motion also discloses a clarity that leaves little doubt as to Haydn's mastery of the neighbor-note technique. The motion from the G major chord through the diminished chord on G♯ to the A minor neighbor chord is balanced by an extended motion from the A minor to the G major chord. This latter expansion in which A passes through F and F♯ to G of the dominant chord is similar to the approach Haydn used in the early B♭ major sonata, in which the G minor neighbor chord returned to the dominant F major through E♭ and E♮. A comparison of these motions shows how much clearer and more convincing are the techniques in the C major sonata.

The expansion of the motion within the A minor chord is equally well defined because of the unequivocal nature of the prolonging techniques. These are: (1) an exchange of voices in the outside parts (measures 21–26); (2) an arpeggiation of the chord through the bass motion A–C–E–A, with D and D♯ as passing tones (measures 21–23); (3) a shift of the two upper voices to a higher register, and (4) the use of applied dominants both in the neighbor-chord motion and in the return from the A minor to the G major chord.

No one can regard this as an embryonic or experimental work or look on it as an imitation of the sonatas of Philipp Emanuel Bach. Not only does it bear the imprint of Haydn's artistic personality, but every aspect of the treatment shows that the classical sonata has emerged.

The second of this later group, the sonata in E major,[4] is outstanding from various points of view. Not only is the material of a more dramatic and intense character than we usually find in the allegro movements of Haydn's sonatas, but the treatment offered by the structural motion of the development section is the only instance of its kind in the thirty-two sonatas of this early period.

The unusual element in the technique is the opening of the section with a repetition of the theme on a chromatic passing chord. This in itself is indicative of the more elastic conception of the form and the greater originality in the style that the works of this period reveal. The structural motion offers a new type of technique, since here Haydn has used a descending motion from the B major chord concluding the exposition to the E major chord opening the recapitulation, in place of the more frequently employed neighbor-note technique.

---

[4] *Kritische Gesamtausgabe*, No. 22; Breitkopf and Härtel Edition, Vol. IV, No. 39; Peters Edition, Vol. IV, No. 34.

Josef Haydn

Example 41

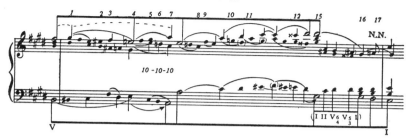

In proceeding directly in an unbroken flow from the exposition to the recapitulation Haydn has achieved a tightness in the motion and an interlocking of the sections all the more remarkable because of the elasticity of the techniques. There is no pause at the close of the development, as in the preceding examples, but the motion is concluded only with the entrance of the tonic E major chord.

The development shows a motion from the root to the inverted position of the B major chord, with a top-voice descent from F♯ into D♯, a middle voice. However, the inverted B major chord at the close is so weak and the A major and G♯ minor chords preceding it are given such prominence that we hear the B major as a passing chord between the G♯ minor and E major chord rather than as a structural dominant.

Because of the stress of the G♯ minor chord, there might be a tendency to hear the bass motion as a descent by thirds from the B major through G♯ minor to the E major chord, an outline of the horizontalized E major chord. This interpretation, however, gives greater force to the G♯ minor than to the A major chord, which the prolonged motion within the A major chord contradicts.

Actually the entire development is an expansion of the space between the B and E major chords, through a descending motion within the two positions of the B major chord. In this the A major and G♯ minor chords serve as passing chords. It is the weakness of the final B chord that permits the motion to continue on to the E major chord and in so doing clarifies the connection between the dominant chord ending the exposition and the tonic chord on which the recapitulation starts.

In addition to the strength and coherence of the structural framework there are other aspects of the treatment that demonstrate the new tendencies in Haydn's technique. One of these is the more fluid treatment of

Challenge to Musical Tradition

the voice leadings and the greater intensity the chromatics provide; another, the parallelism in the smaller prolongations. For instance, notice how the top-voice descent from G♯ to E (measures 1–4) is answered by the ascent from E to A (measures 4–7, 7–9). Again, there is a suggestion that the interval of a third in which the structural top voice moves is paralleled in the smaller prolongations of both the top voice and bass. The top voice shows several examples of descending and ascending thirds, while the bass indicates a similar treatment in the motions E–C♯–A (measures 4–7), A–C♯ (measures 7–10), and F♯–D♯ (measures 11–12).

The treatment of the prolongations shows a dexterity in the technique and a richness and intensity in the chromatic coloring that are lacking in the earlier sonatas. This is apparent in the expansion of the motion from the A major chord (measure 7) to the D♯ major chord (measure 12) by means of which the structural top voice passes from E to D♯, an ascent of a seventh instead of a descent of a half step. However, it is the chromatic nature of the chords that fill this space and the ingenious manner in which Haydn has used them that contribute so much to the emotional aspect of the work. In fact there is reason to believe that Haydn's increased technical facility not only evidenced itself in the various aspects of the treatment, but enabled him to realize a more imaginative and elastic conception of the form and a fuller grasp of the artistic possibilities it offered.

The sonata in F major,[5] the last in this group to be cited, tends to confirm this conclusion. This time it is not the interesting treatment of the neighbor-note technique that is the most significant feature of the treatment. Instead it is the unique role played by the characteristic motive of the exposition both in the melodic and in the structural life of the development section. In this treatment we find undeniable proof both of the organic nature of the fundamental conception and of the ingenious and original manner in which it is expressed.

The structural motion is so clearly defined through the neighbor-note technique that it requires little explanation. There is a motion from the C major chord through the inverted and prolonged chord of B♭ major to the A major chord, which serves as an applied dominant of the D minor neighbor chord. Here the unusual feature is the wide expansion of the B♭

[5] *Kritische Gesamtausgabe,* No. 23; Breitkopf and Härtel Edition, Vol. II, No. 21; Peters Edition, Vol. II, No. 20.

Josef Haydn

EXAMPLE 42

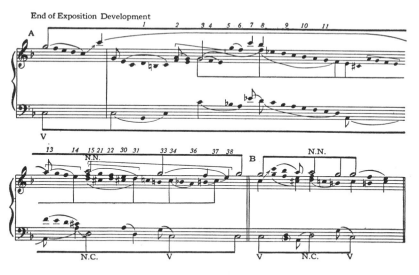

major passing chord. The motion within the neighbor chord and its return through G, the applied dominant of C major, are obvious.

In the top voice we find much of interest because of the influence of the motivic figure on the melodic pattern of the prolongations. First of all we see that the motion from G, the structural top voice of the closing C major chord of the exposition, to its neighbor A of the D minor chord has been widely expanded. This is due to the shift of C, a middle voice, to the top voice, from which the descent to A is made. Thus the ascent from G to A is stretched to fifteen measures. In a similar manner both the neighbor note A and the structural tone G that follows are expanded by means of smaller motions. Since the resemblance of these prolongations to

EXAMPLE 43

the melodic figure of the exposition is the distinguishing element of the treatment, let us turn to various presentations of the motive to see where the similarity lies.

It is apparent in Example A that the melodic material of the exposition is dominated by the descending figure A—G—F—E, which is shown in various rhythmic patterns. How much this motive influences the motions that prolong the structural top voice of the development is revealed in Example B.

This marks a new trend in the growth of the form. It indicates for the first time a tendency to recognize the full possibilities offered by the thematic material in making it a determinate factor in the development section. Here we find how significant the melodic figure can become in engendering the prolonging motions of the development and in linking them with the motivic impulse of the exposition and recapitulation. This similarity is not accidental — nor is it premeditated. It is rather the unconscious expression of a single melodic idea that is so firmly entrenched in the fundamental conception as to dominate every element of the melodic structure and emerge in every aspect of the treatment. Here in truth we see a real development of the thematic material.

Although Example B points out the various entries of the melodic figure in the development, the purpose they serve is more closely revealed in the preceding example (Example 42), in which the motive is enclosed in brackets.

These three sonatas are not embryos. In the treatment of both the melodic and the structural outlines they represent the full-fledged classical form. To regard them otherwise is to ignore their mature conceptions, the fully realized techniques they indicate, and the structural developments they disclose. By comparison with the early works they show the new tendencies in the form that were vital to its growth. In addition they demonstrate the innovations within the structural motion that differentiate Haydn's treatment of the prolongations from Philipp Emanuel Bach's and at the same time foreshadow the trends of Mozart and particularly Beethoven.

The recognition of these facts contradicts the belief of some authorities that Haydn merely reorganized the form. On the contrary his innovations were not of a superficial or purely technical order. They were fundamental in their effect on the cohesion of the sections and in their clarification of the techniques through which the structural unity of the whole movement was achieved. His innovations are due not solely to his technical facility, but to the artistic conception for which the techniques are the means of expression. He used the structural framework of Philipp Emanuel Bach, but he built the scaffolding out of the materials of his own imagination and creative power. This scaffolding was essential to the evolution of the classical form.

Before leaving the sonatas for a study of the techniques in the quartet, it is necessary to touch briefly on Haydn's approach to the recapitulation.

In the Philipp Emanuel Bach sonatas, we found the development section did not always close upon a dominant chord. Sometimes it ended with a neighbor chord or a contrapuntal motion that led from the neighbor chord to the tonic of the recapitulation.

The thirty-two sonatas that come chronologically within Haydn's early period reveal only one instance of the tonic chord of the restatement not being reached through a dominant. The development either concludes on a dominant or, as in the case of the E major sonata (Example 41), shows a direct motion from the dominant of the exposition to the tonic of the recapitulation.

The one exception to the rule is the Bb major sonata,[6] in which the harmonic aspect of the progression is concealed by the contrapuntal nature of the motion. The treatment here is so similar to that demonstrated in the F major, the first of the Prussian Sonatas of Philipp Emanuel Bach (Example 28), that the measures in question are cited for comparison.

EXAMPLE 44

The chord of G minor has served throughout the development as a neighbor of the dominant F major chord. Although the return to the F major chord is suggested in the bass, the contrapuntal impulse is so much

[6] *Kritische Gesamtausgabe*, No. 14; Breitkopf and Härtel Edition, Vol. II, No. 19; Peters Edition, Vol. II, No. 18.

stronger than the harmonic that we hear the motion as from the G minor to the B♭ major chord. In addition the entrance of B♭ in the top voice over D in the bass within this motion tends to weaken further the effect of the F major chord. As in similar instances in the Philipp Emanuel Bach sonatas, the technique in this example is not convincing and undermines the structural stability.

Nevertheless, as this is the only instance in the thirty-two sonatas in which the treatment shows any structural weakness in the approach to the recapitulation, it is apparent that Haydn has strengthened not only the motion of the development section itself, but its structural connection with the final section and hence its organic function in the entire movement.

Further evidence of the stabilization of the form concerns Haydn's treatment of the thematic material in the final section. In several instances, it may be recalled, Philipp Emanuel Bach omitted any reference to the opening theme in the recapitulation and began with the contrasting theme. Haydn, on the contrary, gave the melodic aspects of the form greater symmetry by beginning the final section with a repetition of the opening theme and adhering to it for a longer period before making the changes necessary to the entrance of the contrasting theme on the tonic chord. This emphasis of the principal theme in the restatement not only provided a greater melodic and structural balance between the first and last sections, but accentuated the basic function of the development as a means of creating artistic contrast and variety.

Various aspects of these sonatas, such as the introduction of the minuet and trio, are of primary interest in a study of Haydn's development of the classical concept. But let us first turn to the quartets to continue our discussion of the techniques Haydn used to achieve the characteristic outlines of sonata form.

THE QUARTETS

The transformation of the older forms of the *divertimento*, cassation, serenade, and notturno into the modern quartet based on the classical sonata is one of Haydn's greatest contributions. How gradual the transition was may be realized by the fact that the first eighteen quartets of Haydn bore the older titles and that Haydn himself regarded Opus 9, No. 1, as his first real quartet.[7]

---

[7] Pohl, C. F., *Haydn* (Breitkopf and Härtel, Leipzig, 1878), Vol. I, p. 332.

Josef Haydn

There are indications, nevertheless, in many of these first eighteen quartets, of certain tendencies that were later to become characteristic features of Haydn's style — the irregular accents and metrical phrasing, the emotional quality of the slow movement, and the growing distinction between the minuet and trio. Nor should we overlook the rugged, folk-like quality of the melodic material of these early works, since it is an individual feature of his melodic style. Interesting as these quartets are in foreshadowing the more mature evidences of Haydn's originality, the works of primary importance are those that, in addition to the melodic and rhythmic elements, demonstrate the new structural outlines on which Haydn fashioned the classical quartet.

The quartets to be discussed, Opus 9, Opus 17, and Opus 20, are generally regarded as embryonic rather than fully developed conceptions of the form. By comparison with the six quartets of Opus 33 it is undeniable that there is a wide gap not only in time but in style and treatment between these works. Opus 20 concludes a period in which the quartet was still in a process of evolution and in which Haydn was struggling with the problems of the new medium as well as to free himself from the influence of the transition composers. Opus 33 opens the period of the full-fledged quartet, in which both the structure as a whole and the treatment of the various sectional elements demonstrates the stylistic changes and technical advances that transformed the quartet of the past into the form that has survived for more than a hundred and fifty years. However, the early works are of interest not only because they disclose the various reforms that were taking place in the growth of the quartet technique, but also because they already show certain trends foreshadowing Haydn's innovations in Opus 33.

The six quartets of Opus 9 were composed in 1771, later than the period of the B♭ and D major sonatas, but slightly earlier than the more fully conceived works in C, E, and F major previously discussed. For this reason we should not regard Opus 9 as entirely experimental, since Haydn already had stabilized certain structural techniques in his treatment of the sonatas. This is especially true of the neighbor-note treatment as a means of expanding the motion of the development section. That so many of the examples cited from the sonatas illustrate this technique is not the result of arbitrary selection, but is due to the predominance of this method in the sonatas. In fact none but the works in which the neighbor-note treatment was used offered the opportunity to show Haydn's devel-

119

opment of structural technique. Because of the concentration on this aspect of the sonatas, the discussion of the quartets will center as much as possible on two other types of structural expansion: prolonged motion within the dominant chord and the extended progression from the mediant to the dominant.

The first of these quartets to disclose a different treatment of the development section is Opus 9, No. 3, in G major. Before discussing this work, it is necessary to touch briefly on the unusual manner in which the development section has been achieved in Opus 9, No. 2, in Eb major, even though it shows a further use of the basic neighbor-note technique.

A dominant Bb major chord closes the exposition. The introduction of its altered seventh, Ab, leads to the chord of G major on which the development section begins. That this G major chord is the applied dominant of the neighbor chord to which it directs the emphasis justifies its use, but does not lessen the bold effect created by its entrance. The nature of this motion and that of the prolonging motion that extends it give adequate proof both of the greater fluidity of Haydn's handling of the form and of the technical mastery through which it is achieved.

Turning to the G major quarter, Opus 9, No. 3, we find the treatment less striking in that it follows a more conventional pattern. For this reason it provides an excellent introduction to the technique of furnishing

EXAMPLE 45

120

the entire development section through the prolongation of the dominant chord. Since this is the first instance of this structural technique, we shall discuss the treatment in detail.

The development section as a whole outlines a passing motion within the D major chord. The top voice descends from D to A while the bass ascends from D to A moving on through B, C, and C♯ to D. From this expansion of the dominant chord, emerge a series of further prolongations that give individuality and integrity to the melodic and structural character of the section and that differentiate it from other developments in which a similar basic motion occurs.

First of all we see that the A minor chord, which Haydn has substituted for the A major, is introduced through its applied dominant, the E major chord. The space between the D and E major chords has been widely extended by inverting the ascending second into a descending seventh, which, by its chromatic character, contributes great variety and contrast to the motion. Within the A minor chord we find further smaller prolongations that expand the structural top-voice descent from C to A. These are achieved primarily through a shift of C and B to a higher register, from which the extending motions are made. Furthermore as the diminished chord on A♯ lends emphasis to the B major passing chord that follows, so the exchange of the A minor for the A major chord (measure 18) intensifies the entrance of the D major chord through its effect of an applied dominant, although its actual function is that of a chromatic passing chord.

Both the structural and the prolonging techniques are so clearly indicated that they demonstrate excellently how an entire section can grow out of the expansion of a single dominant chord. Since this is one of the rare instances among the early works in which Haydn has used this type of structure, it is all the more remarkable that he has so fully grasped the essential elements of the technique. It is true that by comparison with the sonatas in C, E, and F major the treatment lacks the boldness that distinguishes the slightly later works. Nevertheless, it is not lacking in ingenuity, since the effect of the chromatics in the smaller prolongations is sufficiently striking to contribute the color contrast that this type of motion within a single chord so greatly needs.

From an instrumental point of view we find that the individual characteristics of the viola and cello have not been fully recognized. They serve principally to provide an accompaniment for the first violin. This is of interest because of the changed status of these instruments in the late quartets, in which the four instruments are welded together into a more equal blending of the voice parts.

Although the three remaining quartets in this group have many points of interest and show a more imaginative treatment than the foregoing example, Opus 17, composed in the same year as Opus 9, offers a far better insight into Haydn's development of the quartet technique.

Of these quartets the last movements of No. 1 in E major and No. 3 in E♭ major and the first movement of No. 4 in C minor provide outstanding examples of Haydn's grasp of structural techniques and of his innovations in the prolongations. Each of these presents a different type of expanding motion and shows the individual characteristics of the technique. Together they demonstrate the various kinds of composition that can evolve out of the same basic form. The treatment differs widely; the prolongations have little in common, since the nature of the thematic material is entirely diverse. Nevertheless, all three evidence the same fundamental principles of coherence, which assure the tonal stability essential to the form.

The last movement of the E major quartet Opus 17, No. 1, offers an illustration of the neighbor-note technique. Although there are no startling innovations in the exposition, the instrumentation shows a definite growth in the use and function of the viola and cello. The two violins give out the theme, for the most part unaccompanied. The viola and cello pick it up in the thirteenth measure, with the two violins now providing an accompaniment. In employing the viola and cello as solo instruments Haydn recognized the possibilities of color and tone contrast offered by these instruments and has taken an important step in instrumentation. It is true that this use of the viola and cello occurs very infrequently, but it nevertheless indicates a tendency that is brought to fruition in the later quartets.

The exposition shows a clear-cut motion from the tonic to the dominant B major chord on which it closes. The unusual aspect of the motion is the E major chord on which the development section begins. What is the status of this E major chord, and what function does it fulfill in the structural motion?

Although the entrance of an E major chord after the dominant B major chord might suggest a dominant-tonic progression, the use of a structural tonic at the start of the development section would be extraor-

Josef Haydn

EXAMPLE 46

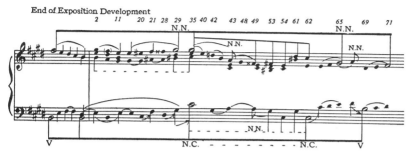

dinary, since it would seriously affect the structural character of the form. Moreover, to impart a structural significance to this E major chord before we examine the music to determine the role it enacts, would give rise to an interpretation that would obscure rather than clarify the function this chord demonstrates in the motion.

Since the E major chord serves the purpose of a contrapuntal passing chord between the chords of B and G♯ major, its presence at the start of the development section is even more striking. The technique proves that although Haydn recognized the melodic value of repeating the theme within the same chord in which it entered in the exposition, he had the vision to give this chord the contrapuntal function that would preserve both the integrity of the primordial progression and the structural outlines of the form. The role this E major chord plays offers convincing proof that the appearance of a chord in no wise defines either its status or function in a specific passage.

Actually the E major chord, with E shown in the bass, comes from D♯, a middle voice of the dominant B major chord. In fact the entire motion created by the E, F♯, and G♯ major chords represents a middle voice, which appears in the bass through the shift of the bass motion B–B♯–C♯ to a middle voice. The basic progression is from the B major through the G♯ major to the C♯ minor neighbor chord; in this the E and F♯ chords serve as passing chords in the expanded space.

This is a most ingenious type of prolongation, which is further expanded through the embellishing motions in the top voice and the introduction of C♯ and D♯ in the bass as applied dominants respectively of the F♯ and G♯ major chords. The prolongation of the C♯ chord indicates

123

Challenge to Musical Tradition

several new tendencies in the treatment. It demonstrates (1) the increasingly important role that the neighbor chord, extended for thirty-one measures, plays in the section; (2) the originality of the expansion through the use of transfer of register and neighbor notes, and (3) the more complex treatment of the voice leadings and the parallelism it offers to the shift in register of the top voice of the B major chord of the exposition. A further parallelism is shown in the melodic figure D♯–E–F♯, which leads to both the development and the recapitulation.

These prolongations of the structural motion reveal not only a mastery of the technical problems, but a conception of the artistic possibilities in contradiction to the theory that the early works represent a period of experimentation. It is true that the quartets from Opus 33 on show greater imagination, through a more interesting type of melodic material and a more ingenious use of it in the development section. But these mature evidences of Haydn's genius are a natural outgrowth of the qualities and stylistic tendencies of the early period. They should not blind us to the various innovations, in such instances as the foregoing example, that had a definite part in shaping the structural character of the classical quartet.

An unusual comparison with the treatment in this work is offered in the last movement of the quartet in E♭ major, Opus 17, No. 3. The first movement departs from the allegro customary in sonata form. Haydn substituted for it a theme with variations. This deviation from the usual treatment indicates that Haydn did not regard the arrangement of the movements as stereotyped. It points to a sufficiently broad and elastic conception of the form to permit the use of whatever type of treatment was best suited to the character of the material and the manner of expression it inspired.

There is a slight similarity between the preceding example in E major and this in E♭ major, since in both a chord that has the appearance of a tonic figures prominently in the development section. But the function of these chords and the nature of the prolongations are entirely different. Here the E♭ major chord enters, not at the outset as did the E major chord, but only after a widely expanded motion within the B♭ major chord. To determine its function and find a justification for its presence let us turn to the example.

To start the development section on a G major chord after the close of the exposition on a dominant B♭ major chord is both daring and original. It is even more striking when we see that the G major chord does not

Josef Haydn

EXAMPLE 47

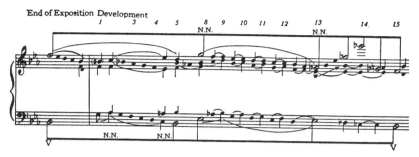

serve as an applied dominant of C minor, but leads instead to the chord of F minor, a neighbor-passing chord within the expanded dominant. What, then, is the status of this G major chord?

We see that Bb, a middle voice of the dominant, passes through B♮ of the G chord to C, a middle voice of the F minor chord. Thus B♮ intensifies the entrance of the neighbor chord, while G in the bass serves as a neighbor of the Ab that follows. Therefore its main purpose is to bring melodic emphasis to the F minor chord. However, its presence as the opening chord of the section gives it added weight and heightens its pressure on the F minor chord. This was a bold innovation in Haydn's day.

The expansion of the F minor chord is also of interest, because through its unfolding it provides Eb in the top voice as a passing tone between F and D of the dominant chord and also provides Ab and C in the bass as under and upper neighbors of Bb. When C appears in the bass, the entrance of A♮ in a middle voice and Eb in the top gives a strong impulse to the following Bb chord.

We come now to the Eb major chord, whose presence offers the unusual element in the treatment. Although it has the appearance of a tonic chord, it is evident that its primary purpose is to prolong the motion of the development section by furnishing G as a structural neighbor note of F of the Bb major chord. Therefore, although the origin of this chord is contrapuntal, its function as a form-making technique is structural.

The prolongation both of this Eb major chord and its return to the Bb major chord is extremely ingenious. Its expansion is achieved by a stepwise descent from G to Gb in the top voice, while the bass outlines a motion from Eb through Bb to Eb in which the space between Bb and Eb is filled with passing tones. The intervening inverted chords, represented

125

Challenge to Musical Tradition

by G, F, E♭, and D in the bass, eliminate the succession of fifths in the outside voices through the 5–6 technique. With the descent to G♭ in the top voice, the E♭ major is converted into an E♭ minor chord. The retention of this G♭ in the top voice while the bass descends from E♭ to C♭ gives it greater emphasis than its function as a passing tone between G♮ and F warrants. Again, the introduction of A♮ into the C♭ major chord, that immediately precedes the dominant, intensifies the return of the B♭ major chord.

Although on the whole the techniques in this example are less convincing than in Opus 17, No. 1, the treatment reveals many daring variations. Its chief interest lies in the use of a G major chord at the start of the section, the neighbor-note motion supplied by the expanded F minor chord, the role of the E♭ major chord, and the prolonged return to the dominant, since each of these brings to light the exceptional nature of the prolonging techniques.

The third example comes from the opening movement of the C minor quartet, Opus 17, No. 4. With this work we come to the outstanding quartet of Opus 17. It is remarkable not only for this early period, but in comparison with many of the later works. The treatment here differs widely from that in the two preceding examples, not only because the development section is based on a prolonged mediant-dominant progression, but also because of the role played by the motivic figure in the unusual character of the expansion. It also emphasizes how much broader is Haydn's conception of the form and the effect of this elasticity on the techniques, and on the other hand it proves how much the distinctive character of the composition owes to the bold and extraordinary treatment of the prolongations.

Except for the B minor sonata very briefly referred to in the opening chapter, this is the first work in which we have encountered a I–III–V–I progression as the structural outline of an entire movement. Hence the technique itself is of primary interest. However, we cannot regard it as representative of the usual treatment because of the prolonged motion from the dominant chord, which normally concludes the development, to the tonic chord of the recapitulation.

Additional proof of the extraordinary originality of the technique is provided by the A♭ major chord that opens the development section and is expanded for twenty-two measures before the dominant G major chord enters. This is a rare example of the use of the neighbor note within a

Josef Haydn

mediant-dominant progression. Equally unusual is the role of the motivic figure in determining the character and nature of the expanded motion from the dominant to the tonic chord of the restatement.

Since the most essential element is the structural motion binding the exposition to the recapitulation, let us consider it before discussing the prolongation of the Ab neighbor chord.

EXAMPLE 48

The problem disclosed by this graph is the status of the Eb major chord that appears between the chords of G major and C minor. What is its function, and why has Haydn delayed the entrance of the tonic chord for seventeen measures? Naturally no definite and authoritative explanation of Haydn's motives can be offered. We can, however, suggest certain possibilities to which the music itself gives rise.

First of all the descent from G to C through Eb, a motion in thirds that outlines the tones of the C minor chord, is not sufficiently unique to create a major problem. It is rather the importance that Haydn gives the Eb chord through its prolongation and also the character of the motive introducing this chord that provide the arresting elements of the treatment. It would be interesting to speculate how far the prominence of Eb, in the thematic material of the exposition as well as in the top-voice motion of the development, was either a conscious or unconscious influence on Haydn's introduction of the Eb major chord into the structural progression.

EXAMPLE 48A

127

Challenge to Musical Tradition

The graph shows the melodic and structural outline of the motion from the G major to the C minor chord. The entrance of the motive E♭–G–C after the dominant chord and the fact that it outlines the tones of the tonic chord suggest that we have reached the recapitulation. This assumption, however, immediately proves false when an F minor instead of a C minor chord appears and passes to an E♭ major chord. Here the function of F minor is that of a prolonged passing chord between the G and E♭ major chords.

We must not overlook the far-reaching implications of Haydn's treatment in this passage or its effect on the music of his successors. Here is a dramatic conflict between what the motive leads us to expect and what actually occurs. The frustrated attempt to gain the tonic chord and the suspense it creates, which is intensified by the prolongation of the E♭ chord, reveal an entirely new element, indicative of the unique possibilities to which Haydn's conception of the form gave rise. How much the passage gains from this conflict between the motive and the delay of the recapitulation may be seen in the following examples, indicating other possibilities that Haydn might have used.

EXAMPLE 48B

Example 48B (1) shows a direct motion from the G major chord, the close of the development, to the C minor chord of the recapitulation, without the dramatic effect offered by prolongation of the intervening measures. However, this arrangement suggests parallel octaves in the outside voices. Example 48B (2) reveals that the motive, instead of outlining the C minor chord, could have entered on the E♭ major chord at the outset, as it actually occurs in the final measure of the development section. But this abrupt entrance of the E♭ chord would have been so striking that it would have weakened the effect of the tonic chord of the recapitulation. Moreover, if instead of presenting the motive as an unaccompanied figure whose outline suggests the entrance of a C minor chord (Example 48A), Haydn had introduced the motive in connection with an E♭ major

Josef Haydn

chord, as in Example 48B (2), he would have sacrificed the dramatic suspense that is attained by anticipating the entrance of the tonic C minor chord long before it actually occurs.

Another unusual feature is the introduction of the A♭ major chord as the opening of the development section and the role it plays in prolonging the mediant-dominant progression.

EXAMPLE 48C

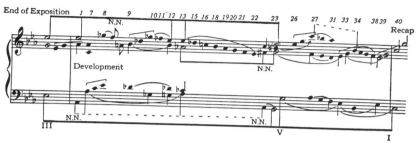

The status of this A♭ chord, which directly follows the mediant E♭ major chord at the close of the exposition, is at first somewhat doubtful. It is only when we see it in relation to the following G major chord that its function as a neighbor chord becomes clear. This function is emphasized by the entrance of F♯ in a middle voice immediately before the G major chord appears.

In prolonging this neighbor chord for twenty-two measures Haydn not only used a neighbor note (measure 8), an embellishing motion (measures 10–12), and a descent from a top into a middle voice (measures 13–22), but also employed the motivic figure as a further means of expanding the different voice parts. This widely extended A♭ chord is in itself an unusual aspect of the treatment, since such a prolongation of the mediant-dominant progression is rare. A more typical expansion of such a progression is shown in the B minor sonata (Example 11) referred to in the opening chapter; there the development section is created by a passing motion leading from the mediant to the dominant chord. The amazing aspect of this section of the C minor quartet is that thirty-six of the thirty-nine measures consist of chords serving in one way or another to expand the basic III–V–I harmonic progression.

In addition we should notice the predominant role the motive plays in these prolongations. It forms a melodic link between the exposition and

129

the development and also between the development and the recapitulation. To indicate its numerous appearances throughout the section, each entrance has been shown in brackets.

Although this work belongs to an early period, it reveals an imagination and breadth of conception that, together with the expertness of the technical treatment, are generally associated with the later quartets. No longer is the quartet in an embryonic stage or the classical form in the process of evolution. Both have emerged through the vision and mastery demonstrated by Haydn in applying the principles of structure and prolongation to his more elastic idea of the form.

However, since this prolongation of the mediant-dominant progression is unusual, let us turn to a more representative although less original example of this type of structural motion — the first movement of the F minor quartet, Opus 20, No. 5. It is to be expected that these works of a slightly later date should disclose certain tendencies differentiating them from the treatment of Opus 17. This is especially true of the instrumentation and the increased importance given to the viola and cello. Although the changed status of these instruments may be attributed in part to the predominance of the fugal technique in the final movements, the fact that they share the melodic responsibility in movements of a different nature suggests a general recognition of their potentialities as solo instruments.

It is only necessary to turn to the affettuoso of the first quartet, the opening theme of the first movement of the C major quartet, No. 2, and the adagios of the third and sixth quartets, in A major and G minor respectively, to realize how large a part the viola and cello play in unfolding the thematic material of these movements. The character of the melodic material and its inherent fitness to the instrument to which it is allotted indicates a new tendency to merge the four instruments into a single unit of sound, rather than to regard the first violin as a solo instrument, with the others providing the accompaniment. Although this trend was to become a definite reality only through the achievements of Beethoven, its presence in these early works should not be overlooked.

There are other evidences of the growth of Haydn's quartet technique. The first of these is the character of the subject matter and its more imaginative use in the development section. This is illustrated by the manner in which the material lends itself to a specific treatment in the first movements of the quartets in E♭ major, No. 1; C major, No. 2; and F minor,

Josef Haydn

No. 5. These development sections show that Haydn no longer uses the theme in its entirety, but only the measures that offer the best possibilities for melodic adaptation. This is important, since it shows the trend toward a genuine development of the material, indicative of the full-fledged form.

Further proof of the adroitness of Haydn's techniques lies in the unconventional nature of the prolongations, both of the structural framework and the melodic line. It is true that none of these works demonstrates the imaginative and artistic conception that underlies the foregoing C minor quartet. Nevertheless, the technical skill and ingenuity revealed by the treatment of the prolonging motions leave little doubt as to the growth of Haydn's ability to express fully the many-sidedness of his artistic personality.

The F minor quartet, Opus 20, No. 5, offers an excellent example of how much interest, color, and intensity the prolongation injects into a I–III–V–I structural progression, even though the treatment employs the more customary techniques. In contrast to the treatment in the C minor quartet the mediant-dominant progression is expanded through a passing motion that delays the entrance of the dominant chord. In short

EXAMPLE 49

131

Challenge to Musical Tradition

it is a typical example of the use of a mediant-dominant progression as the harmonic framework of a development section, but an instance in which the techniques are sufficiently original to show the new tendencies in Haydn's stylistic treatment.

The motion within the A♭ chord is too obvious to require explanation. However, the opening of the development on a D♭ major chord, which has been approached through an A♭ seventh chord, is so daring that if we were examining it from the customary theoretical point of view, it might suggest a temporary "modulation" to the key of D♭ major. The example reveals, on the contrary, that the D♭ chord is a subdominant in the harmonic prolongation of the A♭ major chord.

From a structural aspect the motion that expands the space between the A♭ and C major chords is of primary importance. In this the substitution and expansion of the minor for the major dominant, which is reached only at the close of the section, is further evidence of the unorthodox nature of Haydn's treatment. The use of the C minor chord not only engenders an interesting prolongation of the top voice, but increases the intensity in the structural motion to achieve the climax, the C major chord. This is one of many instances in which we find a mixture of the major and minor chords. It should not suggest the presence of two tonalities or the use of two different chords, since the C minor and C major chords represent two different aspects of the same chord. This use of mixture can be applied to any chord irrespective of its origin, function, or the tonality in which it appears without impairing the clarity or coherence of a basic or a primordial progression. This is proved by the countless instances in which chords belonging to a minor key are introduced into a composition in a major chord. Thus in a work in C major we find many different chords that are indicative of the key of C minor. Although these minor chords usually demonstrate a prolonging function, they sometimes, as in the above example, are of a structural origin as a dominant. Therefore, instead of defining a work as in the key of C major, it would be more accurate to describe it as a work in C, thus allowing for the various expressions of a mixture of the major and minor chords.

In the motion from the mediant to the minor dominant the entrance of the chord of F minor (measure 20) offers a further illustration of the varied function the same chord may exercise in different passages. Because of its emphasis, through the C major chord that precedes it, there might be a tendency to regard it as a tonic. However, a more careful study

132

Josef Haydn

of the graph reveals that such an interpretation would be erroneous. First of all we see that it occurs within a widely extended motion from the A♭ to the G major chord. Here an ascent in tenths in the outside voices leads the A♭ major to the C major chord, an applied dominant of F minor. The introduction of F♯ in the bass intensifies the motion from the F minor to the G major chord. Thus, instead of a direct motion from the A♭ to the G major chord, there is a detour through the chord of F minor. Therefore the status of this F minor chord is clearly defined as a passing chord in the motion. Furthermore, since the motion as a whole defines a mediant-dominant progression, it would be impossible for the F minor chord to function as a tonic without destroying the structural outline of the form.

Melodically the entrance of this F minor chord effects the transfer of A♭ to a higher register, a motion that is paralleled by the shift of G of the G major chord (measure 21) to its octave (measure 25). The stress that the preceding neighbor note B♭ gives to A♭ of the F minor chord suggests that the similar emphasis that B♭ of the dominant chord brings to A♭ in the opening chord of the recapitulation may be an unconscious imitation.

Some points, however, such as the consistent use of an interval of a third to define the smaller motions, recur too frequently to be regarded as accidental. Although this repetition of a specific interval might denote a lack of resourcefulness, the fact that the smaller motions take on the same melodic contour outlined by the structural top voice of the entire movement in the descent A♭—G—F points on the contrary to the strength of the melodic concept that embraces both the structural and prolonging motions.

Since the development section closes with a retained G in the structural top voice and the restatement starts on A♭, some readers might regard this G as an under neighbor note of A♭. It cannot be so, however. G represents a definite break that stops the motion at the psychological point and prevents it from attaining its ultimate goal of F. By so doing, it provides the opportunity for a third section of the form, the restatement. In this the structural line is repeated, but no longer frustrated; it completes the full descent to F.

This conception of the form demonstrates that the sectional elements are created by the structural techniques; they do not arise out of an artificial or accidental distribution of the material, but are an organic necessity. Furthermore, it shows that the structural top voice is an essential factor in determining the fundamental outline of the form, since it is the

Challenge to Musical Tradition

means by which the break or interruption of the motion is achieved. Thus, although the harmonic progression provides the dominant chord on which the interruption occurs, it is essential that the structural top voice combine with it to define the sectional outlines of the form and supply the structural justification for their presence.

Because this example, more than any other we have discussed, offers the possibility of mistaking the interrupting tone for a neighbor note, the explanation of this technique has been purposely delayed so that it could be given at this point. In the graphs, the break in the structural motion has been indicated by separating A♭ of the recapitulation from the preceding G of the development and the tonic from the dominant chord.

This technique of interruption occurs when the structural top voice supported by the dominant chord of the progression creates a break in the motion that necessitates completion in a third section of the form. It is not restricted to sonata form, but is used in binary form as well; there it provides the artistic opportunity as well as the structural necessity for the introduction of a second section. Although not every two- or three-part form is created through the interruption of the structural top-voice motion, it is the most widely used of the form-making techniques. It is, in fact, a type of structural prolongation, since it is the primary means by which a basic one-part form is converted into a two- or three-part form.

The C minor quartet offers a similar use of interruption when the structural top-voice motion is brought to a stop on D of the dominant G major chord. This engenders the repetition of the motion, in which the descent from G to C is achieved in the recapitulation.

In general, however, a comparison of the techniques that expand the I—III—V—I progression, on which the structural motion of the first movement of the C and F minor quartets is based, shows that the treatment in the earlier work is more venturesome and outstanding. This is due primarily to the unusual expansion not only of the mediant-dominant progression, but of the dominant-tonic as well. In the latter motion the motive plays a unique role. It not only serves in its customary melodic capacity, but exerts a strong influence on the nature of the structural prolongation. In short it makes possible the introduction of the E♭ chord that expands the descent from the G major to the C minor chord.

The first movement of the F minor quartet shows a more conventional treatment of the I—III—V—I progression. This, however, points even more sharply to the distinctive nature of the prolongations, the dynamic effect

134

they create, and the richness, interest, and color they contribute. It is particularly true of the treatment of the top voice, which, unlike the motivic figure in the C minor quartet, exercises no pressure on the techniques that prolong the structural motion. Nevertheless, the character of the prolongations and the impetus they give the motion show an originality that, though differently expressed, was a necessary stimulus to the growth of the form.

Thus far we have discussed the first and last movements of the quartets because they most clearly illustrate Haydn's stabilization of the techniques through which sonata form evolved. It is to be expected, for the most part, that these works should not disclose the artistic or technical possibilities that we find in the later works, such, for example, as the opening movement of the B♭ major quartet, Opus 76, No. 4. In this, Haydn's tremendous prolongation of the neighbor chord in the development section, as well as the imitation in the melodic prolongations, of the opening figure of the exposition, reveals a conception of the form and a technical assurance indicative of his increased powers of creation. On the other hand we should not forget that it was his experience with the neighbor-note technique in numerous works of the early period and his extraordinary use of the melodic figure in the F major sonata (Example 42) that were responsible for the full realization of these same techniques in the later work.

The early sonatas and quartets are significant not only in the development of Haydn's own means of expression, but for their influence on the later tendencies in the form. As Philipp Emanuel Bach laid the foundation for Haydn, so Haydn, in these early works, erected the framework of the classical sonata and quartet, which Mozart and Beethoven adapted to their own requirements.

To give a fully-rounded picture of the significance of this early period, it is also necessary to touch briefly on the symphonies.

THE SYMPHONIES

The early form of the symphony was patterned on the style and structure of the three movements of the sinfonia or Italian overture. There was an allegro, followed by a slow movement, with a quick allegro as a finale. Most of the works of the transition composers are based on this general type of structure, although there are a few isolated instances in which a minuet and trio appear as a fourth movement. Although the evolution of

Challenge to Musical Tradition

this suite-like form into the highly distinctive character of the classical symphony cannot be attributed to any one composer, it is nevertheless admitted that Haydn was primarily responsible for the melodic, technical, and structural alterations, as well as innovations in the instrumentation, that converted the varied experiments of the transition composers into a highly developed and clearly defined organism.

Among composers whose experiments in the form pre-date the early symphonies of Haydn and may thus, in one way or another, have influenced the trend the form was to take, are Georg Matthias Monn, Johann Stamitz, Georg Christoph Wagenseil, Karl Friedrich Abel and Johann Christian and Philipp Emanuel Bach. Since this is not a historical discussion of the growth of the symphony, it is unnecessary to point out the differentiating characteristics disclosed by the works of these composers. It is sufficient to recognize that they reveal a change from the motivic to the thematic idea, with themes that comprise several independent motives — a significant step in shaping the melodic tendencies of the form. They also indicate a definition of the sectional elements of the allegro, with evidence of the contrasting effect of the thematic material of the exposition. Thus it is possible that Monn, Stamitz, Wagenseil, Abel, and even Gossec may have directed the general trend the symphony was to take. They may also have influenced Haydn in the instrumentation of his early works. Nevertheless, considerable as their contributions are, there is one vital element that their works do not clearly define — that the various sections of a movement are component parts of an organic whole.

This is a significant fact. It suggests that although the works of these composers may have been instrumental in shaping various smaller aspects of Haydn's treatment, his fundamental conception of the form was based on the principle of structural coherence demonstrated in the Prussian and Württemberg Sonatas of Philipp Emanuel Bach. Haydn's early symphonies show many distinguishing characteristics that differentiate his treatment from immediate predecessors'; none of these was as essential to the stabilization of the form as his definition of tonal and structural unity. In applying to the symphony the techniques of structure and prolongation that he was to use later in the sonata and quartet Haydn laid the foundation for the fully developed classical form. The first movements of his early symphonies do not show such originality in the melodic content, the various smaller prolongations, and the treatment of the structural motion

Josef Haydn

as the later works, but the techniques expanding the harmonic progression are clear and definite.

For example, the symphony in D major, composed in 1759, shows a development section in which the structural motion outlines a descent from A of the dominant chord through G, F♯, and E to D of the tonic chord of the recapitulation. Although the prolongations are less unusual, the structural plan is similar to that used in the E major sonata (Example 41) in which the motion was achieved contrapuntally by means of a descent from B to E.

A more customary prolongation of the dominant-tonic progression is disclosed in the C major symphony, No. 2, written about 1760. Here the development section shows a motion within the dominant chord. Other instances of this type of prolongation may be found in the opening movements of the D and A major symphonies, Nos. 4 and 5.

In the sixth, seventh, and eighth symphonies, which bear the programmatic titles of *Le Matin, Le Midi,* and *Le Soir,* Haydn has used the neighbor-note technique. Singularly enough, in all these examples the prolonged motion to and from the neighbor note is much clearer and more sharply defined than in the early B♭ and D major sonatas, which were written several years later. In *Le Matin* and *Le Midi* the introduction of chromatics in the prolongations creates a richness in the voice leadings and an intensity in the motion that one does not expect in these early works. A quotation from the first few measures of the development section of *Le Matin* reveals the unusual and ingenious technique expanding the motion from the A major to the B minor neighbor chord.

EXAMPLE 50

Le Midi is the most original of these works, not only from a melodic and structural point of view, but also in regard to instrumentation. It is scored for strings, flutes, oboes, and horns, and the instruments are employed to emphasize both their individual tone qualities and the con-

137

trasting effects of various combinations. For example, in some sections the strings alone are used, and in others the oboes take up the theme, while in the adagio the melody is given out by the flutes. The independence of the instruments and the fitness of each group for the specific purpose it serves indicate the new tendencies in the treatment that determined the trend that instrumentation was to take in the future. Here Haydn's use of a first and second violin and cello as solo instruments was so unusual that in writing of this work Pohl says: "Such a scoring was unheard of for Eistenstadt and caused the old Werner [the *Kappellmeister*] to think with justice that Haydn had lost his head." [8] Altogether the score called for two principal violins, two violins ripieno, viola, cello, obbligato, two oboes, horns, bassoon, and continuo.

This symphony is important as a whole because the character of the material, the clarity of the structural motion, the variety in the smaller prolongations, and the unusual effects of the instrumentation all evidence a growing tendency toward an originality and individuality of expression that differentiates Haydn's stylistic treatment from that of his contemporaries. In the adagio that introduces the opening theme; in the emotional quality of the slow movement, intensified by the preceding recitative; in the strong and vigorous character of the minuet with its contrasting trio, emphasized by the use of flutes as solo instruments; and in the distinctive nature of the finale, which Mozart later used to such good advantage, Haydn already defined the characteristic four-movement symphony out of which the mature form was to emerge.

A broad survey shows that the later works reveal the same type of innovations within the structural motion and the same bold use of prolongation that we encountered in the sonatas and quartets of the early 1770's. There is also a more frequent use of folk-song material and a more ingenious treatment of it in the development section. In fact the domination of a single motivic figure throughout the middle section, on which to weave the prolongations of the top-voice motion, suggests that here, as in the sonatas and quartets, Haydn has already achieved the beginnings of a true development. The increasing importance of the introduction and coda in these later works and its effect on the works that were to follow should not be overlooked. Not only do the changes Haydn instituted in the status of the introduction and coda disclose a growth in his own conception of the form, but they led directly to the more radical innovations of

[8] Pohl, C. F., *Haydn* (Breitkopf and Härtel, Leipzig, 1878), Vol. I, p. 285.

Josef Haydn

Beethoven, through which these sections were transformed by the imaginative and significant roles they played in prolonging the structural motion. Although most of our discussion thus far has centered on the first and last movements of the sonatas, quartets, and symphonies, because they are the characteristic elements of the form, we cannot altogether neglect the influence of Haydn on the adagio, the minuet and trio, and the rondo.

THE SLOW MOVEMENT

There are many evidences of Haydn's imprint in the character and treatment of the slow movement. First and most important is his introduction of the theme and variations as an alternative to the customary two-part form. Not only did this supply Haydn with a new stylistic medium that he used successfully, but it opened the way to the later developments by Beethoven and Brahms.

Under Haydn the character of the movement took on greater significance because of the sincere and forthright nature of the material and the genuine emotion it expressed. The simplicity of the melody was compensated for by the intensity of the prolongations; together they resulted in a stylistic quality completely divorced from the sentimental tendencies of the "gallant style." There is warmth and color in the slow movements, at times even a passionate fervor in the later works that links Haydn with Beethoven. Although this element occurs less frequently in the early sonatas, quartets, and symphonies, before 1776, there are sufficient evidences of it to believe that it was inherent in Haydn's own nature and not the result of the influence either of Mozart or Philipp Emanuel Bach.

THE MINUET AND TRIO

There appears to be a diversity of opinion as to whether Haydn was the first to introduce the minuet and trio into the symphony. On the one hand Paul Láng states that "the first complete symphony in four movements, including the minuet, was already present in Georg Matthias Monn's symphony in D major, composed in 1740." [9] Later he says that the minuet was "incorporated into the cyclic form by Stamitz about 1745." [10] Pohl, however, admits that the question is debatable: "Whether Haydn was the first to add the minuet to the three-movement symphony is still to be determined. Many include Gossec with Haydn in this con-

[9] *Music in Western Civilization* (Norton, 1941), p. 607.　　[10] *Ibid.*, p. 613.

nection." [11] Nef attributes the introduction of the minuet to the Mannheim school, but the innovations in character and treatment to Haydn.[12]

Regardless of its origin, there can be little argument as to the transformation the minuet and trio underwent in the hands of Haydn. In fact nowhere is the individuality of his idiom more clearly reflected than in this movement. Even in the earliest quartets and symphonies the minuets are of an entirely different quality from the minuet of the suite. This is due to various aspects of the treatment. The minuet of the suite was a slow, stately dance whose grace and elegance were indicative of its aristocratic origin as a court dance. The minuets of Haydn, on the contrary, are robust and vigorous in style, quicker in tempo, and full of the homely spirit of a folk dance.

Three distinct factors effected this change: the new type of melody, the use of irregular accents, and the number of irregular phrase-groups that characterize the minuet and trio. The melodies are simple and genial and reveal the qualities inherent in Haydn's own personality. They are in striking contrast to the type of melodic material used by pre-classical composers, and they show that, in this respect at least, Haydn was singularly free from the influence of his forerunners and contemporaries. The genuineness of Haydn's melodic style is not confined to this movement, but in association with the irregularities of accent and phrasing that occur more frequently here than in any other section, it effected changes that made possible the later conversion of the minuet into the scherzo.

Although in the symphonies the folk-like quality of the melody contributes so much to the new aspect of the minuet, there are frequent evidences also in the early works of the irregular accents and phrase-groups that appear to such a marked extent in the later ones. The best examples of these tendencies in the early works are found in the quartets. One of the first instances of this metrical freedom is the first trio of Opus 1, No. 1, in which the first part consists of fourteen measures. These are divided into two groups of three measures each and two of four measures each. Here the extension of a customary two-measure phrase to three has resulted in an overlapping that foreshadows, interestingly, an idiosyncrasy that became more marked in later years.

Other evidences of irregularity may be seen in the minuet of Opus 9,

---

[11] *Joseph Haydn* (Breitkopf and Härtel, Leipzig, 1878), Vol. I, p. 276.

[12] *Geschichte der Sinfonie und Suite* (Breitkopf and Härtel, Leipzig, 1921), p. 148.

Josef Haydn

No. 2, with its two five-measure phrases, and the minuet of Opus 9, No. 3, which comprises two six-measure phrases, while the second half of the trio in Opus 9, No. 3, is made up of thirteen measures. The trios of Opus 17, Nos. 2 and 3, show a first part of fourteen and ten measures each. In the Opus 20 quartets the trio of No. 1 has a first part of ten measures; the minuet of No. 2, twenty; and the minuet of No. 5, eighteen. The constant use of such metrical freedom, by comparison with the more or less regular four-measure phrases to which Haydn's contemporaries adhered, shows how little Haydn's natural characteristics were influenced by the prevailing methods of other composers.

Examples of irregular accents are too numerous to cite. A few typical illustrations are in the trios of Opus 2, No. 4; Opus, 9, Nos. 3, 4, and 5; the minuet of Opus 9, No. 6; the trio of Opus 17, No. 4; and the minuet of Opus 20, No. 2.

In general the sonatas, quartets and symphonies show an increasing contrast in character between the minuet and the trio. This was achieved not only through differentiations in the melodic quality and the more vigorous rhythmic treatment of the minuet, but also through the variety of effects provided by the instrumentation. Haydn may not have been the first to introduce the minuet into the symphony, but he was the first to make it a vital and characteristic element of the form.

THE PRESTO

By injecting into the final movement a lightness, gaiety, and humor that emanated from his own genial nature, Haydn imbued it with a spirit that separated it from the past and shaped its future trend. Furthermore, by using the rondo form in many of his works, he provided an additional possibility for stylistic treatment heightening the contrast to the structural outlines of the other movements. The distinction between the allegro or the opening movement and the presto was accomplished not only through the use of the rondo form in the latter, but also by means of the different type of subject matter and the varied treatment he imparted to these movements, even when both defined the structural outlines of sonata form.

Further evidences of Haydn's originality in his treatment of the final movement are to be found in Opus 20, Nos. 2, 5, and 6, and Opus 50, No. 4, in which the fugue form has been incorporated into the quartet. Not content with a single subject, Haydn has written one fugue with four subjects, one with three, and another with two, in order to attain an even

141

Challenge to Musical Tradition

greater variety of material and mood. These fugues do not have the character, the inventive genius, or the technical perfection of a Bach fugue. They are nevertheless interesting, not only because of Haydn's deft handling of the unusual subject matter, but because his experimentation with and inclusion of the fugue form in the quartet brought together the various media used by his predecessors into the larger confines of the classical sonata form — a step that made possible Beethoven's use of the fugal style in the remarkable last movement of the quartet Opus 59, No. 3.

Such are Haydn's contributions to the melodic, rhythmic, and structural elements of the classical form. They show that although he built on the structural outlines already indicated in the works of some of his predecessors, he nevertheless imparted to them the spark of his artistic imagination, the coherence to which his conception of tonality gave expression, and a freshness and sincerity in treatment that freed music from the sentimental tendencies of the "gallant style."

In addition he divorced the symphony from chamber music, recognizing the right of each to evolve its own character along separate and distinct instrumental lines. Finally he stimulated the future trends of instrumentation by giving independence both to the viola and the cello in the quartet and to each and every instrument in the symphony. He discontinued the use of the cembalo in the symphony and in so doing made the orchestra the self-sufficient unit it has remained ever since.

The contribution of Haydn must not be estimated from a twentieth-century viewpoint or by comparing his achievements with those of any of his successors. He must be judged solely with reference to composers of his own day and for the effect of his works on later trends in style and form. By these standards he was the direct forerunner of Beethoven.

The transition composers stressed the effect of a work; Haydn emphasized the impulse out of which the work was conceived. He achieved his effects not through the use of the ornament or the attainment of the "gallant style," but through the expression of honest emotion in language simple and spontaneous. Always close to the common people from whom he had sprung, Haydn wrote out of his own experiences, despite the elevated position to which he rose at the court of Prince Esterhazy. To him elegance and refinement of style were not a goal in themselves. If they were an inherent part of the material, then they were essential to its presentation,

Josef Haydn

but always the choice of style depended solely on the character of the subject matter itself.

A lesser genius than Haydn might have evolved the classical sonata, quartet, and symphony through a mechanical organization of material whose smaller outlines were already indicated. But Haydn's expansion of the form was not an end in itself; it was the result both of his creative need to find expression for the great variety of his musical ideas and of the limitless possibilities offered by the concept of tonality. Craftsman though he was, his imagination rather than his technique was responsible for his innovations, although it demanded technical dexterity of a high order to achieve the results he produced.

Haydn holds a unique position in the world of instrumental music. The translucent beauty of Mozart's style, the power and passion of Beethoven's, the dramatic fervor of Wagner's, and the dynamic changes in present-day music have not lessened the warm human appeal, the spontaneous joy and good will, that radiate from Haydn's music. Haydn should not be compared with these successors, for they were his beneficiaries.

CHAPTER V

Beethoven

IMPACT OF EMOTION *on style and technique. Enlarged structural dimensions of sonata form; the development section. Broader functions of the introduction and coda; effect on the basic structure.*

MANY different explanations have been offered for the new elements in Beethoven's music. Some authorities attribute them to the influence of the French Revolution on the life and thought of the period that immediately followed it. However, if the special characteristics of Beethoven's style have their foundation in the revolutionary spirit of his age, why are not these same qualities found to an equal degree in the works of his contemporaries?

A further attempt to explain the various technical and stylistic innovations of Beethoven has been made by those biographers who have been confused by the many conflicting interpretations offered by analysts, composers, and performers. Unable to find a purely musical solution, they have turned to the latest methods of psychological investigation. They explain the artistic conflicts of the composer in terms of the personal conflicts of the man. In fact they point to the emotional crises in Beethoven's life as the source of those controversial elements in his music that have baffled musicians for more than a hundred years and led them to characterize the works of his last period as enigmatic.

Finally there are some who interpret the bold innovations introduced in the form by Beethoven as foreshadowing the musical revolution that was to follow, the full impact of which was felt only at the close of the nineteenth century.

No one should deny either the influence of the general life of the period or the effect of an artist's personal environment on the character of his works. It is inevitable that the *Sturm und Drang*, sweeping over the world, must leave its imprint on the later art-life. It is equally understandable that certain circumstances in Beethoven's private life, such as his unhappy

144

childhood, his unfortunate relationships with his brothers and later with his nephew, his emotional experiences, and finally, and most important, his loss of hearing, all had an effect on the man that was reflected in his music. Nevertheless, to cite his personal problems as the origin of artistic problems that can be interpreted as due to a natural unfolding of his development is to use the escape method in dealing with the main issue, which is to explain the music itself. The influence of Beethoven the man on Beethoven the composer may easily be overemphasized.

In a similar manner the belief that the revolutionary tendencies in his treatment are early evidences of trends which at the close of the nineteenth century resulted in the overthrow of the tonal system indicates a total misconception of tonality. Such an interpretation arises in a desire to link the present with the past, to find in the music of the early composers the seeds of twentieth-century techniques. It robs Beethoven of his greatest achievement, his contribution to the concept of tonality through his development of the techniques of structure and prolongation.

In the following consideration of Beethoven's influence on the growth and evolution of music we shall dispense with all discussion of questions the answer to which is extra-musical in origin. It is our purpose to confine ourselves to those problems of melody, rhythm, counterpoint, harmony, and form to which certain selected works give rise. We shall treat these problems solely from a musical point of view and solve them with reference to no methods other than those the music itself supplies.

In most studies dealing with Beethoven's artistic development the authors have been guided by the famous treatise of Wilhelm von Lenz,[1] in which the works of Beethoven are divided into three distinct periods of creative activity: (1) the period of imitation, (2) a period in which the traditional forms are given an increasing freedom of style, and (3) the creation of new forms according to the imaginative requirements of the composer. From such a categorical pigeonholing of sonatas, trios, quartets, and symphonies, one would conclude that in the first period Beethoven was merely an imitator of Haydn and Mozart, that in the second he had achieved a style of his own within the classical sonata form, and that in the last period he completely reversed himself by turning into a nineteenth-century musical Lenin, as Robert Haven Schauffler indicates in his title, *Beethoven, the Man who Freed Music.*

[1] *Beethoven et ses Trois Styles* (St. Petersburg, 1852).

145

Challenge to Musical Tradition

The all-important fact that such a division of Beethoven's works sets aside is that while there is in the later works a natural and logical growth in technical mastery, in idiom and style, there is in truth no negation of any artistic principles set forth in the early ones. On the contrary Beethoven's technical and stylistic treatment in the last period is a definite intensification of his earlier methods.

In differentiating among the great number of Beethoven's works one may with justice refer to the early or later compositions, from a purely chronological point of view and without an intention of making any demarcation in the actual artistic devices, which are common to both periods. To understand the music of Beethoven we must see it as a whole, as a growth of individual characteristics of style and treatment, evidencing themselves with hesitation at the beginning of his career and avowing themselves with vigor and clarity as his mastery and conviction increased.

What, then, are these individual characteristics of style and form, which have so profoundly affected the music of Beethoven and have left their imprint on the whole stream of musical consciousness to the present day?

Undoubtedly the most obvious is the new kind of emotional intensity he achieved, which extends not only to his treatment of the material, but to the various elements of the form as well. It is not that Beethoven was the first to find adequate means of emotional expression. Certainly one cannot be unmindful of the heights to which Bach soared or of the numerous instances in which Haydn and Mozart attained moments of sustained emotional stress. Rather, Beethoven created a more passionate, more vehement style, due not so much to the spirit of the age in which he lived as to the type of subject matter he selected, the nature and length of his prolongations, and his unorthodox treatment of rhythmic stress.

The significance of this emotional aspect of Beethoven's style is its influence on the music of the entire century, in the songs of Schubert, the symphonies of Schumann and Berlioz, and the romantic operas of Carl Maria von Weber. In fact this element of Beethoven's art generated the impulse that was to flower in the music of his successors as the spirit of nineteenth-century romanticism. It is not enough, however, to speak in general terms of the new emotional force in Beethoven's style. Even the layman is conscious that there is a sweep to the works of Beethoven that is symbolic of a quality which came into music with him. What techniques have been employed to obtain these new and striking results? Is it the techniques themselves or Beethoven's use of them that is responsible for the effects he has achieved?

BEETHOVEN'S USE OF EMOTIONAL INTENSITY

Although there are indications of this intensity in the early sonatas, such as the *largo appassionato,* of Opus 2, No. 2, and the *largo e mesto* of Opus 10, No. 3, it is in the *"Pathétique,"* Opus 13, that Beethoven reveals himself as the master of this new and powerful technique, especially in the sustained suspense of the *grave* that ushers in the opening movement. Various factors contribute to the mood of these measures, and each of them augments the effect of the others.

One of these is the dotted rhythm. You will realize how essential it is to the character of the melody and the atmosphere of suspense if you replace the complex rhythm with the simpler quarter- and eighth-note values. The use of suspensions and retardations, especially on a strong beat, is a further stimulus to the intensity of the motion.

A more subtle aspect of the treatment is the role that the transfer of register plays in the expansion both of the top voice and of the bass. Here the constant fluctuation in register creates a feeling of unrest and insecurity that enhances the tendencies already suggested by the rhythm.

For example, in the opening measure the outside voices are placed in a low register, two octaves apart. But at the close of the figure the span is narrowed to a fifth, through the ascent of the bass to a higher register. To make this even more effective, Beethoven has prefaced the final chord with a suspension. As this occurs on an accented beat, the suspension brings the whole motion to a climax at the point where the higher register has been attained. Thus two time-worn devices have been combined to create a new kind of intensity and psychological response.

Furthermore, the constant change in register is not confined to the *grave.* It is rather a foretaste of the larger role it is to play in the allegro. Thus we see that a well-known technique has been conceived as part of the basic plan of the whole; not only is it an essential element of the thematic material, but it is a primary factor in the prolongations.

Although these technical agents are important in creating the atmosphere of the *grave,* the most vital aspect of the treatment is the tension created by the expansion of the structural framework. This passage discloses a motion from the opening C minor chord to the E♭ major (measure 5) and G major chord (measure 9) to the C minor chord that ushers

147

Challenge to Musical Tradition

in the allegro, a I–III–V–I harmonic progression. The tonic-mediant progression is clear, but the expansion of the mediant-dominant progression is somewhat complicated and requires explanation.

EXAMPLE 51

The primary factor in the expansion of this space is the horizontalization of the G seventh chord, since it provides the opportunity for introducing various other prolonging techniques. First of all it makes possible the entrance of A♭ in a middle voice as a neighbor of G, to which it finally passes when A♭ is transferred to the bass. The use of this A♭ is most effective, since it temporarily converts the G chord into a diminished seventh chord on B♮ and thus brings an additional suspense into the motion.

Two other aspects of the treatment to which the outlined G seventh chord gives rise are the diatonic and chromatic passing tones that extend the space between the chord tones and the transfer of register that is so important to the melody. Now let us look at the top voice to see if it confirms this reading.

We see that E♭ moves to F, which is enormously prolonged through an ascent strongly outlined by the tones of the G major chord. The motion is further extended by passing tones and shifts of register. These, however, are more apparent in the ascent from F to B♮ than in the concluding motion from B♮ to F. The reason for this is that in the later motion the melodic figure is contracted into two ascending thirds, B♮–C–D and D–E♮–F. This quickening of the melodic impulse accentuates not only the motion to F in the top voice, but the entrance of G in the bass as the climax of the prolonging motions.

The expansion of the neighbor note F contributes greatly to the emotional aspect of the treatment. It enriches the effect of the thematic figure

148

through various repetitions and permits the use of the passing tones within the outlined G seventh chord that both stimulate and intensify the structural motion. Here every element in the prolongations expanding the neighbor note and the mediant-dominant progression serves to build up a growing suspense, until the climax is reached with the simultaneous entrance of G in the bass and F in the high register in the top voice. By applying the older techniques to a more dramatic conception of their functions, Beethoven has opened up a whole new world of stylistic possibilities. Here the melody, rhythm, accent, counterpoint, and tone color not only demonstrate their inherent functions, but have been made to serve an entirely new and different purpose as well, by creating a new and personal means of expression.

However, effectively as these techniques have been used in the introduction, they play a larger and more forceful role in the melodic and structural expansions of the allegro. Here, too, the rhythmic accent, the shift in register, the chromatic nature of the voice leadings, and the character and treatment of the prolongations all tend to convert the basic harmonic structure into a dynamic and impassioned stylistic expression. It is an amazing aspect of the treatment that every element of the technique is an integral part of the structural motion, co-ordinating every section of the movement into a oneness of purpose and design. It would seem as though the function Beethoven conceived for the *grave* were to set in motion the forces of drive and tension that were to be fully unleashed in the swifter emotional tempo of the allegro.

The "Pathétique" is worthy of detailed treatment because it shows Beethoven's early grasp of the possibilities in a new kind of subject matter and a new type of technique. Yet it is only one of a long list of later works in which the emotional element is dominant. This list includes the funeral march of the sonata, Opus 26, as well as the funeral march of the "Eroica" Symphony, the allegro of Opus 57, the allegretto of the Seventh Symphony, the adagio of Opus 81a, *Les Adieux,* and the opening movement of Opus 110. Since a discussion of all these works, even from a superficial point of view, would be impossible, we shall confine ourselves to an examination of two entirely different themes, the one from the slow movement of the "Eroica" Symphony and the other from the first movement of Opus 57, the "Appassionata" Sonata.

Much has been written about the "Eroica" as a whole and the funeral march in particular. In many instances, however, the discussion centers on the effect Beethoven has created rather than on the manner through which the color and mood have been achieved. From Beethoven's sketches it is evident that the opening theme went through a genuine metamorphosis before it acquired the especial characteristics that differentiate it from any other works of a similar nature. Many of the devices applied to the material of the "Pathétique" have been employed with equal success in this movement of the "Eroica." The choice of a low register for the opening measures and the fluctuation between a low and high register in the following phrases, the use of a dotted rhythm, the importance of the neighbor note, the rests, and the introduction of the triplet figure (measure 7) as a new rhythmic impulse are the obvious means that Beethoven has taken to establish and sustain the elegiac mood of this movement. How much they contribute to the poignant quality of the melody can be realized by divesting the opening theme of its rhythmic character and its ornamentations, in a reduction to its simplest form.

EXAMPLE 52

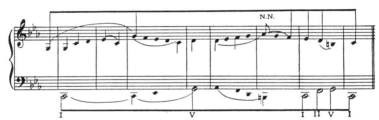

These eight measures show a structural motion built on two harmonic progressions. The melodic outline indicates an ascent from G, a middle voice, to its octave, through the tones of the C minor chord. A similar ascent from D to A♭, with an incomplete neighbor-note motion to F, is achieved through the arpeggiation of the G major chord. In both, the space-outlining motions clearly reveal the simple chord-like nature of the melodic conception and the purely diatonic character of the passing tones. This leads to the conclusion that it is what Beethoven has done with the material rather than the nature of the material itself that has resulted in such a powerful effect.

The instrumentation is an additional factor contributing to the unusual quality of the mood. The theme is given out by the deep, vibrant tones of the strings, with the melody placed in the lowest register of the violin. On its repetition the melody now an octave higher, is taken up by the oboe. Both the transfer of the register and the different timbre of the oboe provide a fresh impetus to the emotional character of the passage. Other contributing agents are the dotted rhythm of the melody and the drum roll in the bass. They heighten the deep solemnity of the mood and provide pulsation of a type that suggests a slow procession.

Since there are many instances that demonstrate Haydn's effective use of rests, we cannot point to Beethoven's treatment of them in this example as a new tendency in the technique. Nevertheless, we should not overlook the fact that as an integral part of the fundamental idea these rests are important factors in creating the special mood Beethoven has designed for this movement.

These are the varied means Beethoven employed to achieve a new stylistic effect. But important as they are in reflecting the new tendencies in his treatment, the most significant aspect of his technique is the absorption of these smaller details into the larger structural ideal.

The opening theme shows a motion within the expanded tonic C minor chord. It is followed by a contrasting theme that starts on a mediant E♭ major chord (measure 17), but carries the motion to the dominant G major chord leading to the tonic, on which the first theme is repeated (measure 30). Thus the first thirty measures outline the structural progression I–III–V–I within the C minor tonality in an expansion of the tonic C minor chord. Although these measures are only a part of the movement, they recur so frequently that they may be regarded as characteristic of both the stylistic and the prolonging techniques.

That Beethoven, through his own experience, was able to glimpse the nature of the dark despair that tragedy brings to all humanity is indicative of his imagination and sympathy as a man. That he was able to express his own compassion in such terms as to make it the personal experience of every listener testifies of his greatness as an artist. How well he succeeded in his task can be realized by comparing the *Marcia funebre* with the funeral march in Wagner's *Götterdämmerung*. It was Wagner's purpose to confine himself to a funeral oration on the death of a hero by narrating events concerned primarily with the life of Siegfried. The dirge, with its succession of motives, deals solely with his birth, his achievements, and the crcumstances leading to his death. We grieve for Siegfried, but we do not identify ourselves with his death. Beethoven, on the other hand, has not given an oration for a superman, despite his original dedication of the work to Napoleon. He has portrayed death as an experience common to the peoples of all nations, all races, and all creeds.

For a third example of Beethoven's use of emotional stress we must inevitably turn to the "Appassionata" Sonata, the most perfect illustration of the new tendencies of his style.

If first of all we consider the material, we find that there are two essential elements to the theme, the arpeggiated-chord figure of the first two measures and the neighbor-note figure of measures 3 and 4. Surely there is nothing new or dynamic in the use of an arpeggiated chord or a neighbor note. There are innumerable examples of both in the works of Beethoven's predecessors. What is it in the treatment of these opening measures that divests the material of its conventional aspects and presents it as a new and thrilling musical experience?

To begin with, the arpeggiated figure, with its descending and ascending motions, presents two forces whose conflicting tendencies themselves provide the first element in the struggle for melodic supremacy. This note of unrest is intensified when, at the climax of its ascent, the arpeggio gives way to a new melodic impulse, the neighbor-note figure, whose quiescent nature is in sharp contrast to the dynamic quality of the arpeggio. However, the triumph of the neighbor-note figure is short-lived, for at the height of its activity a new contender appears in the form of an eighth-note motive (measure 10), injecting fresh rhythmic momentum.

These are the essential factors that provide the melodic material of the opening theme. Their struggle for supremacy and the opposing influence that each exerts create and maintain the dramatic intensity of the mood.

A further element that contributes to the stimulus is the constant shift in register. This is evident in the upward sweep of the arpeggiated figure, the low register in which the eighth-note figure enters, and the tremendous descent of four octaves that expands the dominant C major chord (measures 14–15). The effect of the dotted rhythm and the contrast offered by the eighth-note figure must be recognized as additional factors.

These are the principal means Beethoven has employed to create a new and highly effective stylistic treatment. It is necessary to find out whether they play an equally important role in determining the nature of the structural prolongations.

The example shows how largely the theme is dominated by the neighbor-note figure. We have seen how much its melodic and rhythmic con-

Beethoven

Example 53

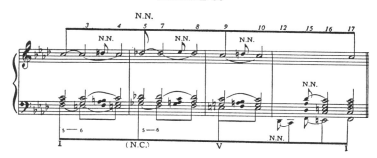

trast to the arpeggio contributes to the interest and suspense of the mood. What, then, is its function in regard to the top voice and the harmonic progression?

Since the inherent characteristic of any neighbor note is to create an embellishing motion, it is obvious that each of these phrases in itself demonstrates an expansion of the embellished tone. However, the example shows that in combination they define a wide extension of a single neighbor-note motion C–D♭–C that the structural top voice outlines. Here it is of interest that although in the basic prolongation Beethoven has used the scale tone D♭, in the smaller motions he has varied the effect by the introduction of D♮. The G♭ major chord, which provides the structural top-voice neighbor note, also demonstrates a somewhat similar function in connection with the harmonic progression.

We see that these seventeen measures rest on a I–V–I progression, a harmonic prolongation of the tonic F minor chord. The motion from the F minor to the G♭ major chord is expanded by the neighbor-note figure within the C major chord. This chord, however, is not a structural dominant such as we find in measure 9, but an embellishing chord that gives rise to the melodic figure. The following G♭ chord is obviously a neighbor chord supplying D♭ as a neighbor of C in the top voice and G♭ as a neighbor of F in the bass. However, it does not return to the tonic chord, but passes through the inverted D♭ major chord in an incomplete neighbor-note motion to the dominant, whose impulse to the tonic is delayed by the entrance of the eighth-note figure and by the neighbor-note embellishments it describes.

Of further interest is the role the neighbor note plays in the contrasting theme, in which it again provides D♭ as an embellishment of C in the

153

structural top voice. How fundamental the conception of the neighbor note is as a basic element in the treatment is indicated in the following example. The constant repetition of D♭ in both the principal and contrasting themes as well as in the smaller and middle-voice motions, shows how essential it is in the prolongation of the structural top voice and its consequent effect on the expansion of the tonic and mediant chords of the basic harmonic progression. Thus there can be no question as to its prolonging function.

EXAMPLE 53A

In addition to the treatment of the neighbor note, the graph offers an unusual instance of the use of mixture in the presence of the A♭ major and minor chords as mediants of the structural progression. Here in contrast to the Haydn quartet, Opus 20, No. 5 (Example 49), in which the major chord of the mixture plays the significant role in the motion, the minor mediant is made prominent through the wide prolongations to which it gives rise in the development section. Furthermore it leads to the structural dominant without a return of the mediant A♭ major chord. The techniques that expand the motion to the dominant chord of the progression are so extraordinary that we shall examine them in detail as indicative of Beethoven's new treatment of the development section and where it differs from that of Haydn.

THE DEVELOPMENT SECTION

The innovations by which Beethoven gave new impetus to the development section, widened its scope, and made it the focal point of the movement is a subject about which much has been written. Many authorities attribute the new character of this section to the subject matter, its organic nature, and its inherent potentialities for development. That the material itself has permitted, if not motivated, the changes in Beethoven's treat-

154

Beethoven

ment of the development section is undeniable. But it is also true that to regard it as the sole factor is to overlook the equally important changes that have taken place in the prolongation of the structural framework.

In concentrating on the melodic aspect of the treatment, Parry has expressed a point of view shared by many other musicians. He says: "Prior to Beethoven, the development of a long work was based upon antitheses of distinct tunes and concrete lumps of subject matter representing separate organisms, either merely in juxtaposition or loosely connected by more or less empty passages." [2]

There can be no argument as to the fitness of Beethoven's subject matter for the new conception of its function in the development. On the other hand, to regard the material in the numerous examples cited from the various works of Haydn as "concrete lumps . . . representing separate organisms" is both erroneous and misleading. It is necessary to point only to Haydn's use of the motivic figure in the development section of the F major sonata (Example 42) and the C minor quartet (Example 48) to prove the misconception under which Parry labors.

The character of Beethoven's material is more flexible than Haydn's. Certain potentialities for adaptation that are inherent in it lend themselves to the broader conception of their function in the development section revealed in his works. For example, Beethoven selects a fragmentary phrase as the germ plasm from which every melodic impulse springs. In short he grasped the full implications of the role the development section plays from both a melodic and a structural point of view.

The acknowledgment of this fact, however, need not blind us to the achievements of his predecessors nor to the conception of organic unity their works demonstrate. To believe that the development sections of Haydn's works were based on separate organisms indicates that they lacked coherence, which the integration of the melodic, contrapuntal, and harmonic factors into a single structural unit contradicts. If, however, Parry means that neither Haydn's material nor his treatment of it in the development section reveals as mature a conception of the possibilities for its organic growth as the works of Beethoven, no one will disagree. The distinction is important, because the statement he makes robs Haydn of the most significant aspect of his contribution — the demonstration of the form as an expression of tonal coherence.

[2] Grove, *Dictionary of Music and Musicians* (Theodore Presser, 1927), Vol. IV, p. 524.

Challenge to Musical Tradition

The development section of the *allegro assai* of Opus 57 illustrates these new tendencies in Beethoven's techniques in regard to the treatment of both the melodic figure and the structural motion.

EXAMPLE 53B

It is apparent that the development section emerges out of a tremendous expansion of the motion from the minor mediant to the dominant chord. Thus, basically, the structural outline is identical with that used by Philipp Emanuel Bach and Haydn. The difference lies primarily in the unique nature of Beethoven's prolongations.

In the contrasting section we have already seen the unusual shift from the major to the minor mediant and the melodic and structural expansion it engenders. A more striking example of the breadth of Beethoven's conception is the exchange of the minor mediant for its enharmonic equivalent, the G♯ minor chord, in the opening phrase of the development section. This was a bold innovation, and it emphasizes anew how strongly Beethoven's instinct for the dramatic motivated his treatment.

However, the effect of this G♯ chord is short-lived, since the D♯ immediately gives way to E, of which it is a neighbor note, while B♮ and G♯ are retained. On this E major chord the entire thematic figure is repeated. The introduction of the E major chord in so conspicuous a place at the start of the section, as well as its wide expansion, through which various repetitions of the neighbor-note figure occur, might be interpreted by some theorists as a modulation to the key of E major. The example shows on the contrary that the function of this chord is neither harmonic nor structural, since it is a passing chord in the motion between the opening A♭ minor and the A♭ seventh chord (measure 87).

Although both of these A♭ chords have the same root and in the con-

156

trasting section represent a mixture of the mediant chord, in the above example their functions are so differentiated that they stand for two different chords. The function of the A♭ minor chord is structural, since it leads to the dominant C major chord. The function of the A♭ major chord is prolonging, since it serves as an applied dominant of the D♭ major chord that follows. The motion as a whole, without the intervening prolongations, is from the A♭ minor through the A♭ major to the D♭ major, the neighbor chord of the dominant. Thus the E major and C minor chords that outline the descent from A♭ to its octave are passing chords in the motion.

It is undoubtedly true that the use of the E major instead of the E♭ major chord was inspired by the contrast which the exchange of A♭ for G♯ offered in providing a new chord environment for the introduction of the theme. The whole atmosphere of these opening measures of the development is enriched by the fresh interest, the suspense and stimulus, provided by the chromatic nature of the prolongation. Nevertheless, significant as is this E major chord for its prismatic effect, its function has been clearly defined as non-structural.

The prominence Beethoven has given to this prolonging chord at the opening of the section is the distinctive feature of the treatment. It offers a concrete illustration of his development of the possibilities inherent in the form through the use of prolongation. He expands the mediant chord for seventy-five measures, but avoids the monotony that such an enlargement might produce by his use of mixture and more especially by the nature of the motion to which the enharmonic exchange gives rise. The descent by thirds from the A♭ minor to the A♭ major chord is the most spectacular aspect of the technique. It provides a wholly new environment to stimulate the fresh impulse of the melodic figure; it unfolds the richness of the color contrasts engendered by the chromatic passing chords; and finally, in spite of its prolonging function, it is the creative element that impregnates the entire section with the distinctive characteristics differentiating it from the treatment in other sonatas.

The introduction and prolongation of the D♭ major chord, to which the A♭ seventh chord leads as an applied dominant, is also of interest, because it stresses the powerful influence the neighbor note exerts on the technique through the entire movement. Here the D♭ major chord serves as a prolonged neighbor chord of the dominant, in which D♭ again appears as an embellishment of C. In the expansion of the C major chord we

Challenge to Musical Tradition

find further references to D♭ as a neighbor note, which point once more to the primary role it plays in the prolonging motion.

In the final measures of the development section the dominant chord of the basic motion is retained, although the top voice has already achieved the repetition of the theme that is indicative of the recapitulation. This technique is reminiscent of the treatment of Philipp Emanuel Bach in the C minor sonata (Example 30), in which a similar overlapping of the sections occurs.

A comparison of the treatment in these sonatas not only emphasizes the imaginativeness and flexibility of Bach's conception, but shows how strongly his definition of the form influenced the techniques of his successors. Although the Beethoven Opus 57 reveals various new tendencies in the techniques, through which the original form was given a broader and more clearly outlined character, it nevertheless is based on the same structural idea as that underlying the C minor sonata of Bach. It demonstrates that in spite of the sharper definition of the structural outlines the sectional elements retain their original character as mutually dependent and well-integrated parts of an organic whole.

It is apparent, nevertheless, that although there is a similarity in the basic conception of the first movements of Bach's C minor sonata and Beethoven's Opus 57, the treatment in the latter reflects those changes, both in form and in technique, that differentiate the more mature from the early stage of the sonata. The growth in general is illustrated by certain definite trends that Opus 57 reveals. The first of these is the essentially new character of the material and the thematic possibilities to which it gives rise. In this instance, which is not unique, it presents an emotional conflict as well, heightening the dramatic aspect of the treatment. The most striking contrast, however, is evidenced in the prolongation both of the top voice and of the basic motion. Here every technical innovation provides an additional stimulus to the fundamental impulse out of which the entire movement is evolved. Thus it has a psychological as well as a structural implication. The increased tension springing from the wider expansion of the harmonic framework, in this instance the mediant-dominant progression, is balanced by a growing intensity in the stylistic tendencies. Thus the greater momentum is due not only to the more obvious aspects of the thematic treatment, but also to prolonging techniques whose boldness has added richness, color contrast, and vitality to the basic elements of the form.

158

There is a final aspect of the treatment that should not be overlooked — the role the neighbor note plays both as a melodic, and as a structural element in welding together the andante and the *allegro non troppo*.

We have seen how strongly the use of D♮ influenced the treatment in the opening movement, in which it figures both as a melodic and as a structural embellishment. Now let us turn to the andante to see the different connection in which it is employed.

The andante has been conceived as a theme with variations, with a key signature of D♭ major. The theme consists of two eight-measure phrases, each of which defines a harmonic prolongation of the D♭ major chord. Since the variations are patterned on the same structural outline as the theme, it is obvious that the entire movement describes a prolonged motion within the D♭ major chord. Customarily this D♭ major chord would represent the tonic chord of the tonality in which the motion of the slow movement is defined. Here, however, the final variation, unlike the preceding ones, does not outline a harmonic prolongation of the D♭ chord, but discloses a passing motion from the D♭ chord to the dominant C major chord in the opening measures of the *allegro non troppo*. This linking together of the two movements by means of a motion connecting the D♭ and C major chords suggests that in this instance the D♭ major chord functions not as a tonic, but as a structural neighbor chord whose enormous expansion provides the structural and prolonging motions that comprise the melodic and harmonic outlines of the slow movement.

Although the use of the neighbor chord to connect the andante and the *allegro non troppo* is unique in regard to Beethoven's treatment of the form, it is typical of the clarity and coherence that his structural and prolonging techniques demonstrate. This is revealed in the clear-cut outlines that define the three movements of this sonata. The *allegro assai* shows a primordial I—III—V—I progression that creates and maintains the F minor tonality. The andante discloses a motion within the D♭ major chord leading through a neighbor motion to the dominant C major chord on which the structural life of the *allegro non troppo* begins. This C major chord stimulates the impulse to the tonic F minor chord whose prolongation melodically, contrapuntally, and harmonically unfolds the three sections of sonata form in which the final movement is cast.

In the following example only the motion of the final variation is indicated, since it is the only one that does not define a completed motion with the D♭ major chord. Therefore, this deviation in the concluding measures of the final variation is the important element for our consideration, since it alone demonstrates the structural means by which the merging of the two movements has been effected.

EXAMPLE 53C

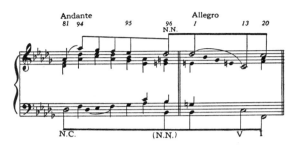

The graph shows a motion from the D♭ major chord in which A♭ appears in the top voice and D♭ in the bass, to the inverted seventh chord on E♮, with D♭ transferred to the top voice and B♭ in the bass. This is achieved through a top-voice descent from A♭ to D♭ due to the shift of A♭ to a higher register and a bass ascent from D♭ to B♭. However, at the close of this ascent B♭ is duplicated in the same low register in which the opening D♭ and the C of the C major chord that follows, appear. The passing motion is clearly defined. The only problem the passage raises is the status of the inverted seventh chord on E♮ and the function of B♭ in the bass.

Since this seventh chord occurs within the motion from the D♭ to the C major chord, its function as a passing chord that delays the entrance of the C major chord is prolonging. Its importance lies in the fact that it contains the neighbor note D♭ which now appears in the top voice, and that it foreshadows the entrance of the C major chord. Yet how does this explain the presence of B♭ in the bass?

The fact that the neighbor note D♭ appears in the top voice as a melodic embellishment of C, precludes the possibility of its presence in the bass as well, since such a motion would have resulted in parallel octaves. Therefore, we may assume that B♭ is a substitute for D♭. Furthermore, since it occurs in the same register as D♭ and C in the bass, it suggests an expanded neighbor-note motion in which D♭, an upper neighbor, passes through B♭, an under neighbor, to C, after which B♭ reappears as the seventh of the C major chord. It is also evident that the prolongation of the neighbor notes in the first twelve measures of the allegro creates a

160

tension that intensifies the entrance of the C major chord and gives it heightened significance as the climax of the motion. At the same time, the treatment emphasizes the importance of the neighbor note, both as a structural and prolonging technique.

A study of this sonata shows that Beethoven introduced many innovations in the techniques, some of which affect the structural outlines of the form. It is also apparent that the new tendencies in his style brought to the treatment a dynamic quality that is not present in the works of his predecessors. It is equally clear that he expanded the harmonic framework and at times even altered the contour of the structural motion through the type of prolongations he effected. These new elements in the treatment were his specific contribution to the development of the form. Of primary importance, however, is the fact that in spite of the various changes he made, the conception of the form as a structural organism was kept intact. Thus, although we find many deviations in the techniques that expanded the structural outline, in those that define the structural outline as an expression of tonal coherence it is obvious that Beethoven adhered to the same principles and demonstrated the same interrelationship of the harmonic and contrapuntal functions as the works of Philipp Emanuel Bach and Haydn reveal.

Although this is only one illustration of the impact of Beethoven's treatment on the form, especially in regard to the new tendencies in the development section, it is sufficiently typical of his inventiveness to indicate the nature of the changes he effected and the unusual techniques he employed. Another example, equally original, although along different lines, will be included in the discussion of the introduction and its enlarged function in the structural life of the entire movement. In this instance the reference to the introduction in the development section offers a unique opportunity to explore an entirely new type of structural prolongation.

There can be little doubt that Beethoven's treatment of the development section brought a tremendous stimulus to the growth of the form. It was a vital factor in shaping the trend the sonatas, quartets, and symphonies of his successors were to take. There are, however, two elements of the form in which the full power of Beethoven's imagination effected changes equal to those in the development section and in which it exerted a similar influence on the later treatment of the form. These sections are the introduction and the coda. Beethoven's expansion of these sections,

161

the new melodic interest that he imparted to them, and the greater significance he attached to their functions are generally acknowledged. However, there has been insufficient discussion of the specific nature of the changes, the techniques he used to achieve them, and the effect the increased importance and the larger dimensions of the introduction and coda have on their structural functions.

Let us begin with the introduction. What is its function, from both an artistic and a structural point of view?

THE INTRODUCTION

Sir George Grove says: "The main purpose of an Introduction in music is either to summon the attention of the audience, or to lead their minds into the earnest and sober mood which is fittest for the appreciation of great things." [3]

This is a definition of the artistic function of the introduction. It explains the simple openings we find in some of Haydn's quartets, in which, with a single chord or group of chords, he seeks to arouse the interest of his listeners. It also accounts for the opening chords in Beethoven's "Eroica" Symphony and describes that type of slow introduction with which Haydn begins the "Surprise" Symphony in G major, offering such a contrast to the theme that follows.

However, Grove does not state that in addition to the effect it creates and the contrast it provides, the introduction in the classical sonatas, quartets, and symphonies is a closely integrated part of the structural motion. For example, the introduction to the "Surprise" Symphony not only establishes a mood that by its dissimilarity heightens the interest of the principal theme, but it is bound up with the theme in prolonging the opening tone of the structural top-voice motion. In other words Haydn regarded the introduction no longer as an appendage, but as an integral part of the structural motion. In spite of the simple character of the introduction and the rather obvious nature of the prolongations, this was a definite contribution to the structural solidarity of the form.

Mozart, on the other hand, seldom prefaced his works with an introduction. The two outstanding examples are the introductions to the C major quartet and the symphony in E♭ major. The striking dissonances on which the quartet opens cannot fail to arrest the attention of the listener. Yet in spite of the bold techniques the passage reveals and their dynamic effect,

[3] *Ibid.*, Vol. II, p. 488.

Beethoven

the introduction has a deeper and more vital musical significance in its structural connection with the movement.

It was Beethoven, however, who in his sonatas, trios, quartets, and symphonies was to bring an entirely new meaning to the introduction. He not only intensified the impulse Haydn had given to it, but realized that it possessed further potentialities for melodic and structural development, which he was the first to explore. We need only compare its treatment in the late works of Haydn and the E♭ major symphony of Mozart with the dramatic opening of Beethoven's "Pathétique" Sonata, the First Symphony, and the quartet, Opus 59, No. 3, to recognize not only the difference in technique, but the more fundamental distinction in the conception of the role the introduction played.

Whether the greater stimulus Beethoven injected into this section actually changed its function as well as its character is debatable. Structurally it was an offshoot of the basic harmonic progression. Yet its impact on the movement in the climactic entrance it provided for the opening theme of the allegro cannot be overlooked. In fact there are some instances, such as the First Symphony and the quartet, Opus 59, No. 3, in which the techniques Beethoven used in the introduction tend to conceal the tonality. As a result, this element of suspense intensifies the entrance of the principal theme of the allegro. Here the power that the introduction exerts on the allegro is so much greater than in the works of Haydn that it is difficult to believe its function is the same. Not only does the tension created by the chromatic prolongations gain such momentum that it gives the principal theme an explosive quality, but it drives the expanded dominant with an equal violence to the first fully emphasized declaration of the tonic chord. Through this type of prolongation Beethoven imparted a new quality to the introduction, which made it a more essential if not a more integral element of the form.

Although we have already discussed the various technical means through which the *grave* of Opus 13 attained such emotional impetus, let us now consider it from a different angle — the effect its repetition in the development section of the allegro has on its original status. In other words does the use of the material of the introduction in various parts of the allegro change its structural as well as its artistic function?

If we examine the harmonic framework that underlies the exposition and development section, we find that it bears a strong likeness to the harmonic progression out of which the *grave* emerged. Both define a mo-

163

Challenge to Musical Tradition

tion outlined by the chords of C minor, E♭ major and G major, a clear-cut horizontalization of the C minor chord. The motion within the allegro is tremendously expanded, with an unusual prolongation of the space between the tonic and mediant chord. This is due to the introduction of the B♭ major chord as an applied dominant of the mediant, whose wide expansion is slightly reminiscent of Philipp Emanuel Bach's treatment in the Prussian Sonata in E Major.[4] Although the techniques prolonging the applied dominant and the melodic aspects of the treatment are totally different, the basic conception of the structural expansion is the same.

This passage within the B♭ major chord not only accelerates the melodic interest through its introduction of a new thematic figure, but stimulates the structural tension by delaying the entrance of the mediant E♭ major chord. On the whole it demonstrates an entirely new treatment of the transition and gives it a melodic importance customarily reserved for the contrasting theme. The long-postponed entrance of the E♭ major chord ushers in the contrasting theme. A bass descent from E♭ to F♯ brings the exposition to a close on an inverted seventh chord on D.

It is at this point that Beethoven introduces the opening measures of the *grave* within the chord of G minor. The use of the G minor rather than the G major chord that the D major chord also suggests not only

EXAMPLE 54

4 See page 80.

Beethoven

preserves the original character of the *grave* figure, but withholds the entrance of the major chord until the motion has reached the structural dominant of the basic harmonic progression. The function of these four measures of the *grave* presents an interesting problem. As a repetition of the opening figure, they are of melodic significance. It is necessary, however, to determine also the specific nature of the prolongation in which they occur as well as the techniques by which the expansion of the mediant and dominant chords has been achieved.

Graph B shows the main outline of the motion from the final E♭ major chord of the exposition (measure 121) to the G major chord, the climax, which leads ultimately to the tonic C minor chord of the recapitulation. Within this motion the F minor chord serves as a neighbor-passing chord, since it provides F as a neighbor note in the top voice and F as a passing tone between E♭ and G in the bass. The space is further expanded by the introduction of the E minor and the diminished seventh chord on F♯ as chromatic passing chords.

In the prolonged motion from the E♭ major to the E minor chord, the B major chord is a vital factor. As an applied dominant it not only brings harmonic emphasis to the chromatic passing chord, but through its melodic intensification it gives additional stimulus to the entrance of the principal theme. However, instead of proceeding directly from the E♭ major to the B major chord, Beethoven moved through the G minor chord, by which the augmented fifth from E♭ to B is converted into two major thirds. This G minor chord ushers in the four measures of the *grave*.

The function of this passage now becomes clear. First of all it provides a great contrast for the repetition of the theme within the E minor chord. Furthermore it recalls the introduction and exposition so vividly that through psychological association it tends to strengthen the organic connection of these sections with the development. Technically its purpose is to prolong the motion to the B major chord through an ascent in major thirds. However, we should not overlook the imagination that conceived the role these measures were to play or the dramatic quality their repetition produces.

It is evident that the status of the G minor chord is contrapuntal, as a passing chord within the motion to the B major chord. Therefore the powerful impression to which this technique gives rise is a remarkable illustration of both the vision and the ingenuity of Beethoven's treatment.

There still remains the problem of the E minor chord, whose empha-

165

Challenge to Musical Tradition

sis through the introduction of the main thematic figure is so marked that it is customarily regarded as the start of the development section. In the accepted method of analysis the entrance of the theme on the E minor chord, preceded by the chord of B major, would be regarded as a modulation to the key of E minor. Were this a modulation from E♭ major to E minor it would seem a bit strange, even though the unexpected is characteristic of Beethoven's treatment. But as we have seen, this E minor chord is actually a chromatic passing chord between the E♭ major and F minor chords, and as such it possesses neither a harmonic nor a structural function. In fact it is of no greater harmonic importance than F♯, the chromatic passing chord between the F minor and G major chords that follow. The difference between these passing chords lies in the melodic emphasis Beethoven has placed on the E minor chord and the use he has made of it to provide the illusion of a modulation when the entire passage consists of a prolongation of a passing tone within the basic motion of the tonality.

The use of the E minor chord instead of the more conventional C major, which the motion to the F minor chord and the presence of E♮ as a passing tone lead us to expect, is illustrative of the scope of Beethoven's imagination and the boldness of his technique. However, it is apparent in the graph that the E minor chord is only an artistic means of delaying the entrance of the C major. Nevertheless, the substitution so heightens the tension of these measures that it creates the illusion that the motion begins on an E minor chord. In fact some authorities are sufficiently impressed to regard it as a modulation to the key of E minor. How erroneous this assumption is becomes evident in the shift to the C major chord (measure 147), which reveals that E, its horizontalized third, has served as the root of the E minor chord.

The top voice shows a motion from E♮ to F of the F minor chord. This ascent has been widely prolonged by an ascent from E♮ to B♭ that engenders the descent from B♭ to its octave, further expanding the C major chord. Here the unfolding of the interval E♮–B♭ of the seventh chord on C is answered by the unfolding of A♭–F within the F minor chord, in which F appears in a lower register. Thus F, the neighbor of E♭ of the mediant chord, the goal of all that has been going on through these forty-one measures, is finally achieved.

The amazing originality and ingenuity of the treatment leave little doubt as to the concrete means Beethoven used to transform a single mediant-dominant progression into a motion of such richness, vitality, and tension. The inclusion of the *grave*, though not as a structural force, demonstrates an entirely new conception of its possibilities that is further evidenced in a second reference to the *grave* in the measures immediately preceding the coda. Other innovations in the technique are the weaving together of the *grave* motive and the opening theme, the substitution of the E minor for the C major chord and the importance that its expansion gives to a chromatic passing chord, and the shift from the E minor to the C major chord, which as an applied dominant lends weight to the long-postponed entrance of the F minor neighbor-passing chord.

Although 'these innovations concern the broader techniques that expand the harmonic framework, the smaller motions prolonging the structural top voice are of an equally daring nature. In fact the treatment throughout, especially in regard to the introduction and development, plainly reveals the effect of Beethoven's enlarged conception of the form on the techniques, as well as the impact of his stylistic characteristics on the structural outline.

This is not the only instance in which Beethoven has set aside traditions in his treatment of the introduction. Although entirely different in every respect from the *grave,* the opening measures of the First Symphony provide a further illustration of the dynamic imprint of Beethoven's genius on the introduction during the so-called "first period," the period of "imitation." It is difficult for us today to appreciate how startling the opening chords in this symphony must have sounded to a nineteenth-century audience. To realize fully the boldness of the conception and the equally dynamic effect of the technique, we should compare this introduction with the opening sections of Haydn's last symphonies. Only then can we recognize how revolutionary Beethoven's treatment was.

We see that instead of beginning in the usual fashion with a tonic or dominant triad Beethoven opened the work on a dissonance, a seventh chord on C, followed by the chord of F major. In addition he stressed the dissonance, while the consonant F major chord is marked pianissimo. The G major and A minor chords in the succeeding measure are given similar dynamics, with the dissonance again accentuated. At this point a D seventh chord leads directly to the dominant, the goal of the first four measures.

The problem to which the passage gives rise is the status of the opening C seventh chord and its function in the prolonged motion.

EXAMPLE 55

Had the work begun on a C major triad, with B♭ entering on the second quarter as a passing tone between C of the C major chord and A of the F major, there would have been no question as to the nature of the harmonic progression or as to the status of the C major chord as a tonic (graph A). Instead, to effect a more dramatic opening, Beethoven combined the passing tone B♭ with the triad as a single chord (graph B). Although this contraction was a startling innovation, it does not alter the character of the chord or rob it of its function as the beginning of the motion.

The top voice strengthens this statement. It clearly demonstrates an ascent from E of the C seventh chord to G of the dominant and thus defines the interval of a third within the harmonic progression. A further indication of Beethoven's intentions lies in the stress he applied to E in the top voice and C in the bass as the initial impulse that stimulates the motion to the G major chord. Accordingly these first four measures outline a I–IV–V progression which, with the concluding motion to the tonic, constitutes a harmonic prolongation of the C major chord.

Beethoven

There may be some readers who hear the C seventh chord only in relation to the F major chord that follows as an applied dominant. This is a possibility that cannot be entirely disregarded. According to this explanation the motion starts on the subdominant F major chord and represents an incomplete harmonic progression (graph C). The fact that both the F and G major chords are approached through their respective applied dominants, the C and D seventh chords, is a point in favor of this interpretation. However, the acceptance of F as the first harmonic factor in the progression also implies that it is the start of the top-voice ascent. This interpretation completely overlooks the stronger dynamics Beethoven used in connection with the C seventh chord to indicate E in the top voice and C in the bass as the obvious start of the motion. Yet the reader may contend that since the C and D chords serve the same function as applied dominants, E in the top voice is a melodic intensification of F, as F♯ is of G. Although theoretically this might appear to be true, our aural impressions differentiate between the roles these two tones enact. We hear E as the start of a motion that ascends to G; thus it defines a space-outlining function. We hear F♯ as a chromatic passing tone within this motion; its function is that of a space-filler. Consequently, although E and F♯ are used to intensify the F and G that follow, their functions are totally different. In addition, to hear the C seventh chord only in its connection with the chord of F major contradicts the dynamics Beethoven used and the aural impressions they create.

On the whole the explanation of this passage in terms of an incomplete harmonic progression is not altogether convincing. In fact it tends to strengthen the first interpretation of the C seventh chord as a contraction of the triad and the passing tone B♭, hence the tonic of a complete I–IV–V–I progression. The reader himself must decide which of these two readings is closer to his own hearing of the passage.

The graph gives an outline of the entire motion within the first eight measures of the introduction through which the basic progression has been expanded. Here the main problem concerns the techniques prolonging the space between the F and G major chords.

The function of the D seventh in relation to the G major chord is obvious. In addition to its harmonic emphasis, it brings melodic intensity to G, the climax both of the top voice and of the structural motion. Less clear is the status of the G major and A minor chords that appear between the F and D major chords.

169

EXAMPLE 56

We see that the melodic outline comprises three parallel figures, E–F, B–C, F♯–G. Although the first two of these indicate the same dynamics, the impulse from E–F toward F♯–G is so strong that we hear the middle figure primarily as a break in the motion. The fact that the B–C is pitched lower than the other figures contributes to this effect. Actually B–C is a middle voice that comes from A of the F major chord and assumes the temporary role of a top voice only through the transfer of F, a top voice, to a lower register. In the motion supporting these figures, the problem centers on the A minor chord, since the status of G major as a passing chord between the F major and A minor chord is obvious.

What, then, is the function of this A minor chord? First of all it points the way to the D and G major chords that follow, through a succession of fifths. Here the A minor and the D and G major chords constitute an incomplete II–V–I harmonic progression that prolongs the G major chord. Furthermore, by stimulating the impulse from the F to the D major chord, the chord of A minor heightens the connection between F and F♯ in the top voice. Thus its function is twofold. As a member of a harmonic prolongation it gives momentum to the extended motion from the F to the G major chord. Through this it so accelerates the impetus in the top voice that it brings the two main figures, E–F and F♯–G, into a single motion of an ascending third. The use of this A minor chord instead of the other possibilities to which the melodic figure gives rise shows how clearly the nature of the motive and the character of the harmonic progression determined the technique.

Graph 1 of this example indicates the customary treatment of this melodic line. It reveals a clearly defined motion within the C major chord through a I–IV–V–I harmonic prolongation. This arrangement, however, tends to bind the first two figures into a unit that separates itself from the

Beethoven

EXAMPLE 56A

final figure and thus weakens the connection betweeen E–F and F♯–G. In addition it gives such a strong declaration of the tonality that the effect of the opening chord is entirely lost. In short it achieves a motion that is contrary to the impression Beethoven wished to create.

In graph 2, we find a different arrangement, a substitution of the inverted F major for the A minor chord. The results of such a prolongation are obvious. It intensifies the power of the F major chord to an extent that minimizes the function of the C major chord as a tonic. In fact it might even lead to the assumption already held by some theorists that the work opens in the key of F major. Furthermore it creates a cross-relation between F, a middle voice of the F major chord, and F♯, a top voice of the D seventh chord.

These two graphs indicate the significance of Beethoven's treatment in clarifying the specific meaning of the passage. It accentuates the top-voice motion through its connection of the F and D major chords; it also brings the F and G major chords into closer association through the harmonic impulse it gives to the drive to the G major chord. Finally, by comparing graph 2 with graph B (Example 55), we see that Beethoven's use of the A minor chord emphasizes the contention that the seventh chord on C represents a contracted triad and passing tone and the start of the motion. It is obvious that, had Beethoven intended the C seventh chord to serve as an applied dominant of F in an incomplete harmonic progression, the use of the inverted F major instead of the A minor chord would have given a clearer demonstration of his intentions.

As a whole the techniques both defining and expanding the harmonic progression are unique. Not only does the contraction of the C major triad and the passing tone provide a daring opening, but the chords that support the melodic figure B–C and also expand the F and G major chords reveal a remarkable technical ingenuity. They indicate the subtlety with which

Challenge to Musical Tradition

Beethoven has emphasized the structural tendencies of the motion while using every artistic means to veil the tonality. This is the extraordinary aspect of the treatment — that the various innovations through which Beethoven created an entirely new kind of emotional suspense have demanded no sacrifice of the basic techniques that assure tonal stability.

Beethoven's bold challenge to the more conservative treatment of the introduction by his predecessors plainly indicates that this "first period" was not a period of imitation. In fact this passage has been the subject of much controversy in the past and still remains a problem for students of analysis and even their teachers. How revolutionary, then, must Beethoven's treatment have seemed in the early nineteenth century!

To show the rich and fruitful development of this technique in a later work, let us turn to the introduction of the quartet in C major, Opus 59, No. 3. Here, as in the First Symphony, Beethoven has departed from the customary tradition of beginning with a tonic or dominant chord. Instead he starts the introduction with a diminished seventh chord on F♯, an unusual opening for a work in the key of C major. But once again, as in the First Symphony, we must differentiate between what Beethoven has written in order to achieve certain artistic effects and what lies behind the artistry in the nature of his voice leadings.

In any discussion of the Beethoven quartets one naturally turns to De Marliave's authoritative study of these works [5] for an interpretation of their structure and meaning. However, as De Marliave frankly admits that he is adhering to Marx's purely technical analysis and as Marx's discussion is fuller and richer in its implications, it seems advisable to go to the original source for the accepted explanation of this introduction.

Marx says: [6] "From the abrupt entrance, far removed from the established tonality, the harmonies wander as in the dark, halting and unsteady in their motion. The voice parts lose themselves in a wide spacing of four octaves until at last they are brought within a narrower register as they reach the chords of B—A♭—D—F and B—G—D—F. Again united, they timidly and gently approach the allegro vivace."

Gerald Abraham [7] gives a similar interpretation of these chords in his description of the introduction: "Mysterious chords, practically all pianissimo, melting into each other almost imperceptibly. Neither theme nor

[5] *Beethoven's Quartets* (Oxford University Press, 1928).
[6] *Beethoven, Leben und Schaffen* (Otto Janke, Berlin, 1875), *Zweiter Teil*, p. 47.
[7] *Beethoven's Second-Period Quartets*, The Musical Pilgrim (Oxford University Press, 1942).

172

key emerges, but the last chord of all is an inverted dominant seventh in C."

These statements bring up a question that must be answered if the introduction is to be explained satisfactorily. Do the harmonies "wander in the dark," or in De Marliave's terms "at will," or have they been directed toward a definite goal, which has been subtly concealed in order to make the entire introduction a long period of emotional suspense?

EXAMPLE 57

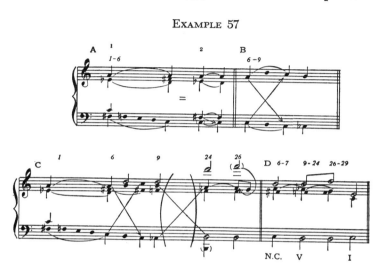

The first six measures (graph A) show a motion in which the diminished seventh chord on F♯ is exchanged for the D seventh chord, with F♯ in the bass descending to C. Graph B indicates a motion within the D major chord through which A in the top voice ascends to C while C in the bass descends to A, an exchange of voices in the outside parts. The passing of A to A♭ in the bass with similar half-step descents in the two middle voices leads to a diminished seventh chord on B, with D retained in the top voice (graph C). In the measures that follow, the top voice ascends an octave while the bass descends to B, the root of the diminished seventh chord; B appears in a higher register than the low C, but this is due to the limitations of the cello, of which C is the lowest tone. The final position of this diminished chord shows F transferred from the top voice to a middle voice (measure 26), after which the resolution of A♭ to G ushers in the dominant seventh chord on G. Thus in measures 9–24 there

173

is a prolonged motion, through the transfer of register and exchange of voices, within the diminished seventh chord on B.

Accordingly the first twenty-nine measures comprise a motion from the D seventh chord to the dominant chord of G major (graph D). However, instead of the customary effect of an applied dominant, the inversion of the D major chord gives it the function of a neighbor chord. This motion is expanded primarily through an intensification of the neighbor-note technique. The opening diminished seventh chord on F♯ (graph A) shows E♭, a middle voice, to be a neighbor of D of the D major chord. In a similar manner the diminished seventh on B reveals A♭ as a neighbor of G of the G major chord to which it eventually resolves. There is an interesting parallelism in the treatment by which the D and G major chords are prolonged. As the passing of E♭ to D converts the diminished seventh chord into the chord of D major, so through the passing of A♭ to G the diminished seventh chord on B is exchanged for the G major chord. Thus each is preceded by its own neighbor chord through which the prolongations are effected.

Thus far we have defined the motion by which the dominant chord of the V–I progression has been extended for twenty-eight measures. However, we have not examined the motion through which the diminished chord ascends an octave in the top voice and descends from A♭ to B in the bass (measures 9–24). This prolongation is the most complex aspect of the treatment and offers many difficulties. They can be explained only through the voice leadings and the suspensions that characterize the techniques throughout.

Example 57A

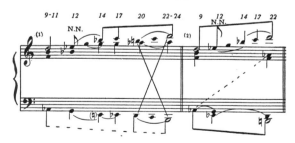

Graph 1 of this example shows the first entrance of the diminished seventh chord on B, with A♭, the seventh, in the bass. The problem here concerns the descent from A♭ to B in the bass, with the necessary transfer of A♭ to an upper voice. Beethoven solves it by again resorting to the neighbor-note technique.

Starting on A♭, the bass shows a descent to B, which outlines A♭–D–B of the diminished chord. In addition it indicates a motion from G to E♭, whose suggestion of the E♭ major chord is confirmed by the presence of E♭–G–B♭ in the top voice. We see that when A♭ passes to G in the bass, D in the top voice moves to E♭, with B♭ in the middle voice, a clear definition of the E♭ major chord. Although the top-voice motion from E♭ through G to B♭ unfolds the tones of the E♭ chord, the bass motion does not demonstrate a similar outline. Here E♮ occurs in combination with B♭, and the entrance of E♭ is delayed until B♭ has passed to C in the top voice. The fact that G and E♮ instead of G and E♭ appear in connection with E♭–G–B♭ of the top voice creates a difficulty that can be explained only by the constant rhythmic retardation of the bass in the preceding measures. In these we see that through the use of suspension the entrances of both G and E♮ in the bass have been delayed. This suggests that the retention of E♮ under B♭ is due to the same technique of suspension through which the seemingly nebulous quality of the tonality has been achieved.

However, since the entrance of E♮ has been retarded, it is logical to assume that under ordinary circumstances E♭ would have appeared in connection with B♭ as well as C of the top voice. According to this reading, G–E♭ represents an arpeggiation in the bass corresponding with the outlined E♭ chord in the top voice. From this point of view the function of the E♭ chord is twofold: to provide E♭ in the top voice, as a neighbor of the D on which the ascent starts and concludes, and to transfer A♭ from the bass to a middle voice.

In the measures that follow we see that the motion from C to D in the top voice (measures 17–22) is expanded through an ascent from B♮ to D, against a bass motion from D to B♮. Through this exchange of voices both the top-voice ascent from the low D to its octave and the bass descent from A♭ to B are achieved.

Because of the suspensions in the voice leadings, it is impossible to substantiate this interpretation of the motion within the prolonged diminished chord. Yet it seems justifiable to attribute the conflict in the voice leadings to the suspensions, since they play so large a role in the treatment of the introduction. However, although there may be a difference of opinion as to how the motion within the diminished chord is expanded, there can be no denial of the fact that in these fourteen measures (9–22)

Challenge to Musical Tradition

the outside voices demonstrate a motion that outlines the prolonged diminished chord. Since this is the case, it becomes evident that the harmonies do not "wander in the dark," as Marx and De Marliave state, but that the key does emerge in spite of Abraham's claim to the contrary. We see that although, to create the mystery and tension of these measures, Beethoven intentionally used techniques that mask the strong basic impulse from the D to the G major chord, the motion itself emphasizes the delayed entrance of the G major chord and thus intensifies its function as a dominant.

To recognize that these twenty-nine measures disclose a widely prolonged motion within the dominant chord of the tonality does not detract from the amazing dexterity of the technique or the highly imaginative conception of the introduction it expresses. Here indeed is an example of Beethoven's originality that demonstrates his transformation of the introduction into a structural force whose tension gives an entirely new and different impetus to the C major chord on which the exposition begins.

This technique is a combination of the treatment of the *grave* of the "Pathétique" and the introduction to the First Symphony. In its prolongation of the diminished seventh chord on B, which is exchanged for the dominant G major chord, it is strongly reminiscent of the *grave*. In opening on a seventh chord instead of a triad and on a dissonance which is striking in its apparent lack of relationship to the tonality, the technique resembles the treatment of the First Symphony. However, the more complex nature of the voice leadings in the quartet and the greater tension they exercise on the harmonic progression are proof of the development both of Beethoven's dramatic instinct and of his technical ingenuity.

No one can regard these measures merely as a preface to the movement. It is true that as a prolongation of the dominant preceding the opening C major chord they are not an essential element of the basic harmonic progression. However, the atmosphere of tension and suspense they create and the stimulus and intensity they inject into the prolongation have a psychological effect on the whole movement that gives these measures an artistic if not a structural function. We recognize this fact when the expanded dominant achieves the C major chord (measure 29). Here the entrance of the tonic chord is so fleeting that we are hardly aware that the climax of the preceding measures has been attained. It is touched on so lightly and disappears so quickly that we feel as though we are being swept along from the beginning of the introduction through

176

the first fourteen measures of the vivace in a growing wave of tension that subsides only with the entry of the main theme in a full-throated declaration of the C major tonality (measure·43).

Thus the first forty-two measures serve as a dramatic preparation for the climactic entrance both of the theme and of the tonic chord of the basic harmonic progression. Nevertheless, the techniques by which this effect is achieved in no wise negate the principles of structural coherence revealed in the earlier works. Instead they disclose a fuller flowering of Beethoven's imagination through a natural development of his artistic and technical resources.

These three examples illustrate the changes that have taken place in the introduction and the various means by which its function has been enlarged. Its original purpose, to set the mood and provide a contrast for the allegro, has been given greater significance through the suspense and tension produced by the bold treatment of the prolongations. Whether its structural function also has been widened, through the added impetus contributed by it to the entrance of the tonic chord and the thematic figure, is a question each reader must decide for himself.

Although it would be difficult to prove that Beethoven gave the pro-longing motion of the introduction a new function, everyone will agree that he so greatly intensified its original purpose that it plays a more vital role in the movement than in the works of his predecessors and contem-poraries. The only example that could be cited as an instance in which the introduction exercises a different function is the *grave* of Opus 13. Here not only does it build up a mood whose suspense provides a dra-matic contrast for the dynamic character of the theme, but in addition the repetition of the first four measures in the development section serves to expand the motion between the mediant and dominant chords of the basic harmonic progression. This demonstrates an entirely new use of the material, in a connection that no one before Beethoven had recog-nized.

Now let us turn from the introduction to another section of the form whose development was due in such measure to the new aspects of Bee-thoven's treatment — the coda.

THE CODA

As the introduction was the preface to the movement, so the coda was a formal close. For Beethoven, however, it was not the point at

177

Challenge to Musical Tradition

which his imagination stopped, but a section that inspired his creative and technical ingenuity anew. It was in no sense an appendage to the movement, but a vital and challenging element of the form. Before discussing in detail some of the techniques Beethoven used, to give a deep structural significance to the coda, let us consider the type of coda the works of his predecessors reveal.

The coda undoubtedly originated in the necessity of bringing a work to a conclusion. In the earlier polyphonic period, when composers adhered strictly to the rules of imitation in their treatment of the voice parts, it was often difficult, because of the imitation, to terminate a work. Therefore a few simple chords, independent of the imitation, were added to provide the desired ending. This type of cadential coda was also applied to such early instrumental forms as the suite, the sonata, and the theme with variations. In the suite, because of the adherence to one tonality throughout, and in the variation form, because of the similarity of all the variations in their dependence on the theme, it was necessary to point out that the end of the work was at hand. Therefore a passage was added to the final movement of the suite or to the last variation to effect a clearly defined close. From this it is obvious that the coda was conceived not as an integral part of the form, but as a supplement to it. It was what the Italian word for "tail" implied, an appendage to the final movement.

In the works of Haydn the original character of the coda is retained, although as a prolongation of the final tonic of the basic structure it has become a component part of the entire movement. These codas, except for some of the symphonies, are chiefly confined to the last movement and are a simple and straightforward assertion that the movement is coming to a close. However, there is a new element in the treatment, since Haydn frequently refers in the coda to the thematic material of the exposition. As a result there is a melodic interest that was lacking in the older suites and theme with variations. Furthermore, because of his use of melodic material, Haydn's codas are no longer confined to a chordal cadence. Nevertheless, the constant repetition of the harmonic progressions that prolong the structural motion of the coda tends to weaken the effect of the contrapuntal chords and thus deprives the motion of the richness and variety they create. As a consequence many of these codas are so obvious in their repetitious declaration of the tonality that they do not hold the interest of the listener.

There is one exception to this — the coda of the finale of the "Farewell"

178

Beethoven

Symphony in F♯ minor. Haydn has treated this section in what for him was a radical departure from his usual method. He emphasized the distinctive character of the coda by employing new subject matter, in a tempo and rhythm entirely disassociated from those of the movement itself. There is even the suggestion of a tonal contrast in the wide prolongation of the A major chord, which is undoubtedly regarded by some theorists as a "modulation" to the key of the relative major. This instance, however, is unique, since in general Haydn's treatment of the coda confines itself to the material of the exposition and a simple statement of the tonality through various repetitions of a clearly defined harmonic progression.

Mozart, on the other hand, in a few but nevertheless important instances, effected a change in the character of the coda. For the most part the codas of Mozart are as simple as Haydn's from a structural point of view. His prolongations also lack the chromatic tendencies that contribute so much color and richness to the outlined motion. But in the treatment of his thematic material Mozart is much more brilliant and effective than Haydn; he envelops the whole within the melodic beauty and freshness characteristic of his style. For an illustration of this point the reader should turn to the codas of the first movement of the C major quartet, the last movement of the sonata in C minor, the first movement of the piano quartet in G minor, and, most important of all, the final movement of the "Jupiter" Symphony. In these the new treatment of the thematic material, the increased tension in the voice leadings, and the enlarged outlines of the structural motion are proof of the new impulse that Mozart injected into this section of the form. But by comparison with the number of his works these instances are extremely meager and are the exception rather than the rule. Nevertheless, in these few works, Mozart opened up new possibilities that Beethoven later was to utilize.

It was Beethoven, however, whose innovations brought about an entire change in the character of the coda and made it a significant element of the form. However, as in the case of the introduction, it is doubtful that these mutations affected its primary function, since the coda retained its original status as a prolongation of the final tonic of the basic harmonic progression. On the other hand the wider expansion of the section, its closer artistic if not structural integration into the movement, and the nature of the prolonging techniques Beethoven employed offer proof of the new impetus he injected into the coda and the means by which he transformed a formal close into a veritable *tour de force*.

Challenge to Musical Tradition

These are the obvious results of the techniques. The underlying cause that gave rise to them was the fundamental difference in Beethoven's conception of the coda as a challenge to the imagination of the composer rather than as the point at which the creative impulse waned.

In these new tendencies we find two opposing forces, one of closer structural co-ordination, the other of wider sectional expansion, which present a natural conflict that is entirely new so far as the coda is concerned, a conflict that is again and again the main factor in stimulating Beethoven's fantasy. This new treatment is not a development of the so-called "last period," but is revealed in his early works as well. It would seem as though the dormant state in which he found both the introduction and the coda offered a challenge to his imagination and technical invention that made these sections in the early works a natural outlet for the full expression of his stylistic treatment.

An illustration of the early evidence of the tendencies in the techniques that were to re-create the coda can be found in the *largo e mesto* of the sonata in D major, Opus 10, No. 3, one of the most beautiful slow movements in all Beethoven's works. This coda begins on a tonic D minor chord, with the theme entering in the bass. At the third measure Beethoven introduces the first of a succession of chromatically altered chords

EXAMPLE 58

that intensify the character of the coda, since they appear to be outside the established tonality. These first eight measures are of special interest, because they demonstrate the type of prolongation Beethoven used to enrich and expand the I—II—V—I progression, the harmonic framework that supports the entire coda, and the new tendencies in the treatment that enhanced the artistic significance of this final section.

Beneath the profusion of chromatics graph A shows a clear-cut I—II—V—I progression, a harmonic prolongation out of which the motion of the coda emerges. Since the structural motion is so clearly defined, it is obvious that whatever problems arise concern only the techniques that expand the harmonic progression. The main problem, therefore, is the status of the E♭ minor chord, on which a new melodic figure enters, that begins the chromatic ascent to the supertonic chord.

Graph A shows a motion from the D minor through the B♭ major to the E♭ minor chord. Ordinarily in such an arrangement the B♭ major chord would serve as an applied dominant of the E♭ minor. Here, however, the inversion of the E♭ minor with G♭ in the bass outlines a descent of an augmented fifth, which the B♭ major chord converts into two major thirds. Thus it fulfills, not its customary harmonic function in relation to an E♭ minor chord, but the contrapuntal function of a passing chord.

We come now to the E♭ minor chord and its status in the motion. There seems to be a connection between the E♭ minor chord on which the ascent begins and the E minor chord on which it ends. This is indicated by the fact that E♭ and G♭, the outside voices of the E♭ minor chord, are exchanged for E♮ and G♮ of the supertonic seventh chord at the conclusion of the ascent. As a result, it is logical to conclude that the E♭ minor is a passing chord between the tonic and supertonic chords, and is responsible for providing the initial stimulus that impels the motion to the higher register.

This leads us to the final point in our investigation, the use of the chromatics that exert such a strong influence on the character of the coda. Graph A shows the different registers in which the tonic and supertonic chords of the progression appear, creating a leap of a ninth in the top voice and an even wider span in the bass. It is obvious that these spaces have been filled in with the chromatic passing chords (graph B). Their function is not only to effect the transfer of register, but, through the intensity their color contrast provides, to create a crescendo whose sweep and momentum heighten the entrance of the supertonic chord and

181

Challenge to Musical Tradition

at the same time impart a rich prismatic quality to the harmonic progression.

Of further interest is the metrical grouping of these passing chords to add a rhythmic impetus to the motion. The bass shows a group of nine chromatic tones that have been distributed over three measures. Ordinarily this would suggest an allotment of three chromatics to a measure. Instead Beethoven has planned their arrangement in groups of two, three, and finally four to a measure. This increased impulse serves to intensify the struggle of the voice parts to attain a higher register and creates a dramatic climax for the entrance of the supertonic chord.

The introduction of this type of motion and the stimulus it brings to the basic progression is the new element that characterizes Beethoven's treatment of the coda. We need only compare this prolongation with the techniques Haydn and Mozart used in order to realize that even in this early sonata the character of this section has already undergone a drastic change. Not only has it gained in stature and distinction, but through stylistic and technical innovations it has acquired a depth and intensity that foreshadow the treatment of the coda in the first movement of the "Eroica."

In order not to limit our evidence to one example, let us take the coda from the first movement of the Waldstein Sonata, Opus 53, in C major, a work from the "second period."

The movement as a whole is illustrative of the power and drive of Beethoven's style as expressed in the motivic impulse of the opening theme in its swift flight of register, the daring use of an E major instead of the customary E minor chord as the mediant in the progression from the tonic C major to the dominant chord, the quiescent beauty of the contrasting theme within the prolonged E major chord and the relief it offers to the dynamic impulse of the main theme, and the extraordinary insight into the possibilities of the material, as demonstrated by the role that the shortened motive of the theme plays in the development section.

Finally, this is one of those instances in which the coda is knit to the restatement so ingeniously that it is difficult to say where the restatement ends and the coda begins. The motion of the coda outlines a basic tonic-dominant progression that Beethoven has stretched to abnormal size, both through the insertion of passing chords and by an extensive prolongation of the dominant G major chord.

In the prolongations, however, the technique differs from that in the preceding example. Here Beethoven introduces the theme on a D♭ major chord (measure 249). It is undoubtedly the melodic significance given this chord that led authorities such as Nagel [8] and Tovey [9] to regard it as the beginning of the coda. However, various elements in the treatment tend to weaken this interpretation.

First of all, since the closing measures of the exposition and the recapitulation are identical, concluding on a C major chord, it is logical to assume that as one C major chord ends the exposition, the other represents both the final tonic in the structural motion of the recapitulation and the opening tonic in the motion of the coda. A further factor that points to the C major chord as the start of the coda is that it begins a four-measure phrase which, except for the use of an F minor for an F major chord, is a repetition of the first four measures of the development section. These parallelisms are too fundamental to be disregarded. Yet Nagel and Tovey indicate the D♭ major chord that enters four measures after the C major as the start of the coda.

To clarify the situation and show the different functions the C and D♭ major chords fulfill, let us turn to the music.

Graph A indicates a bare outline of the motion from the tonic C major chord to the dominant G major, showing a leap from C to G in contrary motion in the outside voices. In graph B we see the unique nature of the passing chords that fill the outlined spaces between the C and G major chords. The use of such a contrapuntal prolongation not only inspired the originality of the melodic treatment, but invested the harmonic progression with a variety of color effects that give distinctive quality to the character of this coda. However, it is apparent that thus far there is no indication of the D♭ major chord or of the purpose it serves in the motion.

Let us turn to graph C, in which the D♭ major chord finally appears. Although the first four measures show a strong mixture of the C major and minor chords, the motion concludes on a C major chord with C in the top voice passing to B♭, the altered seventh. This B♭ serves as a passing tone between C and A♭ of the D♭ major chord that follows. However, in the music A♭ does not appear as a top voice in the same register with C and B♭, but as a middle voice in which the motion C–B♭–A♭ is more

[8] *Beethoven und seine Klaviersonaten* (Hermann Beyer & Söhne, 1903), Vol. II, p. 79.

[9] *A Companion to Beethoven's Pianoforte Sonatas* (Association Board of the Royal School of Music, London, 1935), p. 161.

EXAMPLE 59

clearly defined. This permits the theme to return in the same low register in which it originally appeared. The introduction of the theme within the Db major chord creates three motions of a third; a descent of C–Bb–Ab, and two ascents F–G–Ab and Ab–Bb–C through which the phrase is extended over four measures. It is true that the repetition of the theme gives great melodic significance to the Db major chord, but the graph shows that this melodic emphasis has been placed on a prolonging chord since the Db major chord serves as a passing chord between the C major and C minor chords. Therefore the function of this chord is not structural. It does not outline the start of a motion, but injects fresh stimulus into a motion whose initial impetus comes from the tonic C major chord.

We come now to the C minor chord, in which the top voice has returned to C of the original register. Although structurally this chord is merely part of a motion between the tonic and dominant, it nevertheless has been given a melodic and dynamic emphasis because of the new impulse the melodic figure reveals and the sforzando marking Beethoven has given it. Here the two motives, each of which previously had required an entire measure, have been rhythmically shortened so that, combined, they could appear within the same measure. Furthermore, it is on this C minor chord that the unbroken ascent to the diminished chord on F♯, the neighbor of the dominant, begins.

184

The motion that follows is too clearly indicated to require comment. The bass climbs to A♮, the climax of the ascent, and returns through A♭ to G of the dominant chord. Simultaneously with the entrance of A♮ in the bass, F♯ is achieved in the top voice; together they intensify the long-delayed entry of the G major chord. The shift of register in the top voice offers a further illustration of Beethoven's use of this technique to create melodic interest and suspense.

As in the preceding example, the treatment is entirely new. In both, the chromatic nature of the prolongations enriches and stimulates the harmonic progression. In both, the harmonic outline is expanded far beyond the normal limits of the motion involved. But here the similarity ends, for in each case the technique has been shaped to meet the individual problems presented by the nature of the melodic, rhythmic, and contrapuntal elements.

The ingenious use of the thematic figure and the unusual nature of the prolonging motion demonstrate the new tendencies in Beethoven's treatment. But the significant element of the techniques is the overlapping of the recapitulation and coda. These two sections have been so closely interwoven that there is a difference of opinion as to where one stops and the other begins. This is due primarily to the accentuation of the D♭ major chord through its introduction of the thematic figure, an emphasis that has concealed its function as a passing chord in the structural motion. As a result the D♭ major chord is accepted by some authorities as the opening of the coda.

The boldness of the technique is a reflection of the boldness of the conception. The coda serves no longer as a conventional close, but as the incentive to a fresh creative effort. The result of this new approach was that by heightening the interest it made this section a more vital and prominent part of the movement. Not only was this a definite contribution to the development of the classical form, but it had a tremendous influence on the treatment of the coda by later nineteenth-century composers.

In turning to the works of the so-called "last period" for a final illustration of Beethoven's coda technique, the problem of selection is intensified. The coda of the finale of the E♭ major quartet, Opus 127, has been chosen because it offers so many interesting points for discussion. In addition, in certain outward respects it bears a resemblance to Haydn's treatment of the coda in the "Farewell" Symphony and thus provides the opportunity for comparison. The obvious resemblance between these two sections is that in each the rhythm, tempo, and even material of the coda differ from those of the main sections of the movement. However, insofar as the prolonging techniques and the effects they produce are concerned, the treatment is totally different.

In the Haydn symphony the presto of the movement is changed to adagio and the *alla breve* rhythm to three-eighths. In addition Haydn introduced a figure of sixteenth notes in triplets as the main motive of the coda; this is entirely new and in no way related to any of the material he had previously used. Of primary significance is the technique that provides for the use of the prolonged A major chord for the main ˙section of the coda, before the entrance of the dominant C♯ major chord brings the movement to a close on the F♯ major chord.

EXAMPLE 60

Recapitulation Adagio

The graph shows only a bare outline of the motion that prolongs the I–III–V–I progression binding the recapitulation and the coda into a single structural unit. Here the unusual aspect of the technique is the strong emphasis of the C♯ major that precedes the A major chord of the adagio. Although through its position at the close of the presto it gives the impression of a dominant, its status is that of a passing chord between the F♯ and A major chords. The use of this technique in the coda was extraordinary in Haydn's day, and it demonstrates the boldness with which he explored the various possibilities inherent in the form. However, the impact of the C♯ major chord is so strong and the motion to the A major chord so abrupt and unexpected that they tend to weaken the tonic-mediant connection of the F♯ minor and A major chords. As a result, in spite of its integration into the structural progression the coda has the effect of being isolated from the movement.

Now let us turn to Beethoven's treatment of the coda of the E♭ minor quartet. Here, too, we find a change in rhythm, from *alla breve* to six-

Beethoven

eighths, the adaptation of the motive to the new rhythmic impulse, and the introduction of a new figure in triplets, which is used throughout. In addition, with the entrance of the *allegro con moto* the key signature changes, and the three flats indicating the E♭ major tonality are obliterated.

What is the structural implication of this shift from E♭ to C major? Is it actually an "unprepared modulation to the key of C major," as De Marliave [10] claims? If so, what purpose does it serve? How shall we account for a modulation to C major within the E♭ major tonality? These are questions for which De Marliave offers no explanation.

It is true that through the striking alteration of the rhythm, tempo, and key signature, Beethoven has taken every means to give the impression that the coda is independent of the main structure. However, as we have seen in the preceding examples, there is a difference between techniques that create an outward effect and those that define the function of a chord in the structural motion. Once again it must be clearly understood that regardless of the methods used to conceal its connection with the recapitulation, the coda begins at that point where the restatement has been brought to a close, usually a repetition of the closing measures of the exposition, but within an outlined tonic chord. The decisive point in the motion is the E♭ major chord on which the recapitulation ends

EXAMPLE 61

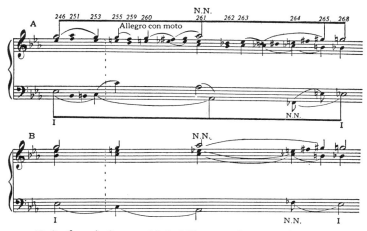

[10] *Beethoven's Quartets* (Oxford University Press, 1928), p. 254.

187

Challenge to Musical Tradition

(measure 246). Usually this chord would also represent the start of the coda. To find out where the coda begins and the status and function of the C major chord, let us turn to the music.

Graph B discloses the main prolongation of the motion from the E♭ major chord on which the recapitulation ends to the reëntry of the E♭ chord in the thirteenth measure of the allegro. We see that the primary factor in this expansion is the A♭ major chord that provides A♭ as a neighbor of G in the top voice. Here the motion from the E♭ to the A♭ major chord is extended by the introduction of C in the bass descent from E♭ to A♭. This converts the perfect fifth into two groups of thirds. This is the C major passing chord, on which the allegro opens, which De Marliave and many others regard as a modulation to the key of C major.

A more detailed explanation of this motion is offered in graph A. Here we see that a small parallelism of the structural top-voice motion G–A♭–G engenders a bass motion from the E♭ major to the C minor chord. This C minor chord is immediately exchanged for the C major chord (measure 255), preceding the *allegro con moto*, on which the allegro also begins.

In referring to the opening measures of the new phrase (measure 256), Roger Fiske writes: [11] "After a trill in thirds on the violins, there is an astonishingly original coda, in a slower tempo — ' Allegro con moto,' a different time — six-eighth, and starting in quite the wrong key — C major. An end like this must have been incomprehensible to its first audience; today it seems pure magic." From this statement it is evident that Fiske understands the C major chord to be a modulation to the key of C major. Yet what does he mean by "the wrong key"? It is true that the entrance of the C major chord is unexpected, but why wrong? It would seem as though the coda were as incomprehensible today as to its first audience.

The function of C major as a passing chord in the motion is clear. To have begun the allegro on this chord and to have altered the tempo and rhythm at this point give the C major chord a prominence out of all proportion to its prolonging function. Yet it is just this deviation from the norm that is the striking aspect of the technique. Here Beethoven effects an entirely new and contrasting environment, not by modulating to a new key, but by expanding a passing chord within the motion from the E♭ to the A♭ major chord.

[11] *Beethoven's Last Quartets, The Musical Pilgrim* (Oxford University Press, 1940), p. 27.

188

Beethoven

The motion from the Ab to Eb chord is equally daring through the enharmonic exchange of Ab for G♯ and the chromatic voice leadings that effect it. For example, the ascent from D♮, a middle, to G♯, a top voice (measures 263–265), not only provides changing colors that contribute much to the passage, but at the same time prepares the climactic effect of the entrance of the E major neighbor chord. In addition it conceals the obvious exchange of Ab for G♯ and thus gives the E major chord greater contrast and distinction. This prolongation also permits the entrance of Fb in the bass, an equivalent of E♮, as a neighbor of Eb, in imitation of the top-voice figure Ab–G.

Thus far we have discussed only the technical means by which the prolongation has been achieved. But this is only one angle of this remarkable work. Of further importance is Beethoven's unusual handling of the thematic material. The adaptation of the two main figures of the allegro to the six-eighths rhythm of the coda and their combination into a single motive shows the imagination and ingenuity with which Beethoven conceived this section.

EXAMPLE 61A

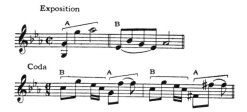

This is a typical illustration of the elastic qualities of the subject matter and the possibilities they provide for use in a different environment. An interesting aspect of the treatment is the manner in which the transition from the four-quarters rhythm of the recapitulation to the six-eighths of the new metrical phrasing is made. The trilled dotted half notes of the violins effect this change without a break in either the rhythmic continuity or the melodic flow. It is a perfect example of the fusion of the imagination of the conception with the originality and dexterity of the technique.

By means of the rhythmic treatment and the motion that leads from the Eb to the C major chord, there is not the abrupt transition to the *allegro con moto* that we find in the adagio of the "Farewell" Symphony. Although this is only one of the many distinctions in the techniques, it

189

Challenge to Musical Tradition

has a vital effect on the connection of the coda with the recapitulation. In fact, although we are conscious of certain deviations in the coda, we hear it as an organic part of the movement and not as an independent entity.

This is the extraordinary aspect of the treatment. Although Beethoven has given great emphasis to the entrance of the C major chord to give the effect of its being the beginning of a new motion, he has bound it so tightly to the recapitulation as a chord of prolongation that it in no wise weakens the tonal implications of motion from the Eb to the Ab major chord.

Here is a challenge to tradition that has been mistaken for a challenge to tonality. Both De Marliave and Fiske assert that the coda begins in the key of C major. But what explanations have they offered to prove this conclusion, and how do they account for such a modulation within the Eb major tonality? Furthermore how can a chord whose function in prolonging the motion to the Ab chord is contrapuntal possess at the same time the harmonic status that a modulation to a new key demands?

Again we see the results to which the purely harmonic approach leads. What is gained by regarding the C major chord as a modulation to a new key that can compensate for the impact of such an analysis on the conception of tonality? Why is it always necessary to attribute the presence of similarly striking effects to modulations outside of the key? Surely, if the only possibility of achieving such original and bold techniques is to leave the tonality and venture into different keys, we must all agree with those contemporary composers who believe that tonality has failed. However, it is conceivable that tonality has not failed, but we ourselves have been ill equipped to comprehend its meaning, and that the accepted system of analysis, based on a theoretical rather than a practical approach, has fashioned our concept of tonality on the teaching of academicians rather than on the music of master composers. It is time that we turned to the music itself instead of to textbooks for our explanations, since the textbooks have failed to give us the means of fully understanding the function of tonality, as it is revealed in the music.

The three examples cited represent a typical work of each of Beethoven's "three periods." In each, the new tendencies in the treatment have centered on the specific means by which a contrapuntal chord of prolongation is given undue emphasis. The conception in all is primarily the same. It is only in the nature of the techniques and the degree of emphasis that they differ. From this it is obvious that these works cannot be placed in separate categories, since the treatment of the coda in Opus 127 is a natural outgrowth of the innovations that Opus 10, No. 3, discloses.

Again, their importance does not lie in the fact that Beethoven has expanded a four-measure phrase into a section of twenty, fifty, or even a hundred measures, since the expansion of the introduction and coda is not significant *per se*. On the contrary it was the function served by these prolongations that was the essential element in the treatment. Not only did they transform the character of the coda by turning a more or less conventional closing section into a motion of great intensity and suspense, but in combination with the melodic treatment they helped to conceal the point that bound the coda to the recapitulation. Consequently they made it appear as though the coda had the structural independence that its melodic, rhythmic, and contrapuntal activity suggest. Thus, within the same structural framework that outlined the codas of Haydn and Mozart, Beethoven extended the whole range of his art and brought into being a new and different conception of the treatment of the final section and the influence its larger stature exerted on the entire movement.

In spite of the more distinctive character, the increased importance, and the wide expansion that he gave it, Beethoven effected an ever closer integration of the coda into the structural organism. He achieved this by a closer union of the restatement and coda, in which the conclusion of the restatement and the opening of the coda are so skillfully interwoven that it is frequently difficult to tell where one ends and the other begins.

In this discussion of Beethoven's techniques we have concentrated on certain important aspects of his work and consequently have omitted others that also have a far-reaching result on the development of the sonata, quartet, and symphony. We have dealt in detail with the new kind of intensity he created and the effect of his expanded conception of the form on his treatment of the development section, the introduction, and the coda.

It would be fruitful to discuss also the means by which Beethoven transformed the minuet into the scherzo, the new type of variation he conceived, the deep and impassioned nature of his slow movements, and finally the great impetus he gave to instrumentation and orchestral coloring. However, since we could not cover in detail the entire range of his art, it was necessary to concentrate on the elements that most clearly indicate those developments within the tonal concept that were of primary importance to his successors and to the future trend of music.

Certainly it was the new kind of emotional intensity that we found in the "Pathétique" and the "Appassionata" that opened the way to the so-called "romantic" style of Schubert and Schumann. Nor can we deny that the atmosphere of suspense that Beethoven's prolongations created was a stimulus to Wagner, especially in his treatment of the prelude to *Tristan und Isolde*. It is equally true that the new and original character of Beethoven's quartets had an undeniable effect on the chamber music of Schubert, Schumann, and Brahms. This may be seen in the nature of the subject matter, the integration of the instrumental lines, the chromatic nature of the contrapuntal expansions, and the unbroken flow of one section into another, without the cadential demarcations that were customary until Beethoven dispensed with them. Again, no one can question the influence that Beethoven's treatment of the introduction and coda had on the symphonies of Brahms, especially the C minor, in which these sections are such a significant part of the first movement.

These are the more obvious aspects of Beethoven's contribution to the future. There are also numerous subtle ways in which he left his imprint on the trend that the music of the nineteenth century was to take. There is the intensification of the rhythmic irregularities we found in the works of Haydn. There are the extensive use of syncopation, the wider distinction in character between the scherzo and the trio, the highly chromatic nature of the prolongations, and the stress of contrapuntal chords, with such dynamic effect on the structural motion. However, over and above these expressions of his imagination and his mastery of techniques is the reaffirmation of those principles of structural coherence through which every element of a work is an integral part of the organism that embraces the whole.

These are Beethoven's greatest legacy to his successors: his majestic conception of tonality as a demonstration of artistic unity, a conception that permitted vast changes within the structural framework without destroying its foundation; countless innovations in the technique without exchanging freedom for license; tremendous expansions of the harmonic progressions without affecting their stability; and an elasticity and flexibility in the treatment that enriched and intensified the significance of each section of the form without sacrificing its organic connection with the larger structural unit.

Beethoven

Beethoven stands out as the most significant figure in the nineteenth century. Like Bach, he is not only the climax of one period, but the beginning of another. Also like Bach, he is not of the past, but the present. We cannot doubt that his works will endure so long as the beauty, nobility, and greatness of spirit they reveal are essential to mankind.

CHAPTER VI

Richard Wagner

THE LEITMOTIV; *its dramatic and psychological significance, its musical function; result on tonal coherence. Innovations in the prolonging techniques. New chromatic tendencies; their effect on the structural motion.*

S o much has already been written about Wagner's life, philosophy, and musical theories, as well as the various aspects of his style, that it would seem no angle had been léft untouched and any further discussion would merely be repetitious. However, since we are not concerned with either his life or philosophy except in so far as they affect his works and since our approach to his music is different from that used in books already written, there should be little duplication.

In spite of the varied theories advanced in explanation of Wagner's "harmonic" treatment and the romantic tendencies of his chromatic style, they express only two basic points of view, generally speaking: (1) that Wagner's conception of tonality, indicated by his use of key center with modulations to closely related keys, is as clearly defined as that of Haydn, Mozart, and Beethoven; (2) that his use of the leitmotiv, his unmelodic declamatory style, altered chòrds, and chromatic techniques, and his method of enharmonic exchange and constant shift of key center tended to violate the principles of absolute music and were essential factors in the breakdown of the tonal system.

Widely as these statements differ in ultimate conclusions, their authors start from a common premise. They believe that the sole basis on which Wagner's music can be evaluated is its confirmation or negation of the established rules that theorists have applied to the absolute forms of the sonata and symphony. As a result Wagner's most devoted admirers regard him as a great genius and place him in the same category with Beethoven, while his critics hold that he is an egoist whose conceptions of grandeur and chromatic deviations from the harmonic norm attest to the influence

Richard Wagner

of the romantic period in which he lived and of which he became the musical symbol.

The fallacy of such arbitrary contentions is that none is wholly right or wholly wrong. No one can deny that Wagner demonstrates his genius in the close association into which he has brought word, action, and tone, in a manner no one else has approached. It is equally true, however, that there are times when he subordinates the music to the text and thus sacrifices the integrity of the music for what he believes to be the more important element, the dramatic or psychological interest. The result is that he sometimes deviates from the principles of structural unity that Bach, Haydn, and Beethoven held inviolate.

In Wagner's music we are not dealing with forms in which music is the sole consideration, as it is in the suite, sonata, quartet, and the symphony. Nor are we discussing that form of opera in which the music is the motivating factor, where arias, duets, and choruses have been conceived entirely from the point of view of the music. On the contrary we are considering a very special type of composition, the music-drama, in which the merging of the words, the action, and the music is the artistic goal. This necessitates a study of the music from two different points of view: first, whether it demonstrates the principles of structural unity; second, whether any sacrifice of these principles is due to the demands of the text. We shall apply the same method of analysis to Wagner's music as to the works of his predecessors, but we shall also consider any deviations in the basic techniques in relation to the text or the dramatic action they represent.

According to Wagner himself, the main factor that led him to find a new medium of expression was his belief that the conventional form of the opera had failed to achieve its initial purpose. He says: "Music, a means of expression, has been made the end, while the end of expression, the drama, has been made a means." [1] Although the music-dramas themselves tend to show that, in spite of Wagner's theories, the music remains the dominant factor, it is undoubtedly true that in many instances it was the dramatic concept that inspired the musical idea.

It must be remembered that unlike Bach, Haydn, Mozart, and Beethoven, Wagner did not turn to composition as a natural means of expression. His initial impulse found an outlet in the drama. In fact, his desire

---

[1] *Gesammelte Schriften* (C. M. Fritsch, 1887), *Band III, Oper und Drama. Einleitung.*

Challenge to Musical Tradition

to compose first evidenced itself when he was writing the tragedy of *Leubold and Adelaïda*. Strongly influenced by performances of Beethoven's music, especially the overture to *Egmont*, he was convinced that what his drama lacked was a musical background.

In speaking of this early period Wagner says: "I was now filled with a desire to compose, as I before had been to write verse. . . . I now wanted to set *Leubold and Adelaïda* to music, similar to that which Beethoven wrote to Goethe's *Egmont*." [2]

It is obvious that in Wagner's early creative attempts music was secondary to his interest in the drama. His own statement helps to explain his unique approach to the problems of music and to his theory that music was a means of expression rather than an end in itself. In fact he appraised all music, whether operatic or symphonic, on the same basis — the effectiveness with which it disclosed the poetic or dramatic concept and the integrity with which it fulfilled the requirements of the extra-musical idea. How strongly his view of the music-drama as a perfect means of expression colored his understanding and judgment of the works of other composers can be seen in his allusions to Gluck, Mozart, and Beethoven: "Gluck and Mozart, together with the scanty handful of kindred tone-poets, serve us only as lode stars on the midnight sea of operatic music, to point the way to the pure artistic possibility of the ascension of the richest music into a still richer dramatic poetry, namely into *that* Poetic art which by this free surrender of music to her shall first become an all-effectual Dramatic art." [3]

In his letters to Uhlig, Wagner writes: "The characteristic of the great compositions of Beethoven is that they are actual poems; that in them it is sought to bring a real subject to representation." [4]

It is apparent from these statements that Wagner's reaction to all music was different from that of any other composer. He could not conceive of music divorced from all extra-musical sources. If we accept this premise, however, the essential point in our discussion must be to determine what effect such an approach had on Wagner's stylistic treatment and on the future trends of music. We must examine various passages to see whether Wagner adhered to the principles of tonality as demon-

[2] *My Life* (Dodd, Mead and Company, 1924), p. 36.
[3] *Gesammelte Schriften* (C. M. Fritsch, 1887), *Band III, Das Kunstwerk der Zukunft. Richard Wagner's Prose Works,* translated by W. A. Ellis (Kegan Paul, Trench, Trübner & Company, 1895), Vol. I, p. 154.
[4] *Letters to Uhlig, Fischer and Heine* (Scribner & Welford, 1890), p. 184.

Richard Wagner

strated through the techniques of structure and prolongation or whether his union of tone, word, and action led him to achieve dramatic crises at the sacrifice of musical clarity.

THE LEITMOTIV

The leitmotiv is the characteristic feature of the new form and most clearly reveals those dramatic and psychological tendencies in the treatment that reflect the merging of the music and text in the expression of a single concrete idea. In addition, the brevity of the motive offers an unusual opportunity to determine its status either as a structural entity or as a prolongation of the basic motion. Furthermore, the various alterations of the motive that occur in the repetitions provide an excellent means of investigating the melodic, rhythmic, and contrapuntal devices Wagner used to effect the transformation.

Since we shall confine ourselves to this main element of the music-drama, we must examine passages in which the motive appears in connection with the text and also in passages in which the text is lacking. Only if we cover every aspect of its treatment can we evaluate the varied techniques Wagner used.

It is true that Wagner did not originate the idea of the leitmotiv. We find evidences of it in the works of Berlioz, Liszt, and even Schumann. Nevertheless, none of them gave it the musical prominence, the dramatic significance or the symphonic quality Wagner assigned to it. How strong an attraction it had for Wagner is indicated by the fact that even in his early opera, *Das Liebesverbot*, he was already experimenting with its possibilities. In *Rienzi* and *The Flying Dutchman* there is a tendency to use an orchestral figure for a person or situation and return to it throughout the scene. However, he does not use it as a link between the scenes or to remind us of a situation that occurred previously. In *Lohengrin*, the leitmotiv has emerged as a concrete characterization, but the repetitions lack the alterations in rhythm and chord texture that have such psychological significance in the later works. As the *Ring* cycle was the first full-fledged expression of the music-drama, it was inevitable that in the *Ring* the motive, as a highly developed technique, should play its first major role.

The character of the motive in the *Ring* differs from that in the early works. It is of an instrumental rather than a vocal nature, and as a result it is shorter than the motives that were conceived along vocal lines. The brevity of the *Ring* figure lends itself more easily to adaptation and altera-

197

Challenge to Musical Tradition

tion and offers greater possibilities for those striking changes in its treatment that parallel the shifting events in the drama.

Although in the repetitions of the motive in the *Ring* we find various deviations in the melody, rhythm, tempo, and chord structure, at no time is there a genuine development of the material as there is in a fugue or a sonata. There are times when Wagner presents a motive in augmentation or diminution or when he combines two or three motives, as, for example, in *Siegfried* and *Die Meistersinger,* to symbolize through contrary motion the conflicting forces at work. But none of these constitutes a real development as we apply that term to the organic growth of a musical idea.

There are many aspects of Wagner's treatment of the leitmotiv that suggest how strongly the psychological element colored his musical expression. His use of the simple arpeggiated triad for the motives of the Rhine, the Rhinegold, the Rhinemaidens, the Valkyries, and the Need of the Gods symbolizes the elemental nature of the river, the gold, or the characters themselves. He employs the consonant Db major triad to portray the stability of Valhalla, but shifting dissonances for the Wanderer motive, a contrast in treatment indicative of the conflicting elements in Wotan's character. Again, the primitive nature of the giants is set forth by the primitive interval of a fourth.

A more subtle indication of the psychological tendencies in the treatment is the similarity in the melodic outline of the motives of Siegfried, the sword, and the curse (Example 62A–C). The dramatic connection is obvious, since it is Siegfried alone who can forge the sword of truth to lift the curse that has fallen on Wotan and through him on the Wälsungs. Another evidence of the technical ingenuity with which Wagner carries out the psychological and dramatic implications of the text is the expansion of the Horn motive, representing the ebullient, undisciplined nature of the immature boy, into Siegfried the hero, the motive of accomplishment as it appears in *Die Götterdämmerung* (Example 62D–E).

However, interesting as it would be to follow the psychological trends through the parallelisms in the various motives, our main objective is the musical treatment and the status of the motive in the scene in which it appears. Is it an independent entity or an integral part of the structural motion? Is Wagner's treatment of the motive consistent or does it vary? Does he subordinate the music to the text or action, and if so, what is the effect on structural coherence?

Richard Wagner

Example 62

A — Siegfried
B — Sword
C — Curse
D — Horn
E — Siegfried The Hero

We must answer these questions before we can properly estimate the significance of Wagner's contribution and the full impact of his techniques on the music that was to follow.

THE MOTIVE IN THE *RING*

In various instances the motive is obviously a prolonged member of the harmonic progression that comprises the scene. We find such an example in the opening motive of *Das Rheingold,* which for a hundred and thirty-six measures rests on an arpeggiated E♭ major chord, the tonic of the tonality. Another illustration is offered by the motive of the Rhinegold. Here the entire passage, consisting of the motive and its repetitions, shows a motion within the expanded G major chord that leads to the C major chord, on which the Rhinemaidens' song enters, in a closely knit dominant-tonic progression.

A less obvious illustration, however, in which the techniques indicate not only the structural but the psychological aspects of the treatment, is the Valhalla motive. Psychologically, Valhalla is a symbol of the security that will envelop the gods as long as they use their power with justice and wisdom. Through its clear definition of tonality, its diatonic voice leadings and rhythmic emphasis, the motive conjures up the picture of a mighty and impregnable fortress, the abode of the gods. Here the tones of

199

the horizontalized D♭ major chord comprise not only the melodic and harmonic outline of the motive, but the repetitions that cover the first twenty measures of Scene II of *Das Rheingold.*

The harmonic framework shows a I—III—V—I progression, a harmonic prolongation of the D♭ major chord. Although the mediant-dominant progression is clear, the less obvious motion from the D♭ major to the altered mediant, the chord of F major, provides an interesting insight into Wagner's technique of prolongation.

In the example, the repetitions of the motive that appear in measures 3–6 and the duplication of measures 7 and 9 are omitted, since the restatements of these phrases in no way affect the prolongation of the motion from the D♭ to F major chord.

Graph A shows a top-voice ascent of a third from A♭ of the tonic to C of the altered mediant chord. This motion has been extended through an

EXAMPLE 63

Richard Wagner

ascent from D♭, a middle voice, to B♭, a passing tone in the top voice, and by the extra motion from B♭ to D♮ that furnishes D♮ as a neighbor note of C. The bass indicates a motion from D♭ through B♭ to F, the root of the altered mediant. This is further prolonged by the entrance of G♭ and F, the former as the root of the G♭ major chord, the latter the fifth of the inverted B major chord. It is simple to account for the B♭ major chord, since it provides the neighbor note D♮ in the top voice; its function, then, is to embellish the F major chord. However, to precede this F major with a B♭ major chord is slightly confusing, since it tends to emphasize the F major chord as a dominant of B♭ rather than as the altered mediant of the D♭ chord.

In turning to the G♭ major chord (measure 8), it is evident that its function is that of a passing chord, since it supports B♭ in the top voice. However, although G♭ and F are shown as bass tones, we see that F is retained as a middle voice of the B♭ major chord and that G♭, which appears as the root of the G♭ chord, actually comes from A♭, a middle voice of the D♭ chord, and passes to F of the B♭ and ‘F major chords. Thus through its function in the middle and the top voice the G♭ chord serves as a passing chord.

This interesting introduction to Wagner's techniques shows that the doubtful element in the motion is the B♭ major chord that originates in the repetition of the characteristic figure of the motive, the ascending third, B♭–D♮. Since B♭ already is present in the G♭ major chord, we see that its repetition forces the ascent beyond the ultimate goal of C to D♮, its neighbor. Thus the B♭ chord provides D♮ in the top voice as a neighbor note and B♭ in the bass as a passing tone between D♭ and F. However, although its purpose is well defined, its entrance immediately before the F major chord suggests a harmonic association that tends to confuse the status of the F major chord as an altered mediant of the harmonic progression.

On the other hand, the psychological aspects of the treatment are remarkable and indicate those tendencies in the technique through which the music became the pictorial representation of a concrete idea. An illustration of this is the use of the F major chord instead of the unaltered mediant for the reëntry of the motive. Since there is nothing in the voice leadings to necessitate the exchange of the minor for the major mediant, we can only assume that the F major chord was substituted because it gave a more realistic picture of the strength and security of which the

201

Challenge to Musical Tradition

Valhalla motive is the symbol. The power of the ascent brings such emphasis to the F major chord that the repetition of the motive within the F minor chord is heard only as an aftermath.

Even more striking however, are the means by which Wagner implies the physical, spiritual, and psychological results of Alberich's curse when he introduces Wotan in the role of the Wanderer.

The span between the events that take place in *Das Rheingold* and the situations to which they give rise in the first act of *Siegfried* are crystallized in this scene between Mime and the Wanderer. Through the different nature of the motive, the highly chromatic tendencies of the treatment, and the more complex technique of prolongation, Wagner has painted a vivid contrast to the security and strength typified by the Valhalla motive. It is in *Siegfried* (Act I, Scene II) that the Wanderer comes to Mime's cave to ask who will re-forge the fragments of Siegmund's sword, a question Mime is unable to answer. Of this Bekker says: "The solemn Wanderer scene is set against the grand introductory scherzo. In plan, it is a companion piece to the Death Prophecy scene (Walküre) consisting of three strophes and anti-strophes, question and answer thrice repeated. . . . The mystic whole-tone sequences of the Wanderer's harmonies, progressing evenly and gravely in chromatic alternation frame the scene." [5]

This too simple explanation of one of the finest examples of Wagner's ability to express in musical language a concrete extra-musical idea will not suffice. It states the result, but not the technical means by which it has been achieved. Nor does Bekker interpret the meaning of the passage, either as an independent unit or in its relation to the entire scene.

The problem for us is not the effect of what Bekker calls the "whole-tone sequences," but the nature and function of these chromatic chords. In short, does this passage have a musical function irrespective of its impressionistic effect, through its organic connection with the scene, or does it serve only as a means of pictorial representation?

We see that there is a motion from the opening B major chord, in inversion, to the B major chord in root position (measure 12), with an exchange of B and D♯ in the outside voices. Thus, the passage indicates a prolonged motion from the opening B major to the concluding E major chord. Since the basic framework is clear, let us turn to the prolongation

[5] *Richard Wagner,* translated by M. M. Bozman (W. W. Norton & Co., 1931), p. 281.

202

to find what technique Wagner has used to expand the space between the two B major chords.

Graphs A and B offer two different explanations of the prolonging technique. Although both indicate the same outlined motion, the means by which it is achieved vary. This is especially noticeable in the first five measures of the motive.

In both graphs we find a top-voice motion of B—A—G which has been extended through the introduction of those chromatic chords that add so much to the pictorial realism of the motive. Graph A shows that the descent from B to G is made through two smaller motions of a minor third, B—G♯, A—F♯, G, in which G♯ and F♯ serve as under neighbors of A and G. The B♭ and A♭ that occur in measures 2 and 4 are incomplete neighbor notes of the preceding A♮ and G, and as embellishments, they have been omitted to clarify the main motion. The bass indicates a motion from D♯

EXAMPLE 64

203

through C♯ to B of the expanded G major chord, in which the chords of E and D major serve as applied dominants.

Graph B reveals a different prolongation of the motion from the B to G major chord. Here the top voice is extended through the intervening passing chords of B♭ and A♭ major, which supply the passing tones B♭ and A♭ in the top voice and D♮ and C♮ in the bass. This gives rise to a succession of sixths in the outside voices.

Since each of these readings coincides with the music, the choice depends entirely on whether we hear the first four measures as two groups of two-measure phrases or four phrases of a measure each.

In the measures that follow, the presence of the G and F major chords, both of which are expanded, provides an interesting insight into certain new tendencies in Wagner's technique of prolongation. Although the G major chord can be accounted for through a mixture of the B major and minor chords, the use of the F major chord cannot be explained so easily.

Richard Wagner

It is clear that the substitution of F♮ for F♯ in the top voice alters the nature of the descent so that we do not hear it as a motion within the outline of the B major chord or as a mixture of the B major and minor chords. In the bass, the descent from D♯ to B does indicate a horizontalization of the B major chord. Customarily, if one of the outside voices defines a motion within the arpeggiated chord, it is sufficient to maintain the tonal characteristics of the prolongation, and thus comes under the technique of horizontalization. In this instance, however, the effect of horizontalization is weakened considerably by the wide expansion of the G major chord and the smaller motions within the C and F major chords, all of which tend to obscure the tonal characteristics of the space in which they occur. Here the impact of these prolongations on the bass descent from D♯ to B, intensified by the ambiguity of the top voice descent from B to D♯, is sufficiently strong to create a conflict between the basic technique that defines the chord-space and the passing chords that provide the intervening motion. Therefore, in spite of the fact that the bass suggests horizontalization, the effect of the passing chords is so marked, that there is a tendency to hear this passage as a motion *between* two chords instead of *within* the outline of a single B major chord. From this point of view, the presence of the F and G major chords as passing chords is understandable, while, if we regard the motion in terms of horizontalization, these chords contradict the tonal character of the outlined space in which they move.

In any motion between two different chords, the passing chords may be of diatonic or chromatic nature, without regard to the character of the chords between which they appear. However, to apply to two positions of the same chord the same technique which previously had been used only in connection with two different chords is a step whose far-reaching implications must be discussed.

Heretofore any expansion of the space such as Wagner has defined has been conceived as a motion within the tones of the chord. Although the passing chords may have been of a highly chromatic nature, they did not affect the tonal clarity expressed through the horizontalized chord, even though the horizontalization was confined to one of the outside voices. If, however, we regard this motion as the result of a passing-chord technique, Wagner no longer moves within the chord, but between two B major chords.

This technique gives rise to many new possibilities. The treatment of

205

Challenge to Musical Tradition

this motive alone illustrates the variety of effect the passing chords can create. In this instance, the passage is sufficiently short to maintain the connection between the chords of B major in spite of the impact of the' intervening chords. If, however, the same technique were used in a more extensive motion in which the character of the passing chords exerted an ever greater pressure on the outlined motion, what would be the effect on tonal stability? Is not the tendency to move between two B major chords rather than within a B major chord a step in the direction of those later techniques that weakened tonal coherence?

The reader may contend that Beethoven used a similar treatment in prolonging the space between the A♭ minor chord and the A♭ seventh chord in the development section of the first movement of Opus 57. The situation, however, is not the same. We found that the A♭ minor had a structural and the A♭ major a prolonging function. This difference in function, in addition to the distinction in their modal characteristics, defined them as two different chords, the usual connection in which the technique appears.

Whether we hear the Wanderer motive as the result of horizontalization through the outline of the bass or as a passing motion between two B major chords, the technique is unique. In one, the character of the space-filling motion is at variance with the character of the chord outline; in the other, the use of a passing-chord technique between two positions of the same chord attenuates their inherent connection. Thus, from either point of view, there is one element in the treatment that engenders a vagueness in the motion.

Since the F major chord is the outstanding contradiction, let us consider the various possibilities that may have occasioned its use in this motion.

First of all the presence of F in the top voice is due primarily to the nature of the motivic figure and the predominance of whole-tone successions. Furthermore, the wide expansion of G in the top voice not only is supported by a prolonged G major chord, but is enriched through the entrance of the C major chord. This motion of G–C leads naturally to the F major chord in a succession of fifths. A different explanation lies in the effect of the F major chord as the Neapolitan sixth of the E major chord at the close of the motive through the progression F–B–E. A final suggestion concerns the text and its influence on the music. Had Wagner used a typical horizontalized motion in which he introduced the F♯ major instead of the F major chord, he would have created a tonal stability that would have been at variance with the instability and unrest of which the figure of the Wanderer is a symbol. Therefore, to intensify the psychological implications of the drama, Wagner injected those elements into the motive that produced a tonal vagueness.

Although these different arguments account for the presence of the F major chord, they are offered as mere conjecture, without any intention of implying that any of them was a conscious factor in the treatment. However, they reveal that there are valid reasons for the use of the F major chord, even though it is a disturbing element in the motion.

As we turn to the smaller techniques that expand the G and F major chords, it is clear that in each instance the prolongations effect an exchange of the root position for the inverted chord. The unusual aspect of the technique is that although the root positions are emphasized by their applied dominants, the chords of D and C major, it is the inversions that define the nature of the structural descent. The entrance of B, the third of the G major chord, in the same register in which D♯ and C♯ of the preceding B and A major chords appear, indicates a bass motion of D♯–C♯–B rather than D–C♯–G. In addition the exchange of voices in the F major chord, through which F of the top-voice descent enters in connection with A, the bass of the inverted chord, substantiates the interpretation of the motion as a succession of inverted chords in which the outside voices move in sixths.

Although we have questioned certain new tendencies in the treatment, we cannot overlook the remarkable ingenuity with which Wagner conveys in the music the essential impression of the text. Nor should we minimize the fact that through conceiving this motion as a succession of sixths, he used the one technical means of concealing the conflicting elements in the prolongation. In other words, the bass motion leads more convincingly to the B major chord through A, the third, than through F, the root of the chord.

The final element in our discussion concerns the status of this motive. Is it a structural entity or an organic part of a larger motion in which it demonstrates a definite connection with the closing measures of the preceding scene?

The thirty-four measures that conclude Scene I indicate a key signature of D♭ major. Since the last seven measures of this passage begin on a D♭ major chord, obviously the tonic of this motion, they are sufficiently representative to disclose whether there is a structural link between the end of Scene I and the opening of Scene II.

Instead of showing these measures as a motion from the D♭ to the G♭ major chord as they appear in the music, they have been exchanged for their enharmonic equivalents, so that the techniques by which the D♭ major chord passes to the B major may be more easily understood.

EXAMPLE 65

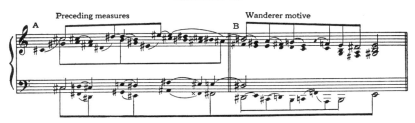

The graph reveals that there is structural motion binding the D♭ and B major chords together. This is the fifth succession outlined by the C♯, F♯, and B major chords. The space between the C♯ and F♯ chords has been extended through the intervening passing chords of D♯ and E♯ minor. Although this prolongation is clearly defined, the top-voice motion is somewhat vague.

There is an ascent from C♯ to E♯, at which point the motive of Renunciation brings a descent from E♯ to A♯, a middle voice. Whether this A♯ is a substitution for F♯ in the top voice or whether the ascent from C♯ to E♯, created by the motivic figure, is a melodic prolongation and embellishment of the motion C♯–B–A♯, is a question to which the music gives no definite answer. The force of the melodic figure that carries the motion to E♯ is so strong that it is difficult not to regard it as of primary importance. On the other hand, there is a parallelism between C♯–A♯ and B–D♯ that suggests a structural motion of C♯ through D♯ of the B major to E of the final E major chord of the Wanderer motive, which is confirmed by the succession of fifths in the bass.

Although the top voice is not clear, there can be little doubt that the bass indicates a well-defined motion that binds the Wanderer motive to the final measures of the preceding scene.

In the measures that succeed the passages shown in the graph, mainly repetitions of the Wanderer motive, the connection is less apparent. Here the first repetition outlines the C major chord, the second the A major chord, the third the E♭ major, and the fourth the B major. If we combine these chords, what is the significance of this motion either as a unit in itself or in relation to the B and E major chords that precede it? Certainly there is nothing to indicate the function of the E♭ major chord, even if we exchange it for its equivalent of D♯ major. Nor do the intervening phrases that lead from one repetition to the next tend to clarify the nature of this chord succession or reveal the status of these chords in relation to the foregoing motion from the C♯ to the E major chord.

Consequently, although the opening measures of Scene II show a connection with the concluding measures of Scene I, the tonal ambiguity created by the repetitions of the motive deprives the scene of any harmonic or structural significance.

Whether this lack of tonal security is due to the nature of the motive and its psychological implications is a question to which no authoritative answer can be given. Nor can we attribute it to a structural weakness that is the beginning of the breakdown of tonality. In fact no conclusions can be drawn until we examine other passages to find out if they too show similar structural tendencies or if this example is an isolated instance.

Although the use of chromatics is so inherent a part of Wagner's style that numerous examples would serve as a basis of comparison, the most interesting in point of technique and its effect on the structural motion is the motive of Magic Sleep from the final scene of *Die Walküre*. Here Wagner is dealing with the supernatural power that Wotan can conjure up at will. He gives us a feeling of the mystery and unreality of this world of gods and half-gods by the shifting chromatics of the motive and the luminous color effect they give out. He makes us aware of the might of Wotan's wrath, which leads him to doom Brünnhilde to endless sleep.

As a whole, the scene is one of the outstanding moments of the entire cycle. The harsh punishment that Wotan decrees is mitigated by the obvious conflict between his love for Brünnhilde and his parental authority. There is a deep and poignant tenderness in the music, which reflects the sadness of Wotan's realization that by Brünnhilde's defiance of his command she herself has broken the tie that bound her to his will. In the Magic Sleep motive, Wagner has injected into the music a hypnotic quality that convinces us of Wotan's supernatural power to cast a spell on Brünnhilde from which she is to awaken only when, as Wotan decrees: "one stronger than I, the god, shall pierce the flames which surround thee."

Challenge to Musical Tradition

What are the techniques Wagner has used to create this effect, and what significance has this motive in addition to its pictorial impression?

EXAMPLE 66

If we isolate the motive from the preceding measures, it gives rise to various interpretations. Eaglefield Hull, for example, points to the basses Ab—B—D and E—G—Bb as successions in minor thirds, but does not explain their meaning or function.[6] Ernst Kurth cites this passage as an illustration of Wagner's use of chromaticism to create iridescent coloring. He suggests that the chromatics tend to lull the senses so that the full power of the Sleep motive may convey itself to the listener.[7] In speaking of the technical aspects of the motive, Kurth points to the fact that although the chromatic chords move freely, they nevertheless tend to demonstrate a tonal connection through a group of tonic and dominant sequences. These successions emphasize the chords of E major (measure 10), C major (measure 12), G♯ major (measure 14), and E major (measure 16). Beginning with the Ab major chord on which the motive opens, which he exchanges for G♯, Kurth finds a descent by major thirds through the basses E—C—G♯ (Ab) to the final E major chord. It is interesting to note that while Hull finds a motion in minor thirds, Kurth points to a succession of major thirds in the same passage.

[6] *Modern Harmony* (Augener, Ltd., 1914), p. 18.
[7] *Romantische Harmonik* (Paul Haupt, Berne and Leipzig, 1920), p. 314.

Richard Wagner

The graph shows a motion of an octave through which the A♭ major chord is transferred to a lower register, where it is exchanged for the chord of G♯ major. This is the important aspect of the motion — that it defines a space of an octave between the A♭ and G♯ chords. In analyzing this motion, the first point to consider is whether these are two different chords or whether they possess the same function and represent two different aspects of the same chord.

Customarily, the exchange would indicate that these chords serve distinct purposes. Here, however, they combine to outline a single space of an octave, which indicates that the enharmonic exchange is not essential to the clarity of this passage, but may have a bearing on the preceding measures.

The motive of Renunciation that precedes the Magic Sleep motive, discloses a prolonged motion from a tonic E minor to a mediant G major chord. The entrance of the A♭ chord of the Magic Sleep motive immediately after the G major chord, suggests that its function is that of a neighbor chord. With the shift of register, however, it is exchanged for a G♯ major chord whose motion to the dominant B major chord establishes it as an altered mediant of the concluding E major chord. Although the A♭ and G♯ chords appear to be two different chords, one with a prolonging function, the other with a structural function, we see that the A♭ chord does not return to a chord of G major in a neighbor-chord motion but is exchanged for a G♯ chord. Had this G♯ chord passed to an F♯ chord, it also would have confirmed the status of A♭ as a neighbor chord; since it moves to the chord of B major, it proves that the A♭ chord describes neither a complete nor an incomplete neighbor-chord function and that its status has been completely absorbed by its exchange for the G♯ major chord. This leads us to question Wagner's use of an A♭ instead of a G♯ chord as the opening of the motive. Had Wagner begun on a G♯ chord, an altered chord on A♯ would have replaced the B♭ major chord to create a top-voice descent B♯–B♮–A♯–A♮ instead of the less convincing succession B♯–B♮–B♭–A♮. The inverted A♯ chord would have created the bass ascent G♯–B–C♯♯–D♯ in which the intervals are not the same as those that comprise the succeeding motions. Therefore it is logical to assume that Wagner used the A♭ chord because it made possible the parallel groupings that define the prolonging technique, it simplified the manner of writing by eliminating the introduction of double sharps, and it gave a clearer expression of the character of the motion than a G♯ chord

Challenge to Musical Tradition

would have afforded. The presence of the A♭ chord can be attributed only to the artistic purpose it serves as a substitute for the G♯ chord, since it fulfills no function until its exchange has been effected.

Since we have found that the A♭ and G♯ major chords represent two different presentations of the same chord, it is necessary to examine the prolonging motion to determine the specific technique Wagner used. The top voice shows a chromatic descent of an octave, but the grouping of the tones does not define a motion within the spaces of an outlined A♭ or G♯ chord. In fact the grouping of the tones in the top voice and bass points to a passing-chord technique that closely resembles Beethoven's expansion of the space between the A♭ minor and major chords in Opus 57. Wagner, like Beethoven, descends an octave through a succession of major thirds A♭ (G♯)–E–C–G♯, in which the chords of E and C major are passing chords. Since the chromatic descent in the top voice outlines a chord space, the customary means of filling this interval would be to horizontalize the G♯ major chord. Instead, Wagner used the passing-chord technique. This leads us to assume that although the A♭ and G♯ major chords are shown to be two expressions of a single chord with the sole function of a mediant, the difference in their appearance has caused Wagner to regard them as two different chords. Here the use of the passing-chord technique, customarily applied to two different chords, to prolong the space between two positions of the same chord, is an intensification of the treatment of the Wanderer motive.

The results of this technique are self-evident. It is inevitable that if a space between two G♯ chords can be filled with any kind of passing chord, without the necessity to prove the connection through a motion within the tone spaces of the G♯ chord, the same technique can be applied to two G♯ chords that open and conclude an entire scene. Here too, the motion could be made up of passing chords, but who would hear it as a link between the two G♯ chords or as a definition of the tonality? Yet there is no difference in the basic conception of the technique, only a difference in the extent of the prolongation. If we admit that in spite of the conflicting tendencies of the passing chords, the technique in the Magic Sleep motive maintains a clear connection between the G♯ major chords, why cannot this same method be used in larger sections, in which the added pressure of an increased number of intervening chords cannot help but weaken, even obliterate, the fundamental connection?

212

Richard Wagner

This is not a criticism but a discussion of Wagner's technique. Its purpose is to point out those new tendencies that differentiate his treatment from his predecessors' and to indicate their possible effect on the future trend in music. It was inevitable that Wagner should have evolved a stylistic idiom through which he demonstrated his theory of the inter-relationship of the musical and dramatic impulses. Whether the innovations in his treatment are the result of this union or whether they are indicative of a different conception of tonality and of the means by which it is maintained are questions which at this point in the discussion we are not prepared to answer. We must recognize, however, in the Magic Sleep motive, that it is the unique aspect of the technique and its lack of tonal implication that intensify the effect of the shifting chromatics and provide a musical complement for the action that dominates the scene.

However, instead of isolating the motive from the rest of the scene, as Hull and Kurth have done, let us examine it in relation to the seven preceding measures, which give out the motive of Renunciation within the E minor chord. These measures may explain the use of the A♭ chord in the opening of the Magic Sleep motive and should reveal the status of this motive either as an entity or as an organic part of a larger structural motion.

EXAMPLE 67

213

Challenge to Musical Tradition

The motive of Renunciation indicates a tonic-mediant progression in the motion from the E minor to the G major chord. The space is considerably expanded by the use of the B major chord as that type of applied dominant that moves not to the tonic, but, in this case, to its own neighbor chord.

The top voice shows two descents from G to B. The emphasis placed on G in these measures might lead us to assume that it represented the structural top voice. However, in the Magic Sleep and Brünnhilde's Slumber motives, which follow, the constant reference to B through its neighbor notes C or C♯ reveals that B is the structural tone and the descent from G is an embellishing motion. This conclusion is confirmed by the presence of G in a middle voice, where it is retained throughout the motion to the G major chord. Therefore, although the descents from G to B are of motivic importance, as embellishments, they have no structural significance.

Here, too, we find two references to C as a neighbor of B (measures 2, 4, and 5). In a similar manner the C major chord on which the second descent to B begins (measure 3) serves as a neighbor of the B major chords that precede and follow. The F♯ minor chord that enters between the C and B major chords is an applied dominant of B major. Thus, by means of an embellishing motion, two types of applied dominants, and the F minor neighbor-passing chord (measure 5), Wagner has achieved a rich and colorful prolongation of the tonic-mediant progression.

We come now to the main point of interest. Is there a connection between this passage and the Magic Sleep motive, or is each one a motivic entity without structural implication?

The graph shows that the motives of Renunciation and Magic Sleep

EXAMPLE 68

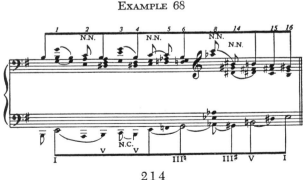

214

Richard Wagner

constitute a prolonged I–III♮–III♯–V–I progression within the E chord denoting an extraordinary mixture of the E minor and major chords. The only problem in the passage is the status of the expanded G♯ major chord. What is its connection with the motive of Renunciation and what is its function within the entire motion?

Since the first six measures of the graph outline a tonic-mediant progression within E minor and the three final measures indicate an altered mediant-dominant-tonic progression within E major, it appears as though the G♯ chord were the point in the motion at which the exchange of the minor for the major chord was effected. In foreshadowing the entrance of an E major chord, the chord of G♯ is a determining factor in the motion and the axis about which the minor-major mixture revolves. It offers a further instance of mixture, since the unaltered mediant of E major is a G♯ minor chord. Therefore, although the G♯ chord provides B♯ as a neighbor of B♮ in the top voice, its intensification of the B and E major chords that follow defines its function as a structural mediant through whose prolongation the mixture of the minor and major characteristics has been so greatly enhanced.

The passage is an extraordinary demonstration of the elasticity of Wagner's conception of tonality and the boldness of his technique. It shows the strength of the tonal structure, to withstand the impact of the expanded G♯ chord. It also reveals that Wagner did not demonstrate the clarity in his prolonging techniques that he achieved in the outline of the harmonic progression. This contradiction between the coherence of the structural motion and the vagueness produced by the passing-chord technique of the prolongation is obvious. It suggests that to achieve the unique character of the motive, Wagner intentionally used a technique that so far departed from the norm that its atonal implications reflect the strange, illusive, supernatural quality dominating the action of the drama.

However, although it is possible to attribute the tonal vagueness of the expanding motion to the demands of the text and thus to justify the technique in this specific instance, we must also recognize that the same technique could be used in passages in which the text was not a salient factor. In short, we must consider the wider implications of this treatment. It is inevitable that Wagner's use of this type of prolonging motion influenced the techniques of his successors, who perhaps applied the same treatment to the theme of a sonata or symphony. Therefore it is not suffi-

215

cient to explain these techniques as they occur within the music-drama. We must also realize that, legitimate as they may be under these circumstances, the use of similar methods in abstract music would necessarily result in a weakening both of the structural motion and of the tonal coherence.

Nevertheless, it is still too soon to determine whether the vagueness revealed by the expanding motions in the three examples we have analyzed is typical of Wagner's treatment, or whether the demands of the text have exerted such pressure on the technique that these instances are more or less unique. Therefore we must examine passages in which the music is separated from the text, even though the motive, as representative of the drama, still predominates. Then, and then only, can we decide whether the methods Wagner used in these three passages are characteristic of his technique, or whether they occur only in situations in which the music is subordinated to the dramatic impulse.

Let us take three totally different examples, one from the prelude to *Parsifal*, another from the prelude to Act III of *Die Meistersinger*, and the last from the prelude to *Tristan und Isolde*. Although the poetic idea is still represented by the motive, the absence of the text offers an excellent opportunity to compare the technique in a passage in which the music predominates with examples in which the motive is definitely associated with the text or the dramatic action.

THE MOTIVE IN THE PRELUDES

The prelude to *Parsifal* is an extraordinary introduction to the conflicts of the drama. Its psychological effect is of tremendous importance to the mood of the opening scene. In it the mystery of the Sacrament, the spiritual longing symbolized by the Grail, the testament of Faith, and the tragedy that the motives of Suffering and Penitence reveal are woven into a musical narrative of the events Gurnemanz discloses in the scene which follows. It shows the power of Wagner's imagination to present these motives in a manner that sustains the mood of the entire act. Even in the prelude we are transported from the world of reality to the world of Mount Salvaat, where we become participants in the drama of the knights of the Grail.

Although the motive of the Sacrament, with its deep, poignant note of suffering, offers a remarkable example of Wagner's unique ability to find a musical equivalent for so illusive a spiritual conception, the varying

216

Richard Wagner

repetitions in the motive of Faith provide a more characteristic example of his stylistic treatment. The motive, given out by the horns and trumpets, is a spiritual call to arms. The strong, vibrant impulse that characterizes this figure is a convincing portrayal of the power of which it is a symbol. Here, as in the Sacrament and the Grail, Wagner has solved the difficult problem of translating a religious or ethical concept into a concrete musical expression.

Once again, to simplify the passage and to clarify the motion it demonstrates, the chords in measures 7 and 8 have been exchanged for their equivalents.

The fundamental aspects of the technique concern the prolongations of the Eb major chord and its exchange for the Eb minor chord at the close of the passage.

In the opening measures there is a motion from the Eb to the Gb major chord. The strong emphasis of this Gb chord and its wide expansion suggest that it functions as a mediant of the Eb chord. If this were the case, we could account for the status of the altered supertonic chord (measure 9) only as a chord of harmonic emphasis of the dominant Bb major chord that follows. This explanation, however, which defines it as a chord or prolongation, is incompatible with its impact on the structural top voice in forcing the line to descend from the long-retained Bb to Ab. Another factor that militates against this reading is that if we hear the top voice as a descent from Bb to Eb, three of the tones Ab–Gb–F occur within the altered chord on F, a chord of prolongation. Here its structural function in connection with the top voice contradicts its prolonging function as a chord of harmonic emphasis.

It seems much clearer, therefore, to hear this diminished seventh chord on F as an altered supertonic of the structural motion, since this accounts for its impact on the structural top voice. From this point of view, the expanded Gb major chord is a neighbor of the supertonic and provides an embellishing motion. Accordingly, the top voice defines a motion of Gb–F–Eb in which the space between Gb and F has been greatly extended by an ascent from G to Bb that is answered by the descent from Ab to F. The ascending motion engenders further prolongation within the Gb major chord. How strongly the interval of a third that defines these main embellishments dominates the techniques in both the top voice and bass may be seen in the graphs.

Turning to the expansion of the Gb major chord (measures 5–9), we

217

again find a type of motion that permits two interpretations. The passage as a prolongation does not alter the nature of the structural progression, but it gives further evidence of the vagueness of Wagner's expanding techniques.

Graph A shows the first of these readings in which we hear the emphasis placed on the first quarters of measures 7, 8, and 9. This gives rise to a top-voice descent of E♭♭–D♭–C♭–B♭, concluding on the same B♭ that appears in the top voice of the G♭ major chord (measure 6). Although for motivic purposes, E♭♭ is given the same stress as D♭, C♭, and B♭, the presence of the D♭ chord between two G♭ chords, suggesting a I–V–I harmonic prolongation, leads to the possibility that the E♭♭ chord is a neighbor of D♭. From this point of view E♭♭ in the top voice, as a neighbor of D♭, is a parallelism of the neighbor motions A♭–G♭ and C♭–B♭ in the preceding measures. In a similar manner A♭, the root of the A♭ minor chord, is a neighbor of G♭, with C♭ in the top voice a passing tone between D♭ and B♭. Through these embellishing motions D♭, a middle voice

EXAMPLE 69

in the G♭ major chord (measure 6), is exchanged for E♭ in the same chord (measure 10).

The second possibility to which the strong emphasis of B♭♭ gives rise (measure 6), is shown in graph B. We see that B♭♭, on which the motive starts, is the same B♭♭ on which it pauses momentarily at the end of the descending motion (measure 8). This suggests that the chord on the fourth quarter of each measure, the end of the descent, is the salient factor in the motion, of which the other tones are embellishments. According to this interpretation, there is a top-voice motion of B♭–A♭–C♭–B♭ in which B♭♭ enters as a passing tone between B♭ and A♭. Here A♭ and C♭ serve as a lower and an upper neighbor of B♭. The bass shows a similar type of embellishing motion, with F♭ and A♭ as a lower and an upper neighbor of G♭.

Although this reading differs greatly from that shown in graph A, both achieve the same end — the prolongation of the G♭ chord, with the exchange of D♭ for E♭ in the middle voice. Thus, instead of hearing this repetition of the motive as a modulation outside of the tonality, we hear it

Challenge to Musical Tradition

as an embellishment of the G♭ major neighbor chord within the harmonic prolongation of the E♭ major-minor chord. In this the use of G♭ instead of G♮ as the root of the neighbor chord foreshadows the entrance of the E♭ minor chord at the close.

The treatment here discloses several inconsistencies. First of all, the basic technique is vague since it gives rise to two different interpretations, either a I–III–V–I or a I–II–V–I harmonic progression. The latter is indicated in the graphs because it coincides to a greater extent with what we hear in the music and at the same time disposes of the conflicting tendencies that the altered chord on F offers in a I–III–V–I progression. Nevertheless, the structural outline itself is not entirely clear. In addition, the prolonging techniques also are indefinite, as they too are capable of two different readings.

It becomes evident, therefore, that even in the absence of the text, the motive remains the dominating factor, since through its repetition the various contradictions in the treatment arise. Undoubtedly the re-entry of the motive in a fresh chord environment intensifies both its role in the prelude and its underlying symbolism, but these extra-musical effects are achieved at the sacrifice of the structural coherence.

However, let us turn to our second illustration, the prelude to Act III of *Die Meistersinger,* to see whether there is a similar impact of the motive on the basic techniques.

DIE MEISTERSINGER, PRELUDE TO ACT III

As in the prelude to Act I of *Parsifal,* the music is made up entirely of motivic phrases. Here, however, the action of the drama is already in motion, so that in addition to creating the mood of the scene that follows, the prelude serves as a connecting link between the situation at the close of Act II and the developments of Act III.

In discussing the psychological implications of this prelude, Ernest Newman takes issue with Wagner's statement that it represents "the bitter moan of the resigned man who presents to the world a strong and serene countenance." He says: "How is anyone to know that this *Vorspiel,* if it has any connection at all with one of the characters of the drama, is to be understood as being associated with Sachs? In the second place, how are we to know that the first theme represents the bitter moan of the resigned man?" [8]

[8] *A Study of Wagner* (Putnam, 1899), p. 313.

Richard Wagner

There is some justification for this point of view. Although the motive of Renunciation occurs twice in the second act, once in the serenade scene between Sachs and Beckmesser and once in the third stanza of Sachs's song, in neither case is the phrase made sufficiently important to connect it with the prelude or to establish its association with Sachs. Nor can we grasp the full meaning of the *Wach' auf* theme that follows, since it is a phrase of the chorale that we hear for the first time in the third act. Consequently, to one unfamiliar with the drama, the connection that Wagner intended to suggest by placing the motive of Renunciation and the chorale theme in juxtaposition is entirely lost. In fact, the psychological association is understood only when we hear the music often enough to recognize these motives and grasp their underlying significance.

The opening motive of Renunciation, which Wagner describes as "a soft and mellow, deeply melancholy strain that bears the character of utmost resignation," [9] implies the sadness with which Sachs has yielded to the claims of the young knight. The entrance of the chorale phrase at the close of this motive suggests that Sachs unconsciously turns to his art as a means of sublimating his love for Eva. Next comes the Cobbler's Song, given out by the strings, which reflects the deeply poetic nature of Sachs. This is borne out by Wagner's description of this passage, in which, according to Newman's translation, he says, "it is as if the man had turned his eyes upward, away from his daily toil, and lost himself in sweet and tender dreams." [10] The winds proclaim a second phrase from the chorale, after which the opening motive of Renunciation is repeated.

Newman argues that Wagner has failed in his intention to conjure up the dramatic and psychological significance of these motives. This is, in part, true, since it would be impossible at the first few hearings to grasp their full connotations. However, although we might not understand the subtle connection of these motives, does not the music itself convey the different moods they express? Is it necessary to know that the opening phrase is indicative of Sachs's renunciation to sense the mood of meditation and sadness it reflects?

The music alone is sufficient evidence of Wagner's intention. Nor need we recognize the succeeding phrase as a fragment of the chorale to sense that the mood has changed. It is no longer one of sadness and dejection,

[9] *Letters to Mathilde Wesendonck,* translated by W. A. Ellis (Grevel, 1911), p. 302.
[10] *Entwurfe, Gedanken, Fragmente,* pp. 104–5. Newman *A Study of Wagner,* p. 313.

221

Challenge to Musical Tradition

but is filled with hope, vitality, and the will to live. In a similar manner, whether or not we realize that the next passage is the Cobbler's motive and as such is suggestive of Sachs, we feel its eloquence and the tender, poetic quality that distinguishes it from the more vibrant character of the preceding phrase.

If Wagner has accomplished this and it is not imposing too much on the listener to believe that he has, then we must say, with all deference to Newman, that Wagner has not failed in his purpose. He has provided his listener with the clues through which the emotional and psychological aspects of the drama are suggested. However, it is also important to find out if there is a structural connection between the motives that bears out their psychological association. If there is, and if Wagner succeeds in depicting, through a single structural outline, the merging of Sachs the cobbler with Sachs the artist, he has achieved a function for music which in its psychological aspects is entirely new.

But now let us look at the music. The prelude opens with the motive of Renunciation which outlines a motion from the G minor to the D major chord that leads to the G major chord, on which the chorale theme enters. In this exchange of the G minor for the G major chord, Wagner has implied a transition from the earlier motive of sadness to the inner strength of the creative artist. Here the interesting prolongations occur that provide the Cobbler's Song and the return of the chorale.

Since the prelude is too long for us to cover every aspect of the treatment, the graph indicates only the larger expansions revealing the structural motion that binds the two chorale phrases and the Cobbler's motive into a three-part form.

The chorale defines a motion from the tonic G major to the dominant D major chord. This motion is extended through the harmonic prolongation, I–V–I and the basic I–(VI)–II–V progression. In the latter, the submediant E minor chord serves as a chord of harmonic emphasis that stresses the entrance of the supertonic chord. The top voice reveals two descending motions. The first of these is a prolongation of G, a retained tone, through a descent to B, a middle voice; the second is a structural motion in which G, a structural top voice, moves stepwise to D (measures 21–25). This structural descent is supported by the I–II–V progression.

Not only does this dominant D major chord bring the motion of the chorale to its climax, but its expansion provides the outline within which

222

Richard Wagner

EXAMPLE 70

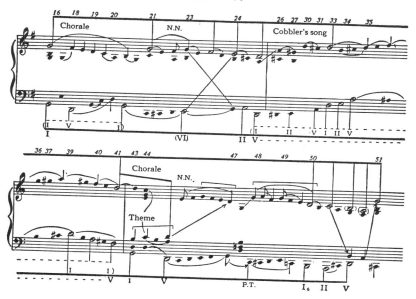

the Cobbler's Song occurs. In fact, this widely prolonged dominant moves on to the tonic G major chord only with the entrance of the second phrase of the chorale (measure 43). This is a remarkable demonstration of Wagner's imagination, versatility, and technical invention. It shows the originality of his conception, through which the prolongation of a single I–II–V–I progression gives rise to a passage of rich melodic interest, colorful contrast, and technical ingenuity without any weakening of the structural outline.

The motion as a whole defines a three-part form of which the Cobbler's Song comprises the middle section. The opening chorale phrase directs the structural top-voice descent from G to D with a bass motion from the tonic to dominant chord. The second chorale phrase completes the top-voice descent of an octave by leading the motion from D to G, while the bass again defines a I–II–V harmonic progression. Within this structural framework the Cobbler's Song, through its outline of the prolonged D major chord, provides a new melodic interest, the rich colors of the passing chords, and the harmonic contrast inherent in the tonic and dominant chords.

223

Challenge to Musical Tradition

The entire motion within this middle section is an embellishment of D in the top voice and D in the bass. The top voice outlines an ascent from A, a middle voice, to D, the structural top voice, transferred to a high register. The motion climbs beyond D, and passes through F♯ and G to A, from which the descent to D is made. In the bass, we find a similar expansion of the motion within the D major chord through the outline defined by two harmonic prolongations. Here for the first time Wagner has clearly demonstrated a motion within the outlined tones of the chord in which every aspect of the treatment, even in the smaller expansions, confirms the nature of the prolongation outlined by the outside voices. However, he has offset the possible monotony of such a chord outline by the highly chromatic nature of the space-filling motions, to whose richness and color the strongly marked syncopations lend emphasis and intensity. Thus, through his unusual treatment of the voice leadings, he has transformed the simple outlining motion into a passage of poignant beauty, full of the warmth and vibrancy of his creative artistry.

It is possible that Wagner's treatment of the Cobbler's Song has a psychological as well as musical significance. Is it too far-fetched to believe that the imaginative impulse that emerges from the structural technique is symbolic of the richness contributed by Sachs the artist to the more prosaic life of Sachs the man?

Whether or not we attach any importance to such a comparison, it is obvious, from the musical point of view, that this is the first passage we have examined in which every element of the technique points to the motion as within the horizontalized chord. This leads to the assumption, which must be confirmed by further investigation, that in those instances in which there is no conflict between the musical and dramatic or the musical and psychological impulses, Wagner preserved the integrity of the musical structure.

In approaching the second chorale phrase, the third section of the form, we find a difference between the treatment here and in the chorale proper (Act III, Scene V). In the chorale, in which there is no interruption between the phrases, the D major chord that ends the first phrase is retained through the first two measures of the second. Here, however, the long extension of the D major chord makes it necessary to terminate the prolongation with the conclusion of the Cobbler's Song and to start the new phrase on the tonic G major chord.

The entrance of the tonic chord ushers in the third section of the form.

224

Richard Wagner

Its structural function, however, connects it with the opening I–II–V progression that it concludes. Thus it is the focal point of the two harmonic progressions underlying these measures. It is the end of one and the beginning of the other and thus binds the entire motion together into a clear-cut demonstration of structural unity.

Since the main point of our investigation was to find out whether the expansion of the motivic phrases affected the coherence of the structural motion, we have found the necessary evidence in the two strongly outlined harmonic progressions and in the sharply defined prolongation of the D major chord in the Cobbler's Song. They demonstrate that in spite of the significance of the motives and the unusual treatment of the Cobbler's Song, ·the structural outline remains intact.

Although from this point of view there is little need for further discussion, there are a few aspects of the technique in the second chorale phrase that are unusual and should not be overlooked. The first of these concerns the repetitions of the structural descent from G to D, in the first chorale phrase, as embellishing motions of D in the third section. Since the top voice has already descended to D, these repetitions cannot have structural implications. Yet Wagner introduced them with such explosive force as to create a doubt as to their actual functions as embellishments and give a momentary impression that they constitute a structural top voice. The extraordinary impulse Wagner has applied to these descents, G–F♯–E–D, is a significant factor in the motion, since it heightens the connection between the two chorale phrases by recalling the structural motion of the first phrase before the further descent from D to G begins in the second. In this way he welded the two motions that make up the top voice into a closer structural unit and clearly indicated the organic nature of the two phrases.

Turning to the bass to confirm this reading, we find a prolonged motion from the D major chord (measure 44) to the inverted G major chord (measure 50), within which the embellishing motions in the top voice occur. Thus in neither of the repetitions of the structural top-voice descent does G appear in connection with a tonic chord, but only with the passing chords that expand the bass descent from D to B. This is significant, since it shows that these repetitions are prolongations of D of the structural top voice just as the chords in which they appear are prolongations of the bass descent from D to B.

We have dwelled on the unusual tendencies in the treatment to prove

225

Challenge to Musical Tradition

that the D, to which the structural top voice descends (measure 24), and the D, on which the descent to G starts (measure 50), are the same in spite of the melodic repetitions that occur in the intervening measures. This defines a structural line of an octave in which the wide expansion of D gives rise to the melodic content of the Cobbler's Song and the first eight measures of the second chorale phrase. It further reveals how the horizontalization of the D major chord provides the middle section of a three-part form.

However, in clarifying the structural aspects of the technique, we should not overlook the originality of the treatment or the amazing ingenuity of the prolongations. Furthermore, the passage reveals a conception of form that Wagner inherited from his predecessors. Here form is not superimposed on the material, but develops side by side with the material in a unity of purpose carried out by the melodic, rhythmic, contrapuntal, and harmonic factors.

Finally, the prelude offers substantial proof of Wagner's technical ability to keep within the structural outlines of a single tonality while enlarging the framework to meet his own specific needs. This structural coherence has a function outside of its musical significance; that is, its psychological implications. The prelude begins and ends on the motive of Renunciation, which serves as an introduction and postlude to the three-part form it circumscribes. Is it not also renunciation, from a psychological point of view, that impels Sachs the man to find an outlet in Sachs the artist? We have seen that the chorale phrases and the Cobbler's Song have been woven together into a single structural· organism through the expansion of the dominant chord of a I–II–V–I harmonic progression. Is it wishful thinking to believe that in this structural unity Wagner has symbolized the fusion of the artistic and practical elements in Sachs's nature, through which the spirit of resignation is turned into a genuine creative effort?

It is quite true, as Newman points out, that no one hearing the prelude for the first time could possibly grasp the subtlety of Wagner's intentions. But who can hear any work for the first time and immediately understand the fundamental significance of the music?

Wagner has clarified his purpose for all those who desire more than a superficial study of this prelude. He has reinforced the psychological associations through his emphasis of the musical connections. He has intensified the dramatic significance without sacrificing the musical integ-

Richard Wagner

rity. Finally, he has written a prelude which, divorced from all relation to the text, stands on its own feet as an illustration of those principles that apply to the forms of abstract music.

In our third illustration we find a work of a totally different nature. Here, as in the two preceding preludes, our interest centers mainly, although not entirely, on the techniques Wagner has used to achieve the dramatic and psychological effects of the music. Is there a clearly defined structural organism, as in the prelude to *Die Meistersinger,* or do the techniques indicate certain contradictions in the structural and prolonging motions such as we found in the prelude to *Parsifal?*

THE PRELUDE TO *TRISTAN*

Although this prelude has long been a bone of theoretical contention, it is admitted that as a whole *Tristan und Isolde* is the most perfect demonstration of Wagner's genius, as it is the greatest achievement of the romantic impulse. We may react differently to it today from the audience of the nineteenth century. For some, it may afford the opportunity for an emotional debauch or serve as an escape drama; for others, the music may be too redolent of the lush and sensuous spirit of a past era, too remote from the realism of present-day thought, or too opposed to the musical credos and techniques of contemporary works to have a definite place in their musical life. Yet whatever quarrel we may have with the romantic nature of the drama or the highly sensual character of the music, once having accepted the premise that it was Wagner's intention to write such a work, there can be no difference of opinion as to his attainment of his goal. Had Wagner written no other work, he would have achieved a type of music that set him apart from every other composer of his time, and it is probable that his influence on the composers who followed would have been equally great. *Tristan* is unique, and its appearance on the musical scene must have had an effect on a nineteenth-century audience comparable to the first performance of Stravinsky's *Le Sacre du Printemps.*

Much has been written about *Tristan,* about Wagner's alteration style, his use of retardations and suspensions, the intense fervor of his chromaticism, the symphonic nature of the scenes and acts, and so on *ad infinitum.* Each chord succession has been the occasion of verbal warfares, each motive the basis of violent discussions, and the whole drama a foundation for hysterical outpourings that divided musicians into two groups — those who were pro-*Tristan* and those who were anti-Wagner.

Challenge to Musical Tradition

In fact it is possible that no other single work of any one composer aroused such stormy and violent reactions as *Tristan*.

There are many good reasons for these reverberations, especially if we conjure up the social as well as the musical conventions of Wagner's own day. First of all there was the natural cleavage between the adherents of the so-called classic and romantic styles. There were even those self-styled romanticists who decried the unconventional aspects of Wagner's *Tristan* technique. There were the puritans, both moral and musical, for whom the loosely-veiled implications of the second act were a sacrilege to art and innocence. In addition there were those for whom music was not a means but an end in itself, who deplored the subjugated state into which it had fallen to serve Wagner's dramatic intentions. These and many additional reactions helped to foment the emotional storm that *Tristan* aroused.

Today when we can approach this work from a calm and unprejudiced point of view, there is no difference of opinion as to the unique quality of Wagner's achievement. No one will deny that *Tristan* is an extraordinary example of the complete unification of the dramatic, psychological, and musical impulses. Although some may contend that Wagners' choice of subject, a historic legend, in which the two main characters show pathological symptoms, is responsible for the new pathological tendencies in the music, this should not affect our estimate of the work as a whole. Wagner chose a situation into which he could pour out his own emotional frustrations, and was enough of a genius to discover a type of music that so adequately portrayed his yearnings and desires that his union of word, action, even unconscious desire, is an achievement of the highest order.

At this time Wagner had turned from the philosophy of conquest to Schopenhauer's philosophy of renunciation. The drama, therefore, becomes a struggle between the worldly and material attitude, as embodied in *Tristan*, and the spiritual ecstasy of renunciation in death, typified by Isolde. We also find evidence of this new spirit of resignation in Wotan's submission to Siegfried, Hans Sachs's yielding to Walther, and King Mark's acceptance of fate in the final scene of the drama.

In *Tristan* this atmosphere of suspense, with the renunciation of earthly joys for the moment of spiritual bliss that comes with oblivion, not only dominates the drama, but is the motivating musical factor as well. It is the origin of the retardations and suspensions, the accented chromatic passing tones, the altered chords, the restless drive that enters with the

Richard Wagner

Love motive in its ascending and descending countermotions. It is the conflict between two forces, of which Isolde through her mystic understanding eventually becomes the stronger, bringing Tristan from the harsh light of day into the still, quiescent beauty of the night, the land of Nirvana.

The prelude, with its exposition of the motives of Love, the Glance, Tristan the Hero, the Love Potion, and Longing for Death, outlines the basic plot of the drama and establishes an emotional chiaroscuro that has been achieved by no other composer. Here it is not so much what Wagner has done as how he has done it. As proof of this, the reader should turn to the *grave* of the first movement of the Beethoven sonata, Opus 13, in which the phrases in measures 7 and 8 bear a striking resemblance to the Love motive of *Tristan*. Yet Beethoven's treatment is so different that by comparison, it highlights those aspects of Wagner's music that are the result of his individual personality.

From the different opinions concerning the tonality defined by the prelude, it would seem as though Wagner's desire to inject into the music the same mood of suspense that dominates the drama has led to the use of techniques that have created some confusion among his interpreters. This is due largely to the fact that he stressed the neighbor notes and passing tones, but gave little impulse to the chord tones that define the motion and the tonality. For example, in the first three measures, F, a neighbor note, bears more weight than E, the fifth of the A minor chord; G♯, the neighbor of A, is accented more than A, the chord tone; A♯, a passing tone, is placed on the strong beat, while B, the chord tone, follows on a weak beat. The same technique used in the succeeding repetitions of the motive is responsible for creating eleven measures of such poignant intensity that the emotional crescendo tends to obscure the tonal reflections. In fact the effect of the prelude is so overpowering that many of the most ardent Wagnerites are more concerned with its Freudian implications than with its musical significance.

For us, however, for whom the prelude is an outstanding example of Wagner's artistic and technical achievements, the music is the all-absorbing question and the discussion of the symbolism secondary. We must find out if, and where, the suspensions and retardations affect the structural motion; why Wagner has repeated the motive three times and then changed to a new rhythmic form; what relation these various motives have to each other and to the structure of the whole; and finally, if there

229

is a motion within the outlined chord that gives expression to the A minor-major tonality.

EXAMPLE 71

Although the illustration is limited to the first twenty measures of the prelude, it is sufficiently typical for us to regard the techniques as representative of Wagner's treatment in the remaining measures.

To clarify this passage and the top-voice motion it defines, the chord tones have been differentiated from the passing tones by indicating them as half notes irrespective of the time values they denote in the music. When combined, these half notes reveal an ascent from A of the opening measure (shown in a lower register) to A of the F major chord (measure 17), a space of an octave. This ascent is attained through four phrase-

Richard Wagner

groups, which, shorn of neighbor notes and chromatic passing tones, show a motion of A–B (measures 1–3), B–C–D (measures 6–7) D–E–F♯ (measures 8–15), G♯–A (measures 16–17). Since measures 12–15 are a duplication of measures 8–11, they have been omitted in the illustration.

Because these seventeen measures should define the start of a structural motion, if one emerges, and because they introduce the most significant motive of the music-drama and build up the emotional suspense that is the keynote of the prelude, it is essential for us to understand their musical as well as psychological meaning.

The problems to which they give rise are: (1) By what technical means has Wagner converted an ascent of an octave into a motion of such power and tension? (2) What is the structural motion that supports the top-voice ascent? (3) What is the function of the F major chord that provides the climax of the ascending motion? Let us take up each question in turn.

The dynamic character of the top voice has been achieved through the tremendous stress applied to the chromatic passing tones, as well as to the inherent contrast between the ascending and descending figures that together comprise the motive. In addition the half-tone descents in the bass, F–E, A♭–G, and C–B, exert a pressure on the second chord in each group that also stimulates the tension in the motion.

We come now to the second point, the harmonic framework underlying the top-voice ascent. The salient points emphasized in the three statements of the motive are the veiled A minor chord (measure 1), the E major chord (measure 3), the G major chord (measure 7), and the B major chord (measure 11). Here the emphasis of the B major chord is much stronger than that of the preceding chords. First, the two measures that comprise the motive are repeated in a higher register, after which E♯ and F♯ in the top voice are given out twice, thus prolonging the motive to six measures. This points to the B major chord as the direct goal of these fifteen measures, in a motion from the tonic A minor to its altered supertonic. From this point of view, the E major chord (measure 3) is not a structural but a prolonging dominant, through which the motion from the tonic to supertonic is expanded. In the fifths outlined by the A minor and E and B major chords, the fifth between E and B has been converted into two thirds by the introduction of the G major chord.

The entrance of the F major chord after the dominant chord, E major, offers a problem for which the music is not the only solution. This is a typical Wagner substitution of the submediant for the tonic, to inject into

231

EXAMPLE 72

the music the tension and suspense of the drama. The use of the tonic, which the progression I–II–V leads us to expect, would represent a complete fulfillment of the motion within the A minor chord. This would be contrary to the note of frustration that provides the primary plot interest and the conflicts of the drama. Therefore the presence of the F major chord undoubtedly can be attributed to Wagner's desire to express in the music the same lack of resolution and fulfillment that motivates the drama. It delays the conclusion of the motion by replacing a chord of structural import with a chord of prolongation and thus leaves the motion incomplete and pendent.

This F major chord introduces the motive of the Glance, a vital factor in the unfolding of the drama and also a means of prolcnging the space between the F and A major chords (measures 17–22). The motive starts on A, a middle voice of the F major chord, and climbs to G, the top voice of the inverted C major chord (measure 20), and thus stimulates the descent into C♯, a middle voice of the A major chord.

The question that now confronts us is: What is the status of this A major chord to which the motion is directed? Is it the long-delayed tonic of the progression for which the F major chord is a substitute, or if not, what is its function in the passage?

232

Richard Wagner

Although this A major chord is a tonic, it gives no feeling of bringing the motion to a conclusion. On the contrary, it is so closely interwoven with the motivic impulse and its appearance is so transitory that its weak effect does not support its status as a structural chord of the main harmonic progression. In fact, as we hear this passage, the A major chord is touched on so lightly that it gives us no feeling of stability, but on the contrary carries the motion on to the B major chord that follows. Since its function, according to our aural impression, is not structural, what purpose does it serve?

First of all it has a psychological significance that cannot be overlooked. The doubt surrounding its status is in itself a fresh stimulus to the suspense and tension of the motion, since it provides a momentary glimpse of the fulfillment that is to come only with the strongly outlined motion to the final A major chord, the structural tonic. In addition it gives the effect of a second attempt to achieve the tonic, which also is frustrated. There is, however, a musical explanation of its function that justifies its psychological value. Since the structural tendency of this A major chord is doubtful, let us examine the motion from the F to the B major chord to see whether it reveals a different and more convincing role for the A major chord to play.

Graph B indicates that the descent from A into C♯, a middle voice of the A major chord, introduces C♯ as a passing tone between C and D♯ of the F and B major chords. According to this reading, the A major chord exercises not the harmonic function of a tonic, but the prolonging function of a passing chord. The bass motion tends to confirm this explanation, since it shows a clear-cut descent by fifths, F—B—E—A, which points to the connection of the F and B major rather than the F and A major chords. But this motion offers an unusual type of harmonic progression. The submediant F major chord does not return to the dominant in a conventional deceptive cadence (in reality only a neighbor-note motion), but instead passes to the supertonic B major chord. The F major chord is too strongly stressed, both as the goal of the top-voice ascent and through its motion to the B major chord, for it to be regarded as a harmonic prolongation or a chord of harmonic emphasis. It is so clearly the *deus ex machina* of the entire motion, the means of achieving the dramatic suspense, that we cannot deny its structural status as a submediant. On the other hand, coming after a well-established I—II—V progression, how can we account for the F and B major chords as of structural significance?

233

It is apparent that there is an inconsistency in the motion, which is the result of Wagner's use of the F major chord; that it is due primarily to the psychological effect produced by this chord is equally evident. It is clear that the F major chord creates a kind of interruption in both the structural top voice and the bass that gives an entirely new function to the submediant chord. Because of this effect, it is impossible to hear this chord only as a prolonging fifth to the B major chord or to hear the motion from the E major chord (measure 16) to the final dominant as a prolongation of the E major chord. To accept the A major chord (measure 22) as a structural tonic would solve the entire problem of this motion. However, the impulse of the A major chord as a passing chord to the supertonic is so much stronger than its effect as a tonic that to regard it as a structural agent would provide a solution contradicted by its function in the music.

Therefore we must attribute the extraordinary character of the progression to the psychological results of the F major chord. In fact it so obviously injects into the music the dramatic implications of the text that it is fair to assume that the deviation from the structural norm was not the result of technical vagueness, but rather a deliberate attempt to convey in the prelude the suspense and frustration that dominate the entire drama. There is a clarity to the motion that leaves little doubt, in spite of its unusual character, as to either Wagner's intentions or the nature of the progression. Therefore the meaning of these measures is obscured only if we regard each chord as a harmonic entity and each neighbor note and passing tone as an integral part of a chord structure.

The new and original aspects of the treatment are the result primarily of Wagner's conception of music as a pictorial and emotional agent. It is his intuitive recognition of the fact that music can penetrate beyond the spoken word and convey an impression for which words are inadequate that differentiates the nature of his treatment from any other composer's.

In view of this achievement Wagner's structural deviations may appear to be of little consequence, since they reflect the major issues of the drama. Their importance, however, lies in the influence they may exert on Wagner's successors and the effect the application of such techniques to absolute music may have on tonality.

The prelude provides the most typical example of Wagner's chromatic style, but there are other passages in *Tristan* that offer an opportunity to determine the effect of such intense chromaticism on the structural motion.

Richard Wagner

WAGNER'S USE OF CHROMATICISM

Since the general characteristic of the treatment in *Tristan* is the intense use of chromaticism, the problem of selection is difficult. Almost any passage chosen at random would illustrate the chromatic tendencies in the technique, but it is necessary to show instances in which the chromaticism does not affect the structural clarity as well as some in which its imprint is evident. Therefore we have taken two illustrations, each based on a different technique with varying effects on the tonal coherence, as indicative of the general tendencies in the treatment.

The first of these is the motive of Tristan the Hero on which the fifth scene in Act I opens. This is Tristan's first entrance. Consequently the motive that heralds his appearance suggests the qualities indicative of his character and his worldly position. In the treatment, however, Wagner has indicated the tension and agitation with which Tristan meets Isolde.

In his interesting study of Wagner's techniques, Ernst Kurth [11] has cited this passage and offered an explanation of its meaning. Since the author is not in agreement with Kurth's conclusions, the motive also serves to demonstrate two different means of approach, one based entirely on a harmonic analysis, the other on the principles of harmony and counterpoint as providing the chords of structure and prolongation that establish tonality.

Let us first turn to Kurth's explanation of the passage. His analysis is given directly below the music. "The cadence here is not simple. Eb minor is the underlying tonality, the tonic of which does not appear at the beginning, the end, or in the middle of the phrase. The sequence of the harmonies is developed under the static organ-point effect of Ab, which, therefore, should not be considered as a note in the harmony if one is to understand the tonal relationships. Accordingly the first chords are Cb—Eb—Gb and Bb—D—F (Eb VI and V); the end of the fourth measure and the first two quarters of measure 5 bring the chord of Bb—Db—Fb, a diminished triad, as an applied dominant, followed by the two positions of the Cb major chord in measures 5 and 6, again the submediant. In this same sixth measure the chord of F—Ab—Cb—Eb (Eb II) enters on the second quarter, and measure 7 closes with the dominant Bb major chord." [12]

Although Kurth has made a valuable study of Wagner's chromatic style, in this instance he begins his analysis with a chord in the third

[11] *Romantische Harmonik* (Paul Haupt, 1920).   [12] *Ibid.,* p. 125.

235

Challenge to Musical Tradition

measure and ignores the opening F minor chord on which the motive starts. Yet the music shows that this F minor chord has been approached from the C major chord of the preceding passage with its effect of an applied dominant. Brushing aside this F minor chord and the strongly emphasized A♭ that follows, Kurth selects a second inversion of the C♭ major chord as the point on which to establish a progression within the E♭ minor tonality.

There might be some justification for this reading if Kurth were consistent, showing that measures 3–6 represent a motion from the second inversion (with G♭ in the bass) to the root position of the submediant C♭ major chord. Instead, he has regarded each chord as a harmonic entity, without defining the motion within the phrase or its connection in the passage. The most flagrant omission, however, is the lack of any reference to the opening F minor chord on which the motivic impulse starts.

The close of Scene IV on a C major chord brings so much emphasis

EXAMPLE 73

236

to this opening chord of F minor that we cannot disregard this F minor chord in a discussion of the measures that follow. It is clearly the start of a motion that concludes on a B♭ major chord. Whether its function is that of a supertonic of the E♭ minor chord or a minor dominant of the B♭ major, we cannot tell from these measures. It is only in the subsequent repetitions of the motive that its definite function is revealed. However, irrespective of its specific status, as the start of a motion to the B♭ major chord, it is a vital factor in the motive. Furthermore, since it reappears in an altered form directly before the B♭ major chord enters, it is logical to assume that the measures that separate the opening F minor chord from its altered form are prolongation and thus without harmonic significance.

These intervening measures (3–6) can be understood as a motion within the C♭ major chord, from a second inversion with G♭ in the bass to its root position. From this point of view the chords of B♭ major and minor, which occur between two positions of the C♭ chord, do not have the harmonic significance, Kurth has indicated, since they are passing chords within the outlined C♭ chord. The question that now arises concerns the status of this expanded C♭ major chord and its function in the motion.

The top voice of this C♭ chord outlines a motion from E♭ to G♭ (graph A). Since G♭ passes to F of the altered F chord, it appears as though E♭ and G♭ are neighbor notes of F in a widely expanded embellishing motion. It is also possible to regard the C♭ chord as a means of introducing C♭ as a passing tone between C♮ and B♭ in the middle voice of the F minor and B♭ major chords.

There is a second explanation, however, and to the author, at least, this is more convincing. It is based on the recognition of A♭ not only as an organ point, but also as an essential element of the chord structure. This interpretation of the status of A♭ is borne out by its role in the repetitions of the motive in which the top voice begins on A♭.

Graph B shows A♭ in two connections, the first as the third of the F minor chord. Its retention, however, in combination with the tones C♭–E♭–G♭, suggests that it also serves as the root of the seventh chord. The horizontalization of this chord, in which there is a descent from G♭, a middle voice, through E♭ and C♭ to A♭ in the bass, provides the prolongation that expands the space between the opening F minor and the altered seventh on F (measure 6). We have seen that E♭ and G♭, which outline the top voice, are neighbors of F, to which G♭ passes when A♭ is reached in the bass. This suggests that the entire prolongation is due to the substitution of G♭, a neighbor note, for F, the root of the chord. Thus the entire passage consists of a motion from the F minor through the diminished seventh chord on F, to the B♭ major chord at the close. Since the prolonging chord provides E♭ and G♭ as neighbor notes in the top voice and C♭ in the middle voice as a passing tone between C♮ and B♭, its function is that of a neighbor-passing chord.

In the treatment of this motive, there appears to be none of the contradictions that Kurth found because of the omission of the E♭ minor chord. This brings up the question of tonality and whether the omission of the E♭ chord is not an indication that, in connection with the succeeding phrases, the motive constitutes a prolonging motion rather than a motion within the E♭ tonality. To find a solution to this problem, let us examine the three repetitions of the motive that follow.

EXAMPLE 74

Graph A represents the actual motion within each of the three statements of the motive. It is obvious that the motion F—B♭, outlined in the first phrase, is paralleled by the motion A♭(G♯)—C♯ in the second phrase. The final progression, however, differs in that the motion of B—F♯—B defines a completed motion within the B minor-major chord. Each of these phrases can be explained in terms of its own motion, but what is their structural significance if we link them together?

In graph B it becomes clear that the B♭ and C♯ major chords, which show the tendency of a dominant in their respective phrases, appear as neighbor chords if we consider them in relation to the chords that follow. Their embellishing function is indicated in the motion from the F to the B minor chord. Here, the A♭ minor chord is the essential factor in that it divides the space into two groups of minor thirds, F—A♭, and through its enharmonic exchange, G♯—B. Here the A♭ chord serves as a pivot on which the motion between the F and B minor chords is effected.

It is apparent that there is no evidence in this larger motion of the E♭ minor tonality suggested by the opening phrase. Instead of serving as a supertonic of the E♭ minor chord or as a minor dominant of the B♭ major, the opening F minor chord functions as a prolonging fifth through which Wagner moves from the C major chord that concludes the preceding scene to the B minor chord of the final phrase, the dominating influence of the measures that follow. The use of the F minor rather than F major chord is exceptional, but it may be due to the greater tension the F minor chord injects into the motion. The unusual aspect of the treatment, however, is the contradiction between the strength of the B♭ and C♯ major chords that conclude the motion of their respective phrases and their non-essential character in the structural motion of the whole. This leads us back to Kurth's analysis and his explanation of the opening phrase.

Kurth's acceptance of this passage as a complete entity is responsible for his hearing it within the E♭ minor tonality. This is typical of the harmonic approach that tends to isolate each phrase rather than to stress its function as part of a larger organism. To regard the opening measures as indicative of the E♭ minor tonality also points to an F♯ major tonality for the second phrase and B minor-major for the closing motive. In twenty measures Wagner would thus have used three different tonalities, no two of which disclose the "harmonic relationship" that is the significant factor in this type of analysis.

Instead, we have heard these measures as an expansion of a motion from the F minor to the B minor-major chord, with the possibility that the F minor chord functions as a prolonging fifth between the preceding C major and the succeeding B minor chords. This accounts for the technique in the smaller phrases and brings these three statements of the motive into a single structural framework. However, although we can integrate these phrases into a small organic unit, it is impossible to determine whether the C major and B minor chords are part of a larger structural motion or whether they are merely connecting links between two scenes.

We found a similar lack of clarity in the status of the C♯, B, and E major chords that bind the Wanderer motive to the preceding scene, and there is an equal uncertainty as to the function of the prolonged E♭ major chord of the Faith motive if we consider it in relation to the passage that follows. This suggests, in some instances at least, that although Wagner has defined the harmonic impulse that outlines these motions, he has not demonstrated whether it is of a structural or prolonging nature. In short, although we can explain a brief passage as a connection between two scenes or as a prolongation of a chord, there is no evidence of the tonality these motions represent, since there is no indication of a structural organism of which they are offshoots. Consequently we can evaluate the techniques only in so far as they define the circumscribed motion within each passage.

We should not regard this as evidence of structural weakness or tonal indecision. It is obvious that in the music-drama, with a constant shift of scene and action, it would be impossible to achieve the structural unity that sustains the larger motions in a movement of a sonata or a symphony. Therefore we have no means of judging Wagner's techniques outside of the motion they define, since the link they form with the preceding scene has neither a structural nor a tonal implication.

Let us turn now to our second illustration, the prelude to Act III. The prelude of fifty-two measures is based entirely on the use of two motives, the four ascending tones of the Love motive and the motive of Longing. As the Love motive is the life-force of Act I that brings ever-increasing momentum to the dramatic climax, the drinking of the love potion, it is fitting that it should be an equally significant figure in the prelude to Act III.

Although the main part of our discussion centers on the latter half of the prelude and the prolongation of the dominant chord, it is also necessary to touch on the opening measures to grasp the full meaning of the passage. Since the motion of the prelude consists only of the repetitions of these two motives, we have an excellent opportunity to find out whether Wagner has used each as a structural entity or whether their psychological connection has been carried over into the music, in which they function as integral parts of a basic structural framework.

Richard Wagner

EXAMPLE 75

Let us start with the first twenty-nine measures, which define a complete motion within the prolonged tonic chord.

Whether we hear the first chord as a subdominant in which the opening tone F has been replaced by a rest to preserve the four tones of the Love motive, or as a supertonic seventh, in neither case does it demonstrate a harmonic function. It serves two purposes, however, both of which are important from a melodic point of view. It provides the first three tones of the Love motive, G—A♭—B♭, and introduces D♭ in a middle voice as a neighbor note of C. Through the new treatment of the Love motive and the dissonant effect of the opening measures, Wagner sharpens the contrast between the world of night, with the quiescent beauty of the preceding act, and the grim reality of the daylight to which Tristan awakens. He achieves this through the effect of the seventh chord, ushering in the motive, and the rhythmic arrangement by which B♭ (measure 2) is heard in connection with the chord of F minor rather than in combination with the preceding chord to which it belongs. These alterations are so subtle that it is easy to overlook the artistry with which Wagner has adapted the motive to reflect the new mood of sadness that pervades the entire act.

The bass motion outlines an expanded I—V—I progression, a harmonic prolongation of the tonic F minor chord. The structural top voice, however, is less clearly defined. The ascent to C in the opening measures suggests that it is the tone on which the top-voice motion begins. On the other hand, the strong emphasis on G in the measures that follow, in which C is revealed as a middle voice, complicates the voice leadings. However, the entrance of D♭ in a higher register, where it appears as a neighbor note of C, as well as its sustained emphasis in the latter half of the prelude, point to C as the structural top voice and G as a middle voice. It is the conflict for supremacy between D♭ and G that offers the main

241

melodic interest in the following example, the concluding measures of the prelude.

The graph in Example 76 indicates that these measures combine with the prolonged tonic chord of the first twenty-nine to outline a widely expanded I—II—V—I progression.

The treatment of the Love motive in these measures differs from that in the preceding example. At the start of the prelude the motive is distributed between two different chords, while in the above passage it occurs within a single horizontalized G minor-major chord. This suggests that the E♮ on which the motive begins is a neighbor of F, the seventh of the chord. This motive provides an interesting problem in the nature of the space it outlines. There is a motion from F to A♭ in which G, the root of the chord, enters as a passing tone between the seventh and ninth. In this instance the dissonances define the space-outlining motion, with a consonance as a passing tone, a reversal of the usual procedure. However, although A♭ is obviously a neighbor note of G, its retention for six measures emphasizes its status as a ninth, leaving little doubt that it is a vital factor in the motive and that G serves the less significant function of a passing tone.

Nevertheless, although A♭ is retained as a middle voice, we see that the top voice climbs to D♮. This ascent from F to D♮ within the G minor-major chord is an answer to the descent from D♭ to F in the final measures of the preceding passage. Thus D♭ to F, a motion from a top into a middle voice, is balanced by a motion from F to D♮, an ascent from a middle to a top voice, which together provide the technical means by which the top-voice motion from D♭ to D♮ has been prolonged.

In the following measures the dominant is achieved through horizontalization, in a parallelism of the supertonic technique. Again the neighbor note D♭ is given greater melodic importance than the chord tone C, with the result that we hear a motion from D♮ of the preceding phrase (measure 37) to D♭ that is retained throughout the entire prolongation of the C major chord and passes to C only with the entrance of the F minor chord. The expansion of the dominant chord is due primarily to the struggle for supremacy between D♭ and G, in which D♭ first enters as a middle voice (measures 39–46) and then is shifted to the bass (measure 47) and finally to the top voice (measure 49), after which a descent of an octave brings it into its proper register in connection with C of the final F minor chord. There is a similar transfer of E♮ from a middle voice to the

Richard Wagner

Example 76

243

bass (measures 43–45), after which it again appears as a middle voice when Db enters in the bass. Here the ascent from G to its octave is paralleled by the descent from Db to its octave.

The graph indicates this exchange of voices and shift of registers and shows how these techniques stress the neighbor note Db as an important melodic factor by its entry in one or another of the voice parts.

It is also necessary, however, to get a clear impression of the motion that underlies the entire prelude, so that we may realize both the organic nature of the conception and the ingenious means by which the basic structure is expanded to fifty-two measures. The following graph, in which only the essential elements of the melodic and harmonic outlines are indicated, demonstrates the structural foundation of these fifty-two measures.

EXAMPLE 76A

This illustration of Wagner's use of two motives to prolong a I–II–V–I progression is a remarkable instance of his creative artistry and technical facility. It is an amazing development both of the neighbor-note treatment and of the possibilities offered by the exchange of voices and the transfer of register. Although no one of these techniques is an innovation in itself, as we have seen in the variety of works in which they already have occurred, nevertheless Wagner has found a means for adapting them to his own specific needs that differentiates his treatment from that of preceding composers.

In contrast to some of the passages we have examined, this prelude shows a closely knit structural organism, which, through the harmonic progression, outlines and maintains the F minor tonality. Furthermore, although it is the repetitions of two motives that effect the prolongation of the F minor, G minor-major, and C major chords, the emphasis of these motives neither obscures the clarity of the motion nor infringes on the tonal boundaries established by the progression. In short, the con-

244

Richard Wagner

stant use of the motives has not led to techniques that weaken the structural unity, but, on the contrary, to techniques that, as we have seen, heighten and intensify the prolonging motions. This is due mainly to the use of chromaticism and the color and richness it brings both to the melodic figure and to the basic harmonic progression. The emphasis of Ab and Db instead of the chord tones G and C is one aspect of the treatment that reveals not only the strong chromatic tendencies in the technique, but their predominance in the prolongation of the structural outline. The expansion of these neighbor notes within the chords they embellish and the retention of Db so that its resolution comes with the F minor instead of the C major chord are innovations whose results are too important to overlook. In view of these new trends in the technique and the marked chromaticism of the motivic figures, the clarity of both the prolonging and the structural motions stands out in contrast to the treatment in those examples in which the strong chromatic influence of the motive left its imprint on the expanding and structural techniques.

Among the various examples we have examined as the basis of our discussion, we have found some in which the structural motion is clearly outlined and the prolonging techniques unclear. In others there was a structural ambiguity that resulted in a vagueness in the expansions. In the example from *Die Meistersinger* and in this last prelude, both the structural and the prolonging motions are sharply defined. However, although there are many conflicting elements in the technique as a whole, one aspect of the treatment is consistent throughout — the fidelity of the music to the text and action.

To achieve this identity of the impulses that underlie the various music-dramas, there are times, as in the Wanderer and the Magic Sleep motives, when Wagner has sacrificed the clarity of the tonality to the dramatic necessity, with a resultant weakening of the prolonging motions. There are other instances, as in the motive of Faith, in which the repetition of the phrase gains such melodic momentum that it creates a confusion as to the actual nature of the harmonic progression, or as in the opening prelude to *Tristan*, in which, to achieve a mood of emotional intensity, the melody and rhythm have been robbed of their normal balance and clarity and Wagner has invested them, together with the structural motion, with a purposeful co-ordination of abnormal intentions that sets forth the mood of conflict and suspense.

In this discussion there have been more allusions to passages from

Tristan than from the other music-dramas because *Tristan* is the climax of Wagner's struggle to make music "a means of expression" in which it became the end as well. The music of *Tristan* is unique; it has no counterpart. It not only represents the world of tone; it is a combination of tone, emotion, drama, symbolism, and association. It is not subordinated to the drama in the sense that the text predominates, since the music itself is an embodiment of the emotional conflicts of the drama. This is the all-important point. Although, by intensifying its potentialities as a dramatic and emotional agent, Wagner extended the range of musical expression, at the same time he undermined its strength and emasculated its function as an independent and wholly self-sufficient force. Therefore, although on the one hand Wagner invested music with qualities and characteristics it never before had possessed, on the other he robbed it of its inalienable right to remain within the confines of its own territory and to function according to those principles that govern the tonal world, divorced from all outside influences.

No one can deny that Wagner attained his artistic goal, since the music of *Tristan* is itself emotion, its ebb and flow, its rise and fall in the transformation of physical attraction into spiritual exaltation. In addition, it is the climax of chromatic daring within the stronghold of tonality, as it is the final word in the chapter of nineteenth-century expressionism.

As *Tristan* is the end of all that was, so it is the beginning of all that followed. It was the close of a period in which diatonicism still remained the dominant factor, with chromaticism as a contending element adding richness and color, motion, suspense, and intensity to the structural foundation. But those who were to succeed Wagner did not view the struggle as the final conquest of diatonicism, but instead they saw only the newly won gains of chromaticism and erected it as the standard to which they rallied. Nor did they recognize what strong tonal tendencies in the treatment survived the impact of these chromatics, even though the chromatics themselves frequently complicated the prolonging motions. These composers saw *Tristan* as the road to the future; for them the past was gone — dead. They failed to realize that Wagner's connection with the past alone sustained those innovations that were his contribution to the future.

Although our discussion has centered on only one aspect of Wagner's treatment, the influence of the motive on the principles of structural coherence, it is clear that within a given area, the preludes in the examples cited from *Die Meistersinger* and *Tristan,* Wagner did remain

246

Richard Wagner

within the boundaries of tonality. That these boundaries have been narrowed, that in many cases the tonality shifts with the changing environment of a new scene, is equally true, but it is more or less inevitable in a work such as a music-drama, in which the principles that apply to a sonata or symphony cannot be maintained. Therefore, that Wagner, in his new conception of music, achieved coherence even within the smaller outlines of the motive is in itself the measure of his artistic strength.

The influence of Wagner on the music that followed was due to the fact of his creating an idiom that was an individual expression of his musical credo. Others made those aspects of his technique that originated in his use of music as emotion a point of departure from the so-called traditions of the past. Unfortunately, however, they mistook his extreme use of chromatics for a negation of diatonicism, his enharmonic exchanges for a denial of tonality, and his adaptation of the musical to the dramatic or psychological impulses for an overthrow of the principles of structural unity.

This is the tragedy of Wagner — that in spite of his amazing extension of the older techniques, he invalidated their function; in spite of his adherence to tonality, his lesser deviations have led to its breakdown; and in spite of his use of chromaticism within the realm of diatonicism, he gave rise to a form of chromatic supremacy that resulted in atonality.

CHAPTER VII

Debussy

EXTENSION AND ADAPTATION *of older techniques within tonality.*

Conflicting interpretations of techniques offered by present-day musi-

cians. Use of old technique outside the tonal framework. Experiments

in new techniques; their effect on structural coherence.

DISCUSSION of the music of Claude Debussy projects us into a world far removed from the legendary figures that peopled Wagner's music-dramas. It brings into juxtaposition two composers with completely contrasting musical personalities and equally diverse musical styles. This dissimilarity is all the more interesting in view of the fact that both of these composers found their musical inspiration in an extra-musical source. Many personal and artistic factors made for the individual stylistic expression of these composers. Basic elements of contrast are the differences in emotional stimulus and emotional reaction.

Wagner is concerned with the dramatic and psychological aspects that give rise to conflicts in human relationships. He interprets these with an emotional surge, an overwhelming power and vitality, that engulf the listener in the ebb and flow of his music. Debussy, on the other hand, is motivated by a poetic concept. His style has a delicacy and restraint that are inherent in his natural reserve, just as the passionate outpourings of Wagner are a natural outlet for his emotional experiences. Again, Debussy, on the whole, is stimulated by the ever-changing moods of nature rather than by human conflicts. It is the clouds, the sea, night, a sunset, reflections on the water, the forest, that arouse in him an aesthetic and emotional response to which his music gives expression.

Debussy frequently voiced his recognition of the strong kinship between music and nature. For example, he said: "Music is the expression of the movement of the waters, the play of curves described by changing breezes. There is nothing more musical than a sunset. He who feels what

Debussy

he sees will find no more beautiful example of development in all that book which, alas, musicians read too little — the book of nature." [1]

This, together with other statements of Debussy, serves as a clue to his art. It is a frank admission that his creative urge was largely stimulated by visual and other sensory impressions. His problems arose from the necessity of achieving a musical style in which he could describe these impressions rather than from problems that lie within the realm of abstract music. We need only turn to the titles of his works, even the smaller preludes, to find evidence of the fact that it was in extra-musical ideas that Debussy found the source of his inspiration.

Much has been written about the effect of the symbolist and impressionist movements on the nature of Debussy's art. His intimate association with poets and painters who were to foster these new trends in literature and art may well have led him away from the Wagnerian influence, reflected in his early works, to find a new and personal stylistic idiom. Yet, although these movements may have been contributing factors, the individual aspects of Debussy's treatment can be traced to certain definite personal and national characteristics that shaped both his approach to music and the individual quality of his style.

Although many composers before Debussy had reflected the various aspects of nature in their music, their reactions found a more realistic manner of expression in that they attempted to reproduce actual sounds connected with nature. Debussy, on the contrary, was not concerned with finding a musical analogy for a storm, the wind, a bird singing in the forest, raindrops, dawn or sunset, since he was interested primarily in the effect of these phenomena on his emotions. In short, he did not paint a picture of a storm, but through his reaction to it he conveyed his impression of its power and majesty.

This conception of music, in its kinship with nature and painting, was entirely new. Therefore it was inevitable that Debussy should find a means of expression through which he could connote the individual and original aspects of his musical ideas. To blend the raw materials of music, the tones, as a painter mixes the colors on his palette to achieve effects of iridescent light, of shadowy haze, and of dank darkness, demanded either a new use of older methods or the creation of entirely new ones. It is the extension and adaptation of the old as well as the origin of the new that form the basis of our discussion.

[1] Vallas *Theories of Claude Debussy* (Oxford University Press, 1929), p. 8.

Challenge to Musical Tradition

EXTENSION OF THE ESTABLISHED TECHNIQUES

The established techniques were evolved and developed through the use of tonality. They embrace the various means by which a basic structure is transformed into a rich, colorful, and artistic work through the cooperation of the melodic, motivic, rhythmic, contrapuntal, and harmonic functions; in short, the various techniques of structure and prolongation. They are the foundation on which the works of Bach, Haydn, Beethoven, Wagner, and innumerable other composers are built, and they are necessarily an essential element in any expression of the concept of tonality. These concern the arpeggiation of the chord, the neighbor note, transfer of register, passing chords, and the various types of harmonic prolongation.

In examining the works of Debussy, let us start with the use of the arpeggiated chord as a means of expansion, to see how this aspect of the older techniques has been extended to meet the individual characteristics of Debussy's style.

THE HORIZONTALIZED CHORD

The first of these examples is the motive of Golaud's love from the opening scene of *Pelléas et Mélisande*.[2] Here, although the entire motive consists of a single chord, Debussy's treatment of each of the chord tones offers an unusual illustration of the added effect of his extension of the older techniques.

EXAMPLE 77

The bass shows a well-defined outline of the E major triad. In combination with the upper voices, however, we find that with one exception, the triad on E, each of these bass tones serves as the root or member of a seventh chord. Thus the horizontalized triad has become the means of erecting a succession of sevenths.

[2] Vocal score, p. 7. Copyright 1907. Permission for reprint granted by Durand & Cie, Paris, France, and Elkan-Vogel Co., Inc., Philadelphia, Pa., copyright owners.

Debussy

An interesting insight into Debussy's use of the neighbor note is offered in the second chord, in which C♯, the neighbor note, and B, the chord tone, are both present. As a harmonic entity, this chord would indicate a third inversion of the C♯ chord. In relation to the chords that constitute the motion, this chord is shown to be an inverted E major chord, with C♯, a neighbor note of B, in the chords that precede and follow.

Another characteristic feature of the treatment is the retention of F♯ as an unresolved suspension in the final E major chord. This use of a ninth, which does not pass to the chord tone, but is left pendent, is typical of Debussy's technique in many other instances and may be regarded as a form of elision in which the resolution tone is supplied by the listener.

Although Debussy has used the arpeggiated triad as the foundation of the motive, it is obvious that he has employed it to achieve an entirely new and different purpose from what it formerly served. Here the succession of seventh chords, a vertical effect, is stronger than the horizontal effect sustained by the outlined E major chord. The result is that the unity inherent in the chord tones is overshadowed by the dissonant character of the seventh and ninth. Whether or not, in adapting the technique of horizontalization to this purpose, Debussy has weakened the association of the chord tones, is a debatable question, but that he has demonstrated a new possibility to which the outlined chord gives rise cannot be denied.

A further instance of this same treatment occurs in the opening measures of the sarabande in the suite *Pour le Piano*,[3] in which the arpeggiation of the D♯ minor chord is responsible for a succession of sevenths.

EXAMPLE 78

II ————— V

The motion outlined by these two measures is from the seventh chord on D♯ to the G♯ minor chord, a supertonic-dominant progression within

[3] Copyright 1901. Permission for reprint granted by Jean Jobert, Paris, France, and Elkan-Vogel Co., Inc., Philadelphia, Pa., copyright owners.

the C♯ minor tonality. Here the use of the minor dominant is indicative not of a mixture of the G♯ minor and major chords, as we found in the works of Haydn, Beethoven, and Wagner, but of the modal dominant that appears so frequently in Debussy's treatment.

As in the preceding example, the chord on A, the fifth òf the horizontalized D♯ chord, includes both the chord tone and its neighbor note B. The difference, however, lies in the fact that here the neighbor note is stressed, while the chord tone A, to which it returns, enters as the second of a group of triplets. Although in the motive of Golaud the function of C♯ as a neighbor note was more clearly defined, it is equally apparent in this example that B serves in a similar capacity. In fact it is just this deviation in the rhythmic stress that makes for the originality of Debussy's style. It should also be noted that the interval of a third, which outlines the essential tones of the motive F♯–A, E–G♯, is carried out in the emphasis of D♯–F♯ and the inverted third E–G♯ in the bass.

The use of a succession of parallel fifths not only is typical of Debussy's treatment, but is a device which many of his successors, Ravel among others, employed extensively. In this instance the fifths tend to sharpen the individual character of the chords as harmonic entities rather than to emphasize their common origin in the horizontalized D♯ chord. Thus they give a purely contrapuntal technique the effect of a vertical treatment. It is by such means that Debussy has obtained a new and original effect from the use of the arpeggiated chord.

Another instance in which the horizontalized chord gives rise to a typical Debussy treatment is offered in the motive of the Forest from the opening scene of *Pelléas et Mélisande.*[4] The passage is of further interest because it provides an illuminating insight into Debussy's use of the neighbor note.

EXAMPLE 79

Debussy

Although the chord on A (measure 2) might seem to be a minor dominant, the fact that it passes to the F major instead of to the tonic D minor chord negates the possibility that it fulfills a structural function. In this instance it serves only as a chord of prolongation between two F major chords. Its melodic function, however, is to supply G, an essential element in the motive, as an under neighbor note of A, and D, a middle voice, as a passing tone between E and C of the F major chords. Thus its function is that of a neighbor-passing chord. This is an unmistakable illustration of horizontalization as a means of expanding the mediant chord of a tonic-mediant progression.

We come now to Debussy's use of the neighbor note. In the first F major chord, E, a middle voice, appears to be the seventh of the chord. In fact Lenormand explains this F major and the succeeding A minor chord as "chords of the seventh without preparation." [5] Yet if we examine this middle voice closely, we find that E serves as an embellishment of D of the preceding D minor chord. There is a motion from D to E, after which E passes through D to C of the succeeding F major chord in an incomplete neighbor-note motion. Therefore we regard E not as an unprepared seventh, but as an embellishing tone that is identical with the seventh of the F major chord, but whose function is entirely different. Although there is actually nothing new in the role the neighbor note plays, the treatment is sufficiently original to be cited by Lenormand as an illustration of the modern use of discords without preparation. The passage as a whole is built on the outlined tones of the D minor chord, but the characteristic elements of the treatment tend to obscure the horizontalization through the vertical effect that the embellishing and passing tones create.

A more orthodox use of E as a neighbor occurs in the opening measures of this scene, in which there is a complete neighbor-note motion of D—E—D, with E appearing in connection with the C major chord, preceded and followed by the chord of D minor. In the succeeding measures E again appears as a neighbor note of D in the melodic outline of the Fate motive. Since in these two motives, which comprise the first six measures of the opening scene, the status of E is already defined, there is no reason to believe that in the above example, which immediately

---

[5] *Study of Twentieth Century Harmony* (B. F. Wood Music Co., Boston, 1915), p. 44.

Challenge to Musical Tradition

follows measure 6, its function has been changed. It is all the more interesting that in this repetition of the Forest motive Debussy has varied the treatment so that instead of a complete neighbor-note motion we find an incomplete one. Therefore, as a melodic embellishment, there is no reason why E should require preparation.

However, interesting as this passage is, the best illustration of Debussy's use of the neighbor note as an extension of the older technique may be found in the prelude, "The Girl with the Flaxen Hair."

THE NEIGHBOR–NOTE TECHNIQUE

In the preceding chapters we have seen that the neighbor note can serve in both a prolonging and structural capacity. Although Debussy did not invest it with new or different functions, he used it in a manner that, engendered by his own stylistic idiom, deviates from the treatment of his predecessors.

In referring to this work in her brief discussion of the preludes, Mlle Boulanger says: [6] "Like the *Blessed Damozel*, a 'pre-Raphaelite' composition . . . the influence of Chabrier is apparent in the melodic turn of the theme and in the frequent use, in one form or another (measures 9–10, 12–13, 15–16, 18–19, 19–20, 20–21), of the cadential formula which we have previously cited in connection with Chabrier."

Although no one will deny the influence of Chabrier on Debussy, the reference to the cadential formula is hardly an explanation of Debussy's technical treatment in "The Girl with the Flaxen Hair." However, that the reader may judge how large a part this formula does play in the prelude under discussion, the example used by Mlle Boulanger [7] is given below.

EXAMPLE 80

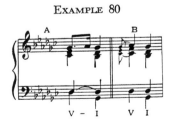

It is obvious that the formula shown in Example 80A is a contraction of Example 80B, in which the change of emphasis applied to the appoggia-

[6] *Rice Institute Pamphlet* (April, 1926), p. 172.   [7] *Ibid.*, p. 168.

turas has given the treatment a new quality, though not a new meaning. However, in addition to Debussy's use of the Chabrier idiom, the main point of our discussion of the following prelude [8] concerns his ingenious use of the neighbor note to prolong the structural motion.

EXAMPLE 81

The melodic figure shows E♮ as a neighbor of D♭, but instead of appearing in the same register, E♮ occurs a seventh below. This might lead to the assumption that E♮ should be heard in connection with G♭–B♭–D♭ as the root of a seventh chord. However, it is obvious that the six tones that constitute the melodic figure are arranged as two triads that have G♭ and B♭ in common. The only distinction between them is that E♮ has replaced D♭, the chord tone, and appears in a lower instead of a top voice.

Challenge to Musical Tradition

The function of E♭ as a neighbor note is evident. The manner in which Debussy has used it is the distinctive feature of the technique. You may recall that in the Valhalla motive (Example 63) Wagner employed a somewhat similar treatment. B♭, the neighbor note, also appears in a different voice and register from A♭, the chord tone, and also gives a faint suggestion of a connection with the preceding triad. The effect, however, is less striking, since B♭ and the A♭ to which it returns lie in the same register. Furthermore, it is the constant reference to E♭ throughout the prelude as an integral part of the melodic figure, an embellishment of the middle-voice motion, and as the root of the E♭ major neighbor chord, the climax of the first six measures, that reveals the originality of Debussy's neighbor-note technique.

The prolongation of the D♭ major chord (measures 5–7) offers some interesting parallelisms in the treatment. There is the use of both the B♭ minor and B♭ major chord as applied dominants, the one in relation to E♭ minor, the other to E♭ major, both neighbor chords. Furthermore, the E♭ major chord does not return to the dominant it embellishes, but proceeds directly to the tonic G♭ major chord. It is possible to hear this E♭ chord as an altered submediant, but its melodic function is so clearly outlined by the status of E♭ in the outside voices that defining it as a neighbor chord gives a truer interpretation of the music.

In the measures that follow, the voice leadings are typical of Debussy's stylistic treatment. The tonic chord enters as a seventh, with F♭ in the bass and G♭ in a middle voice. However, the descent from F♭ to D♭ of the succeeding G♭ major chord (measures 8–10) reveals that F♭ is actually a middle voice, which appears as a bass only because the real bass, the low G♭, shown in parentheses, is withheld until the entrance of the following G♭ chord. Undoubtedly the substitution of F♭ for G♭ gives a new quality and greater tension to the repetition of the melodic figure.

The dominant chord (measure 9) is cited by Mlle Boulanger as an example of the cadential formula. It is clear, however, that G♭ has been retained from the preceding E♭ minor chord, but instead of passing to F it is carried over into the G♭ chord. It is equally obvious that E♭ serves in its customary capacity as a neighbor note. Therefore, although the presence of G♭ and E♭ can be explained from the point of view of voice leading, the effect as a whole is that of the formula. We cannot agree, however, with Mlle Boulanger's reference to measures 12 and 13 as representing a similar use of the Chabrier idiom.

256

Debussy

In the example given by Mlle Boulanger, the two chords show a dominant-tonic relationship in the form of an applied dominant. In measures 12 and 13, both chords are the same G♭ major, so that the term "cadential formula" is not applicable. The first of these chords contains the tones E♭–C♭–A♭, all foreign to the G♭ major chord. Of these, E♭ is again a neighbor of D♭, to which it passes in the next measure; C♭ a neighbor of B♭, from which it comes and to which it returns; and A♭ a neighbor of G♭, which flanks it on either side. These tones are clearly embellishments of the tonic G♭ chord and as such bear no resemblance to the dominant-tonic progression in the preceding measures, of which it is supposed to be a parallel example.

Before concluding this discussion, it is necessary to point out the characteristic seventh chords through which Debussy moves from the G♭ to the C♭ major chord (measures 13–16).

Example 81A

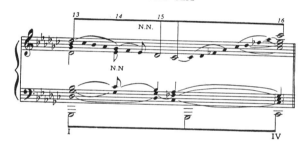

The graph shows that measures 13 and 14 define a motion within the expanded G♭ major chord. Here, E♭ again enters as a neighbor note of D♭ with C♭, a middle voice, an embellishment of B♭. In the music both D♭ and C♭ in the top voice (measure 15) are shown in connection with C♭–F♭–A♭ in the bass. In the graph D♭ appears with D♭–G♭–B♭ as a member of the G♭ major chord to which it obviously belongs. Since its entrance over D♭ in the bass would have resulted in parallel octaves in the outside voices, it is possible to attribute the shift of D♭ to the succeeding chord to the principles of voice leading. As the entire measure is concerned with a motion within the G♭ major chord, it is clear that the seventh chords that effect the descents are passing chords and thus of a contrapuntal origin. This fact does not detract from the new and striking aspect of the treatment, but it negates the theory that these

257

seventh chords have a harmonic function. Thus the innovations are in the prolonging motions, but not in the structural technique. It is also clear that in the following measure, the tones F♭–A♭–C♭, all of which are foreign to the G♭ major chord, can be accounted for on strictly orthodox grounds. The graph shows A♭ to be a passing tone between B♭ of the G♭ chord and G♭ of the C♭ major chord. F♭ functions similarly as a passing tone between G♭ and E♭, while C♭ appears prematurely as an anticipation of C♭ of the C♭ major chord. Thus, instead of waiting until the entrance of the subdominant to reveal C♭ as a structural top voice, Debussy introduced it within the G♭ chord, at the same time retaining D♭, from which it came. Although the effect is new and arresting and reflects the individual tendencies of Debussy's style, it is nevertheless an extension of the older techniques to the requirements of a new and different idiom.

Although the two final measures have been cited as further evidence of Debussy's use of the cadential formula, the fact that the tones in question are passing tones between the G♭ and C♭ major chords makes it problematic whether we should regard this as an example similar to the one offered by Mlle Boulanger. On the other hand the presence of A♭ and F♭ does impart to the G♭ major chord a quality that emphasizes its fifth connection with the C♭ major chord.

The use of the cadential formula, however, is the least significant element of the treatment. Of far greater importance is the extraordinary use Debussy has made of the neighbor note.[9] It gives a distinctive character to the melodic figure, it expands the prolonging motions, and it is the primary means by which the I–V–I–IV progression is extended to sixteen measures.

Although Debussy has injected an entirely new quality into the prelude through the treatment of the neighbor note and the new tendencies in the prolonging motions, these stylistic characteristics have neither obscured nor weakened the essential outlines of the harmonic framework or the basic elements of the tonality. The changes he has made have not negated the older techniques, even though he has adapted them to a different type of musical expression. However, the use of seventh chords, such as we found in the passing motion within the G♭ major chord, is so typical of Debussy's treatment in general that a single example within a small motion is not sufficient evidence for drawing a conclusion as to the effect of such

[9] See *Clair de Lune* and Book II, Prelude V, for a similar emphasis of the neighbor note technique.

passing chords on the structural coherence. Therefore we must turn to other passages, in which the motion is more widely extended, to see whether the nature of the passing chords that fill the space between two members of a harmonic progression intensifies or enervates the function of these members in maintaining the tonal stability.

PASSING CHORDS

The concluding measures of the prelude from the early suite *Pour le Piano* [10] offers an interesting illustration. Here we find a motion that suggests a I—V—I progression in which Debussy has replaced the major with the minor dominant. However, there are two factors that tend to obscure the tonal characteristics of the motion and thus weaken the tonal stability of the progression. These are the passing chords that fill the space between the A and E minor chords and the low bass tones that give a different quality to the chords with which they appear.

EXAMPLE 82

Although these bass tones occur throughout, their presence is so fleeting and their effect so momentary that we must regard them as color tones of embellishment rather than as the roots of their respective chords. From this point of view there is a motion from the tonic A minor to the E minor chord in which the bass descends from A through G♭ and F to E. We come now to the main factor in the treatment — the passing chords that fill the space outlined by the tonic-dominant progression.

The first of these passing chords is an altered seventh on A♭. If this A♭ chord appeared between an A minor and G major chord, we could easily account for its presence. Here, however, it leads to an altered chord on E♭. Since both of these chords are altered, it is impossible to find the connection that exists between the unaltered forms of these same chords.

[10] Copyright 1901. Permission for reprint granted by Jean Jobert, Paris, France, and Elkan-Vogel Co., Philadelphia, Pa., copyright owners.

The entrance of an altered seventh on E♮ further complicates the motion. Why has Debussy introduced B♭ in this E chord when it so obviously weakens the effect of the E minor chord that follows? Furthermore, although the altered chords on A♭ and E♭ are passing chords, do they not create a conflict in the motion that greatly enervates the inherent strength of the tonic-dominant progression? A final contradiction is disclosed by the presence of F in the bass in connection with the E♭ chord. Although it is obvious that F is a passing tone between ˙G♭ and E♮, its entrance in connection with the E♭ chord denotes a new use of a passing tone. It suggests that a passing tone in a space-filling motion may occur in combination with any chord, irrespective of the fact that it is entirely unrelated to the chord in which it appears. This is not an extension of the old technique, but a totally new tendency in the treatment. It might be possible to explain the presence of F as the seventh of an altered G chord by exchanging E♭ for D♯ but for the fact that the preceding A♭ seventh chord points so strongly to the chord of E♭ major.

We must admit that although Debussy has outlined a clear-cut I—V—I progression, the passing chords that fill the space create a prolonging motion whose lack of tonal conviction weakens the structural framework. By means of the passing chords, Debussy has invested the motion with a rich and lustrous color effect, but he has achieved this effect at the expense of tonal coherence.

Let us look further to see whether this is typical of this passage only or whether there are instances in which the passing chords provide a much clearer definition of the structural motion.

Turning to Act IV, Scene III, of *Pelléas et Mélisande*,[11] we find an unusual prolongation of the dominant-tonic progression through the adaptation of various older techniques.

In graph A the repetitions of measures 1, 2, 5, and 6 have been omitted.

We see that the motion from the B to the E major chord is expanded through the introduction of passing chords. The top voice ascends from F♯ to G♯, while the bass climbs from B to E, moving on to G♯, the third of the E major chord. The top voice is extended through the arpeggiation of the tones of the B, C, and A♭ major chords, the enharmonic exchange of A♭ for G♯, and the embellishing motion to which it gives rise.

---

[11] Vocal score, p. 265. Copyright 1907. Permission for reprint granted by Durand & Cie, Paris, France, and Elkan-Vogel Co., Inc., Philadelphia, Pa., copyright owners.

Debussy

EXAMPLE 83

Since the bass also reveals a similar use of arpeggiation, it is apparent that Debussy was employing certain techniques of the past as a means of expanding the progression. The most interesting aspect of the treatment, however, is the adaptation of these techniques to the demands of Debussy's style.

The opening measure is an illustration of this point. Although the top voice indicates the three tones of the B major chord, each of these tones

261

in combination with the lower voices comprises a different chord. Thus Debussy has achieved the color contrast of three different chords within the outline of a single chord. The unusual element in the treatment is that although the inverted F♯ seventh chord has the effect of a dominant of B major, it moves to the inverted G♯ minor passing chord. However, it is a question whether this F♯ chord actually fulfills a harmonic function. The A and C♯ in the middle voices are retained from the preceding D♯ seventh chord, while E in the bass, preceded and followed by D♯, appears to be a neighbor note. Since it comprises two suspensions, a neighbor note and F♯ of the arpeggiated B major chord, its origin seems to be of a contrapuntal nature.

We find a somewhat similar treatment of the arpeggiated tones of the C major chord. For example, G in the top voice is combined with D, a passing tone between D♯ of the B, and C of the C major chord; B♭, a passing tone in the motion from B♮ to G; and F in the bass, a passing tone between F♯ and E. Again it is the passing tones that convert the outlined tones of the C major chord into three different chord effects.

The treatment of the altered seventh chord on D, though different, is equally original. Here the descent from A♭ to E♭ in the outside voices shows E♭ as a neighbor of D♭ in the upper voice, with E♭ in the bass as a passing tone between D and E♮. Furthermore, the retention of C—D—A♭ in the upper voices, while the bass moves to E♮, is an ingenious device through which the embellishment of A♭ delays its exchange for G♯. Thus, although we find the equivalent of the E major chord when E♮ enters in the bass, the retention of A♭ in the top voice permits the introduction of B♭ and C, which preserve the character of the A♭ chord. This postpones the full emergence of the dominant chord until the final measure, when the exchange is made.

This is indeed a remarkable instance of the new possibilities inherent in the older techniques. It shows a use of passing chords that is highly characteristic of Debussy's style. Although there are various innovations in the treatment, each of which indicates an extension or an adaptation of the established techniques, the passing chords that result from the voice leadings neither impede the structural motion nor contradict the nature of the harmonic progression. Herein is the unusual aspect of the treatment — that, while adhering to the older tonal techniques, Debussy has created a rich and colorful effect bearing the imprint of his own artistic personality. He has retained the principles that govern structure and prolongation, but through the character of the prolongation he has invested the structure with a quality reflecting the new tendencies in his style.

The final point in this discussion of the extension of the older methods concerns a vital factor in maintaining the tonal coherence. This is the use of harmonic prolongations.

HARMONIC PROLONGATIONS

Numerous examples of this technique can be found in Debussy's works. A passage from *Jardins sous la pluie* has been selected, because it contains so many of the characteristics of his idiom within so few measures. Furthermore, it shows both the strength and the weakness of his stylistic trend.

As a whole, the passage indicates a III–V–VI progression within the E major tonality. It is apparent, however, that the G♯ minor mediant chord has been expanded through the use of its own harmonic prolongation. The use of this technique is of special interest in view of those aspects of the treatment that are so typical of Debussy — the doubling of the outside voices, the broken chord, the altered passing chords, and the delicate quality of the mood, his so-called impressionistic style.

EXAMPLE 84

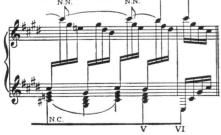

The first three measures [12] show a motion from the G♯ minor to the C♯ minor chord (measure 2), the subdominant, which pushes on to the D♯ major, the dominant, with a return to the G♯ chord. In this motion the A♯ major and B major chords in the opening measure are passing chords that fill the space between the G♯ and C♯ minor chords. In the second measure, however, the A♯ major chord fulfills a different function as an applied dominant of the D♯ chord. With the entrance of the G♯ chord (measure 3) there again is an ascent to the C♯ minor chord, which in this instance is not a subdominant, as in the harmonic prolongation, but a neighbor chord of the structural dominant, the B major chord, which follows. This difference in function is due to the fact that in measure 2 the C♯ chord directs the motion to the dominant of the harmonic prolongation, while in measure 4 it serves as an embellishment of the dominant B major chord of the basic progression. This is an excellent instance of the distinctive functions that the same chord may fulfill within a single III–V progression.

It is possible, however, that the presence of the A♯ major chord on the third quarter of measures 1 and 2 might suggest that it is of greater importance than the C♯ minor chord and that the intervening chords of B major and C♯ minor are embellishments. According to this hearing, the A♯ major chord would serve as an embellished supertonic leading directly to the dominant D♯ major chord. Because of the emphasis of the C♯ minor chord, this interpretation seems a little far-fetched and much less convincing than the one offered in the analysis. The fact that the passage gives rise to two different readings indicates that there is a lack of definiteness in the treatment and a certain vagueness in the technique. However, whether we hear the A♯ major as a passing chord to the subdominant or as a supertonic of which the C♯ minor chord is an embellishment does not affect the prolongation of the G♯ minor chord. Thus it is somewhat startling to come upon the reference Marion Bauer makes to this passage.

In speaking of three measures from *Reflets dans l'eau,* she says: "In this example the sequence is not based on perfect triads but on thirteenths or sevenths according to the enharmonic reading of the chords. The following from Debussy's *Jardins sous la pluie* with the broken chord, is the same in principle." [13]

---

[12] Copyright 1903. Permission for reprint granted by Durand & Cie, Paris, France, and Elkan-Vogel Co., Inc., Philadelphia, Pa., copyright owners.

[13] *Twentieth Century Music* (Putnam, 1933), p. 144.

Debussy

This statement is completely bewildering, since the passage consists entirely of perfect triads. Yet "the same in principle" can only mean that, like the *Reflets*, this example is based on thirteenths and sevenths. Is it possible that Miss Bauer combines two different triads, such as the A♯ and B major chords in measure 1, into a single chord? This is the only means of hearing a thirteenth. Yet why should we combine triads in Debussy's music when we regard them as separate chord structures in the works of Haydn, Beethoven, and Wagner? Perhaps the author has not fully understood the point of Miss Bauer's comparison, but it appears that there is no connection whatsoever between the techniques used in these two passages. Let us look further to see if the prolongations in other works are of a different nature.

The opening measures of the prelude *Danseuses de Delphes* [14] offers an interesting illustration of Debussy's technique.

EXAMPLE 85

The passage shows a clear-cut I—II—V harmonic progression, which outlines the motion from the B♭ to the F major chord. This has been expanded through the use of the neighbor note, horizontalization and transfer of register.

In the very first measure we already see evidences of the imprint of Debussy's style on the older technique. In filling the space from B♭ to F in the bass to support the passing tone G in the top voice, we would immediately think of the G minor or the inverted E♭ major chord as the natural possibilities. Instead we find A, the horizontalized third of the F chord, serving as the root of its own seventh chord. To offset the similarity between the A minor and F major chords, Debussy exchanges C for C♯ in the F chord and thus creates an altered chord on the dominant. It is by such simple and effective means that the motion takes on a distinctly new and different quality.

The top voice moves from F to G, a neighbor note (measure 3), returning to F, while the bass ascends chromatically from B♭ to D. Thus the first four measures disclose a prolongation of the tonic chord through which the root position is exchanged for a first inversion. Through the melodic figuration F is shifted to a higher register while B♭, a middle voice, passes to A over a retained D in the bass, an ingenious device by which the B♭ major is converted into a D minor chord. Again F in the top voice is embellished by G which does not return to F but passes in an incomplete neighbor-note motion to E of the C major chord. The expansion of this supertonic chord is achieved through a descent from E, a top voice, to C, a middle voice, and by an embellishing motion in the bass in which D and B♭ appear as upper and lower neighbors of C.

Although the prolongations that expand the structural motion show the imprint of Debussy's stylistic idiom, they nevertheless are convincing in the type of passing and embellishing motions they create. In fact this is one instance in which the extension of the older techniques results in an enrichment of the structural motion without affecting the tonal stability demonstrated by the I—II—V harmonic progression. Although the passage shows fewer deviations in the treatment than any of the preceding examples, there are, however, certain elements of the technique, such as the nature of the passing chord in the opening measure and the emphasis of dissonant passing tones, that reflect the individual characteristics of Debussy's style. Here again is evidence that the older techniques can meet the demands of a new age and express the qualities of a new stylistic idiom without sacrificing their former function in maintaining the structural unity. This fact is important. It demonstrates that the art of prolongation is not static, confining the composer to a prescribed set of rules. On the contrary, its elasticity is its greatest artistic asset so long as the effects it achieves are not gained at the expense of tonal stability. The structural security the horizontalization of the chord provides permits the intervening voice leadings to take on the color and characteristics of each composer, so that every prolongation is the expression of an original artistic style.

In the examples we have discussed we have seen that the techniques vary. For the most part they adhere to those principles of structure and prolongation through which the concept of tonality was evolved. There are instances, however, in which the stylistic tendencies have weakened the structural outline, and the nature of the passing chords has deterred rather than impelled the motion to its harmonic goal. At these times the techniques have been extended so far beyond their original purpose that instead of clarifying the structural meaning, they obscure it. As a result, some of these effects have led present-day composers to believe that Debussy had already stepped outside the boundaries of the tonal world.

Analyses of Debussy's works by contemporary composers and theorists not only reflects the present-day evaluation of his contribution, but the present-day approach to the problems to which his music gives rise. Since it is as essential to understand the techniques of twentieth-century composers as it is to grasp the techniques of the past, the second part of our discussion will center on the analysis of various passages from Debussy's works by contemporary musicians.

THE PRESENT–DAY APPROACH TO DEBUSSY'S MUSIC

In the examples that follow, Debussy is one step further away from the older methods than in those passages we already have discussed. This undoubtedly accounts for the fact that in some instances the only explanations offered are that Debussy has used a pentatonic, whole-tone, or twelve-tone scale.

To know the special scale in which a work is composed may be an aid to our aural impressions, but it neither clarifies the technique nor demonstrates what is happening in the music. Therefore, when contemporary composers or theorists analyze a work by stating that it is in the whole-tone or twelve-tone scale, it indicates either that the music is incapable of further explanation or that the analytical approach to works in the tonal system is inadequate in solving the problems of present-day techniques.

As a first illustration, let us take a passage from one of the preludes, *Minstrels*, of which Marion Bauer states: "Like the Ravel citation [the Pavane] it is harmonized in the twelve-tone scale." [15] Since this is the only explanation offered, the use of the word "harmonized" is not altogether clear. It suggests that the melody is tonal but that the chords that provide the setting are of an atonal nature.

Although Miss Bauer starts with the A major chord in the third measure

[15] *Twentieth Century Music* (Putnam, 1933), p. 144.

of the following example, it is easier to understand the techniques if we begin with the tonic G major chord that enters two measures earlier.

EXAMPLE 86

As a whole, we see that the graph [16] shows a motion from the G to the D major chord, a tonic-dominant progression. This is a strong indication of the G major tonality. It remains to be seen, however, whether the techniques that expand the space bear out the tonal implications of the progression.

The first four measures define a motion from the tonic to the altered mediant. The space is extended through the arpeggiation of the A major passing chord, whose outlined tones serve as the roots of their own chords and engender the embellishing top-voice motion.

One aspect of the technique, although not new, appears here for the first time. This concerns the direct approach of the mediant to the tonic, without the usual dominant. Here the mediant provides the harmonic impulse that directs the motion from one tonic chord to another. Thus it temporarily assumes the role generally played by the dominant. Although it cannot fulfill the function of a dominant, since it does not demonstrate the primary relationship of a fifth, it serves as the climax of a structural motion and thus intensifies its own function as a structural force. There

Debussy

are instances, however, in which the mediant chord in a I–III–I progression supports a neighbor note of a tone of the tonic chord. In such cases the mediant does not exercise a structural but a prolonging function. Although the I–III–I is used not too frequently as a structural progression, it can be found in passages in the works of the older composers as a type of harmonic prolongation.

With the entrance of the G major chord (measure 5) there is a clearcut I–IV–V progression in which the bass descends by thirds from G through E to C. Here the use of an E major rather than an E minor chord between the G and C major chords is both striking and unusual. However, since this chord fulfills a contrapuntal and rhythmic but not a harmonic function, it does not affect the nature of the motion.

It is true that the presence of the A, E, B major, and C♯ minor chords in a short passage in G major tends to obscure the inherent characteristics of the tonality. On the other hand, since the A major chord is a chromatic passing chord through whose horizontalization the C♯ minor and E major chords emerge, and the B major chord can be accounted for as an altered mediant that immediately passes to the tonic, the motion is between two G major chords, in which the top voice has moved from G to B. The transfer of B to an inner voice, which is due to the demands of the motive, has no effect on the structural meaning. It is evident that the imitation of the top-voice figure E–C♯–A–B, in the same succession of intervals G–E–C♮–D, necessitated the transfer of B to a lower voice.

In view of these facts, it is difficult to agree with Miss Bauer's reference to the twelve-tone scale, since the top voice outlines a diatonic ascent from G to D and the bass a prolonged I–IV–V progression. Both interpretations are offered so that the reader may decide which more accurately represents his own understanding of the passage.

Another interesting reference to Debussy appears in Horace A. Miller's [17] discussion of modern chord structures. He cites the following passages from *Pelléas et Mélisande* [18] (Act II, Scene I) to illustrate the use of a dominant eleventh.

If we listen to these measures, we hear the chords on the second quarter as neighbors of those on the first and third quarters. Mr. Miller recognized this by indicating that the two D minor chords were the same.

[17] *New Harmonic Devices* (Oliver Ditson, 1930), p. 61.
[18] Vocal score, p. 69. Copyright 1907. Permission for reprint granted by Durand & Cie, Paris, France, and Elkan-Vogel Co., Inc., Philadelphia, Pa., copyright owners.

EXAMPLE 87

Nevertheless, he regards the intervening chord, which consists entirely of neighbor notes of the D minor chords, as a dominant eleventh. Although the root tone C is the dominant of the F major chord, in this instance it serves only as a neighbor chord and thus should not be mistaken for a structural dominant, which demonstrates a totally different function as a member of a harmonic progression.

The chords that prolong the tonic-mediant progression are of a contrapuntal origin, although the final E seventh chord has the tendency of an applied dominant of A minor. They are due to the embellishing motion in the top voice, which engenders the counterpoint in the bass. The new aspect of the treatment lies in the constant conflict between the outside voices, and it is this element of the technique that tends to obscure the meaning of the passage and the coherence of the basic motion.

Although Mr. Miller offers no explanation of the function of these chords or the meaning of the passage, he makes a statement regarding chords of the ninth, eleventh, and thirteenth that is important in connection with the next illustration. He says: "The exact time and place, when and where a combination of notes becomes a chord and not a group of suspensions and appoggiaturas has been a subject of much discussion. It is largely the matter of elision in our listening. Certain implied chords whose statement comes to be superfluous in progressions, are no longer desired by the advanced composer, and he reveals to us newer methods." [19]

This reference to elision brings up a technique that not only is characteristic of Debussy's treatment, but also influenced the music of his successors — the elimination of the resolution tones to which the ear is so accustomed that it compensates for their omission.

As an illustration, let us take a passage from *Pelléas et Mélisande* for which George Dyson offers a different explanation. Instead of regarding

[19] *New Harmonic Devices* (Oliver Ditson, 1930), p. 59.

Debussy

these chords as a typical instance of elision, he calls them "harmonic side slips." He says: "He [Debussy] takes, for example, a chord of the ninth, and slides away with it whole, in any direction, until whatever tonality it originally had, is, to say the least, highly attenuated." [20]

EXAMPLE 88

The leap of a fifth in the first two chords of this passage [21] suggests that it forms the basic technique of the following measures, but that these applied dominants have been omitted.

Although the graph in Example A defines this succession as the origin of the elision, it is intended, not to suggest that Debussy heard the passage in this form, but to show the connection between the earlier and later techniques. In fact this explanation is based on the more orthodox treatment in a different passage (Example B), in which the intervening fifths are present.

It must be admitted at the start of this discussion that the passage

[20] *The New Music* (Oxford University Press, 1923), p. 65.
[21] Vocal score, p. 45. Copyright 1907. Permission for reprint granted by Durand & Cie, Paris, France, and Elkan-Vogel Co., Inc., Philadelphia Pa., copyright owners.

itself is so vague and the motion it describes so unclear that no explanation, regardless of the type of analysis used, could pass unchallenged. Therefore, the suggestions offered in the graph should be regarded only as a means of indicating the possible source to which the new aspect of the treatment can be traced. If elision is the underlying factor that creates this striking succession of ninth chords, we must admit that there is a connection between this technique, in which the intervening chords have been eliminated, and the older technique, in which they have been retained. Although this connection does not bring clarity to the tonal character of the passage or reveal its structural significance, it is a clue to the origin of those chords Dyson regards as "side slips."

The graph indicates a motion from the C♯ minor, the tonic of the scene, through the ninth chord on C♮ to the ninth chord on B♭. In this the motion from the C♯ minor to the passing chord on C♮ has been prolonged by an embellishing motion that widens the space between E and D in the top voice and C♯ and C♮ in the bass. As embellishing chords we can account for the ninth chords on F♯, E, and D♮, but how shall we explain the final ninth chord on B♭ when there is nothing in the measures that follow that reveals its function either as an embellishing or passing chord, or as a chord of structural import?

Although it would be impossible for anyone, irrespective of the analytical approach used, to prove that the technique in example A is an extension of the technique used in Example B, there is a certain similarity in the treatment, although in the one instance the fifths are lacking, and in the other, Debussy used triads instead of ninth chords. However, since in the one example the fifth successions are present, are we not justified in regarding the other instance as based on the same technique instead of as a complete break with the past, as Dyson suggests?

Two different explanations of this passage have been given, so that the reader may decide whether he hears these ninths as "side slips" or as elisions. He must recognize, however, that although the term "side slips" is extremely indicative of the effect of these chords, it does not explain the origin of the technique, nor does it provide a possible clue to the motion the chords describe.

Another interesting passage that gives rise to a difference of opinion is cited by Lenormand [22] as an illustration of Debussy's use of the whole-

[22] *A Study of Twentieth Century Harmony* (B. F. Wood Music Co., Boston, 1915), p. 102.

tone scale. The example is taken from the opening measures of the prelude from the suite *Pour le Piano*.[23]

EXAMPLE 89

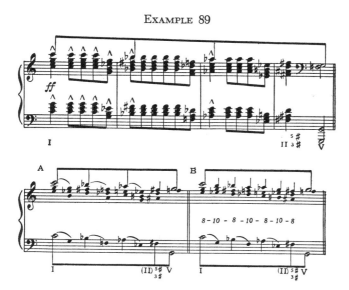

It is unfortunate that Lenormand has not gone beyond the altered chord on D in the first quarter of measure 4. Although his illustration discloses the whole-tone chords that fill the space between the C major and the altered chord on D, it does not include the dominant G seventh chord, which not only clarifies the status of the D chord, but at the same time defines the function of the whole-tone chords.

There are two ways of explaining the motion from the C to G major chord. We can attribute the whole-tone progressions to a mixture of the C major and C minor chords (graph A). It is also possible, however, to regard them as the result of the chromatic technique shown in graph B, in which the intervening half tones, concealed in a middle voice, have been shifted to a top voice. The effect is entirely different, but the presence of B♮–A♮–G♮ in the inner voice suggests that it is derived from the chromatic technique.

The significance of the passage, however, does not center on the fact that Debussy has used a whole-tone sequence, but rather on the function

[23] Copyright 1901. Permission for reprint granted by Jean Jobert, Paris, France, and Elkan-Vogel Co., Inc., Philadelphia, Pa., copyright owners.

of these chords as space-fillers within the tonic-dominant progression. Whether we hear the altered D chord as a supertonic or merely as a passing chord that has the tendency of an applied dominant is a matter of personal choice.

The significant aspect of the treatment, which Lenormand has not pointed out, is that these whole-tone chords appear within a clearly outlined space between the C and G major chords. Thus, although we must recognize the new aspect of the treatment, we also must acknowledge that since the passing chords are indicative of a major-minor mixture of the tonic chord and occur within a well-defined progression, they in no wise impair the clarity of the structural motion. However, Debussy's use of these chords in so early a work is indicative of his preoccupation with the new possibilities to which tonality gives rise, and it is prophetic of the later trends in which the further emphasis of such tendencies leads to the breakdown of the tonal system.

In connection with the various examples of contrapuntal prolongation that our investigation of Debussy's techniques has already revealed, this statement by L. Sabaniev is interesting:

"This harmonic world of Debussy is the genuine element of pure harmony. . . . Each of his harmonies is a self-sufficing sensation and independent color and light. The absence of counterpoint and polyphony are more marked than in any other composer." [24]

Since the various authors to whom we have referred have cited only a few brief measures from which to draw their deductions, the examples have been of a fragmentary nature. To determine fully whether the technique of counterpoint, as we have applied the term to the works of Bach, Haydn, and Beethoven, is confined only to a few isolated passages from Debussy's works, let us take a larger section from the sarabande [25] on which to base our conclusions.

Although the sarabande is an early work, it contains many of the innovations characteristic of Debussy's later treatment. It is perhaps these deviations in technique, extensions of the older methods, that give the sarabande a distinction and invest it with a quality that has little in common with sarabandes of old.

Since we already have referred to the first four measures of this pas-

---

[24] Translated by S. W. Pring, *Music and Letters* (January, 1929, Vol. X).

[25] *Pour le Piano.* Copyright 1901. Permission for reprint granted by Jean Jobert, Paris, France, and Elkan-Vogel Co., Inc., Philadelphia, Pa., copyright owners.

sage in the discussion of Debussy's use of horizontalization (Example 78), we can begin with the tonic C♯ minor chord (measure 6).

The unusual element in the I—II—V—I harmonic progression is the wide expansion of the supertonic chord. The D♯ seventh chord first appears with a raised fifth A𝄪 (measure 9), then is exchanged for the major triad (measure 14), and finally enters in its unaltered form in connection with the dominant G♯ major chord. In the expansion of both the tonic and supertonic chords, we see how significant a role both horizontalization and the transfer of register play.

An interesting aspect of the treatment is the stress placed on the B

EXAMPLE 90

major chord (measure 8). As the end of a phrase, with the additional emphasis of a fermata, the chord would seem to be of structural importance. Yet its actual function is that of a passing chord between the C♯ minor and A major chords. It is part of a prolonging motion that expands the space between the tonic and supertonic chords. The remaining chords in this motion, A and F♯ major, represent the horizontalized fifth and third of the D♯ chord, each of which serves as the root of its own chord. Here the B, A, and F♯ chords support the passing tones in the ascent from C♯, a middle voice, to F♯, a structural top voice. Therefore, although the B major chord is strongly accentuated, we see that its function is solely prolonging. It is characteristic of Debussy's treatment, however, that he emphasized a passing chord rather than the structural supertonic of the progression.

In the prolongation of this D♯ chord, the presence of the altered fifth, A♯, gives rise to the F♯ major instead of the F♯ minor chord and to the diminished triad on A♯ instead of the A major chord. The exchange of the altered D♯ chord for D♯ major concludes the phrase, but it is immediately replaced with the unaltered supertonic seventh in the repetition of the melodic figure on which the sarabande begins.

The use of the various forms of the supertonic and the unusual nature of the chords engendered through horizontalization are indicative of those tendencies in the treatment that foreshadow the later techniques. On the other hand, the older methods are represented by horizontalization, passing chords within the tone-spaces of the outlined C♯ and D♯ chords, transfer of register, and the neighbor note. These are all contrapuntal techniques, since they concern the leading of voices in connection with the prolonging motions that expand the harmonic progression. They have nothing whatsoever to do with harmony, but only with those aspects of the treatment that provide melodic and contrapuntal interest through the color effects they inject into the structural motion.

We can agree with Sabaniev that the emphasis is on the vertical rather than the horizontal style. It is equally true that various tendencies in the treatment conceal both the character and function of the passing chords. Nevertheless, to regard each chord as a "self-sufficing sensation and independent color and light" negates the structural coherence the passage reveals and the nature and function of the prolonging motions.

Had Sabaniev qualified his statement by applying it to certain works in which the impact of the whole-tone successions broke down the sense of tonality and replaced the techniques of structure and prolongation with techniques that no longer achieved tonal coherence, we could understand his attitude. As a general statement, however, it is entirely disproved both in the smaller examples and in the larger passages from "The Girl with the Flaxen Hair" and the sarabande.

These various opinions by present-day musicians have been presented to show what different readings result from two opposing approaches. In the one, each chord is regarded as an entity without consideration of its status in the passage or its connection with the chords that precede and follow. The new tendencies in the treatment are indicated, not by showing how these chords function in the passage or how they affect the tonality, but by pointing out the use of the twelve-tone scale, the whole-tone scale, and chords of the ninth, eleventh, and thirteenth. In short, the scale systems and the chord structures are defined, but there is no attempt to explain the role they play or the result of their impact on the tonal stability. In the other approach the function of these chords is the main point of interest. For the most part they are shown to be either passing or embellishing chords that prolong the basic harmonic progression. In most instances the new tendencies have been defined as an extension or an adaptation of the older techniques, but a differentiation has been made between those examples in which the new tendencies clarify the progression and those in which they obscure the structural motion. The fragmentary examples cited by two authorities to show Debussy's use of the whole-tone and the twelve-tone scale have been supplemented with the additional measures that give meaning to the passage and reveal the tonal character of the harmonic progression. In the one case the twelve-tone theory has been exploded; in the other the whole-tone chords have been disclosed as passing chords within a dominant-tonic progression.

Again it must be emphasized that to state that a work is in this or that scale and that the composer has used chords of the eleventh and thirteenth, altered chords, polyharmonies, and impressionistic or expressionistic effects does not constitute an analysis of the music any more than describing a word as a noun, verb, adjective, or adverb explains the meaning of the sentence in which it appears. To grasp the significance of the sentence and its connection in the paragraph we have to know something more than grammatical terms. In a similar manner, it is not enough to know the musical terms that define a scale or the structure of a chord. We also must understand the function of a chord and the purpose for which the scale is used if we want to grasp the musical meaning of the passage. If tonality is a means of expressing structural unity, it is necessary to find out what elements constitute the unity and what elements maintain it. This requires more than a knowledge of chord structure or scale. It demands a recognition of the different functions a chord can fulfill within a single phrase or passage irrespective of whether it is a triad or a thirteenth.

The originality of Debussy's technique does not lie only in the fact of his employing chords that do not appear in the music of Beethoven, Wagner, and Brahms. It is rather the ingenuity with which he used these chords so as not to destroy the principles of tonality in works in which the tonal concept still prevailed. This is evidence of his artistry, the significant aspect of his innovations in the passages we have examined.

There are instances, however, in which either his adaptation of the old techniques to entirely new situations or his use of totally new techniques has led outside the boundary of tonality. It is difficult, sometimes impossible, to clarify the meaning of these passages. Either the motion is too unclear to permit of any interpretation for which a technical explanation can be offered, or no motion at all is indicated. Examples from such works occupy the third part of our discussion.

Debussy

THE TENDENCY TOWARD ATONALITY

These techniques stem primarily from Debussy's use of the whole-tone scale and the augmented chords to which it gives rise. There is no reason to dissertate on the origin of this scale and how Debussy became intrigued with its possibilities. It is enough that he was primarily responsible for its introduction into the music of western Europe and that he gave it a totally new and original treatment. Yet it is necessary to consider whether his experiments in the whole-tone system did not offer a greater blow to tonality than is generally conceded.

We have seen that although in most instances Wagner adhered to techniques that made for structural unity, there were also times when the chromatic motion or the nature of the prolongations definitely weakened the tonality. In fact there was evidence in a few of the illustrations cited that the theory of chord relationships that led to keys outside the tonality had replaced the older recognition of tonality as axiomatically within one and only one key, through the motion within a single horizontalized chord. This can be regarded as the first step away from the tonal stronghold, a step magnified out of all proportion by the chromatic daring of *Tristan.*

In turning from the grandiose romanticism of Wagner to evolve a style more compatible with his artistic ideals and stylistic tendencies, it was logical that Debussy should find in the simple and more restrained treatment of Couperin and Rameau an expression of qualities with which he was in close sympathy. He looked on this early period as the golden age of French music, and his intense desire to free himself of German influence revived his interest in these early composers, whose works were essentially French in both character and spirit.

However, although Debussy turned to the past for his inspiration, he was too great an individualist to believe that the treatment of these composers could serve to express the later trends in art and life characteristic of his own day. Again he turned from the gods of Valhalla to the French symbolists and impressionists, in whose works he found a confirmation of his own artistic credo. Thus, in evolving a style of his own, he was influenced to some degree at least by the music of Couperin and Rameau, by the poems of Verlaine, Rossetti, and Mallarmé, and by the paintings of Monet and his circle. As a result, the tendency to reproduce in music effects similar to those gained by poets and painters led Debussy to stylistic innovations which in many instances were a definite negation of the principles of tonality. In fact, the more personal his idiom became, the more devastating was its impact on the tonal stronghold.

It is the aesthetic appeal of Debussy's works, the purity of his style, and the sensuous play of colors that are both his strongest assets and his greatest weapons, since it is impossible to believe that such translucent beauty as he has drawn from musical tones could undermine an artistic concept that had served the very composers whose works he so revered. However, let us turn to four examples illustrating the impact of these techniques on tonal coherence.

The first is a short passage from *Pelléas et Mélisande*.[26] It shows a top-voice descent of an octave between two F minor chords rather than within a single F minor chord. Thus it calls to mind Wagner's treatment of the Magic Sleep motive (Example 66), although the techniques that provide the motion are entirely different.

Wagner proceeded from an A♭ minor to a G♯ major chord by a descent in major thirds, thus applying to a motion between a chord and its enharmonic equivalent, both of which fulfill the same function, the technique previously used only in connection with two different chords. Debussy on the other hand makes the top-voice descent by two groups of fourths C–G and F♯–C♯, with the final C♮ appearing within the F minor chord.

EXAMPLE 91

How should we understand this motion? Do the descents in the top voice and the ascent of a fourth in the bass indicate that there is a motion from C♮ to C♯, a neighbor note in the top voice, against a motion from F to B in the base? If so, why C♯ in connection with the B major chord? The other possibility is to hear the entire motion as a descent

[26] Vocal score, p. 52. Copyright 1907. Permission for reprint granted by Durand & Cie, Paris, France, and Elkan-Vogel Co., Inc., Philadelphia, Pa., copyright owners.

of an octave, with the ascending bass a counterpoint for the chords in the upper voices. Accordingly the A major chord with E in the top voice that appears in connection with B belongs to the preceding A in the bass, while the chord on the final eighth note of the measure is a passing chord between B major and F minor.

Although this latter explanation seems closer to the music, there is no means of proving that it is correct, since the fourths are so clearly outlined in the motion. However, interpreting the passage as a motion to the neighbor note C♯ is equally debatable, since C♯ seems to be a passing tone between D♯ and C♮, while D♯ is obviously the chord tone. Since neither the measures that precede nor those that succeed this passage throw any light on its meaning, we must assume that Debussy has gone one step beyond Wagner's technique in expanding the motion between two F minor chords. Here, neither of the outside voices nor the descent and ascent in fourths in any way define the tonal characteristics of the F minor chord, or is the motion as a descent of an octave confirmed by the bass ascent to the B major chord.

The fact that this is a brief passage does not minimize the effect of its vagueness. On the contrary, the tendencies it reveals are significant, because they are the seeds out of which the later trend away from tonality was to emerge.

If this were the only instance in which the tonal implications of a motion were obscured by the techniques, it would be futile to discuss it, since it would have little meaning as an isolated example. However, we can find many other passages in which there is a similar confusion in the prolonging techniques.

In his discussion of the various types of seventh chords, Lenormand [27] cites a case from *Pelléas et Mélisande* [28] as an example of the substitution of the minor sixth for the augmented fifth. He says: "Chords of the seventh with an augmentation of the fifth, may proceed, in descending, by similar and conjunct motion." [29]

The analysis offered by Lenormand is limited to the single measure shown in graph A. By citing this fragmentary passage he has overlooked

[27] *A Study of Twentieth Century Harmony* (B. F. Wood Music Co., Boston, 1915), p. 23.

[28] Vocal score, p. 10. Copyright 1907. Permission for reprint granted by Durand & Cie, Paris, France, and Elkan-Vogel Co., Inc., Philadelphia, Pa., copyright owners.

[29] *A Study of Twentieth Century Harmony* (B. F. Wood Music Co., Boston, 1915), p. 26.

the primary function of F as a neighbor of E, which accounts for its presence as a minor sixth instead of the augmented fifth he suggests. This is an essential point in the passage, since it shows a connection between the two A major chords that otherwise is lacking.

EXAMPLE 92

In the opening measure of graph B, F, retained from a middle voice of the preceding chord, appears as a suspension that moves to E, the chord tone. This F reappears in measure 2 and is explained by Lenormand as E♯ an augmented fifth of the A major chord, passing to F♯ in the succeeding chord. A similar exchange of D for C𝄪 results in an augmented chord on the third eighth note of this measure. Yet Lenormand gives no indication of what these exchanges accomplish or in what way they bring greater clarity to the music. The main factor in the motion, the bass descent of an octave from one A major chord to another, has been entirely ignored in Lenormand's analysis, since he cites the measure in which only the first A chord enters and thus breaks off in the middle of the descent.

The presence of two inverted seventh chords on A that are identical except for a shift in register, leads us to assume that these chords define a space of an octave that has been filled with passing chords. We also see that F, the top voice of the first A chord, reappears in a lower register in the final A chord where it passes to E, the fifth of the chord. This suggests that Debussy introduced F as a neighbor of E, in imitation of the opening measure in which it occurs as a suspension over E. The fascinating aspect of this technique is the subtlety and ingenuity by which the two phrases are invested with the same melodic embellishment.

We come now to the passing chords that expand the space between the two A major chords. Although the bass defines a space of an octave, the passing tones do not outline a motion within the A major chord nor can we regard the motion as a mixture of the major and minor characteristics of the A chord. It is clearly a passing motion within an octave, without regard to the tonal nature of the chords that outline the space. The top-voice motion is totally unconvincing whether we hear it as starting on F, as the opening measure suggests, or on the C♯ indicated in the A major chord. In fact the upper voices completely negate the motion defined by the bass. Here is another instance in which two identical chords in different registers are treated as two different chords between which any type of passing chord may appear without the need of clarifying the means by which the motion is effected. In fact there is no possible way of hearing this motion except as a descent from the A major chord to its octave with F substituted for E, to which it returns in a middle voice.

The main element in the treatment, therefore, is not the use of the augmented fifth in the A seventh chord, as Lenormand suggests, since this denies F its function as a neighbor note and as a link between the two A major chords. Although it is important to recognize the function that F fulfills within the melodic figure, it is even more essential to realize the implications of the techniques that prolong the A major chord. They indicate a growing tendency to fill the space between two positions of the same chord with a group of heterogeneous passing chords rather than with a motion within the tone-spaces of the outlined chord. The exchange of a new technique for an older one and the extension and adaptation of older methods to new situations are healthy, normal indications of progress and development if they fulfill their purpose. In various examples we have seen that Debussy has greatly enriched the older techniques without affecting the structural clarity. In the two last illustrations, however, it is obvious that in each case the substitution of the passing-chord technique for the horizontalized chord has weakened the connection between the two chords that outline the motion. The result of this same technique when applied to a larger expansion would necessarily create a vagueness in the structural motion that would impair the tonal coherence. Therefore, here are two examples in which the use of a new technique may have far-reaching results on the stronghold of tonality. This gives rise to the question whether these passages are not more closely allied to those works that show Debussy's trend away from the tonal orbit than they are to those examples previously discussed, that demonstrate the tonal concept through the principles of structure and prolongation.

Various examples could be cited as illustrative of the new tendencies in the treatment, but the discussion will be limited to representative passages from two totally different preludes, *Voiles* and *Les tierces alternées*.

Voiles is frequently mentioned as the work in which Debussy used the whole-tone scale with greatest consistence. Yet no one has given an explanation of its structural meaning. Marion Bauer has gone further than anyone else in providing a clue to the motivic figures on which a large part of the prelude is built. In speaking of Debussy's use of the whole-tone scale, she says: "The most patent example, however, is *Voiles*, which is written entirely in the whole-tone scale with the exception of one section of six measures in the pentatonic scale. . . . Both the accompanying figure (a) and the melody (b) are in whole tone." [30]

There may be some difference of opinion as to which is the accompanying figure and which the melody, but there can be no argument as to the prominence of these two motives and their importance in the prelude. However, no attempt has been made to show the function of these figures, the nature of the motion in which they appear, or the effect of the whole-tone scale on tonality. Thus, we must assume either that the techniques are too unclear to provide an explanation of the motion or that the use of the whole-tone scale invalidates the system of harmonic analysis applied to works of a tonal nature.

This prelude has a delicate, elusive quality, a distinction of character and treatment, and differs so greatly from other works that it remains a unique experiment in the whole-tone idiom. In a brief allusion to this quality, Mlle Boulanger says: "It is extraordinary for the vagueness of its atmosphere and the manner in which it suggests — to me, at least — the paradoxical sense of mobility in immobility." [31] This statement shows a remarkable grasp of the essential conflict in the technique. However, from the point of view of the author, the final words should be "the paradoxical sense of immobility in mobility," since the motion, although con-

---

[30] *Twentieth Century Music* (Putnam, 1933), p. 148.
[31] *Rice Institute Pamphlet* (April, 1926), p. 170.

Debussy

stant, is frustrated by its own limitations. Like wheels in a rut, it keeps
going, but never actually moves.

EXAMPLE 93

The thirteen measures cited above [32] show the two main figures that
in one form or another dominate the first thirty-eight measures of the prelude. As outlined in the graph, it is apparent that both of them may be
combined into a single chord of the whole-tone scale, C—E—G♯ or
A♭—C—E.

[32] Copyright 1910. Permission for reprint granted by Durand & Cie, Paris, France,
and Elkan-Vogel Co., Inc., Philadelphia, Pa., copyright owners.

Challenge to Musical Tradition

If first we examine the figure (a), which Miss Bauer calles the accompanying figure, we see that, although at the beginning there is a suggestion of a neighbor-note motion from G♯ (A♭) to B♭ back to G♯, in measure 3 there is a whole-tone descent from G♯ through C to E that outlines the tones of the augmented chord, just as in the works of the earlier composers we found an arpeggiation of the triad. In fact, the first thirty-eight measures of the prelude are provided solely by this augmented chord, with or without embellishments, over a pedal point on B♭. There is a difference, however, between Debussy's technique and that of Haydn or Beethoven.

In the older works, we have seen that the horizontalized chord provides both the melodic and the harmonic framework within which the motion occurs. It is the generator of all further melodic, contrapuntal, and harmonic activity. In *Voiles,* however, the horizontalized augmented chord remains static. There is no motion outside the boundaries defined by the two melodic figures, nor any motion within the chord except the passing tones within the two motives. Thus, for thirty-eight measures there is a repetition of the same chord outline, within which no further activity occurs. This itself is indicative of passivity rather than mobility.

However, the larger problem to which the passage gives rise is the status and function of this augmented chord. What type of structural motion does it define, and where does it go at the end of thirty-eight measures?

The B♭ seventh chord, with an augmented fifth, F♯, follows. It is possible that the concentration on this chord for the next four measures (39–42) serves to emphasize the entrance of the E♭ seventh chord, the B♭ chord having the tendency of an applied dominant. Can we assume from this motion that the chord C—E—G♯ passes through the altered B♭ seventh to the E♭ seventh chord? Do we hear these forty-three measures as an expression of such a progression, and if so, what connection is there between the chord C—E—G♯ and the E♭ minor chord? Even were we to regard the augmented chord as A♭—C—E, the presence of E♮ weakens the possibility of considering the chord in a fifth relationship to the chord of E♭ minor. Furthermore, the concluding measures of the prelude point to the chord as an augmented triad on C, through the use of G♯ instead of A♭.

Any attempt to explain this motion in terms of a structural progression is inconsistent with what the music defines and what we hear. In fact, it could be regarded only as wishful thinking, since there is nothing in the nature of the chord structures or in the chord successions to indicate that the principles that create the coherence inherent in tonality are also demonstrated in the whole-tone technique. We can accept the predominance of the augmented chord that contains the two motivic figures; we might even assume that the altered B♭ seventh chord is connected with the E♭ minor chord that follows. We cannot, however, explain the meaning of these measures either as a structural top voice or as a basic motion.

There is a suggestion of melodic unity in the shift of the motivic figure (b) from the bass to a top voice (measure 51), but this is a mere outward manifestation and is entirely different from the organic unity that Debussy has demonstrated in other works.

Here is a work that is most significant because it introduces an entirely new medium. The substitution of the whole-tone for the tonal system was an important step in a new direction. Yet no one has regarded the problems that emerge from the new technique as sufficiently important to solve them, or, if that was impossible, to admit the far-reaching results of their atonal implications. Certainly to point to the prelude as an experiment in the whole-tone scale is no explanation of the techniques and in no way clarifies their functions.

It is possible that the whole-tone scale, in its substitution of an augmented for a perfect fifth, does not provide the same kind of structural coherence that is inherent in the older system. If this be true, we cannot apply the same form of analysis to the prelude that we used in connection with compositions that emerged out of the tonal concept. Yet in the thirty-three years after *Voiles* was composed no new type of analysis has been evolved, and the work still remains shrouded in mystery.

The reading suggested in the above graph and amplified in the discussion is by no means a final solution of the problem. It should be regarded primarily as an initial attempt to find out what the prelude means and whether we can apply to the techniques the same principles that were exercised in the works of Debussy's predecessors. As a result, we must recognize that although Debussy has used the technique of horizontalization to outline the motivic figures, he has expanded the chord not by the various techniques of prolongation, but only by repetition of the melodic figures. Furthermore, the status of the augmented chord is not defined. It may represent the fundamental of the whole-tone scale on C, but its function is not demonstrated in the motion to the altered B♭ and E♭ minor chords, which, in a return to the original augmented chord, comprise the entire prelude.

It is evident, therefore, that the principles of structure and prolongation that express the tonal concept are not applicable to the whole-tone system. Furthermore the graph discloses that the two motivic figures dominating the prelude, although contrapuntally opposed, are derived from the same chord structure and in combination define the outline of the augmented chord on C. The analysis also reveals a type of unity in the motivic figures that is not demonstrated in the bass motion.

Whether Debussy intended this melodic coherence to offset the structural vagueness is a matter of conjecture. Here the motivic figures provide the only link between the first and third sections of the prelude. Thus they have a structural significance in defining the melodic parallelisms characteristic of these sections in a three-part form. Whether this or any other type of melodic coherence is an adequate substitute for structural coherence, and whether the unity created by a structural design can compensate for the absence of a basic structural framework, are fundamental considerations that each reader must decide for himself.

Historically the work is pre-eminently important as an essay in a medium that not only rejects but negates the principles of tonality. It is a definite step in the direction of further experimentation with different theoretical concepts that had a more dynamic effect on the tonal stronghold. Thus, although the prelude may be less representative than works in which the techniques are more clearly defined, it is important because of its implication of the general trend of the times.

Since the arpeggiation of the augmented chords plays such a prominent role in the prelude, there is a tendency to regard this technique as allied to the past. The use of an augmented chord, however, as the dominating melodic figure is more indicative of the new technique to which the whole-tone scale gives rise than of Debussy's adaptation of the older techniques to meet the requirements of a new idiom. To show the full impact of his treatment on the principles of tonal coherence we must turn also to a work in which the chords are so indicative of the major-minor system that they offer convincing proof of Debussy's use of the older techniques. Then we will have a well-rounded picture of the two different means Debussy took to give expression to the new tendencies in his style; a new technique, and an adaptation of the older to a completely new concept.

Although several of the preludes offer conclusive evidence of the

288

Debussy

structural vagueness to which the adaptation gives rise, the chord structure of *Les tierces alternées* [33] is so strongly suggestive of the past that it provides the clearest demonstration of how the same technique may be used to achieve tonal coherence or tonal ambiguity. It is evident that the basic problem of the work is the consistent use of thirds throughout, a problem with which Chopin also coped, but in an entirely different way. Here the opening measures present a figure reminiscent of Mime's motive of Reflection heard in the introduction to Act I of *Siegfried*. Whether Debussy also intends the first ten measures to serve as an introduction to what follows can be decided only after a study of the passage.

Since the prelude begins on the third C–E, gives some stress to the G major chord, touches briefly on a succeeding C minor chord, and closes on the same third on which it opens, some interpreters might assume the work to be a mixture of the C major-minor tonality. For us, however, tonality is not a passive factor that can be defined by casual references to a tonic or dominant chord, with modulations to so-called related keys, but an active generating force that dominates every element of the structural and prolonging motions.

Now let us turn to the music.

The leaps in the music have been eliminated in the graph by placing the chords that form each group within the same register. This gives a clearer idea of the motion that each group defines.

The first nine measures show three ascending successions. In taking each of these separately, the first two groups indicate an interval of a fifth; the third group, a fourth. The motion is well outlined in each, but how shall we regard the motion that results from their combination? Is it possible to hear measures 5–10 as a prolongation of the space between the G major chords in measures 4 and 11? Surely there is nothing in the music to support such a reading, nor do we sense any connection between these two G major chords. In fact, we hear this group as a succession of independent chords rather than as part of any sustained motion.

However, let us assume that the third, G–B (measures 2–4) passes through G♭–B♭ (measure 9) to F–A of the inverted ninth chord on G as an expanded motion within the G major chord of which the intervening thirds are prolongations. Here A♭–C (measure 5) appears to be an embellishment of the preceding G–B and the G♭–B♭ to which it

---

[33] Copyright 1910. Permission for reprint granted by Durand & Cie, Paris, France, and Elkan-Vogel Co., Inc., Philadelphia, Pa., copyright owners.

EXAMPLE 94

ascends (measure 9). The problem that now confronts us is that the G
major chord moves not to the chord of C major but to an E major chord
(measure 12) which in turn passes through the inverted seventh chord
on D to the G major chord.

Although there may be a connection between the third, G—B (measure 2) and the B and G chords in measures 11 and 15, there is nothing to
prove that this is a reality rather than a possibility. It is equally uncertain whether this final G major chord moves to a C minor chord in the

succeeding measures. Furthermore, in order to find a connection between G—B (measure 2) and F—A (measure 11), we must hear F—A as a passing third to E—G♯, the end of this motion. Yet what function does an E major chord fulfill, occurring between two G major chords? If the succeeding chord were an A minor instead of an inverted seventh chord on D, the status of the E major chord as an applied dominant of an A minor embellishing chord would be clear. Here the use of a seventh chord on D negates any such possibility. It would seem as though the inverted seventh chord on B (measure 11) and the inverted seventh chord on D (measure 13) expressed the same function in regard to the succeeding chords as chords of embellishment. This is not the case, however, if F—A in the bass is a passing third to E—G♯, in which motion it exercises a passing rather than an embellishing function.

The status of the E major chord is not revealed either in these measures or in the single reference to this passage (measure 92) in which the treatment varies greatly. Its function remains an unsolved problem whether or not we recognize a connection between the G major chords that precede and follow.

In this prelude Debussy has been occupied with a succession of thirds, an old device, which he has adapted to an entirely new purpose. The manner in which he has used these thirds so that the motivic pattern predominates over all other factors and considerations results in a motion that is totally unclear, if we regard the prelude as indicative of the C major tonality. Thus, although the basic interval is allied to the past, the treatment is totally divorced from the past in the absence of any tonal implications. Perhaps, as in *Voiles*, the repetition of the motivic figure creates a melodic coherence that was meant to compensate for the lack of structural coherence. It is far more probable that the main object, to use a series of alternating thirds, was the motivating factor and that the techniques were determined by the character of the motivic figure. If the structural uncertainty in this prelude were an isolated example, we might regard it primarily as due to an interesting and unique experiment. However, as one of several instances of which *Feuilles mortes*, *Général Lavine-eccentric*, and *La Cathédrale engloutie* are typical, it shared in a cumulative effect that was potent in the later trends of music.

We have pointed out that the unclarity of the techniques used in the last four examples makes it impossible to offer what we regard as a satisfactory explanation of their meaning. Not content with a description of the melodic figure and the type of scale and chord structure, we believe it is as important to comprehend the full significance of Debussy's techniques as it is to understand the techniques used by earlier composers. Since the purely harmonic approach has not differentiated between the origins and functions of chords within the tonal concept, there is no reason to believe that the same method will prove successful in illuminating the meaning of the more complex techniques the whole-tone, polytonal and twelve-tone systems present. Although we admit that the Schenker approach has not revealed as much as we would like to know about these two last preludes, it has enabled us to understand that the problems to which they give rise are concerned not only with scales and chord structure, but with the fundamental principle of coherence, whether tonal or otherwise. It is the broad and elastic concept of tonality this method provides that permits the inclusion of works within the tonal system that some authorities regard as in the whole-tone and twelve-tone scales. It establishes a basis on which to differentiate between the old and new techniques, not on grounds of chord grammar but on the more important factor of chord function and chord significance. The reader must grant that the problems for which this method provides not a full solution are problems that are entirely ignored in the harmonic approach. The explanations we have offered go far beyond scale and chord structure; they penetrate the heart of each work in pointing out the specific instances in which the new techniques, through the structural vagueness they create, depart from the old. It is true that these explanations do not provide the final solution to these problems, but in what single book on contemporary music do we find a frank discussion of these new tendencies and their impact on the structural framework?

The main point involved is not whether these techniques lie within or outside the tonal concept. It is rather the necessity to understand them, irrespective of the idiom they express. To indicate that *Voiles* is based on the whole-tone scale and *Les tierces alternées* on the structural design of a third provides a clue to our hearing and a means of indentifying the melodic patterns. It does not, however, reveal how the chords function in a whole-tone system or whether the thirds constitute a melodic figure only or define a structural motion as well. Granted that Debussy's primary idea in the one case was to experiment with the new system, and in the other to use an old device in a totally new way, it is still necessary to know whether the experimental aspects of the treatment emerge out of a

292

Debussy

well-defined structural framework or whether, as the fundamental consideration, they have been achieved through the sacrifice of coherence — tonal or otherwise. Therefore, as both harmonic analysis and the Schenker method were evolved out of the tonal techniques, it is probable that a new system of analysis is needed to understand the new concepts defined by the whole-tone, polytonal, and twelve-tone systems and the new and different techniques they disclose. If we believe in the growth and expansion of musical techniques, we must also recognize that they require a form of analysis to cope with problems to which the new systems give rise. Since we grant that twentieth-century composers have added other systems to the major-minor through which the tonal concept was evolved, would it not be more realistic to admit that the differences between the old and new systems are too fundamental to be able to apply the same method of analysis to both with equally satisfactory results?

There can be no doubt that in our investigation of Debussy's techniques we have come in contact with a new and subtle musical personality whose ingratiating qualities concealed the strength behind its attacks on the tonal stronghold. It matters little whether these attacks were unconscious or premeditated, since the results are the same whatever their origin. Their imprint on the trends of early twentieth-century composers is reflected in the works of Schönberg, Stravinsky, Ravel, and many other of Debussy's contemporaries.

It is equally necessary, however, to recognize the other aspect of Debussy's art, his contribution to tonality through the extension and adaptation of the techniques inherent in its expression. We have observed many instances in which he molded these techniques to his own artistic style without losing the essential characteristics either of tonality or of his personal idiom. Therefore we must consider the new impulse he brought to music within the tonal principle, as well as the impulse he gave to the final breakdown of the concept. He achieved an originality of expression within the realm of tonality which, despite differences in treatment and style, is based on the artistic methods of the past. In severing his connections with the past, in his experiments with new techniques, he instituted practices that were to influence the future. Whether Debussy's chief contribution lies in extending the past into the present or in rejecting the past to lead into the future can only be decided by an examination of those works that are a natural outgrowth of his technical and stylistic innovations.

293

CHAPTER VIII

Stravinsky

NEW TENDENCIES *within the tonal concept. Implications of bitonal tech-*

niques. Is bitonality an outgrowth of tonality? Linear counterpoint;

comparison with contrapuntal techniques of Bach.

N the works of Stravinsky and Schönberg we are dealing with a type of music in which the older concept of unity no longer prevails. This is true of those early works in which tonality is still indicated, as well as of those in which it has been replaced by the newer concepts of poly-tonality and atonality. Yet analysts who attempt to explain these tech-niques continue to employ the same descriptive methods that they use for works within the tonal system.

If we accept the assumption to which the application of one form of analysis to all systems gives rise, we must conclude that there is a connec-tion between the older and newer concepts out of which the systems emerge. Such a deduction is both dangerous and misleading. It is danger-ous, because it re-establishes the past as the pattern on which we evaluate the present and thus unconsciously influences our reactions and responses. It is misleading, because there is no connection between the principles on which the foundations of the old and new systems are laid. The concepts underlying these systems are totally opposed to and have nothing whatso-ever in common with the concept of tonality.

Although both the atonal and polytonal systems grew out of a general protest against the romanticism of the nineteenth century, the two tech-niques express diametrically opposed points of view. Atonality, as the term implies, rejects the tonal concept and the harmonic principle of structural coherence on which it is based. Instead it recognizes the tone-series as a complex in which all twelve tones of the chromatic scale have equal status. In thus disposing of the fundamental tonic-dominant rela-tionship, the primary principle of tonal coherence, atonality frankly dis-avows its connection with the past. Polytonality, on the contrary, retains the textbook requirements for tonality, key center and harmonic relationship, but applies them to two or more tonalities simultaneously. Thus polytonality is regarded as a natural outgrowth of the methods of the past.

It is obvious that these systems necessarily employ the same raw material, the twelve half tones comprised in the octave. It is equally true, however, that the organization of this material and the original premise on which this organization is founded are totally dissimilar in every respect. To attempt to correlate these systems to show the natural development of the new out of the old not only negates the principles that govern tonality, but robs the newer methods of their distinctive and original characteristics.

Although Debussy weakened tonal coherence through the vagueness of his structural and prolonging techniques, his introduction of the whole-tone scale, and his substitution of melodic for structural coherence, there also are many instances in which he extended the older techniques within a clear-cut demonstration of tonality. Thus, though opening the door to the techniques of the future, he did not sever his connection with the principles of the past. Stravinsky, on the other hand, at times gives lip service to the older techinques, although he rejects the principles out of which they evolved.

In our discussion of polytonal and atonal techniques we shall apply to the early works in which the tonal system is evidenced the same type of analysis that we have used so far. For works in which it is replaced by the newer systems, we shall offer an explanation of the theory and point out the distinction between the old and new concepts of unity; we shall not, however, regard the name of a chord or the character of the chord structure as an adequate analysis of the music. Either we must explain the function of these chords and their significance in the passage, or we must admit that, due either to the vagueness of the motion or the lack of a new form of analysis, the music is incapable of explanation in accordance with the principles of harmony and counterpoint.

It is not sufficient to point to passages in Stravinsky's works as illustrative of his use of bitonality or polyharmony. This describes a method, but does not demonstrate the purpose it serves or the results it achieves. Nor shall we solve the problems of linear counterpoint by comparing Stravinsky's medium with Bach's, since the principles underlying their techniques are totally opposed. To understand the new idiom, we must try to find out the laws that govern its principles of voice leading and then contrast these with the contrapuntal principles that demonstrate the tonal concept.

The music of Stravinsky and Schönberg reflects the impulse of twentieth-century thought and life. To comprehend the theoretical principles that underlie the new concepts requires a serious and unprejudiced approach and an earnest desire to fathom the complexities the works disclose. The importance of the atonal and polytonal systems does not rest on personal likes or dislikes, nor on the growing assimilative capacity of the ear. The sole factor by which these systems can be judged is whether the techniques they provide demonstrate a new type of artistic unity to replace the principles of structural coherence that constitute tonality.

What principles govern the music of the twentieth century? For one answer, we can turn to the works of one of the outstanding contemporary composers, Igor Stravinsky. The techniques of Stravinsky may be sorted into two different categories — the extension of the old techniques and the creation of entirely new ones. Under the latter head come the experiments in polytonality and linear counterpoint.

It is not our intention to divide Stravinsky's works into different periods to find a comparison between the various stages of his development and the stylistic evolution of Picasso, as so often is done. It seems more logical to consider Stravinsky's work as a whole, since the seeds of the later techniques are already present in the early ones. It is true that in *Le Sacre du Printemps* and the Piano Sonata, the tendencies are more pronounced and the techniques more definitely outside the tonal concept than in *L'Oiseau de Feu* and *Petrouchka*, but this is a matter of degree rather than of basic distinction. The transition from the style of the *Sacre* to that of the *Octuor* was not a rejection of the earlier technique nor a rejection of the vertical for the horizontal treatment. It was rather a realization that a preoccupation with Russian legends and certain aspects of Russian life had resulted in a type of rhythmic treatment and chord structure in the *Sacre* beyond which further development was impossible. Consequently Stravinsky turned to problems of a more abstract nature. Basically, however, the inherent qualities of his musical language are the same, in spite of the different idioms in which they are expressed. These are the primary characteristics that have made Stravinsky a dominating force in twentieth-century music. They demonstrate that his contribution is an organic whole, the result of a natural development of his musical personality, rather than a series of conflicting theories and stylistic trends.

EXTENSION OF THE OLDER TECHNIQUES

The logical starting point of our discussion is *L'Oiseau de Feu*. Although it was preceded by the symphony in E♭, "Faun and Shepherdess," a suite for voice and orchestra, "Fireworks," and the *Scherzo fantastique,* these works are more or less in the academic style and cannot be regarded as typical. Granted that *L'Oiseau de Feu* reflects the influence of Rimsky-Korsakov, there are nevertheless various passages in which the treatment reveals those characteristics of Stravinsky that become more pronounced in the later works.

It is true that these innovations in rhythmic stress and chord structure are only pallid indications of the more dynamic changes that are to follow. Yet their very presence is proof that in spite of the conventional aspects, the seeds of the future already have been sown. There is the intense chromaticism of the Kastchei and Firebird motives which is later to dominate the linear style; the irregular rhythms and syncopations in the dance of Kastchei's suite that are brought to a climax in *Le Sacre du Printemps;* the canonic imitations in the Dance of the Princesses, which already show Stravinsky's interest in contrapuntal devices, and the conflicting voice motions in which the note of dissonance is strongly affirmed. In addition to these, and even more important, there is the unusual nature of the prolongations and their effect on the tonal structure.

Most authorities regard Stravinsky's treatment of *L'Oiseau de Feu* as typical of the nineteenth century and lacking in originality. They place it in an entirely different category from those later works in which the characteristics of his style are more strongly evident.

Superficially, it might appear as though the romantic quality of the legend, the highly chromatic style, the presence of key signatures, the use of tonic-dominant progressions, and the lush nature of the instrumentation were proof that Stravinsky was totally in accord with nineteenth-century methods. Yet even in the delicate and tender Lullaby, the most fitting movement of the suite in which to reveal the influence of the past, Stravinsky demonstrates tendencies in the prolongations that already point to the techniques of the future.

THE HARMONIC PROGRESSION

Not only does the Lullaby bear a key signature of E♭ minor, but the first twenty-five measures show an expanded I—V—I harmonic progres-

EXAMPLE 95

sion. Thus far, it appears as though Stravinsky were thinking in terms of tonality. However, to find out whether the prolonging chords confirm or negate the structural motion, it is also necessary to examine the techniques he has used to extend the progression.

In the graph [1] the Firebird figure, the predominating motive both of the top and of the middle voice, is enclosed in brackets. Although there is a clear indication of a motion from the tonic E♭ minor to the dominant B♭ major chord, the effect of the passing chords is to attenuate rather than intensify the tonal implications of the progression. This is due to the fact that these prolonging chords do not impel the motion from the tonic to the dominant chord, but through their own vagueness rob it of its inherent clarity.

The bass outlines a motion from E♭ to B♭. Although the E♭ minor chord passes to the D♭ minor, the entrance of F♯ and G (measures 17–19) before C♯ enters, tends to weaken the effect of the enharmonic exchange of D♭ for C♯ of the inverted A major chord (measure 20). Furthermore, had C♯ passed through C♮ to B♭, its status as a passing tone in the motion from E♭ to B♭ would have been clarified. Instead it moves to D♮ and then proceeds to B♭. Here is a contradiction that we must consider in relation to the motion of the top voice.

In the top voice E♭ of the tonic chord passes to D♮ of the dominant, returning to E♭ of the final E♭ chord. This motion is extended by the introduction of D♭ of the D♭ minor chord (measure 24) as an under neighbor of the opening E♭, with E♮ of the A major chord (measure 20) as an upper neighbor of D♮ of the B♭ major chord (measure 23). In other words, the motion E♭–D♮–E♭ has been expanded to E♭–D♭, E♮–D♮, E♭. If we accept this possible interpretation of these measures, we must examine the prolongations to find out whether they confirm it.

Since the first fifteen measures are concerned entirely with an extension of the tonic chord, we may begin with the D♭ minor chord which follows. According to the graph, D♭ in the bass is exchanged for C♯ of the A major chord. How has this been accomplished?

First of all we see that A♭, a middle voice, is shifted to a higher register, where it is exchanged for G♯. Then it passes through F♯ of the F♯ minor to E♮ of the A major chord. This motion is extended through the embellishing tones of the Firebird figure and the middle voice ascent through which E in the top voice is reached. Accordingly the F♯ minor and G major chords supporting the top voice prolongations can be accounted for as passing chords. However, since the F♯ chord (measure 18) is the start of a new phrase, at which point in the score the flats in the signature are replaced with naturals, it is questionable whether we should hear this F♯ chord in connection with the preceding phrase as a passing chord between the D♭ minor and A major chords, or whether we should regard it only in relation to the A major chord that follows. Yet what function has the F♯ chord if we consider it as the start of a new motion, and where does it go? What significance has the top-voice descent F♯–E unless we hear it in connection with A♭, whose exchange for G♯ introduces the melodic figure in which F♯ appears? These doubtful aspects of

Stravinsky

the treatment are partly clarified by the motion from the D♭ minor to the A major chord disclosed in the graph. Yet there is no definite means of proving that this reading coincides with Stravinsky's intentions.

We come now to the altered seventh chord on D (measure 21), in which D in the bass is the conflicting element in the descent from C♯ to B♭. Under ordinary circumstances, the A major chord would serve as an applied dominant of this D chord. Here, however, the function of this D chord is so unclear that it is problematical whether the A major chord is meant to demonstrate this connection. If C, the seventh of the chord, had been placed in the bass instead of in a middle voice, as a passing tone between C♯ of the A major and B♭ of the B♭ major chord, it would have clarified the status of the D chord as a passing chord in the descent from the tonic to the dominant. However, the presence of D in the bass tends to obscure both the function of this chord and the nature of the bass descent. In fact, the only clearly defined function of this altered chord on D is to prolong the top-voice motion from E♮, a neighbor note, to the structural D♮ of the B♭ chord. This expansion is the result of an embellishing motion for which the repetition of the motivic figure within the altered chord is responsible. Yet it is doubtful whether the prolongation this chord effects compensates for the confusion its presence brings to the motion. Not only is its own status unclear, through the presence of D in the bass, but it also obscures the function of the D♭ minor and A major chords. Moreover, because of the insecurity it brings to these chords, it tends to weaken the stability of the structural motion.

It is important to recognize this fact, since it indicates that the prolongations, instead of intensifying the structural motion by giving it greater force and momentum, enervate its inherent strength and attenuate its tonal implications.

This passage is significant. It shows that although a tonic-dominant relationship is the primary expression of coherence, such unity is attained only if the prolonging techniques demonstrate how the motion is achieved. The introduction of a B♭ major chord twenty-three measures after the entrance of a chord of E♭ minor assures a connection that can withstand the impact of any type of passing chord only if the status of these passing chords is clearly outlined in the prolonging motion so that their function within the extended space is well defined. It is equally true, however, that such a tonic-dominant progression cannot maintain its inherent unity if the intervening chords either negate the character of the progression

301

Challenge to Musical Tradition

or create a confusion in the motion. These chords may be of a highly unusual nature. As we have seen in the works of J. S. Bach, Philipp Emanuel Bach, Beethoven, Wagner, and Debussy, they are frequently so rich in their chromatic coloring, so varied in their intensity, that for the most part they are regarded as "modulations" to a new key. It does not matter whether the passing chords are dissonant or consonant, chromatic or diatonic, striking or conventional. The only requirément is that they demonstrate their function by clarifying the techniques that expand the structural progression. It is in this aspect that the treatment in the Lullaby falls short and indicates a definite weakness in the techniques creating and maintaining tonal coherence.

In contrast to the Lullaby, in which the unorthodox treatment is regarded as conventional, let us take another passage in which a basically orthodox treatment is attributed to the use of polyharmony — the Easter Song from *Petrouchka*.

THE NEIGHBOR–NOTE TECHNIQUE

It is apparent that striking developments in Stravinsky's rhythmic and prolonging techniques have taken place. Not only do we find an extension and adaptation of the past, but also the new tendencies that were to reach their climax in *Le Sacre du Printemps*.

As in *L'Oiseau de Feu*, Stravinsky has drawn freely on Russian folksongs for much of his melodic material. The following example from the opening scene at the fair is based on an Easter song sung by the peasants of Smolensk.[2] Both the original (example A) and Stravinsky's version [3] (example B) are given below for comparison.

Although Stravinsky has retained the original simplicity of the melody, the use of chords that at times conflict makes the adaptation far more complex than the original folksong. It also should be noted that through repetition the first four measures of the song are expanded to twelve in *Petrouchka*.

The characteristic figure C–B♭–A–G first enters in the bass, after which it is transferred to the top voice and extended by the embellishing figure A–F–G. The same type of embellishing figure is suggested in the bass in the motion A–E–F–G (measures 4–5). The unusual aspect of the treatment is the combination of triads such as the C major and G minor

[2] Rimsky-Korsakov collection (1876), No. 47.
[3] Copyright 1910–11. Used by permission of the Galaxy Music Corporation, representative of the publisher, Edition Russe de Musique, Paris.

EXAMPLE 96

(measure 1), C major and A minor (measure 2), and D minor and F major (measure 4), which obviously create a conflict in the motion. As a consequence, this passage is frequently cited as illustrative of the simultaneous use of two different triads — polyharmony. It is obvious that these independent triads are combined, but whether their presence represents an experiment along totally new lines or whether it is due mainly to the influence of the neighbor-note and embellishing techniques remains to be seen.

In the first two measures the chords of C and B♭ major and A and G minor appear in the lower voices against a G minor chord in the upper parts. We hear these chords not as harmonic entities, but as extensions of the G minor chord, a pivot around which all the motions throughout the passage revolve. This may be seen in the bass motions that embellish G, C–B♭–A–G, E–F–G, A–E–F–G, G–F–E–F–G. Although each moves around G as a center, the G appears more frequently as the second inversion of the C major than as the root of the G minor chord. In addition this C major chord is combined with a G minor chord in the upper voices. Such a combination is regarded as a use of polyharmony.

Challenge to Musical Tradition

This is one interpretation, based on the conflicting elements of the opposing triads. But do we actually hear this chord as an inverted position of C major? Are we not more aware of G as the root of the G minor chord than as the fifth of C major, with C—E temporarily replacing the chord tones B♭ and D? The motion from the C major to the G minor chord is given so much stress in the main figure that it seems much closer to what the music reveals to regard C—E as substitutes for the chord tones of the G minor triad than to hear these chords as two separate entities. Furthermore, the fact that in some instances the inverted C major chord is followed by G minor (measures 12, 15, and 16) bears out the suggestion that the former serves as a neighbor chord of the latter.

It is obvious that this combination of triads is the result of a neighbor motion of chords, rather than of single tones. As such, it is less an experiment in polyharmony than an ingenious extension of the older neighbor-note technique. The effect it creates is due to the simultaneous presence both of the neighbor notes and of the chord tones. Both, however, represent the same basic chord, one with melodic ornamentation, the other without.

The original and daring aspects of the treatment are not lessened by hearing this passage as an extension of the neighbor-note technique rather than as a venture along totally new lines. On the contrary, the innovations are more striking by comparison with the earlier results produced by the neighbor-note treatment. In fact it is much simpler to discard an old technique and invent a new one than to extend the old in so clever and original a manner that it gives the effect of a new one. The challenge is always more forceful when it attacks the tradition rather than the principles out of which the tradition evolved. It is always more revolutionary when it molds the older techniques to the requirements of a new age than when it overthrows and completely destroys them.

A further illustration of Stravinsky's extension of the older techniques to express an entirely new and different musical idiom may be seen in the Russian Dance,[4] also from *Petrouchka.*

HORIZONTALIZATION

The main technique employed is horizontalization, although the neighbor note again is an important element. However, instead of hori-

[4] Copyright 1910–11. Used by permission of the Galaxy Music Corporation, representative of the publisher, Edition Russe de Musique, Paris.

zontalizing the triad as the earlier composers did, or the seventh chord as Debussy did in *Pelléas et Mélisande*, Stravinsky goes further, to the chord of the, ninth. The sharp, dissonant effect of these ninths cleverly suggests the mechanical origin of the puppets rather than the human characteristics with which they have been invested.

EXAMPLE 97

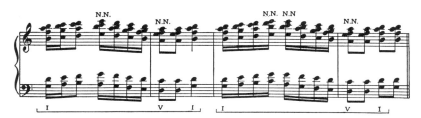

In the first two measures the top voice ascends from B to D passing to E, a neighbor note, which does not return to D but descends a fifth to A of the dominant chord. Thus the ascent outlining the tones B—D is embellished by a descending motion outlining the tones E—A, of which E is a neighbor of D, and A, a neighbor of the succeeding B. Parallel motions are carried out by the middle voices. Only in the bass do we find a slight deviation. Here G climbs to B the horizontalized third of the chord, but instead of continuing to C, a.neighbor note, in imitation of the top voice, the ascent stops at B, at which point the descent to D begins. As a result of this, instead of the fifths that the two lower voices of the ascent reveal, the descent outlines a motion in sevenths. In measure 3, however, the bass does reach C, a neighbor note, but it immediately falls back to A in duplication of the descent in measure 1. Undoubtedly the return from C to A in an incomplete neighbor-note motion is due to the fact that it provides for a step-wise descent to D; a direct return to B would have necessitated either a leap from F to D at the end or a break somewhere in the motion.

The basic technique is so simple that the dynamic effect it has achieved can be attributed only to the consistent use of ninth chords. Even the resulting dissonances are somewhat lessened because we hear the entire passage as a motion within and around a single horizontalized G major ninth chord. This illustration not only reveals Stravinsky's expansion of an old technique to new dimensions, but in addition clearly demonstrates the unlimited and still unexplored potentialities that the technique offers to contemporary composers.

Although horizontalization evolved out of the organic nature of the consonant triad, it has been applied to a dissonant chord of the ninth with such success that we are conscious of the existence of only one structural chord and thus can explain the status of the other ninth chords as passing or neighbor chords within the horizontalized motion.

The Russian Dance is usually cited as an illustration of polyharmony or a succession of ninth chords. Such explanations, however, do not actually clarify the motion or disclose the function of such techniques. Nor do they point out that the enormous ingenuity and boldness of the treatment lies in the extraordinary use Stravinsky has made of the horizontalized G ninth chord.

We come now to a work of an entirely different character, which, although indicated to be within the framework of tonality, is a product of linear counterpoint — the Finala from the *Sérénade èn La*. The discussion of the Finala at this point rather than later, as an example of linear counterpoint, is logical because of the use of horizontalization and also because there might be a tendency to hear the motion as outlined by a tonic-dominant progression, even though the tonic chord never appears in root position. However, even though the motion is not altogether clear, certain tendencies in the treatment place the work in the category of the older techniques rather than among the later techniques in which the tonal principles no longer prevail.

Although Stravinsky calls the work a serenade, "in imitation of the Nachtmusik of the eighteenth century," [5] he has stated that he did not intend the title, *Sérénade en La*, to indicate a tonality. Instead, it refers to the fact that he made "all the music revolve about an axis of sound which happened to be La."

Now let us turn to the music [6] to see what he means by "an axis of sound."

Starting on an inverted A minor chord, the top voice descends from C to C♯ while the lower voices descend an octave. The use of G♯ and F♯ in the top voice and of G♮ and F♮ in the other parts creates an ambiguous descending motion that is only partly clarified by the entrance of C♯ (measure 3) as a mixture of the A minor-major chord.

[5] *Chronicles of My Life* (Simon and Schuster, 1936), p .203.

[6] Copyright 1926. Used by permission of the Galaxy Music Corporation, representative of the publisher, Russischer Musik Verlag, Berlin.

Stravinsky

EXAMPLE 98

If we examine the bass, we find that at no time does the root of the A minor-major chord appear. Only the third, fifth, and seventh are disclosed, providing the two figures that are repeated through measures 3–10.

Challenge to Musical Tradition

The fact that these same figures reappear either in their original form or with slight alterations at various points throughout the passage (measures 13–14, 18–22, and 24–25) seems to indicate that they constitute the main chord outline, with all other tones passing or neighbor notes.

The top voice meanwhile outlines the melodic figure (a) as a motion within the A major-minor chord except for those instances in which neighbor or embellishing tones appear. However, whether these melodic patterns have a structural significance and what connection such a motion would have with the bass cannot be stated. For example, how can we explain a voice leading in which E♯ and G♯ in the bass are opposed by E♮ and G♮ in the top voice (measure 20), when neither of these voices demonstrates a clear-cut motion to a definite goal?

It must be obvious that an "axis of sound" revolving around an A minor chord produces a vastly different result from the expression of an A minor-major tonality. Undoubtedly Stravinsky achieved his purpose, but it is evident that the techniques either are too indefinite to reveal the meaning of this passage or else require an entirely new form of analysis, based on totally new principles of voice leading. All that we can deduce is that Stravinsky's counterpoint consists entirely of arpeggiated chords, the A minor-major, its neighbor and passing chords.

Although the presence of B and D♯ in the upper voices of the closing measure stresses the effect of the E minor chord as a dominant, is its connection with the opening A minor-major chord so clearly defined that we hear the motion as an outline of a tonic-dominant progression? Can we regard these thirty measures as an expression of the A minor-major tonality or is the progression itself too unstable to withstand the impact of the prolonging techniques?

Since Stravinsky has stated that the work was conceived around A rather than within the A tonality, there may be a difference of opinion whether he intended to suggest a connection between the A minor-major and the E minor chord, and whether the prolonging and structural techniques underlying tonality are applicable to this passage. Although it is possible that the structural implications are unintentional, the predominance of the A chord in the motion and the stress of the E minor chord at the end bring these chords so strongly into the spotlight that they indicate a connection in the form of a tonic-dominant progression irrespective of whether the work gravitates around A or expresses a mixture of the A tonality. Therefore, since these chords suggest a structural motion, it is logical to regard the intervening chords as prolongations whether or not they offer a convincing demonstration of their functions as passing and embellishing chords. Furthermore some readers may claim that because of the linear aspect of the treatment, Stravinsky's main concern is to preserve the integrity of the independent voice parts even at the sacrifice of the structural clarity. It is a question, however, whether we can regard this passage as typical of the linear technique because of the uncharacteristic nature of the counterpoint. Here the individual voice parts result not from the customary melodic impulse but from a harmonic impulse, through the constant use of chord arpeggiation. Thus counterpoint has been robbed of its inherent function as a purely melodic technique by exchanging its melodic origin in a succession of intervals, for a harmonic origin, in a succession of arpeggiated chord tones.

The reader may argue that the horizontalized chord is also the origin of Bach's counterpoint. This is true. However, Bach fills the space between the members of a harmonic progression not with a motion consisting of further arpeggiations of chords whose nature and status are unclear, but with voice leadings that provide a definite stimulus to the structural motion. In short, Bach's counterpoint is based on the horizontal principle although the space it fills is outlined by the structural progression.

It is also questionable whether Stravinsky has achieved new effects through the new tendencies in his treatment. Certainly the presence of G♯ and E♯ in one voice and G♮ and E♮ in another is not an innovation, since there are innumerable instances of such dissonances in the works of Bach, with this difference — that Bach's use of dissonance can be accounted for through the voice leadings. In the Stravinsky example, on the contrary, the dissonances cannot be explained either by the nature of the voice parts or by the necessities of the structural motion.

To prove the truth of this statement, let us take a few brief examples from various works of Bach in which we find dissonances similar to those that occur throughout the Finala.

In the first two measures of the passage from the Finala, Stravinsky has created a rich and unusual color effect through the mixture of the A minor and A major chords. This is due primarily to the presence of G♯ and F♯ in the top voice, with G♮ and F♮ following closely in the bass. However, the impressionistic result is attributable not to the counterpoint, but to the inherent conflict between the outlined A major and A minor chords. The originality lies in the simultaneous use of the major and minor forms

Challenge to Musical Tradition

of the same chord. Here the primary impulse is of a harmonic rather than a contrapuntal nature.

There are numerous instances in Bach's works in which an altered and unaltered form of the same tone appear in different voices within the same measure. In these, however, the presence of the altered tone is due entirely to a melodic impulse and can be explained by the contrapuntal principles that govern the laws of voice leading.

The first of these examples is a passage from the sarabande of the English suite in A major.

EXAMPLE 99

We see that Bach has used G♯ in the top voice and G♮ in the bass. If we examine these voices, however, it is apparent that G♯ and G♮ demonstrate two entirely different functions. G♯ occurs as a passing tone in a scale-wise ascent from F♯ to its octave. As an expression of the F♯ minor chord, it was logical to employ G♯. In the bass, however, G♮ serves as a neighbor note of F♯ and is more indicative of this embellishing function than G♯. Thus the roles that these two tones play in their respective voices account for the simultaneous presence of the altered and unaltered tone.

The allemande from the English suite in G minor reveals various instances of a similar conflict between the voice leadings. One of the most daring is a passage in which E♭ occurs in the top voice with E♮ following closely in a middle voice.

We can understand Bach's reasons for using these two tones in such proximity if we differentiate between the functions they exercise. The passage shows a motion from the C minor through the inverted seventh chord on D to the G minor chord. The top voice discloses an unfolding of E♭–G of the C minor and F♯–D of the D major chord, through which the motion from E♭ to D is prolonged. As indicated in the graph, E♭–D represent the top voice and G–F♯ a middle voice shifted to a higher

EXAMPLE 100

register. Thus we hear a motion in thirds. The E♭ that appears above C
and D is the same E♭ on which the passage opens and is retained as a
suspension until it passes to D. Actually E♭ is held while G moves to F♯,
after which it gives way to D.

In the bass, however, we find E♮ instead of E♭ as a passing tone between D and F♯ of the D major chord, to strengthen the impulse that F♯
gives to the following G minor chord. Although Casella might attribute
the use of E♭ in the top voice and E♮ in the bass to the simultaneous use
of the harmonic and melodic minor scales, as he did in his explanation
of a somewhat similar passage, we cannot agree with this point of view.
The fact that E♭ and F♯ occur within the harmonic minor and E♮ and F♯
within the melodic minor does not account for the presence of E♭ and E♮
since their position in the scale is secondary, while the differentiated functions they fulfill are primary factors that necessitated the use of both
the altered and unaltered tones. Thus the underlying cause that explains
these tones is the distinctive roles they play in the prolonging motion as a
passing and an embellishing tone.

The next example appears in the Christe Eleison from the Mass in B
minor.

Here we find G in the top voice against G♯ in the bass, the same dissonance Stravinsky used in the Finala (measure 16).

The graph indicates that the entire passage outlines a motion within
the A major chord in which the top voice descends from G to C♯, while
A in the bass is embellished with B and G♯ its upper and lower neighbor

311

EXAMPLE 101

N.N N.N.   N.N.

notes. Although there might be a tendency to hear G♯ on the fourth quarter of the measure in combination with E in the top voice as an inverted E major chord, it actually belongs with F♯, D, and B of the preceding chord. However, it is possible that to maintain the eighth-note figure in the bass rather than have an eighth and two sixteenths on the third beat and A, a quarter note, on the fourth, G♯ has been shifted rhythmically so that it enters on the final quarter of the measure in connection with the tones of the A major chord. Thus B and G♯ serve as neighbors of A, while F♯ in the top voice is a passing tone.

From this point of view, the use of G in the top voice is easily understood, since it is the seventh of the A major chord. In addition, it should be noted how cleverly the embellishing figure around E imitates G–F♯–E of the structural descent before passing through D to C♯.

In the final measure the G♯ chord again enters in the same capacity in which it served in the preceding measure, as a neighbor-passing chord. Its repetition gives weight to the explanation of the earlier G♯ as the root of the seventh chord.

If we listened to this passage without recalling its source, it would be easy to believe that it had been written by Stravinsky or any other contemporary composer. Certainly it is as dissonant and full of conflict as the Finala. Yet the technique is remarkable because every element in the motion is clearly defined, and we can explain every dissonance in the passage. Here the dissonances do not confuse or weaken the tonality, but

Stravinsky

lend richness, color contrast, and intensity to the outlined A major chord. Where in present-day music can we find a more striking and dynamic effect within or outside of the tonal concept? Yet in spite of the twentieth-century aspect of the treatment, in so far as the conflicting voice leadings are concerned, there can be no doubt as to the meaning of the motion or the techniques by which it has been achieved.

The final example from the fugue in E♭ major needs little clarification.

EXAMPLE 102

It is obvious that the first three quarters of the measure define a motion within the C minor chord. The top voice shows a neighbor motion of E♭—D—E♭ and the middle voice an outlining motion from G to C. This space has been filled with the passing tones A♮ and B♮ to intensify the ascent to C, since B♮ in combination with D of the top voice has the effect of a leading tone and points more conclusively to the connection between G and C than if B♭ had been employed. The use of B♮ accounts for the presence of A♮.

In the bass, however, B♭ and A♭ appear in the descent from C of the C minor chord to G of the G major. As a passing tone in the motion, Bach used B♭ to differentiate its function from that of B♮, the third of the G major chord. The use of B♮ would have indicated a motion from C to B♮, with the space between B♮ and G outlining the horizontalized G major chord. To indicate that the space is from C to G, Bach introduced B♭ and A♭.

Furthermore, there is no conflict between this B♭ and the B♮ that follows in the middle voice, since the distinctive function of each is clearly defined.

Although the underlying reasons for the use of B♮—A♮ in one voice and B♭—A♭ in another are fully demonstrated, this does not minimize the bold and original aspects of the treatment. It only proves that striking effects can be achieved within the fundamental principles which govern the leading of voices.

These four examples are only a few of the innumerable instances prov-

313

ing that Bach's treatment is as daring and unconventional as Stravinsky's. The difference lies in the fact that Stravinsky arbitrarily employs an A major against an A minor descent, a G in one voice against G♯ in another, to attain full independence of the melodic lines. Bach, on the other hand, appears to achieve an equal contrast in the voice parts, but by methods that are not arbitrary but can be justified by the different functions the voices demonstrate. The primary distinction, however, is one not only of treatment but of conception. For Stravinsky the conflict between the melodic lines seems to be the main objective, since structural coherence is lacking; for Bach structural coherence is the goal, and the conflicting motions are incidental. In short, with Stravinsky counterpoint is an end in itself, while with Bach it is rather a means by which tonal stability is maintained and structural motion enriched.

In examining the preceding passages from Stravinsky's works, we have found evidence that these early works disclose an extension and adaptation of the older techniques to the requirements of a new and different stylistic expression. In some, Stravinsky has enlarged and intensified their former function without affecting the tonal clarity. In others, he has used prolonging chords whose vagueness definitely weakens the structural motion outlined by a harmonic progression. There is evidence in all these passages, however, of a dynamic impulse stretching out in all directions to meet the demands of a vital and robust musical personality.

The ingenious treatment of the motivic figure, the neighbor note, and the ostinato in the example from the Lullaby; the new use Stravinsky has made of an embellishing motion and the neighbor chord in the Easter Song, and the application of the technique of horizontalization to a ninth chord in the Russian Dance suggest that he will continue to mold the older methods to express the new tendencies of a new age. On the other hand, the vagueness of the passing chords that prolong the harmonic progression in the Lullaby indicate a weakness in the interlocking of the harmonic and contrapuntal principles that, carried further, would endanger tonal coherence. Finally, the nature of the counterpoint in the Finala is too closely identified with chord arpeggiation to be regarded as having a melodic origin and too unclear in its definition of the voice leadings to demonstrate its function as a prolongation of the harmonic progression. Thus the trend it indicates, if confirmed by the later linear technique, also foreshadows an unmistakable attenuation of tonal unity.

It must be admitted that Stravinsky has reached a stage in his development from which he may proceed in either of two opposite directions. He may become more daring and original within the framework of tonality, or he may seek unrestricted freedom outside the scope of tonality. He can achieve the former only if the basic motion is so clearly defined as to permit use of any type of prolonging chord, however striking and unusual, without impairing structural coherence. The alternative leads to a more consistent use of those techniques whose impact on the harmonic framework will result in an ever-increasing weakening of coherence and the ·tonal concept.

In *Petrouchka* the experiment in bitonality already indicates one direction Stravinsky is to take. Were this the only instance of such a technique, we could attribute this fragmentary adventure to the dramatic influence of the ballet. However, we find an even more extended use of conflicting chords in the *Sacre,* in which the treatment must be regarded no longer as experimental, but as a full-fledged technique in which Stravinsky's originality seeks expression.

Although these essays in bitonality and polyharmony must be classed among the new techniques, there are aspects of the treatment that obviously stem from the older method. For example, the triad is still the harmonic symbol on which the bitonal technique is based. Unlike Schönberg, Stravinsky has not altered the structure of the chord as built on thirds, but has combined chords that originate in different fundamentals and thus indicate two distinct and unrelated keys.

The retention of the triad, the chord structure that prevailed within the tonal system, is undoubtedly responsible for the claim that the new system is an outgrowth of the old. Nevertheless, although the triad and various other aspects of the older treatment have survived, the principles which they demonstrated in the past are not the principles they now serve, since the fundamental concept of tonality no longer prevails.

To understand where the difference lies, let us examine some examples in which the techniques, although allied to the older system, must be regarded as new because their functions are changed even though their outward appearance is the same.

THE NEW TECHNIQUES

Since most authorities agree that it is in *Petrouchka* that Stravinsky first experiments with the bitonal technique, let us take a well-known example from the scene in Petrouchka's cell. Although the passage is frequently cited as an example of bitonality, so far as the author knows no explanation of the techniques have been offered, nor has there been any attempt to find out what Stravinsky achieved by the treatment. This may be due to a fact that Aaron Copland has stated,[7] although not in this connection: "No one has tried to set up any logical system based on polytonal writing. For the most part, composers have used it in an incidental way, rather than trying to apply the principle in large works."

Should we infer from this statement that since the polytonal system is regarded as an outgrowth of tonality, there is no necessity to establish a new constructive principle, or that since it is used only "in an incidental way," it is not sufficiently important to require a logical system of its own? However, even in such passages as the Petrouchka motive, it seems pointless to call attention to the use of a new idiom without indicating the innovations in the technique, the type of motion they create, and the new concept to which they give rise. Otherwise the example merely describes the meaning of polytonal harmonies, but does not demonstrate how it differs from the older system.

The questions that must be answered are: (1) What constructive principle underlies this new system? (2) What characteristic element replaces the horizontalized chord? (3) What similarity is there between the tonal and bitonal techniques? (4) How has Stravinsky achieved artistic coherence through the use of two simultaneous keys?

Let us turn to the passage from *Petrouchka* [8] for a demonstration of the bitonal techniques.

First of all, we see that Stravinsky has used an F♯ major and a C major chord. It is possible that in combining these totally different triads, he intends to suggest the irreconcilable aspects of Petrouchka's nature. However, we can regard the selection of such conflicting chords as a deliberate attempt to make music a means of Freudian expression only if an analysis reveals that the motion itself does not demonstrate the musical function these chords serve.

The most striking aspect of the treatment is the antagonism inherent in the C and F♯ major chords and the dissonances to which the arpeggiation of these chords gives rise. The use of the outlined chord is reminiscent of the older technique, but the simultaneous unfolding of two diametri-

[7] *Our New Music* (Whittlesey House, 1941), p. 61.

[8] Copyright 1910–11. Used by permission of the Galaxy Music Corporation, representative of the publisher, Edition Russe de Musique, Paris.

EXAMPLE 103

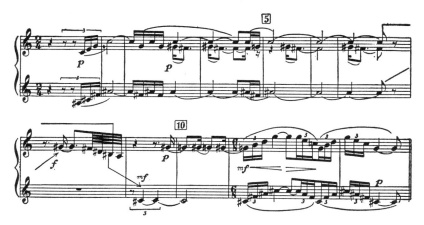

cally opposed and unrelated chords is a definite departure from the older treatment. The fundamental purpose behind horizontalization was to create motion within the spaces of the outlined chord. Let us find out whether the same idea prevails here.

The first seven measures show a static C as a top voice, with a middle-voice motion from G to F♯ in which F♯ is embellished by its neighbor, G♯. In measure 8, C disappears, but B♯, its enharmonic equivalent, enters in the descending figure and passes to C♯ in the bass. Thus C, the top voice of the C major chord, moves to C♯, the fifth of the F♯ major chord.

In a similar manner A♯, sustained in the bass throughout the first seven measures, seems to vanish entirely, but instead it moves to G♯, which now enters as a top voice and later moves to G♮ of the G and C major chords. Thus the C of the C major chord passes C♯ of the inverted F♯ major chord, while A♯ of the F♯ chord moves through G♯ to G♮ of the G and C major chords. This is actually all that occurs within these twelve measures. There is no motion either within or around the outlined chords, but only a juggling of voices that leads to a new conflict between the G and F♯ major chords. The effect of the contrasting chords, so ingeniously conceived, is so striking that it conceals the fact that there is no motion to prove the function of these chords as tonics, since there is no motion demonstrating either the C or F♯ major tonality.

This brings up a pertinent question. If we accept the premise that a chord or a group of chords within the same key do not automatically create tonality, but that tonality is achieved only if these chords define a structural motion demonstrating tonal coherence, and if we accept the definition of bitonality as the simultaneous use of two tonalities and two keys, then can we regard a passage built solely on two static fundamental chords lacking both structural and tonal definition, as an illustration of bitonality? Is the mere presence of two opposing chords sufficient to create bitonality, or is it essential that each proves its tonal character through a well defined structural framework? In short, if bitonality is a product of tonality, have we not the right to expect that although there will be many changes in the treatment and various innovations in the technique, the fundamental principles that demonstrate the connection between the tonal and bitonal concepts will be preserved? If not, then why cling to the term "tonality"? Is it not a contradiction?

Although this passage is always cited as illustrative of bitonality or polytonal harmony, it seems to be an ingenious treatment of two different chords without any tonal implications. As an acknowledged attempt to portray, by means of conflicting chord structures, the schizophrenic tendency in Petrouchka's nature, it is a highly original and successful experiment. As an example of the use of two tonalities it is totally unconvincing, since it offers no proof whatsoever of the existence of those structural elements that are essential to the definition of the C and F♯ major tonalities.

In this same scene, however, Stravinsky has given an extraordinary demonstration of his imagination through techniques that are equally new but that carry out his intention to use conflicting chords in such a manner that they produce the effect of a new type of structural motion.

The principal struggle arises in the antagonism between the tones F♯ and G, sometimes altered to F♮ and G♯. The manner in which Stravinsky has used these tones to build up a scene of growing intensity until they are brought together into a dynamic climax is the amazing aspect of the treatment. Not only is this dissonant interval given a new function, but through it the whole concept of dissonance has undergone a drastic change.

In these five excerpts [9] from the scene in Petrouchka's cell, the struggle between G and F♯, which is only suggested in Example A, shows itself with growing strength until it becomes the sole issue of the eight meas-

[9] Copyright 1910–11. Used by permission of the Galaxy Music Corporation, representative of the publisher, Edition Russe de Musique, Paris.

Stravinsky

EXAMPLE 104

ures of the final passage. That these tones are shown first in succession, then simultaneously, and again in Examples C and D in succession before the major conflict begins, emphasizes afresh the problem that is solved only in the final resolution chord of D major. Again there are times when G♯ replaces G♮ in the war for supremacy. Irrespective of the form, the struggle is constantly being renewed.

There is a similarity between the preceding illustration (Example

319

103) and the passage shown in Example E, since in both the two opposing chords appear. In Example E, however, the fact that the phrase concludes on a consonant D major chord is indicative of a difference in the techniques that may also be indicative of a difference in their functions. Is it not possible that although the F♯ and C major triads are unrelated, in the final measure they have been combined to give the feeling of an altered dominant seventh chord on A♯? According to this reading, F♯, which at the beginning of this passage appears in combination with G and E, of which tones it is a neighbor note, in the last four measures enters as a passing tone between the extended motion from G to E indicated in the top and middle voice.

The nature of the passage and the major role played by the C and F♯ major chords in other sections of the scene make it impossible to offer any explanation that can be fully substantiated. However, there is definite proof that Stravinsky differentiated the treatment here from that in the earlier use of the C and F♯ major chords, since the presence of the D major chord gives a feeling of finality that is lacking in the other instance. In addition, the motion G–F♯–E in the upper voices over A♯ in the bass points to G and E as chord tones, with F♯ as a passing tone.

If Stravinsky intended to suggest a dominant-tonic feeling, he has achieved his purpose in a most striking and unusual manner. On the other hand, if he meant to duplicate the earlier unresolved conflict between the C and F♯ major chords, the D major chord defeats his plans. Nevertheless, whether accidental or premeditated, there is a suggestion that the prolonged struggle represents a form of suspension, resolved only when the chords are combined so as to give the effect of a dominant of the D major chord that follows.

The building up of an entire scene on the conflicting elements outlined in the C and F♯ major chords, of which G and F♯ are the principal antagonists, is far greater evidence of Stravinsky's creative artistry than the mere use of so-called "bitonality." Here we see what he has accomplished through the combination of these chords and the means by which it has been attained. In fact, this latter passage is so necessary to the clarification of the preceding techniques that the opening passage should not be cited without a reference to what follows.

There can be no doubt as to the originality of the conception or the boldness with which it is expressed. Furthermore, the scene as a whole is a remarkable instance of how the use of contrasting chords can transform certain aspects of the older techniques into a new and arresting but musically sound treatment.

In *Le Sacre du Printemps* we approach a work that became the storm center about which musical opinion raged. The adherents of Stravinsky acclaimed it as the dawn of a new era in music that would clear away the obsolete traditions of the past and establish the artistic credo of the future. The anti-Stravinsky faction regarded it as equally revolutionary, but in a direction that they believed to be catastrophic. Yet in spite of these diverse opinions, both groups recognized that it was a work in which the musical values were so new, the techniques so revolutionary, that it shook the very foundations of the tonal world. It not only challenged the concepts and structural principles of the past, but, through the violence of its impact, questioned the direction the music of the future was to take. No one could listen to the *Sacre* without realizing that Stravinsky had given an entirely new function to the vital elements of music — melody, rhythm, counterpoint, harmony, and tone color.

In the *Sacre* the polyharmonic tendencies that were ascendant in *Petrouchka* are brought to a climax. No longer is the technique in an experimental stage, nor can we regard it as entirely incidental; it occurs too frequently.

The opening measures of the introduction [10] provide an interesting illustration of Stravinsky's treatment of a simple folk tune.

The melodic figure, built entirely on the unfolding of the A and E minor chords, possesses a lyric quality whose inherent simplicity is emphasized by the repetition of a single descending third, C—B—A. Here the elemental character of the melody and the use of repetition constitute the musical expression of the primitive nature of the ritual that follows. That the melodic figure is a perfect embodiment of the fundamental aspects of the scene is again evidence of Stravinsky's artistic vision.

The entrance of a middle voice, however, on C♯, as an indication of the following C♯ minor chord, offsets the motion in the top voice by a contradictory motion of its own, which is shown in the graph as a chromatic descent from G♯ and C♯ to their octave. The enharmonic equivalents have been used to clarify the motion.

We see that C of the top voice is prolonged for four measures and then begins a descent to B, a ninth below. Whether this denotes an ex-

---

[10] Copyright 1921. Used by permission of the Galaxy Music Corporation, representative of the publisher, Russischer Musik Verlag, Berlin.

EXAMPLE 105

tended motion from C to B or whether it is exchanged for C♯ in the final
measure, passing to D, an upper neighbor, before moving to B, is not disclosed in the music. All that is evident is that the top-voice motion is completely independent of the two lower voices and the space they outline
from C♯ and G♯ to their octaves below. This space is filled by a scale-
wise descent, further enriched by chromatic passing tones. Thus the top
voice outlines a motion indicative of the A minor-major chord in a descent from C♮ to B, while the lower part moves within the two tones implying the C♯ minor chord.

What does this motion within two totally unrelated chords· signify?
It might be possible to interpret it as representing primitive man's strug-

gle with nature, except for Stravinsky's statement that the *Sacre* must be regarded as absolute music, not influenced by the program.

To explain this passage as a use of polytonal harmonies does not clarify the technique or indicate the structural principle that lies behind it. The essential function of any system, tonal or otherwise, is to provide a means of expressing a musical idea. No system is complete, however, unless it evolves its own principle of unity in the form of artistic coherence. Since Stravinsky has replaced the old techniques with new ones, the fundamental problem his music presents is whether in discarding the older concept of coherence he has formulated a new one, based on a structural principle that clarifies the polyharmonic technique.

The reader may refute this statement by claiming that we are looking for some of the same characteristics in contemporary music that we found in the music of the past. Our answer is that if the terms "bitonality" and "polytonal harmony" are properly named and if the reiterated statement that the techniques they engender are an outgrowth of tonality is true, then we have a right to look for tendencies proving that such a connection exists.

However, we must turn to other examples to see if there are passages in the *Sacre* in which the techniques do establish a motion within each of the individual tonalities.

In the "Dance of the Adolescents," [11] which has the key signature of three flats, we come to a striking illustration of the conflict between two totally diverse chord structures, the triad of F♭ major and the seventh chord on E♭.

We can regard this conflict from three different points of view. It may represent a musical equivalent of the primitive nature of the ritual that is being enacted on the stage. As a realistic expression of the choreography, it lies outside the realm of pure music and consequently stands only in its relation to the ballet. Yet if, as Stravinsky claims, the *Sacre* must be judged solely on musical grounds, we cannot accept this explanation as valid. A second possibility, if the key signature is indicative of the E♭ major tonality, is that the F♭ major chord is a neighbor chord and appears simultaneously with the chord it embellishes. However, if this is a fact rather than a theory, we must find evidence to prove that the F♭ chord serves in this capacity. A third supposition is that Stravinsky has combined two con-

---

[11] Copyright 1921. Used by permission of the Galaxy Music Corporation, representative of the publisher, Russischer Musik Verlag, Berlin.

EXAMPLE 106

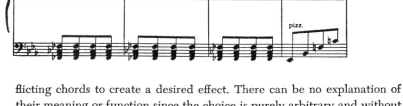

flicting chords to create a desired effect. There can be no explanation of their meaning or function since the choice is purely arbitrary and without tonal or structural implication. It is sufficient that these chords express Stravinsky's intention.

Since the first interpretation is invalidated by Stravinsky's claim that the *Sacre* is absolute music, our discussion is limited to the two other possibilities. There is no element in the treatment to substantiate the assumption that the F♭ major chord is a neighbor of the E♭ chord. Although the passing of F♭ and A♭ to E♭ and B♭ in the final measure at first seems to confirm the reading of F♭ major as a neighbor chord, the entrance of F♮ and C♮ in the same measure immediately negates this possibility. This leaves no alternative but to regard the passage as an experiment in polyharmony, for which no present method of analysis has offered an explanation. The reader may claim that as an arbitrary combination of chords producing the harsh, naked effect the composer desired, the passage fulfills its function without further explanation. This may be the case, but if we accept this theory, we must also acknowledge that the fundamental conception of music as coherence no longer prevails. If we admit that these techniques are totally divorced from the past and create a new type of music in which a structural principle is not required, the passage becomes an interesting experiment in dissonance that results in ar amazingly realistic expression of stark primitivism. On the other hand, to regard the treatment as an outgrowth of the past and the techniques as allied to the techniques of the tonal system denies the older techniques their structural and prolonging functions and robs the tonal concept of its fundamental principle — coherence. The passage lacks structural unity and tonal clarity. Therefore as a by-product of the older methods, it is inexplicable and totally incomprehensible.

Another passage from *Le Sacre du Printemps* that is illustrative of the so-called polytonal system comes from *Jeu du Rapt* [12] (*The Play of the Rapt*).

EXAMPLE 107

[12] Copyright 1921. Used by permission of the Galaxy Music Corporation, representative of the publisher, Russischer Musik Verlag, Berlin.

325

Challenge to Musical Tradition

The two upper groups of intervals provide the main conflict in the motion. This is due to the inherent antagonism between the embellishing motions generated by the major third, F♯–A♯, and the major sixth, A♯–F𝄪, throughout the first four measures. In the fifth measure this same struggle is renewed when F♯–A♯ moves to F♮–A♮ and the major sixth A♯–F𝄪, becomes the minor sixth, A♯–F♯. However, the conflict is not confined to these intervals, but permeates every aspect of the descending and ascending motions. For example F♯ and A♯ in the opening measure descend to B♯–D♯ and then ascend to F♮–A♮ (measure 5). In a similar manner A♯–F𝄪 descend to D𝄪–B♯ before F𝄪 is replaced by F♯. As a result, we find F𝄪 against F♯, D𝄪 against D♯, C♮ in opposition to C♯, and F♯ against F♮.

How shall we explain these measures? Should we regard them as indicative of contrasting melodic lines, which derive their impulse from the embellishment of the F𝄪 and F♯ chords, or should we look at them solely from the contrapuntal point of view as representing two different tonal planes, with F𝄪–C♯ in the bass as a kind of pedal point? However, does not the consistent use of thirds and sixths in parallel motion in the upper parts more or less negate the contrapuntal possibility?

On the other hand, if we regard these intervals as indicative of the F♯ and F𝄪 chords, can we explain the passage as an embellishing motion around these chords when the status of these chords is itself so unclear?

These questions arise only if we assume that the intervals are indicative of two different tonalities. It is possible, however, that they are without tonal implication and have been used not to demonstrate the functions they exercise in a structural motion, but to serve an entirely new purpose. According to this assumption, these opposing intervals, when combined, create a harsh, dissonant effect that intensifies the impact of the rhythm as the primary factor in the treatment. They are merely the tone combinations whose sole function is to reinforce the rhythmic impulse. From this point of view, their function as rhythmic agents accounts for their presence. Yet whether the reader accepts this explanation or regards the passage as indicative of bitonality, he must admit that the techniques have no connection with the past, since in neither case do they define a structural principle. As an example of bitonal treatment, the passage is unconvincing, since the presence of two conflicting intervals does not automatically constitute bitonality. As a demonstration of a new method in which the melodic and harmonic elements have been subordi-

nated to a purely rhythmic impulse at the sacrifice of their inherent functions, there can be no doubt that the technique is totally divorced from
the older treatment in which these functions are maintained to create the
structural principle of tonal coherence.

This same figure occurs in a later section of the work, *Jeux des Cités
Rivales* (Games of the Rival Tribes),[13] and reveals a similar contradiction
between the thirds outlined in the upper and lower voices.

EXAMPLE 108

In his detailed discussion of the *Sacre,* Herbert Fleischer offers this
explanation of the above example:

"The figure is introduced by two groups of horns in thirds which are
frequently separated by a difference of a minor second and in such a way
the melody is harmonized chromatically. . . .

"With this, a constructive harmonic principle is established which in
later works, especially the *Story of a Soldier,* has found its final form."

"The principle of the harmonic coupling of chromatically adjacent
tones and tonalities is an essential element in the understanding of this
dance. The tonality of this passage despite its mystic earth-gray colors is
very close to the character of F major — D minor."[14]

Here at last is a concrete statement of what Fleischer believes is a
principle underlying Stravinsky's technique. But what does Fleischer mean
by the term "principle of harmonic coupling" and why does he apply it to
this passage when in the preceding example, he referred [15] to a similar
group of thirds as "melodic lines"? Does "harmonic" denote the interval

[13] Copyright 1921. Used by permission of the Galaxy Music Corporation, representative of the publisher, Russischer Musik Verlag, Berlin.

[14] *Stravinsky* (Russischer Musik Verlag, Berlin, 1931), p. 120.

[15] *Ibid.,* p. 114.

of a third as an element of the chord structure, or does it indicate the chord function out of which each tonality emerges? If, on the other hand, it represents a new principle, as Fleischer seems to imply, that is expressed through the use of adjacent thirds, why ally it through terminology with an older concept to which it is basically opposed?

We have pointed out that the presence of a static fundamental chord does not constitute tonality, but that tonality is achieved only through a clearly defined structural progression in which the prolonging chords cooperate with the structural chords to produce tonal coherence. If we accept this concept of tonality, why should we regard the mere presence of two adjacent thirds as sufficient evidence of a harmonic principle to establish two diverse tonalities? Furthermore, what connection is there between the structural principle that demonstrates tonality and the harmonic principle derived from two adjacent thirds?

There is no reason why Stravinsky should not combine these adjacent tone groups if he so desires. But there is also no reason for claiming that they represent a harmonic principle and constitute a tonal framework. It is possible to present F and F♯ or F♯ and F𝄪 simultaneously and still remain within a single tonality, if one of these tones is shown to be of melodic origin, such as an embellishment or a passing tone, while the other defines some element of the tonal structure. It is equally possible to combine these tones as Stravinsky has done if we admit that they represent a technique that is entirely without tonal implication.

To call the use of adjacent thirds a harmonic principle is misleading. It is not a principle, since there is no clarification of the artistic concept of which it is an expression. It is a technique that, based on the same interval that served to define the character of a chord structure or the space within the outlined chord in the older system, is linked with the older techniques. However, the purpose it serves and the results that Stravinsky attains through the combination of adjacent thirds show that there is no connection between the techniques. Why not recognize the new aspects of the treatment as the expression of a totally new concept that justifies their use rather than force them into a category to which they obviously do not belong?

A final example from *Le Sacre du Printemps*,[16] in the dance *Rondes*

[16] Copyright 1921. Used by permission of the Galaxy Music Corporation, representative of the publisher, Russischer Musik Verlag, Berlin.

Printanières (Spring Rounds), is indicated to be within the E♭ minor tonality. Here at least we have the right to look for the melodic and harmonic outlines that define the structural framework of the tonality.

EXAMPLE 109

The top and lower voices outline a motion within the E♭ minor chord. In the middle voices, however, we find a B♭ major chord with B♮ added, a B♭♭ major chord with B♭ also present (measure 2), an A♭ major chord with A♮ (measure 3), and the introduction of G♮ in combination with G♭ of the G♭ minor chord (measures 3–4). How are we to understand these extraneous tones? Is B♮ a neighbor of B♭, which appears simultaneously with the chord tone? Yet even if we accept this solution, how can we account for a middle-voice motion within the B♭ major chord when the upper and lower voices define the E♭ minor chord?

In spite of the difference in conception and style, this use of the combined E♭ minor and B♭ major chords might call to mind the famous passage in the "Eroica" Symphony in which, at the conclusion of the development section, the horns rush in with an unexpected entrance of the principal theme in E♭ major, while the violins are maintaining B♭ and A♭ of the dominant chord. The situations, however, are not parallel. Beethoven introduced the premature entry of the theme as the climax of the entire development section, after the status of the B♭ major chord had been firmly established. Thus we are immediately aware that the early entrance of the E♭ chord does not constitute a conflict in the motion or the tonality, since its primary function is to announce the return of the principal theme, which immediately follows. Here the climax is achieved through the momentary combination of two chords, one of which, purely for its dramatic effect, enters prior to its normal appearance in the recapitulation.

In the Stravinsky example there is also a clash of chords, but the ambiguous nature of the chord B♮—D—F—B♭ does not permit us to state that it serves as a dominant. However, even if its status were clarified, there is no point, as in the "Eroica" example, at which the dominant yields to the tonic chord, thus demonstrating the outcome of the conflict. In fact, the static appearance of the E♭ minor chord for thirty of the first thirty-two measures of this section suggests that it is used as a pedal point rather than as the tonic of an E♭ minor tonality.

Neither the E♭ minor chord nor the chord suggesting B♭ major defines a motion within these thirty-two measures that outlines a clear-cut harmonic progression necessary to the definition of the E♭ minor or B♭ major tonality. Thus there is no demonstration either of tonality or of bitonality. There are two opposed chord structures, each of which is the centripetal point of a motion. This motion, however, is entirely ornamental and lacks all harmonic implication of the structural framework necessary to the demonstration of tonality.

Although the *Sacre* is the climax of what is generally regarded as Stravinsky's early period, many of the same tendencies are revealed in *Les Noces*. This is undoubtedly due to the fact that although *Les Noces* did not appear until 1923, it was begun in 1914 and practically completed by 1917. Many authorities regard it as Stravinsky's most significant work. Victor Belaiev [17] believes that "it is the nearest approach which Russian music has ever made to Russian peasant life." Assuredly there can be no questions as to the realism with which Stravinsky portrays the ceremonies of a Russian wedding. Nor can there be any doubt as to the originality of the conception or the extraordinary ingenuity with which it is expressed.

However, at this point we are concerned primarily with the techniques Stravinsky has used and the manner in which he has obtained his effects. In speaking of the character of the music, Belaiev says: "As already mentioned, it is a purely Russian melos, and its peculiarities — on the one hand alienating it from the tonic-dominant European melos, and on the other, approximating it to the oriental melos — are seen in the use of the flattened seventh and in the inclination for scales of an original form, based to a considerable extent on the introduction of the tritone." [18]

[17] *Igor Stravinsky's Les Noces* (Oxford University Press, 1928), p. 2.
[18] *Ibid.*, p. 14.

Stravinsky

As an example, Belaiev cites the melody of the following passage from the opening scene.[19]

EXAMPLE 110

In considering the vocal line apart from the instrumental accompaniment, we find the motion centers around A—C♯—F♯, the tones of the F♯ minor chord. However, when we turn to the setting, there is no confirmation of the top-voice motion. Is this lack of co-operation explained by Belaiev's statement that Stravinsky regards the vocal masses "as the upholders of the 'consonant' principle, and the instrumental accompaniment as harmonic 'overtones' "?[20] Yet even if we examine the setting by itself, what is its meaning? The phrasing emphasizes the same combination of tones, which might be regarded as an inverted seventh chord on C♯ three different times (measures 1, 3, and 5). However, it would be far-fetched to hear this C♯ chord as a dominant leading to the final F♯ chord, especially in view of the conflicting nature of the chord on F♯.

Perhaps we should consider these measures as the result of linear counterpoint, in which the horizontal lines move independently and without regard to the result of their combination. Yet the fact that they move in parallel fifths and sixths indicates not the type of motion characteristic of the contrapuntal technique but the intervals which through chord structure are allied to the vertical techniques. Such use of parallel and augmented fifths constitutes a problem of voice leading, not because it has been tabooed by theorists, but because it creates a weakness and confusion in the motion.

The reader may claim that the lack of clarity is due to the method of analysis rather than to Stravinsky's techniques. Yet what concrete

[19] Copyright 1922. Used by permission of the Galaxy Music Corporation, representative of the publisher, J. & W. Chester, Ltd., London.
[20] *Ibid.*, p. 30.

explanation has Belaiev or any other interpreter of Stravinsky's music offered that clarifies the meaning of such a passage? To discuss the melos or to point to the "consonant" principle in the voices and the use of the instruments as harmonic "overtones," provide interesting commentaries on the treatment, but they do not explain the techniques or reveal the new concept out of which they emerge.

Again it must be emphasized that there is no reason why Stravinsky or any other composer should not express his artistic ideas in any manner or form that is best suited to his personal idiom. The only objection is that we should not confuse the student and listener by connecting an entirely new medium with techniques to which it is in no way related and at the same time deny Stravinsky the invention of a totally new system.

The second example from *Les Noces* [21] gives a clearer demonstration of the absolute divorce of the new treatment from the old.

EXAMPLE 111

Here we find an upper-voice motion in thirds against a motion in fourths. This would seem to indicate two different melodic patterns conceived on two equally diverse planes. One centers on B♭–D, indicative of the B♭ major chord, the other on A–D, which suggests the chord of D minor. In spite of the constant change in time signature, these chords are more or less static, since the embellishing motions return to the same intervals from which they started. There is no definition of their status or function. The motion merely gravitates to B♭–D and A–D. Yet if we regard this passage as within two tonal planes, in which the motion is an embellishment of A–D and B♭–D, how shall we account for the intervals C♯–F♯ and G♯–C♯ as indicative of the tonal plane of D minor? On the other hand, to regard the treatment as contrapuntal, in which the voices move in parallel thirds and fourths, offers an even less convincing explanation of the technique.

[21] Copyright 1922. Used by permission of the Galaxy Music Corporation, representative of the publisher, J. & W. Chester, Ltd., London.

Stravinsky

The only statement for which the music supplies adequate proof, is that the motion outlines a pattern in thirds and fourths. What Stravinsky has achieved through this combination of intervals, outside of its emphasis of the rhythmic effect, it is impossible to say, since this type of motion does not clarify the technique as either bitonal or linear. It merely states a fact that is obvious to any first-year student of harmony.

Some musicians admit the ambiguity of Stravinsky's techniques and the inorganic nature of his conception. Others accept the music as a demonstration of genius and find no necessity for explaining the revolutionary tendencies they acclaim. However, the influence Stravinsky has exerted on the music of the present day demands that we discover the principles on which his music is based, even if a new system of analysis is required.

A final illustration from *Les Noces* [22] brings up an interesting question as to whether the rhythmic arrangement is perhaps responsible for the conflict between the bass and upper voices. If this be true, it would constitute the first instance we have found in either the *Sacre* or *Les Noces* in which the techniques could be definitely linked with the past.

EXAMPLE 112

The three upper voices present no problem, since they comprise a group of consonant triads defining a motion in parallel sixths. Although the motion itself lacks structural implications and we are uncertain of the status of the C minor chord, which the final measures do not clarify, yet

[22] Copyright 1922. Used by permission of the Galaxy Music Corporation, representative of the publisher, J. & W. Chester, Ltd., London.

the character of the technique is familiar. The bass, however, has no relation to the upper voices, and in constant conflict with them, it destroys the nature of the motion they express.

However, if we examine the first measure closely, we see that although the bass tone is not connected with the upper voices with which it appears, it is an integral part of the chord defined by the upper voices that immediately precede it. For example, C, the second eighth note in the opening measure, is totally opposed to the B♭ minor chord with which it is heard, but is the root of the opening C minor chord. This is equally true of the relation of every bass tone to the tones of the preceding chord. This suggests that the incompatibility of the bass and the upper voices that appear in combination is the result of shifting the root of the chord to the following eighth note, so that it does not enter with its own chord but with a chord to which it does not belong.

This is one explanation, which may or may not be a solution of the conflict in the voice leadings. On the other hand, it is equally possible that the rhythmic arrangement was not at all responsible for the dissonant character of the bass, but that Stravinsky conceived it in total disregard of the connection of each tone with the upper tones of the preceding chord. We could also interpret the presence of D♭ in combination with the tones of a C minor chord as an appoggiatura of C in the bass. Instead of sharing this eighth note with C, the chord tone, D♭, is retained and thus shifts C and every succeeding bass tone an eighth beyond the chord of which it is the root.

It is difficult to believe that Stravinsky was so naïve as to employ so obvious a rhythmic device to transform old-fashioned consonances into a more arresting and unconventional treatment. However, irrespective of the cause, what are the results of these conflicting motions? Again, what explanation has any author of a book on contemporary music offered for this technique?

The inability to account for the treatment in this and the preceding examples indicates either that Stravinsky's techniques are unclear and incoherent òr that the present-day approach is unfitted to cope with the problems his music poses. A system of analysis based on a concept of tonality that acknowledges distinctions between consonance and dissonance and between structure and prolongation provides no answer as to the nature of Stravinsky's techniques and the constructive principle they demonstrate; neither does the accepted method of harmonic analysis, which also springs from a tonal concept, although of a different nature. This may be due in part to the unique tendencies of the treatment or to the fact that dissonance has supplanted consonance as the primary factor both in the chord structure and in the voice leadings. Whatever the reason, it is essential for contemporary composers to evolve a new system of analysis based on principles that the new techniques define or else for them to admit that the polytonal techniques are not governed by a constructive principle.

As to the dissonant aspect of Stravinsky's treatment, it should be clearly understood that the presence of dissonance, even to such an extent as in this and the preceding passages, is an argument neither for nor against bitonal techniques. It is inevitable that dissonance should assume a much larger role in contemporary music than it played in the music of the past. With this conclusion no one can disagree. But the essential element in this discussion, as in that of the works of eighteenth- and nineteenth-century composers, is to find what principle governs the passage and the function these dissonances fulfill in the structural framework.

The use of dissonance does not create bitonality or atonality any more than the use of consonance automatically constitutes tonality. Consonance, in the form of the triad, is a symbol of unity through which tonality may be attained, but its mere presence cannot establish tonality. There must be an active demonstration of coherence in the basic motions that the horizontalized chord provides.

However, even if we had discovered a clear-cut motion within the outline of two different tonalities, how can two opposing structures, with two different organisms, be regarded as an extension of the principle that demonstrates tonality? How can two diverse tonalities express the concept of structural unity?

The terms "bitonality" and "polytonality" are a misnomer. The presence of two basic structures does not automatically enlarge the scope of tonality, but destroys its primary concept of unity in the conflicting aims that each denotes. In fact the bitonal and polytonal systems bear no more relation to the tonal system than does the twelve-tone series of Schönberg. The difference between polytonal and atonal composers is the means by which they achieve their end. From the point of view of tonality, however, the end is the same.

George Dyson has given expression to this same conclusion in his discussion of multiple tonality. "Multiple tonality," he says, "must, in the last analysis, mean no tonality at all in the accepted sense of that term." [23]

There are, nevertheless, authorities on contemporary music who differ widely from this view. Boris de Schloezer is one of these. He claims: "In Stravinsky's music there is always a strongly affirmed fundamental tonality to which melodic lines and harmonic complexes belonging to a different key temporarily join themselves. But the foreign key is either, in the end, abandoned, or else it melts, in modulating, into the fundamental tonality. . . . Beneath the complexities of a harmonic tissue where two or three different keys are woven together, one always distinguishes the plane of the principal tonality, which finally absorbs all others and affirms itself by a cadence which destroys all doubt." [24]

First of all one may ask if the term "principal tonality" does not imply more than one. If so, does the existence of one principal tonality, with two or three others functioning simultaneously, constitute Schloezer's concept of tonality?

It would seem, however, as though the presence of more than one tonality, even though one were emphasized to a greater degree than the others, immediately nullified the principle of coherence, the essential characteristic of tonality. The difference between Schloezer's conclusion and that of our analysis arises from a fundamental disagreement regarding the nature and function of tonality and the principles it demonstrates.

Let us be clear about one thing. Tonality is the demonstration of one key through the motion in its representative chord, the tonic. It admits of nothing more. To regard it as giving rise to two or more keys or fostering modulations to other keys denies its function and its meaning.

There is no reason why Stravinsky should not use all twelve keys simultaneously to express his musical idea if he so desires. This discussion is not a diatribe against the methods he uses, but an attempt to understand them. There is every reason, however, to object to explanations that distort the fundamental purpose of tonality as it has been demonstrated in the past in order to include contemporary techniques that are in direct opposition to its artistic concept. Why force these techniques into a category into which they do not belong? Why attempt to explain them in terms

[23] *The New Music* (Oxford University Press, 1923), p. 88.

[24] *Revue Musicale* (Paris, December, 1923), translated by Mlle Boulanger, *Rice Institute Pamphlet* (April, 1926), p. 187.

of principles that no longer are demonstrated? Why hold on to the past, crying for its support, when the past is dead?

Why not admit that Stravinsky has rejected the past and instituted a new era in which new techniques have replaced the old and new harmonic combinations have swept aside the tonal boundaries? At least give us the right to judge his innovations on their own merits and by their own results. Cut the musical umbilicus that ties these methods to the older concepts, and free Stravinsky of the fetishes that his interpreters have imposed on him.

The type of explanation offered by Schloezer and several other contemporary writers may be traced to two distinct factors: the textbook conception of tonality, which permits a modulation to various keys, and the psychological fear that to alienate the present from the past will weaken the security of the present.

Let us throw aside these musical and psychological inhibitions and admit that Stravinsky represents the present, that we can find no explanation of the meaning of these examples from the *Sacre* and *Les Noces*, and that the older methods of analysis no longer serve to interpret the new techniques. Let us agree that according to the principles that defined the concept of tonality in the past, this music is neither bitonal nor polytonal and that we cannot attempt to classify it until we understand its technical significance better. Let us confess that if this music has established a new structural principle, no one has explained it. This does not necessarily mean that such a principle does not exist. It simply acknowledges that although much has been written about Stravinsky's music, no one has demonstrated the new constructive principle it enunciates.

Thus far we have considered only one aspect of Stravinsky's treatment — the nature of his harmonic and contrapuntal techniques. We must also take note of his extraordinary use of rhythm and the stellar role it plays in so many of his works.

In *Le Sacre du Printemps* and *Les Noces* especially the new rhythmic tendencies are apparent. Here we find passages in which the time signature changes with every measure. In addition to such irregular meters as 5/4, 7/4, 11/4, and 3/16, 5/16, and 7/16, there is frequent use of syncopation and the stress of a usually unaccented beat. This creates a rhythmic conflict among the voice parts intensifying the antagonistic chord structures they define.

In the final section of the *Sacre*, the *Danse Sacrale*, the signature is altered so persistently that it is impossible to hear the changes in meter, since there is nothing in the melodic, rhythmic, or harmonic impulse to differentiate one measure from another. We can recognize the repetitions of certain patterns but cannot grasp such rhythmic transitions as 3/16, 5/16, 3/16, 4/16, 5/16, and so on *ad infinitum*. In fact, since there is no obvious reason for these variations in meter, they seem somewhat arbitrary. This brings up the question of what effect such an undefined group of pulsations has on the inherent function of rhythm.

Cecil Gray considers this point in his discussion of the metrical changes in the *Sacre*. He says: "The time signature changes from bar to bar, but the music itself does not. . . . Strip the music of the bar lines and time signatures which are only a loincloth concealing its shameful nudity, and it will at once be seen that there is no rhythm at all. Rhythm implies life, some kind of movement or progression at least, but this music stands quite still in a quite frightening immobility." [25]

Constant Lambert has expressed a similar opinion, only in different words: "Stravinsky's rhythm is not rhythm in the true sense of the term, but rather 'metre' or 'measure.' In many sections of *Le Sacre du Printemps* the notes are merely pegs on which to hang the rhythm, and the orchestration and harmony are designed as far as possible to convert melodic instruments into the equivalent of percussion instruments." [26]

Lambert has gone to the very heart of the question.

In the preceding illustration from *Les Noces* (Example 112) there are five changes in signature within six measures, in spite of the fact that four of these measures disclose four statements of the same melodic figure. To overcome the monotony of these repetitions of both the melodic line and the three other voice parts, Stravinsky has altered the time signature. For example, in measure 2 he changes the 4/4 of the preceding measure to 5/4 so that the first two eighth notes of the third figure fall on the final quarter of measure 2 instead of the first quarter of measure 3. Yet when we listen to this passage, who is conscious of this change in meter? We recognize the same melodic figure, but it is only on paper that the rhythmic variation is apparent.

This is due primarily to the fact that there is nothing in the melodic, contrapuntal, or harmonic treatment that necessitates such a rhythmic distribution or emphasizes it either through phrasing or through the im-

[25] *A Survey of Contemporary Music* (Oxford University Press, 1927), p. 143.
[26] *Music Ho!* (Charles Scribner's Sons, 1935), p. 42.

pulse of a prolongation. Consequently these alterations are arbitrary and not perceptible to the ear. We hear the same rhythmic pattern four times and are utterly oblivious of Stravinsky's varied rhythmic effects.

Although Stravinsky stressed the importance of rhythm through constant changes in the signature, it is a question whether he achieved as great and subtle rhythmic variation as Bach, Beethoven, and more especially Brahms, secured without change of signature. This is due to the fact that in the music of these composers the rhythmic impulse is more clearly defined because of the stronger emphasis of the melodic, contrapuntal, and harmonic functions. Rhythm co-operates with melody, counterpoint, and harmony as essential elements in the growth and expansion of the musical organism. All are integral parts of the whole, and each of these elements sharpens the activity of the others in their individual and collective functions. Therefore any deviation from the rhythmic norm is brought into focus through its effect on the three other factors.

With Stravinsky, however, the emphasis of rhythm at the expense of the melodic and harmonic interests not only results in a loss of the functional activity of these two elements, but, through their impoverishment, in an attenuation of the rhythmic impulse as well. When rhythm is divorced from melody, counterpoint, and harmony to the point at which it becomes motion *per se*, it is shorn of its organic necessity and deteriorates into mere meter.

The constant hammerlike pulsations that dominate so many passages in the *Sacre* may be justified by the primitive nature of the ritual and the elemental character of the participants. To regard them, however, as indicative of a new and fresh impulse pointing the way to the rhythmic treatment of the future, applicable to every type of musical expression, shows reasoning both illogical and unsound. The use of incessant and stereotyped pulsations does not constitute rhythm any more than the presence of two conflicting chords demonstrates bitonality.

As a final approach to the new elements in Stravinsky's style, let us turn to those works in which the trend is toward a more abstract.form of music, based on the linear treatment. Here we must consider the technique, the new problems to which it gives rise, and the claim, so frequently made, that these techniques are an outgrowth of the contrapuntal methods of Johann Sebastian Bach.

Challenge to Musical Tradition

THE LINEAR TECHNIQUE

Linear counterpoint is a purely horizontal technique in which the integrity of the individual melodic lines is not sacrificed to harmonic considerations. The voice parts move freely, irrespective of the effects their combined motions may create. The harmonic element is completely eliminated, since the lines are subject to no restrictions of either tonal or harmonic nature. Here we are dealing entirely with melody and the problems of voice leading.

Strangely enough, this contrapuntal technique, which Stravinsky introduced in his *Octuor for Wind Instruments,* was heralded as a movement "back to Bach." Yet here again the psychological impulse to bind the present contrapuntal techniques to those of the past resulted in a slogan that is as misleading as the terms "bitonality" and "polytonality."

The principle that dominates Bach's contrapuntal style is the principle of tonality, through which the contrapuntal and harmonic factors combine their individual functions to create a single organic structure. Here the function of counterpoint is to prolong a structural progression; although the voice parts enjoyed the greatest freedom, the motion in which they appear is stabilized by the harmonic framework of the tonality. There is no instance known to the author in which the contrapuntal element denies the existence of harmonic considerations.

As Jepperson so aptly expresses it in his differentiation between the contrapuntal methods of Palestrina and Bach: "Bach's and Palestrina's points of departure are antipodal. Palestrina starts out from lines and arrives at chords; Bach's music grows out of an ideally harmonic background, against which the voices develop with a bold independence that is often breath-taking." [27]

If linear counterpoint must be identified with earlier techniques, it should be regarded as a movement back to Machault or Okeghem, perhaps, but certainly not back to Bach.

As the *Octuor* is Stravinsky's first avowed experiment in linear treatment, it is logical to examine it in order to determine the characteristics of the new counterpoint, wherein they differ from the older technique, and the constructive principle they define.

In discussing these opening measures of the finale, we must first con-

[27] *Counterpoint* (Prentice-Hall, Inc., 1939), preface, p. xi.

EXAMPLE 113

sider the two essential factors — the leading of the voices and the ostinato figure in the bass.

Throughout, there are leaps in the top voice that raise the question whether in this treatment the leaps represent a motion within a single voice or whether, according to the older principles, they outline two different voices. For example, does the opening G in the top voice move to F♯ a ninth below (measure 2), or should we regard this F♯ as a middle voice that comes from an unexpressed G in the same register? In short, do cer-

341

tain principles that govern the older method prevail, have they been re-placed by new and different principles of voice leading, or is the linear treatment entirely free of all necessity to define clearly the nature of the voice motions?

The bass also offers a problem that confuses the meaning of the pas-sage. Due to the entrance of the ostinato figure on a different beat of the measure, the rhythmic emphasis in the second figure varies from that in the first. Does this change of stress affect the character of the motion so that it coincides with the meaning of the upper voice or voices, or does it continue along its original lines, independent of the other parts? More concretely, does the second figure ascend to C, as in the first two measures, with D as a neighbor note, or does it move to B and up to D as outlined tones of the G major chord, thus coinciding with the upper-voice motion?

In speaking of the *Octuor,* Miss Bauer states: "Stravinsky wrote articles concerning his ideas on music in which he said that his *Octuor for Wind Instruments* was a musical object, and that the individual timbre of each instrument without nuances was reason enough for the music without look-ing for extraneous causes and emotions." [28]

This is perhaps an answer to our question whether linear counterpoint demonstrates either the older or a new principle of voice leading.

The accompanying graph is offered, not as a solution to the problems of linear counterpoint, but only to indicate the possible voice leadings. It defines the motions described by the independent voices, but offers no conclusion as to their meaning. It follows the music as it is shown in three different registers and consequently discloses three voice parts.

Although there appears to be some relation between the two upper voices, the motions defined by the outside voices have few points of con-tact. This may be due to the use of an ostinato figure in the bass or to the fact that no connection between these parts is intended. As an illustration of this, the top voice suggests a motion from G to C (measure 9). When C is reached, E appears in the bass. However, this E does not end the bass motion as C concludes the top-voice descent, but instead serves as a passing tone in the ostinato figure. Although the top and middle voices combine to achieve this descent, the bass figure stands aloof and thus in no way clarifies the meaning of the upper-voice motions. Again, in the third entry of the ostinato (measure 10), C ascends an octave, thus out-lining a space indicative of the C major chord. During the ascent from

[28] *Twentieth Century Music* (Putnam, 1933), p. 194.

C to F, the middle voice in sixteenth notes climbs from F♯ to its octave, so that F♯ in one voice and F♮ in another move simultaneously to G.

What are the function and the meaning of these motions? Each of the voice parts is understandable as an individual melodic line, but what is their significance when they are combined? Should the ostinato be read differently each time it appears, to bring out the significance of the upper voices? If not, is it mere accident that the emphasis in the second figure falls on B (measure 7) and G (measure 9), which in conjunction with the upper voices suggests a motion within the outlined G major chord? If the emphasis is purposeful, then why do the voice leadings in the following measures contradict rather than affirm this intention?

To accept Stravinsky's statement that the *Octuor* is a musical object should not automatically prevent us from looking for the constructive principle that governs the counterpoint. Where it is and what it is are not evident, but again the fact that we have not found it does not mean that it does not exist. If however linear counterpoint does not demand that the independent voices move so as to demonstrate both their individual and combined functions, what is its primary purpose?

In a discussion of "The Newer Counterpoint," Alfred Einstein supplies us with an answer. He says: "This contact with the pre-classical enabled the new music to approach the abstract. Two musical elements could be almost completely excluded — harmony and rhythm. When two or more purely autonomous melodies are brought together their harmonic relationship is to be ignored, they may go their own way in entire independence. The conception of the interval has completely lost its meaning, for from the simultaneous sounding of two or more tones, there has vanished every association of tension, every memory of consonance and dissonance." [29]

This statement is so clear a definition of the basic elements of the new technique that it explains why we have been unable to find a constructive principle.

We will agree that rhythm and harmony can be almost completely excluded from this type of music. But in a return to the contrapuntal style of the pre-Bach period, in which the interval was an essential element of the technique, how can the interval have lost its meaning? It was from the interval as a melodic, not a harmonic factor, that the distinction between consonance and dissonance arose. It was the interval that governed the

[29] *Modern Music* (November–December, 1928).

principles of voice leading and provided for the use of dissonance so that it was both prepared and resolved. How can the interval be eliminated from melodic motion when the passage from one tone to another automatically involves the use of an interval?

There are works, however, such as the *Sérénade*, the piano sonata, and *Perséphone*, in which the linear treatment is used within an acknowledged tonality. This raises the question whether the tonality influences the nature of the counterpoint or whether the counterpoint affects the nature of the tonality. To answer this, let us turn to the piano sonata. As there appear to be conflicting views regarding the type of sonata Stravinsky has used for his model, the period that his treatment represents, and the character of his technique in general, it should be of interest to consider some of these diverse opinions before beginning a study of the work.

Mlle Boulanger, for example, believes that the sonata reflects the influence of Bach, in its "architectonic character." She finds the two-part writing in the first and last movements "a development and modernization of the two-part contrapuntal writing that we associate with Bach's "French and English Suites." [30]

In sharp contradiction to this statement, Marc Blitzstein, in speaking of Stravinsky's techniques in general, denies that Stravinsky is a contrapuntist. In fact he claims that Stravinsky is interested "in the vertical aspects of music — harmonic timbre, chord spacing." He says: "A dozen things may happen at once in his works; they do not constitute counterpoint any more than the seven mixed colors make a spectrum. Harmony is the element through which to find Stravinsky." [31]

A still different point of view is held by Eric Walter White in his discussion of the piano sonata. He bases his argument on Boris de Schloezer's claim that the piano sonata is not a sonata but *the* pre-Mozart sonata, in which Stravinsky adapted the formulas of Philipp Emanuel Bach. In voicing his disagreement with Schloezer, he points to the second movement as containing "the most ill-sounding clashes between two opposing lines of consecutive thirds," and a passage in the third movement, whose "chromatic sentimentality can only be compared to the worst of Victorian tunes," as evidence that the sonata is not *the* pre-Mozart sonata. Instead, he says: "It is a sonata by Stravinsky." [32]

[30] *Rice Institute Pamphlet* (April, 1926), p. 192.
[31] "The Phenomenon of Stravinsky," *Musical Quarterly* (July, 1935).
[32] *Stravinsky's Sacrifice to Apollo* (Leonard & Virginia Woolf, London, 1930), p. 104.

Stravinsky

How can we reconcile these various opinions, which differ so widely in their basic premise? Is this sonata based on the principles demonstrated by Philipp Emanuel Bach, but conceived technically from the angle of Johann Sebastian Bach, or is it, as White claims, a work that represents a combination of Victorian chromaticism and twentieth-century dissonance? Or should we regard it, as Blitzstein suggests, solely from the harmonic angle?

The following example from the third movement has been selected because it is one to which Mlle Boulanger [33] refers in her discussion of Stravinsky's polyphonic technique.

In comparing the sonata with Bach's preludes and fugues and French and English Suites, Mlle Boulanger has touched on many aspects of the treatment, indicating, among other factors, the use of augmentation, appearing in this instance as a technical *tour de force*. Yet, even though these outward characteristics may bear a certain likeness to the techniques of Bach, they do not represent the basic factors in the treatment and are therefore not the fundamental elements on which to make a comparison. If the similarity is genuine, there must also be a fundamental agreement in the principles that underlie the techniques — that is, Stravinsky must demonstrate the principle of structural coherence, either through the cooperation of the harmonic and contrapuntal functions, or by means of a new concept. Any basis of comparison demands that the objects have some common denominator. In this case, is it the basic concept of tonality to which Stravinsky's and Bach's contrapuntal techniques give expression, or the similarity of techniques that demonstrate two entirely different constructive principles?

Let us turn to the music for our answer.[34]

It is clear that both voices state the same melodic line, but that through the augmentation of the bass, the voices meet on different segments of the melodic figure. Thus it is the augmentation that is the distinguishing element of the treatment. But what are the results? Does the augmentation serve to bring these voices together at points that clarify the tonality, or does it intensify the individual nature of the motions by eliminating points of contact that affirm the tonality?

The first measure shows that while the bass is still engaged in a state-

---

[33] *Rice Institute Pamphlet* (April, 1926), p. 92.
[34] Copyright 1925. Used by permission of the Galaxy Music Corporation, representative of the publisher, Russischer Musik Verlag, Berlin.

EXAMPLE 114

ment of E and G of the opening figure, the top voice has completed this figure and moved on to a new one. Thus F♯—C—A—B appear in the top voice·against E and G in the bass. How shall we read this top-voice motion? Should F♯ be heard as the structural tone, coming from G of the opening figure, with A taken out of the lower register in its connection with C and B, or is this A the structural top voice, to be heard as a neighbor of the preceding G? In the second measure the top voice shows a motion of F♯—E—D during which the middle voice passes from A through G to F♯. But although the motion in these upper voices is clear, the voice leading in the bass is so ambiguous that we are in doubt as to its meaning. Shall we hear it as a motion from F♯ through A to B, or are C and B to be regarded as the bass, with F♯ and A indicating a tenor voice?

These questions deal only with the problems of voice leading. They have nothing to do with harmony or tonality, but belong to the province of counterpoint and are based on principles that both Bach and composers of the fifteenth and sixteenth centuries regarded as the foundation of their contrapuntal technique.

We have only to turn to the preludes and fugues of Bach, to which Stravinsky's treatment has been compared, to recognize that although the function of counterpoint is to achieve motion, the motion is never purposeless. On the contrary, however freely the voices may seem to move, they always represent, within an outlined space, a clearly defined melodic line that indicates both a beginning and an end. In spite of all the detours and dissonances, Bach's counterpoint has both meaning and direction, and through them it co-operates with the structural forces to strengthen and intensify the tonality.

Stravinsky, on the contrary, is concerned primarily with maintaining the full independence and integrity of the voice parts. The melodic lines neither indicate a tonal allegiance nor demonstrate the principles of horizontal motion that governed the works of the fifteenth- and sixteenth-century composers. They are absolutely free to move when and as they please. Therefore to compare this technique with Bach's implies that only superficial characteristics such as the outward resemblance to the E minor fugue have led to such a conclusion.

Again it must be pointed out that the argument is not directed against Stravinsky, but against those interpreters who, by comparison with the techniques of Johann Sebastian Bach and the sonatas of Philipp Emanuel Bach and the pre-Mozart period on the one hand, stifle the creative impulse they wish to acclaim; and on the other, sacrifice the fundamental principles of the past in order to link them to the techniques of the present.

Judged entirely as a demonstration of linear counterpoint, divorced from the older horizontal method, what new principles does Stravinsky's music enunciate to replace the principles that Bach's counterpoint so clearly reveals? Can motion indicate its function when it lacks a clear sense of direction, tonal boundaries, and coherence both in the individual and in the combined voices, even if it is governed by a new principle of voice leading? This undoubtedly is a matter of opinion. For those for whom sound for sound's sake is a new artistic credo, motion alone is sufficient. There are others, however, who believe that clarity of technique, in the form of unity and coherence, will always remain a prerequisite of art, whether it be music, painting, sculpture, literature, or architecture.

Although our examination of Stravinsky's linear techniques has been limited to passages from the *Sérénade*, the *Octuor*, and the piano sonata, additional illustrations from the piano concerto and the later works, *Apollon Musagète* and *Perséphone*, would serve only to confirm the results we have deduced from the examples discussed. Although the stylistic treatment differs, the techniques evidence the same absence of a clearly defined structural principle.

We have seen that in order to achieve a form of expression representing his own musical personality, Stravinsky has divested melody, rhythm, counterpoint, and harmony of the artistic functions they previously exercised. In spite of this, there are many who will agree rather with Schloe-zer that "there is nothing revolutionary in the art of Stravinsky" and that he "makes innovations, but inside the framework set up by his predeces-sors." [35]

To believe this, however, disclaims both the underlying foundation of the framework and the unique and ingenious character of the innova-tions. To deny tonality its constructive principle so that we can bring the old and new techniques within the same category is as unjust to Stra-vinsky as it is untrue of his predecessors. To regard conflicting tonalities as an extension of tonality, or linear counterpoint as a development of counterpoint, is to blind ourselves to fundamental characteristics and to indulge in wishful thinking.

If Stravinsky is great, if his innovations are to extend the boundaries of music, and if his techniques are to shape the trends of the future, why not grant the twentieth century its contribution to the development of music, free from connection with the past? Why are not Stravinsky's inter-preters as daring in their explanations as Stravinsky has been in his music? Why bind him to an artistic credo in which he does not believe and refuse him the right to assert his own?

Let us admit that Stravinsky is a revolutionary, not within the frame-work of his predecessors, but outside it; that although he may have enun-ciated a new constructive principle, no one thus far has defined it or ex-plained how it functions. Let us admit that the roles enacted by melody, rhythm, counterpoint, and harmony are totally different from what they were formerly, when their combined efforts created and maintained an organic whole. Let us admit that whether Stravinsky goes back to Bach, Handel, Pergolesi, or Tchaikovsky, whether or not he indicates a tonality, whether the treatment implies a vertical or horizontal style, the funda-mental characteristics of his art, however intensified or tempered, are es-sentially the same.

In evaluating Stravinsky's works, it matters little whether we like or dislike his innovations. The sole consideration is the effect of these inno-vations on the clarity and coherence of the music.

Their effect has been obvious. They were vital factors in the break-down of a basic principle — the concept of tonality; they changed the functions of the essential elements of music; and they engendered new vertical and horizontal techniques. What new structural principle they

[35] *Modern Music* (November–December, 1932).

provide to supplant the older concept, and what functions, both individual and combined, these new techniques fulfill, neither Stravinsky nor any of his interpreters has revealed. There can be no doubt that through the originality of his rhythmic treatment, the ingenuity of his polyharmonic techniques and the striking effects of his new method of orchestration, Stravinsky has had a tremendous influence on twentieth-century music.

The question, however, to which his music gives rise does not concern these outward manifestations of his artistic personality; it is of a fundamental nature, since it underlies a concept that is common to every form of expression — the law of unity and coherence. Can a system, however new and inventive it may be in reflecting the thought and life of its period, be an adequate substitute for tonality, unless it replaces the older principle of coherence with a structural principle of its own? This is a question the reader must decide for himself.

CHAPTER IX

Schönberg

HIS CONCEPTION *of tonality; its influence on interpretation of tech-*

niques of Bach and Beethoven. Challenge to tonality in twelve-tone

system. First attempt to organize a new theoretical approach. New con-

cept of unity in the motive relationships of series. New theories of conso-

nance and dissonance; their effect on voice leading.

As Stravinsky challenged the older system through his use of the polytonal and linear techniques, so Schönberg made his protest, in the form of the twelve-tone scale, the basis of the atonal system. Schönberg, however, has formulated a new concept of unity, which he expressed through the twelve-tone row, as a substitute for the older principle of coherence. Whether the twelve-tone series will determine the future trend in music cannot be decided at this time. That it has already exerted an enormous influence on contemporary music, however, cannot be denied. Therefore, to understand the evolution of the new system and the various factors responsible for its inception, we must find out the specific elements in his conception of tonality that motivated Schönberg's experimentation along lines that contributed to its breakdown. His own statements concerning the principles of tonality, his analysis of works of the past, and his own demonstration of his concept in various early works are the most valuable clues to Schönberg's new and personal medium. To comprehend the nature and result of his experiments, we must begin with the cause.

Much has been written about the various changes in style found in works of Schönberg's different periods. There is the "romantic" style of *Verklärte Nacht, Die Gurrelieder,* and *Pelleas und Melisande;* the new trend toward chromatic independence in the quartets in D minor and F♯ minor and the *Kammersymphonie,* in which the use of key signatures indicates the intention of expressing a tonal concept. There is the break with tonality and its replacement by the twelve-tone scale with its equality of tones, first demonstrated in the "Three Piano Pieces," Opus 11, and the organization of the "tone row," the clearly defined patterns that, as a complex, provide the material out of which every aspect of the treatment is derived, as revealed in Opus 23. That the treatment in the later periods is a logical development of the early tendencies is the premise of our discussion.

SCHÖNBERG'S APPROACH TO THE PROBLEMS OF HARMONY AND COUNTERPOINT

First of all, what is Schönberg's conception of tonality? Let us turn to his own words for an answer. He says: "This coincides to a certain extent with that of Key, in so far as it refers not merely to the relation of tones with one another but much more to the particular way in which all tones relate to a fundamental, especially the fundamental of the scale, whereby tonality is always comprehended in the sense of a particular scale. Thus, for example, we speak of a C major tonality." [1]

There is a further explanation in the *Harmonielehre:* "Tonality is an artifice . . . the practice of which has as its chief object the imitation of that formal satisfactory effect which satisfies so much in a well-formed thought. Into each key (this is called enlarged tonality), one can bring under pretext of modulation, nearly everything that is proper to the scale of any other extraneous key. Yes, a key can be expressed as exactly and absolutely by other chords as by the chords proper to the scale. But does it really still exist then?" [2]

Schönberg has pointed out the basic fallacy in the concept of tonality presented in most textbooks on harmony. Yet, although he has recognized the negation of the tonal principle in the admission of other and extraneous keys to a work definitely stated to be within a given tonality, he has not attributed this to the inconsistencies between the demonstration of tonality in the music and the theoretical explanation offered by the analysts. In short, he has not attacked the primary cause, the system of harmonic analysis, but has questioned the value of a concept whose function has been so misunderstood.

Schönberg and Schenker are in agreement at this point, but, starting from the same premise, they have moved in opposite directions. Recogniz-

---

[1] *Schoenberg,* edited by Merle Armitage (G. Schirmer, 1937), p. 268.
[2] Translation by R. Cort van den Linden (*Music and Letters,* October, 1926).

ing the contradiction between the definition of tonality, as an expression of the potentialities inherent within a single key, and the modulatory principle that admits the use of many keys, Schönberg abandoned tonality to devise a new system. Schenker, on the other hand, explored the works of the masters to prove that our concept and explanation of tonality were not in accord with the function of tonality revealed in the music. He then evolved a concept and explanation from the music, based on fact rather than theory.

Schönberg is quoted as saying: "Tonality, tending to render harmonic facts perceptible and to correlate them, is therefore not an end but a means." [3] This is true in part, but what is the end? Schönberg does not answer this; Schenker, who does, defines tonality as a means of demonstrating the artistic principle of unity through the interlocking of the harmonic and contrapuntal functions. Schönberg recognizes only the harmonic aspect of tonality, while Schenker finds both the harmonic and contrapuntal principles essential to the preservation of tonal coherence.

How, then, does Schönberg explain the functions exercised by the vertical and horizontal techniques? He says: "The mutual saturation of these two disciplines is so complete, their distinction and separation so incomplete, that every result derived from voice leading may be a harmony and every harmony may have its foundation in voice leading. Apparently we are turning to a new era of the polyphonic style, and chords will be the result of voice leading, justified through melodic content alone." [4]

In this statement we find a wide divergence between Schönberg's and Schenker's points of view. Although Schenker recognizes chords that are the result of voice leadings, he regards them as prolonging chords, without harmonic or structural functions. Schönberg, however, believes that such contrapuntal chords will eventually absorb chords with a harmonic function, since he already finds little or no distinction between them.

Since the major part of this book is devoted to an exposition of the difference between chords of structure, or harmonies, and contrapuntal chords of prolongation, as well as the results of their combined functions, we cannot let Schönberg's statement pass unchallenged. Is it not as arbi-

[3] International Cyclopedia of Music and Musicians, edited by Oscar Thompson (Dodd, Mead and Company, 1939).

[4] Adolph Weiss, "The Lyceum of Schönberg," Modern Music (March–April, 1932).

trary to attribute a chord of structural significance to voice leading as to regard all chords, irrespective of their origin, as harmonies? This approach is the opposite of the harmonic procedure offered in the harmony text-books, but it is equally misleading. Unless harmony and counterpoint demonstrate separate and distinct functions, both of which are essential to the art of composition, why continue to teach them in our music schools? However, if each serves its own purpose, why rob them of their individual rights by regarding as harmonies chords that emerge from voice leadings and are of melodic origin and by attributing to voice leadings chords that are of a structural nature and harmonic origin? What is to be gained by accepting the mutual saturation of these techniques as so complete that their individual functions have been exchanged?

The origin of such sophistry lies in Schönberg's approach to certain techniques, commonly regarded as within the realm of counterpoint, that give rise to neighbor notes, passing tones, suspensions, retardations, chang-ing notes, and so on. He argues [5] that such tones, free or foreign to the harmony, do not exist. In other words, there are no prolongations what-soever. He says: "Foreign tones are supposed to be accidental additions to the chords of the established harmonic system. . . . Free tones are not really foreign to the harmony for they are parts of chords (a sounding to-gether of three or more tones) and the effects that result through their use are harmonies, like all tonal combinations which sound simultaneously. These foreign tones give rise to harmonies which might indeed be for-eign to the system built up on thirds. Yet some chords of that system have originated in the same manner as these 'foreign' combinations; . . . Tones foreign to harmony ought not exist in any harmonic system, for a harmony is a sounding together of tones." [6]

This final statement is altogether misleading and beside the point. These foreign tones do belong to a chord, but not necessarily the chord in which, through a rhythmic displacement, they appear.

For example, let us take a commonplace illustration of suspension, in which C, retained from a preceding chord, enters into combination with G—D—F. Do we hear C as an integral part of the G major chord, or do we recognize it as a substitute for the delayed entrance of the chord tone B? The retention of C, let us say in the melody, while the three other

[5] *Harmonielehre* (Universal Edition, 1922), p. 372.
[6] Adolph Weiss, "The Lyceum of Schönberg," *Modern Music* (March–April, 1932).

voices move to the G major chord, indicates a rhythmic problem that has nothing whatsoever to do with harmony, but only with the delayed motion of one of the voice parts. The same is true in the case of retardation. But what of passing tones?

If we take the motion E—D—C in the top voice over a static C major chord, D appears as a dissonant passing tone. However, as it is obvious that there is a descending motion of a third within the C major chord, shall we regard the foreign tone D as an integral part of the chord? Schönberg does just this in his reference to the Bach motet cited in Chapter II (Example 22). However, to regard every passing or changing tone as a chord tone rather than as creating a motion within the chord-spaces robs counterpoint of its distinguishing characteristic — motion — and places all tones, irrespective of their functions, within the same category.

The role of the passing tone as a space-filler has been demonstrated in the numerous examples offered in the preceding chapters. Its function as a motion between two chord tones is defined in the second species of counterpoint. Thus it belongs to a technique that is concerned only with a melodic principle. Although it complements the harmonic principle, it has nothing in common with it. To regard D, in a motion of E—D—C within a C major chord, as an integral part of the chord, denies the existence of the motion provided by counterpoint and attributes the presence of this tone, and all other tones of a melodic origin, to a harmonic impulse.

Undoubtedly, it is Schönberg's recognition of the complete mutual saturation of the harmonic and contrapuntal disciplines that leads to such a conclusion. The result seems to be the absorption of the contrapuntal into the harmonic technique, for what function is left to counterpoint when all suspensions, retardations, and passing or changing notes are regarded as integral parts of the chord structure with which they appear?

The value of Schönberg's theories, however, cannot be determined by a mere refutation of his arguments. More than a difference of opinion is needed to demonstrate whether his conception of tonality, his approach to the problems of voice leading and harmony, and his theory of the non-existence of foreign tones should be accepted. The test of any explanation is whether it provides a fuller and clearer interpretation of the music, through its analysis of the interplay of the melodic, rhythmic, contrapuntal, and harmonic forces, than has yet been offered. It is fortunate that Schönberg himself, in his discussion of several works that adhere to the tonal concept, has demonstrated the application of his theories, since the analysis is the most adequate presentation of the practical results of his theoretical approach.

THE APPLICATION OF SCHÖNBERG'S THEORIES

One of the most interesting of these explanations deals with the Bach chorale, *Was mein Gott will, das g'scheh' allzeit* [7] ("The will of God be always done"), from the Passion according to Saint Matthew.

The main points of Schönberg's discussion center on the organic nature of the passing tones and the vacillation of the tonality between B minor and D major. In referring to the passing tones in the bass, tenor, and alto of the first verse, he says: "It is therefore clear that these are chords; for their harmonic function is: to so harmonize the melody, which appears three times, that the harmonization, which could easily result in somewhat poor progressions, on the contrary always emphasizes in strong strokes the important intervals of the tonality (I, IV, V), but not so abundantly with the first entrance that a later repetition cannot appear richer and even more astonishing." [8] A little later, in referring to the tonality, he says: "In the next to the last moment, (°) A appears in the bass as though a major chord should follow. The reason is clear; the chorale vacillates between D major and B minor, the purpose of which is revealed at the end; a too secure or definite B minor in the beginning would hardly be appropriate. The decision [as to the tonality] comes only later. It is the function of this A to delay this decision. But it is no ornament!" [9]

Schönberg has chosen a chorale in which the voice leadings present problems whose solution is extremely difficult. The question is whether regarding the passing tones as organic chord tones and the tonality as shifting between B minor and D major offers a satisfactory explanation.

Let us turn to the music to understand Schönberg's remarks.

First of all he says the passing tones in the first two measures are organic chord tones. According to this statement, the chord on the third quarter of measure one is D–E–F♯–G–A, on the fourth quarter F♯–G–A–B–D–E, and so on. Graph A, however, explains these tones differently. It shows a motion from the opening B minor to the inverted D major chord that follows as a tonic-mediant progression. This D major chord is expanded through a harmonic prolongation I–V–I to the third

[7] *389 Choral-gesänge* (Breitkopf and Härtel Edition), No. 342.
[8] *Harmonielehre* (Universal Edition, 1922), pp. 414–15.
[9] *Ibid.*, p. 415.

EXAMPLE 115

quarter of measure 2. The passing tones in question occur within this motion. E in the alto enters between the chord tones D and F♯; in the tenor,
G appears between F♯ and A, with B as a neighbor note of A, while E and
G in the bass fill the spaces within D—F♯—A. It would seem as though
the function of these tones were so clearly defined through their position
within the tone-spaces of the outlined D major chord that there could
be no doubt as to their status. The point graph A emphasizes is that
neither their presence nor absence would alter the fact that through
horizontalization the mediant chord is prolonged. These tones, by filling
in the chord-spaces, merely give impulse and interest to motion already
outlined. Therefore, why regard these tones as organic chord tones when
it is obvious that they do not belong to the chord, but serve as passing
tones in a motion that outlines the chord?

The next point in Schönberg's analysis concerns the eighth-note A in the bass (measure 3). Of this he says that it suggests that "a major chord should follow. . . . It is no ornament." From this it is clear that Schönberg believes that A should be followed by a D major instead of a B minor chord. Why? Before considering this aspect of the treatment, let us examine the motion, to determine the status of the E and B minor chords between which this A occurs.

Graph B indicates a motion from the mediant D major to the dominant F♯ major chord. Here the E minor chord provides E as a passing tone in the bass, with B and E in the top voice furnishing the end and the beginning of two parallel motions that expand the descent from D to C♯. In the first of these, B appears at the close of a top-voice descent of a third, while in the second, E serves as an incomplete neighbor of the preceding D, since it does not return to D as a structural top voice, but passes through D to C♯. Here the passing tones enter as dissonant sevenths of D and E respectively. In graph C, these passing tones appear as consonances, C♯ as the third of the A major, and D as the third of the B minor chord. Thus the function of these chords is that of passing chords within the respective motions, although the A major chord has the tendency of an applied dominant of the E minor chord that follows. Consequently, although the B minor chord has the appearance of a tonic, its function as a passing chord is prolonging, so that it exerts no structural influence on the motion.

The inverted C♯ seventh chord that next enters (graph D) is of interest because it illustrates the type of supertonic that, coming between a mediant and a dominant of the harmonic progression, serves as a harmonic emphasis of the F♯ major chord and intensifies the connection between the mediant and dominant. However, the function of this C♯ chord concerns only its harmonic stress of the dominant. Therefore, although an E in the bass supports both the E and C♯ minor chords, these two chords demonstrate entirely different functions. The status of the E minor chord is disclosed in the basic outline of the motion from the D to the F♯ major chords (graph B). In spite of the more complex nature of the prolongation, its character as a passing chord remains unchanged. Due to the expansion of the harmonic progression, Bach introduced the C♯ minor chord to heighten the effect of the dominant and thus strengthen the structural motion. Although the E and C♯ minor chords are both prolonging chords, one demonstrates a contrapuntal function, the other a harmonic.

Challenge to Musical Tradition

This brings us to Schönberg's statement regarding the appearance of A in the bass, which, he says, should lead to a major chord and which is not an ornament. It is obvious, at least from one point of view, that A serves as a passing tone between G and B. As such, it has no harmonic implications. By the words "no ornament," Schönberg undoubtedly means that A is an organic part of the E minor chord, an interpretation that graph A disputes. It is part of a step-wise ascent that fills the space between the E and B minor chords. Consequently it is of contrapuntal origin.

The question whether a passing tone is a melodic or harmonic agent is fundamental. Even more vital to the problems of musical structure is the statement that it does not exist. If we hear all passing tones as organic, as integrated elements of the chords with which they appear, motion, the essential function of the contrapuntal discipline, is completely obliterated. We no longer hear horizontally, but only vertically, from chord to chord. There is no feeling of motion within a well-defined space in which the harmonic and contrapuntal factors demonstrate their individual and combined functions, but motion of an indeterminate nature, which has neither structural significance nor coherence.

Schönberg's final contention is that the chorale vacillates between B minor and D major. This is an inevitable result of his conception of tonality; it is not borne out by the interpretation offered in the graphs. It is true that Bach gave greater prominence to the D major chord in the first verse of the chorale than to the D major chord in the last, whose effect is much weakened by the chromatic prolongation that expands the motion to the dominant chord. This variety in the treatment, however, is not an evidence of tonal instability. On the contrary, it demonstrates the possibilities inherent in Bach's conception of tonality and the contrasting types of contrapuntal motions that the same structural progression affords.

No one can state authoritatively that any given interpretation is right or wrong. The fundamental premise by which an explanation must be judged is whether or not it corresponds to what we hear. Therefore the reader is left to make his own decision regarding the two readings of the Bach chorale that have been offered — Schönberg's and the author's. If he denies the existence of passing tones and regards them instead as organic chord tones, if he believes that all chords, irrespective of their diverse functions, have the same status, and if he hears the mediant D major chord as indicative of a tonality in opposition to the fundamental tonality of B minor, he will agree with Schönberg. If, on the other hand, he recognizes that passing tones are an essential element of the contrapuntal technique, if he admits the diverse roles played by harmony and counterpoint in defining and prolonging structural motion, and if he realizes that the expanded D major chord does not indicate a conflicting tonality, but accentuates the structural function of the mediant chord of the basic tonality, he will agree with the explanation outlined in the graphs.

Let us go on to a second example that Schönberg cites as evidence of the weakness of the tonal concept — the last movement of Beethoven's quartet, Opus 59, No. 2. It is of great concern to Schönberg that a work supposed to be in the E minor tonality should start with a theme "in C major." In discussing this he says: "For example, the last movement . . . is in E minor. But it begins in C major with a theme which uses every means to establish this key. After a few measures it turns to the key which Beethoven decides to make the main tonality of the piece. I beg you to give due consideration to this case: by every ingenious means, C major is at first stressed in the harmony and in the melody; and the subsequent turn to E minor can be taken even at that point as the third degree of C major. How unconvincing is a key under certain conditions, if such a group can still be taken as the main movement in E minor!" [10]

The graph shows that instead of beginning on the customary E minor chord, Beethoven used a daring innovation, an incomplete VI–V–I harmonic progression as a prolongation of the E minor chord. Here the omission of the opening tonic chord gives rise to the introduction of the main theme within the submediant C major chord. Although the unfolding of the opening theme within the outline of the submediant chord is a subtle deviation from the usual treatment, it is not necessarily indicative of tonal inconsistency, if its function as a submediant is clarified by the nature of the structural motion. In this instance, the VI–V–I progression, regardless of the emphasis of the VI, demonstrates a motion within the E minor tonality.

A structural top-voice motion discloses a descent of a third, G–F♯–E against a bass motion of C–B–E instead of the usual E–B–E. Since the C major chord is expanded for six of the eight measures that set forth the theme, it is inevitable that the characteristics of this chord are more pronounced than those of the E minor chord. Yet is this not evidence of Beethoven's instinctive recognition of the possibilities of contrast that lie

[10] *Schoenberg*, edited by Merle Armitage (G. Schirmer, 1937), p. 279.

EXAMPLE 116

in this type of progression rather than evidence of the unconvincing use of tonality? It is just this shortening of the harmonic framework that demonstrates his daring innovations within the tonal concept. It is so easy to achieve the unusual by destroying the principles of structural coherence that we at times misunderstand the artistic boldness, through which an equally revolutionary effect is attained within the tonal boundaries.

This is a remarkable illustration of the distinction between tradition and principle. It is indeed a challenge to tradition but not to the tonal concept. On the contrary, Beethoven has availed himself of the potentialities that are basic to tonality and has developed them according to the needs of his melodic and structural framework.

The indefiniteness of key lies not in Beethoven's music, but in the type of aural reactions the accepted method of analysis has engendered. The training in harmony and harmonic analysis has accustomed the ear to hear vertically, in a fragmentary motion from chord to chord, to concentrate on modulations, in a shift from one key to another, and to accept the presence of many diverse keys as an expression of tonality. As a result, it has fostered a way of hearing that cannot perceive that an opening theme within a prolonged C major chord can come within the boundary of an E minor tonality. Structural motion of such a type, however unconvincing it may seem to Schönberg, is proof both of the elasticity of the tonal concept and the bold and original treatment through which Beethoven demonstrated structural coherence.

To offer it as an illustration of tonal ambiguity and inconsistency indicates that there is a discrepancy between what the music actually tells of Beethoven's conception of tonality and the conception of tonality that has evolved out of the purely harmonic approach. It is typical of the wide gulf between harmonic analysis and the Schenker method, that Schönberg points to this example as evidence of the unconvincing nature of tonality, while Schenker uses the same passage to demonstrate the rich and ever new possibilities to which tonality gives rise without weakening the coherence or the clarity of the structural framework.

A final reference to Schönberg's discussion of the unconvincing effects that tonality engenders concerns his remarks about the closing measures of the allegretto of Beethoven's Eighth Symphony. Schönberg's reaction to the final measures of the coda is perhaps the most conclusive evidence of how largely his approach to the music of the past is responsible for his rejection of the tonal concept and his experimentation in the twelve-tone system. In this instance his arguments rest entirely on the introduction of A♭ as the seventh of the B♭ major chord, the tonic, and its accentuation of the E♭ major chord that follows. The effect of this, he claims,[11] gives the final B♭ triad the character of a dominant of the E♭ major tonality rather than the tonic of the established tonality.

Before discussing this passage, it should be realized that the measures in question occur in the coda at a time when the structural life of the movement has been concluded on a strong harmonic progression within the B♭ major tonality. It seems incredible, therefore, that the introduction of A♭ in a few measures of the coda could make so profound an impression as

[11] *Ibid.*, p. 275.

to overcome the clearly defined structure within the outlined B♭ major chord that dominates every harmonic and structural prolongation in the three main sections of the movement. However, let us look at the music. Our starting point is the final dominant and tonic chords of the recapitulation; this tonic is also the opening of the coda.

EXAMPLE 117

It is apparent that A♭ serves as a passing tone between B♭ of the B♭ major and G of the E♭ major chord. In combination with the B♭ major chord, however, it heightens the character of this chord as an applied dominant of E♭ major, the subdominant of the harmonic progression. Undoubtedly it is this aspect of the treatment, the use of the B♭ seventh chord as an applied dominant, that impresses Schönberg as weakness of tonal definition.

The emphasis and prolongation of the E♭ major chord bring it into greater prominence than the tonic B♭ major chord, but does this automatically indicate a tonality of E♭ major? We need only recall the various instances in which a supertonic, mediant, or subdominant chord of a basic harmonic progression or of a harmonic prolongation has been even more widely expanded without affecting the tonal stability, to recognize that the technique in this example is not unusual enough either in its conception or in its results to justify Schönberg's conclusion. The main cause of Schönberg's aural reactions is the weakness of the tonic triad by comparison with the stress Beethoven has applied to the B♭ seventh chord. It is logical to assume, however, that having established the status of the B♭ major chord throughout the main sections of the movement and confirmed it in the strong dominant-tonic progression that concludes the recapitulation, Beethoven felt free in the coda to add

A♭ to create a seventh chord and thus intensify the structural role of the subdominant.

The status and function of both the B♭ seventh and the E♭ major chords are clearly demonstrated in the motion from the tonic to the dominant F major chord. It is difficult, therefore, to comprehend Schönberg's claim that the final B♭ major chord has the character of a dominant of the E♭ major tonality instead of the tonic of the key. We can attribute this interpretation only to a way of hearing based primarily on a predetermined conception of vagueness and inconsistency inherent in tonality.

In the three examples under discussion, Schönberg has given us an insight into his analysis of works within the tonal system that clarifies his approach to the problems of musical structure. As a result of his own concept of tonality and what it led him to deduce from the music of Bach and Beethoven as well as other composers, it is not surprising either that Schönberg found the system failed to satisfy his individual needs or that he turned to the twelve-tone series as a new medium. The step from his interpretation of the bitonal tendencies in Bach's and Beethoven's use of tonality to his own use of atonality was inevitable.

It is not fair to Schönberg, however, to judge his concept of tonality only by his own definition of it or by his explanation of the works of other composers. We must also turn to his compositions for a practical demonstration of his use of the tonal system. Unfortunately, this limits our discussion to his early works, since they alone are based on techniques identified with the principles of structure and prolongation. Let us examine various passages from these compositions to see whether Schönberg adheres to his theories or whether, in practice, he observes the distinction between the harmonic and contrapuntal functions negated by his theoretical explanations.

THE EARLY PERIOD

The sextet, *Verklärte Nacht*,[12] is the logical starting point of our investigation, since it is Schönberg's first important work, in spite of the interest and originality of the earlier songs. Although many aspects of the stylistic treatment link it to the Wagnerian influence of this period, there nevertheless are various evidences of the tendencies that were later

[12] All Schönberg examples are quoted by permission of the Associated Music Publishers, representative of the publisher, Universal Edition, except where otherwise indicated.

to find full expression in the twelve-tone system. The fundamental idea itself is of an experimental nature. Here Schönberg conceived of an entirely new use of chamber music and applied to this sextet the programmatic character of an orchestral tone poem. The work is divided into five sections, the first of which serves as the basis of our discussion.

EXAMPLE 118

Since it is impossible to quote the entire section, the example opens at the sixteenth measure, where a D minor chord serves as the tonic of a harmonic progression. Although the preceding measures are of thematic interest, they are not essential to the structural significance, since they center entirely on a static D minor chord.

The graph, as a whole, shows a prolonged I–II–V–I progression within the D minor tonality. Thus the structural motion is clearly defined. The problem now concerns the nature of the prolongation, which, we see, occurs within a widely expanded supertonic seventh chord. What is the character of this motion, and what are the status and function of the tones that provide the prolongation? In short, are the passing tones organic chord tones, or do they serve as space-fillers?

In looking at this prolongation we find a bass motion from E to G, the third of the chord. This is achieved not directly, but through a middle-voice descent in which E in the bass passes to E♭, which leads chromatically to the G below. At the same time G of the structural top voice descends to E, a middle voice. Again this motion is prolonged both through a shift of register and through the use of a middle-voice descent to the bass. Here G enters in the bass simultaneously with the passing tone F in the top voice (measure 24), so that G appears as the root of the G minor seventh chord before it achieves its goal as the third of the inverted supertonic. However, it is obvious that the G minor chord has no harmonic function within the motion, since it is due entirely to the presence of F in the top voice, which delays the entrance of the chord tone E.

This main section of the prolongation discloses the use of a horizontal motion to prolong the top-voice descent of a third and the bass ascent of a third, through which an exchange in the outside voices is effected. Is it not clearer to recognize this technique as a passing-chord motion within the outlined E minor seventh chord than to hear each of the intervening chords as a harmonic entity? In fact, in this motion, has not Schönberg demonstrated a distinction between the harmonic and contrapuntal functions that is in direct contrast to his statement regarding the mutual saturation of these two disciplines? Furthermore, it reveals a much more artistic approach to the problems of harmony and counterpoint than his analysis of the works of other composers would lead us to expect. Nevertheless, there are some aspects of the treatment that are not altogether clear.

In his treatment of the theme, for example, there is a constant stress of apparent passing tones within an outlined space, which might be regarded otherwise if we accept Schönberg's statement concerning the non-existence of passing tones. This is true not only of the opening measures of this section, in the disposition of the thematic figure, but also of other measures indicated in the graph.

The emphasis of E and A on the strong beat of the first,two measures is a case in point. It is the accentuation of these tones that to a great extent weakens the effect of the descent from F to G, a prolongation of the struc-

Schönberg

tural top-voice ascent of a second. In a similar manner the strong impulse toward A in the succeeding measures, indicated as a neighbor note in the graph, raises the question whether Schönberg heard it in this manner or as an organic tone of the E minor chord and of the altered chord on E. The problem itself does not arise from the fact that a passing tone and a neighbor note have been given greater emphasis than the chord tones, since we have found a similar technique in the works of other composers; it is rather that Schönberg's statement regarding passing tones makes us hesitate to attribute a prolonging function to tones that he regards as organic members of the chords in which they appear.

In general, however, there is sufficient evidence of the prolonging techniques to justify our conclusion that in this early work Schönberg discloses a concept of tonality having little in common with his theoretical approach to the problems of harmony and counterpoint.

Another passage from this same work provides a further insight into Schönberg's technical treatment, the exquisite cantilena, which Wellesz says "reflects the verse which speaks of the longing for maternal happiness." [13] Although the emotional character of the theme suggests its Wagnerian heritage, many aspects of the treatment are indicative of Schönberg's individuality. For instance, in the theme the substitution of A♯, an under neighbor, for B, the fifth of the E major chord, is an intensification of the *Tristan* technique. Yet Schönberg has used this device in a manner that gives an entirely new and different quality to the theme.

The harmonic framework rests on two well-defined progressions outlining a motion within the E major chord. The top voice reveals several of the prolonging techniques that we found in the works of the earlier composers. For example, we see the technique of unfolding, by which the motion from B of the tonic chord to its neighbor C♯ of the supertonic seventh chord is prolonged. Here B and G♯ of the E major chord are unfolded with an answering motion from F♯ to C♯ within the F♯ minor chord. One, however, is a space-outlining motion, while in the other the space between F♯ and C♯ has been filled with passing tones. A strongly outlined bass motion of A–C♯–F♯ accentuates the descent in the top voice.

With the entrance of B in the bass, the root of the dominant chord, we find an interesting treatment of the voice leadings. C♯ is retained as a suspension in the top voice while E♯, a passing tone, and A, the seventh

---

[13] *Arnold Schönberg* (E. P. Dutton, 1925), p. 68.

of the chord, appear as middle voices. Since C♯ passes to B and E to F♯ while the bass moves from B to A, these "foreign tones" appear to result from the use of a suspension and a passing-tone motion. If, as Schönberg claims, such contrapuntal devices give rise to organic chord tones, this interpretation does not coincide with the composer's intention. However, the fact that Schönberg has treated these tones as though they were of a contrapuntal origin, by resolving the suspension and completing the pass-

EXAMPLE 119

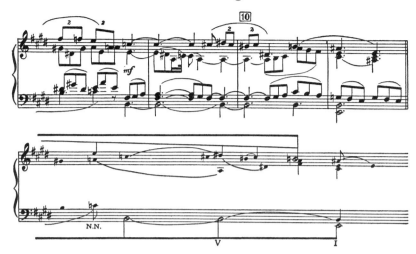

ing-tone motion, suggests that in practice his artistic instinct is stronger than his theoretical credo.

The reader may ask what difference it makes in the interpretation whether we hear C♯ and E♯ as a suspension and passing tone or as organic chord tones. This is a significant question, since it is the crux of the entire discussion.

If we hear a clearly outlined motion from the F♯ minor to the B major chord, in which the entrance of B and F♯ of the dominant chord are delayed through the presence of C♯ and E♯, we recognize that these tones, through their contrapuntal origin, create a tension in the structural motion. It is just because we do not hear them as chord tones that they intensify the supertonic-dominant progression. If, however, we accept them as organic chord tones, this tension is lost, since we no longer await the delayed entrance of B or F♯, inasmuch as C♯ and E♯ are integral members of the dominant chord. As a result we hear them not within a clearly outlined space in which the intervening tones or chords enrich and heighten the motion, but only from one chord to another, the nature and function of which are not revealed. Thus we not only rob the harmonic agents of their structural significance, but in so doing denude the progression of the tension and suspense that C♯ and E♯ generate if we recognize their contrapuntal and non-organic status. To perceive the difference between these two interpretations fully, the reader should experiment with both and satisfy himself as to which defines his aural reactions more clearly.

Challenge to Musical Tradition

With the entrance of the inverted tonic chord (measure 7), the graph shows an unfolding of the interval B–G♯. In the music, however, this G♯ appears in combination with A and C♯ of the succeeding chord. Although from Schönberg's point of view this G♯ is an organic element of the altered chord on A, it would normally be regarded as in connection with the E major chord, but shifted for rhythmic or motivic reasons. Accordingly, it is G♮ that we hear in association with the altered chord on A, as its seventh.

Since there is a similar unfolding of B and G♯ of the tonic chord in the preceding motion from tonic to dominant, the reader should examine the different treatment Schönberg has used in each to prolong the structural progression. They indicate how varied are Schönberg's solutions to the problems of voice leadings.

Undoubtedly, there will be objections to the explanation offered in the graph, because it represents a type of motion that Schönberg has negated in his theoretical discussions. Although the justice of such an argument must be admitted, have we not the same right to offer an explanation of our understanding of Schönberg's music that Schönberg has assumed in his interpretation of the examples from Bach's and Beethoven's works? We have indicated the function of certain tones as neighbor notes, suspensions, or passing tones because we hear them in this capacity, not as organic chord tones. In a similar manner the graph reveals a coherent structural motion; in its definition of the E major tonality, this motion affirms a distinction between the harmonic and contrapuntal techniques that Schönberg maintains does not exist. To believe that in this work he has adhered to the principles of the past and has perhaps unconsciously given a genuine artistic expression to his instinctive concept of tonality does not in any way minimize the originality and individuality of the treatment. It merely proves, as in the case of Debussy and Stravinsky, the elasticity and adaptability of the tonal principle.

In the *Gurrelieder*, which follows the sextet chronologically, the influence of Wagner is again discernible in the emotional quality of the treatment, the tremendous orchestral framework in which it is conceived, and the psychological use of Tove's love song as the main theme dominating the entire work. Here, too, we find an intensification of Wagner's use of accented neighbor notes, suspensions, retardations, and passing tones, all of which inject the tension of dissonance into the harmonic progressions. Yet here too, we are aware of certain tendencies in the treatment that disclose a more pronounced kinship with the later techniques than the sextet revealed.

There is an intense use of chromaticism, with the chromatics playing a more and more important role as in Tove's love song and Waldemar's song, *Es ist Mitternachtzeit*. There are the growing independence of the individual voice parts and the widely spaced intervals in the melodic lines, as in Tove's love song, both characteristic of the later style. There are other passages, however, such as the exquisite *Du wunderliche Tove*, in which the techniques are less complex and reflect the tender beauty of the mood evoked by the text. Yet even here, there are times when the chromatics tend to overshadow the more significant elements in the prolongations.

It is impossible to quote this song in its entirety, but the first nineteen measures are sufficient to give an idea of the poignant quality of the melody and the unusual treatment Schönberg provides through the retention of the dominant B♭ seventh chord throughout the passage.

First of all, we see the interweaving of the vocal and instrumental lines and the effect of continuity that the orchestra supplies while the voice is silent. The prolonged motion from the root position of the B♭ seventh chord (measure 6) to its inversion with A♭ in the bass (measure 9) is an illustration of this point. It also reveals the highly chromatic nature of the prolonging chords that fill the space between A♭ and D in the top voice and B♭ and A♭ in the bass.

Throughout the passage, the retention of the dominant B♭ seventh chord is the result of embellishing motions in the form of neighbor notes rather than a prolongation within the horizontalized chord. In the first of these the motion from the B♭ seventh chord to its neighbor, the inverted A♭ major chord, is effected through a bass motion of B♭—A♭—G—C (measures 6–11). This is further extended by an ascent from B♭ to its neighbor note C (measure 8), which returns to A♭, an incomplete neighbor-note motion. However, it must be admitted that although the tones G—C define a fifth association, the status of these tones as the fifth of the C minor chord and the third of the A♭ major is an extremely weak expression of this relationship and raises some doubt as to the nature of the motion.

There is also a question as to the interpretation of the measures that follow. It is logical to assume that the A♭ major chord returns to the dominant seventh (measure 12), a supposition that the voice bears out. Yet a return to the inverted A♭ chord in the succeeding measure and the phras-

371

EXAMPLE 120

ing in the top instrumental line suggest the possibility that the B♭ chord is a lower neighbor of the two A♭ chords that appear on either side. However, the inverted A♭ chord is indicated as a neighbor of B♭ because there seems to be an ascent from C to E♭ in the bass (measures 13–15), an embellishment of the outlined space from B♭ to D within the dominant chord (measures 12–16). Although this reading is fairly well borne out by the motion described by the melody, the voice leadings are sufficiently vague to give rise to a different interpretation. Therefore the reading must be regarded primarily as a possible rather than a clearly defined explanation of the techniques.

There can be no doubt of the ingenuity with which Schönberg overcame the possible monotony of retaining a B♭ seventh chord for nineteen measures. It is equally apparent, however, that although he achieved a variety of effects through the chromatic nature of the passing chords and the neighbor-note motions, the techniques he used to attain this result are by no means either clear or convincing.

Although the melodic line shows traces of the wide leaps that characterize the later treatment, we find a more pronounced tendency in this direction in the D minor quartet, Opus 7, and the *Kammersymphonie*, Opus 9. The opening theme of the D minor quartet,[14] which insinuates itself in one form or another into each of the movements, offers an excellent illustration of this point.

EXAMPLE 121

Here we see the wide spacings that we find in the piano pieces, Opus 11 and Opus 19. It is true that this melody has been conceived within a tonal framework, while the later compositions indicate the use of the twelve-tone system. Nevertheless, although the idiom is totally different, the seeds of the later melodic style are present already. Other aspects of the technique also foreshadow the later tendencies. Here, too, we find a use of chromatics that indicates their growing importance and prophesies their final supremacy over the diatonic system. In addition, the other voice parts disclose an independence of action resulting in a series of chord combinations that obscure the structural meaning and thus weaken tonal coherence.

[14] *Dreililien Verlag*, Berlin.

A brief allusion to the entrance of the contrasting theme of the first movement (measure 97) demonstrates both the unusual nature of the material and the tonal vagueness that arises in the intricate treatment of the voice leadings.

EXAMPLE 122

Although this example is a mere fragment of the section and does not reveal the many and varied ways in which the principal theme is used as a counterpoint to the secondary theme, it does offer an insight into the highly chromatic nature of the material and the confusion that results from the voice leadings. It would be futile to attempt any explanation of this passage in terms of tonality, since the voice parts, both individually and in combination, are too vague to indicate a well-defined motion with either structural or prolonging implications.

The reader may claim that for a work of this nature, in which the horizontal technique is so obviously the predominating impulse, there is no need to define a structural motion and that the primary factor in the treatment is to preserve the independence and integrity of the individual

Schönberg

voices irrespective of the results of their combination. In short, he may contend that this is a passage in which the sole consideration is the use of two thematic figures in imitation, a purely contrapuntal device. If we turn to the works of the pre-Bach period in which a similar technique is used, we find that the melodic figure not only outlines a clearly defined space, but at times merges with the other voice parts and thus gives rise to chords that clarify the nature of the motion even if they lack structural significance. This is the salient point that the reader must recognize, since it shows that any motion, whether it be of a contrapuntal or harmonic origin, must have direction and purpose.

Jepperson has recognized this same characteristic in these works. He says: "In the sixteenth century there existed a polyphony which grew into a unified whole from single lines by virtue of the artistically controlled relation governing them." [15]

In spite of the horizontal aspect of the treatment, the chords resulting from the single lines should demonstrate their functions within a clearly outlined motion, if we are to regard the passage as within the D minor tonality. Yet it must be admitted the chords themselves are so uncharacteristic of the key, and the motion they create so vague, that it is impossible to offer any explanation of how the passage expresses the tonality of D minor.

This lack of tonal clarity is due not to the constant use of chromatics, but to the manner in which they are employed. So far as the chromatics are concerned, the treatment is merely an intensification of the *Tristan* technique. As we saw, in the prelude to *Tristan und Isolde* there is a marked distinction between the basic progressions that outline structural motion and the prolonging chords that expand the structural motion. This distinction is lacking in Schönberg's technique.

Were this the only instance of weakened tonal stability in the quartet, it could not be offered as indicative of the new trends in Schönberg's treatment. However, since there are other passages in which the techniques are also ambiguous and indefinite, with a similar effect on tonal coherence, it is apparent that the principles of unity demonstrated in the sextet and the *Gurrelieder* have been replaced by techniques in which the germs of atonality already have been sown.

In a valuable article on Schönberg, César Saerchinger makes the following statement about the D minor quartet: "The first quartet, definitely

[15] *Counterpoint* (Prentice-Hall, Inc., 1939), Preface, p. xi.

classical in form, already shows tendencies to atonality, but also betrays Schönberg's uncertainty at this period in its diatonic platitudes and the conventional cadences with which many otherwise daring passages conclude. Inversely, simple melodic phrases culminate in curious passages destroying all feeling of tonic centrality or dispersing into vagueness." [16]

In the *Kammersymphonie* also we find evidence of tendencies prophetic of the later treatment. The opening theme given out by the horn (measure 5) is one such instance. Built on five ascending fourths, it foreshadows the technique characteristic of the "Three Piano Pieces," Opus 11, Schönberg's first acknowledged experiment in the twelve-tone scale. The use of this theme and the prominent role it plays throughout show a trend away from the triad to a group of intervals that do not demonstrate either in succession or in combination the type of coherence indicative of tonality.

Although the argument that the chord is a man-made and consequently artificial device is often advanced in support of chords consisting of intervals of the fourth and the fifth, it is equally true that the choice of the triad as a symbol of unity was neither arbitrary nor accidental. [17] Furthermore, the fact that the intervals of a fourth and a fifth were in common usage long before the third was accepted as a consonance, does not in itself justify a return to the technique of tenth-century organum, when the development of music was in its early stage. There is no need for justification if we frankly admit that the retrogression is an experiment to explore the hitherto unknown possibilities of a system built on fourths. Otherwise it is only an arbitrary selection of intervals, among which the inherent association represented by the tones of the triad is entirely lacking.

The presence of a theme of this nature in the *Kammersymphonie* is an indication that tonality is at the crossroads. In referring to it, Wellesz points out that the theme "appears at all the important points of departure in the development, and thanks to its peculiar composition it is capable of discarding tonality and also, through its fanfare-like character, of bringing into a polyphonic texture of the voices a contrast that has immediate effect." [18]

The first movement of the quartet in F minor, Opus 10, is a contradiction of the tendencies disclosed in various parts of the *Kammersymphonie*.

---

[16] *Schoenberg*, edited by Merle Armitage (G. Schirmer, 1937), p. 96.
[17] See Chapter I for a discussion of the origin of the triad.
[18] *Arnold Schönberg* (E. P. Dutton, 1925), p. 105.

Schönberg

Here the opening theme shows a clearly defined harmonic progression, even though the prolongations reveal many of Schönberg's characteristic techniques. However, in contrast to the clarity of this movement, the third and fourth, in which a soprano voice is added to the strings, bring fresh proof of the growing struggle between tonal and atonal methods.

Let us first examine the theme of the opening movement. In his reference to this passage, Wellesz gives the following analysis:

"The very first theme with which this movement begins, without any preparation, is wonderfully unified and concise.

"The B♯ is enharmonically exchanged to C, which at first becomes the fifth of a passing F minor chord and then the third of an A minor chord, with which the principle theme appears a second time." [19]

In the graph we see a top-voice ascent from A to C♯ against F♯ in the bass (measures 1–3). There is a descent from C♯ to its octave while the bass ascends from F♯ to A, still within the F♯ minor chord. At this point B♯ enters in the top voice, later to be exchanged for C♮.

Wellesz reads A♭ (measure 5) as the third of an F minor chord that passes to the chord of A minor. However, it also is possible to hear this A♭ as G♯ in conjunction with B♯ and the preceding D♯ as the root of the G♯ major chord, a passing chord between the F♯ and A minor chords. Therefore D♯–G♯ and B♯ are indicated as the horizontalized tones of the G♯ chord, whose third B♯ is exchanged for C. Again, the interpretation depends on how we hear this motion, but since D♯ and B♯ are present, it seems clearer to regard it as an ascent of F♯–G♯–A than, as Wellesz indicates, F♯–A♭–A♮, with A♭ representing an F minor chord.

The status of the A minor chord is also somewhat unclear. It is not convincing as a minor mediant in the progression, because C♮, the top voice, enters after C♯, the structural tone in the ascent, already is attained within the F♯ minor chord. Therefore, instead of stimulating, it retards the top-voice motion. This suggests a prolonging rather than a structural function. However, it is equally difficult to account for the A minor chord as a passing chord between the tonic and dominant chords. The graph defines it as a mediant, but as the parentheses indicate, there is a doubt as to its actual status in this functional role.

In the final measures, the entrance of an F major chord between the minor and major dominant offers an interesting use of a neighbor-note

[19] *Ibid.,* p. 111.

EXAMPLE 123

chord. The function of this chord is somewhat concealed by the top-voice leap from C♯ to A instead of to G♯, the fifth of the C♯ minor chord. However, it is the omission of G♯ that intensifies the effect of an F major chord between the chords of C♯ minor and major. Here, instead of the indefiniteness surrounding the function of the A minor chord, we find a clear-cut definition of the status of the interposed chord of F major.

Through this motion from the F♯ minor to the C♯ major chord, Schönberg demonstrates a structural progression that outlines the F♯ minor tonality. Within this motion, however, the prolonging chords are of a nature that tends to weaken the structural stability. This is evidenced in the doubt whether A♭ represents an F minor chord or whether we should hear it as the root of the G♯ major chord. If it is indicative of F minor, why is F omitted? On the other hand, if it has a connection with D♯ and B♯, why is it expressed as A♭? There is the further uncertainty of the function of the A minor chord, which is in conflict with its melodic importance in repeating the thematic figure. These are all elements that attenuate rather than fortify the structural coherence. Yet the fact that the motion is outlined by a tonic-dominant progression shows that there is a strong tonal impulse dominating the structural framework, even though it is weakened by the vagueness of the prolonging chords.

In the two final movements of the quartet, in which a soprano voice is added to the strings, there is a marked difference in the treatment. The third, the slow movement, is in the style of a theme with variations. The theme, an eight-measure phrase, consists of four motives, all of which have appeared in the preceding movements. We recognize the first two as coming from the principal and contrasting theme of the first movement; the third, from the contrasting theme of the scherzo; and the fourth, as an augmentation of the closing group from the first movement. Yet in spite of the ingenious use of this material, the complexities to which the technique gives rise completely obscure the nature of the structural and prolonging motions, through the confused and conflicting character of the voice leadings.

This lack of tonal stability is intensified in the final movement, in which Schönberg dispenses with a key signature. Although this in itself is not necessarily indicative of a lack of tonal definition, the constant use of chromatics in connection with chord tones suggests that the influence of the twelve-tone scale is so strong that it has overcome the natural tendencies of the diatonic and tonal system. In fact, it is possible to believe that Schönberg no longer differentiates between chord tones and tones of a passing or ornamental nature and that he regards them primarily as equally organic and significant members of the twelve-tone scale.

It is true that the movement concludes on an F♯ major chord, a reference to the opening movement in F♯ minor. However, there is nothing in the structural framework that defines a motion within the F♯ major tonality or a mixture of F♯ minor and F♯ major. In fact, the few passages in which the motion might lead us to assume that Schönberg is touching on the F♯ major tonality are so unclear, both in their own outline and in their relation to the passages that precede and follow, that it is impossible to regard them as an expression of tonal coherence. The following example is an illustration of this point.

EXAMPLE 124

The passage starts on an F♯ major chord. The B♮ would ordinarily be explained as a passing tone between C of the preceding measure and A♯. Here, however, there are so many tones unrelated to the chord in which they appear and impossible to account for as passing tones, embellishments, suspensions, or retardations that Schönberg obviously regards them as organic tones. The older conception of their status as foreign tones no longer applies.

Schönberg

The main problem for our consideration is: What motion does this passage define? Is the F♯ major chord the starting point, or is it an under neighbor of the altered seventh chord on G that follows, in a motion to the altered A and D chords (measures 10–11)? The factor that motivates this question is a possible connection between two seventh chords on G, one in measure 2, the other in the second half of measure 9. If so, how shall we explain the top-voice motion and account for the contradiction in the voice leadings?

Although it is possible to point out certain factors in the measures following this passage to the close of the movement as indicative of the importance of the F♯ major chord, there is no motion that demonstrates its function either as a tonic or as a neighbor chord. Nor is there any reason to believe that the chord of G–B–D♯–F is the start of a motion that leads to the final D chord of this passage. Various theories can be advanced, but there is no means of proving any of them.

We need only examine the new role the chromatics play to realize that their former status has been completely transformed. For example, take the chord B–G–D♯–F♯–D♮ (measure 5), in which D♯ in the viola and voice appears against D♮ in the first violin, and the similar contradictions between F♮ and F♯ (measure 7), G♭ and G♮ (measure 9), and E♮ and E♭ (measure 10), in none of which is the function of either of the conflicting tones apparent. In fact, there is every reason to believe that both are conceived as organic chord tones, with no distinction as to their status. This is the all-important change that has taken place — the inclusion of all foreign tones in the chord with the status of chord tones.

Although such combinations occur in the works of Johann Sebastian Bach, Philipp Emanuel Bach, and Beethoven, we have seen that the conflicting tones have different functions in their music. One may be a chord tone, the other an embellishment; or one may be a neighbor note, the other a passing tone. In every instance, however, their presence can be justified on purely technical grounds. In short, the motion in which they appear is so clearly outlined that their status as chord tones, embellishments, passing tones, or suspensions is well defined. There is a definite distinction between the tones that represent the chord structure and those that are the result of various contrapuntal devices. This distinction no longer prevails in the above example.

Schönberg's acceptance of all foreign tones as chord tones is the ultimate step leading to the twelve-tone system. It is responsible for the difference in treatment between the opening movement and the outlined motion within the F♯ minor tonality and for the lack of tonal clarity in the final movement. In the first movement chromaticism is subordinated to the larger demands of the structural motion. In the last movement it pushes the motion outside the tonal orbit in order to gain its own independence and free itself from its former subjugation to the diatonic scale. The quartet marks both the end of one period and the beginning of a new stage in Schönberg's development. It is the climax of the tonal era, in which chromaticism reached its furthermost limits within the concept of tonality, and it is the forerunner of the new period in which the twelve half tones are recognized as equal and independent members of the twelve-tone system.

THE TWELVE–TONE SYSTEM

It is customary to divide the works in this medium into two periods. The first includes the "Three Piano Pieces," Opus 11, through the "Four Songs with Orchestra," Opus 22; the second, the "Five Piano Pieces," Opus 23, through the "Six Small Pieces for Men's Chorus," Opus 35.

The "Three Piano Pieces," Opus 11, already indicate the trends the later works are to take. They are an open declaration of Schönberg's acceptance of the twelve-tone system as the new medium of expression. They are definite proof of his rejection of the older principles and techniques associated with tonality and represent his first experiment in the so-called atonal system.

It is logical that, in turning from the tonal concept, Schönberg should relinquish techniques that were an integral part of its evolution, to find an equally characteristic means of demonstrating the possibilities of the new system. The development and stabilization of the new techniques occupy him during the main part of this first period.

It is also logical that the principles of form that had grown out of the concept of tonality could not serve as the structural basis of the twelve-tone system. First of all, they were historically associated with the techniques used to achieve tonality, techniques in which the harmonic principle embodied in the triad was the dominating factor in attaining structural coherence. As the triad itself is no longer an element in the new system, it was natural that Schönberg should turn from an emphasis of the harmonic to an emphasis of the melodic impulse as the foundation of his technical treatment. The result, as Saerchinger aptly states, was that

382

Schönberg

Schönberg "logically went back to a time when music was as essentially polyphonic as his own." [20] It is not surprising that we find many of the contrapuntal devices used by sixteenth-century composers playing a major role in Schönberg's technique.

The basis of this system is the recognition of the twelve tones of the chromatic scale as of equal importance. No longer are they dependent on the seven tones of the diatonic scale for their existence, nor are they subordinated to them in the new treatment. All twelve tones possess the same status and demonstrate the same function. There is no tonal center; consequently we cannot look for the tonic-dominant relationship, which is the foundation of the tonal system. We not only are dealing with a new type of chord structure, new techniques, and a new set of musical values, but we are confronted with an entirely new conception of the function and status of the same twelve tones that have constituted the raw material out of which the music of the past has been fashioned.

We need only turn to the "Three Piano Pieces," Opus 11, to realize how revolutionary are the fruits of Schönberg's experimentation along totally new lines. The first of these pieces shows a three-measure melodic phrase built on the twelve-tone scale. It is the basic pattern that, through various adaptations, furnishes the main melodic and harmonic material of the entire work. It is regarded as the germ plasm from which all further activity springs. Thus it constitutes a new type of unity in its relation to the repetitions it engenders. Accordingly, tonal coherence demonstrated by the structural top voice and the basic harmonic progression is no longer the artistic symbol of organic oneness. Instead, Schönberg has conceived of a single phrase or a group of smaller patterns as a melodic and harmonic unit that gives rise to the variations in the treatment that comprise the essential elements of the work.

If we examine the motive dominating the first of the "Three Piano Pieces" as the entity Schönberg indicates it to be, what is its meaning, and what type of melodic and harmonic motion does it outline? To answer this question, we must first understand the principles that have evolved out of the twelve-tone system. We cannot apply to this new technique the principles of structure and prolongation, since they no longer prevail. We are dealing with a new type of chord structure, a new concept of unity, and a system in which harmony and counterpoint no longer exercise their former functions. Therefore, since no explanation of their new function has

[20] *Schoenberg*, edited by Merle Armitage (G. Schirmer, 1937), p. 102.

been offered, we can only assume that the sole principle on which coherence rests is the use of a main motive as the life-giving force out of which the material of an entire work is derived.

It is not our purpose at this point to discuss either the advantages or the disadvantages of this system. Our sole aim is to clarify the basic distinctions between the tonal and atonal techniques. The results of these differences and their influence on contemporary music can be estimated only after we understand the significance of the later developments.

THE TWELVE–TONE ROW

The second period, which begins with the "Five Piano Pieces," Opus 23, is no longer one of experimentation, but one of organization. It reveals the fruits of Schönberg's earlier labors in the establishment of a new theory of composition, the twelve-tone series. Here it must be recognized that whether or not we agree with the premise on which this system is built or whether we accept the principles out of which it evolved, it nevertheless represents the first systematized approach to a new theory of composition. We must recognize that of all present-day composers, with the exception of Hindemith, Schönberg is the only one who has organized his theories into a definite and concrete system in which he frankly divorced the principles and techniques from those governing the tonal concept.

Although the principles of the twelve-tone technique have been discussed at length, both by Schönberg and by other composers, it is perhaps necessary to define them, as they are revealed by Schönberg in his own works.

In the twelve-tone row or series, the tones are used not in the flexible manner of the "Three Piano Pieces," but in well-defined groups whose set arrangement remains intact throughout an entire work, whether it be in one movement or in several. These groups make up the series which Erwin Stein regards "as a tone-complex, whose successions and intervallic relations always recur, though in manifold variations and combinations." [21] The series constitutes the melodic and harmonic nucleus out of which the composition is evoked. In addition to the primary grouping, the series appears in three other forms: (1) the inversion of the primary grouping; (2) the crab or retrograde succession from the last tone to the opening tone; (3) the inversion of the crab. However, since the intervallic relations

[21] "Schönberg's New Structural Form," *Modern Music* (June–July, 1930).

remain the same, Stein claims that these different presentations effect a change in "the melodic physiognomy but not in the harmonic structure."

An excellent illustration of the use of the tone-row is the *Suite* for piano, Opus 25. Here throughout the six movements, the row consists of the same three groups of four tones each. It is interesting, however, to see that although the idiom indicates Schönberg's break with the past, the title of each movement — prelude, gavotte, musette, intermezzo, minuet, and gigue — is closely associated with the older dance suite.

The opening measures of the gavotte have been selected to illustrate the use of the series, because they offer a clear demonstration of the techniques to which the row is subjected and of the adaptation of the older contrapuntal devices to the use of the new medium.

EXAMPLE 125

The three groups of four tones each of which the series consists, are indicated in the music and in the graph as A, B, C. The transformation of the first group E♮—F—G—D♭ into B♭—C♭—D♭—G♮, appearing simultaneously with the primary row, is the result of inversion. The inversion of the three groups, as it first appears, is shown directly below the original row in the graph, as A¹—, B¹, C¹. In measures 3 to 5, the series appears in a different form of inversion and is designated in the graph by the markings, A²—, B², C². The two groups in measure 5 that appear as B³ and C³ in the graph, represent an inversion of the crab form. Thus in these five measures, the series is presented in its primary form and in three different adaptations. Although these are only a few of the many forms in which the row is revealed throughout the movement, they are sufficiently indicative of the treatment to illustrate how the series is used, how the changes effected by the techniques provide new and different arrangements within the groups, and how the three groups, through transformation, serve as the germ plasm out of which the movement is developed.

In the *Suite,* Schönberg has evolved a new conception of unity by his use of the series as a tone-complex, the single reservoir that furnishes the material not only of a movement, but of the entire work. The principle of unity to which this concept gives rise has nothing in common with the older principle of coherence, since the organic nature of the work depends, not on the clarity of the structural outline and the prolongations, but solely on the common bond among the twelve equal tones and the guaranty of unity it affords, so long as the integrity of the complex is maintained.

In short, the series does not demonstrate the unity among these tones through an active structural principle, but accepts the origin of these tones in a single fundamental as a sufficient though passive expression of coherence. Yet what does this type of unity achieve when the primary series itself lacks structural meaning, when the techniques, although of musical origin, are employed in a purely mathematical manner, and when the melodic, rhythmic, contrapuntal and harmonic elements have been robbed of their inherent functions?

A further point of interest is Schönberg's use of the tone-row in connection with the seventeenth- and eighteenth-century suite, since it brings up a question that concerns all composers who find expression in a new medium whether the system be the twelve-tone series or so-called bitonality.

Is it not incongruous, to say the least, to employ such forms as the suite and sonata, which were evolved and expanded only through the growth of the tonal concept, in works in which the techniques negate the principles of tonality?

In this instance, Schönberg reverts to the suite form. Stravinsky, using a different technique, equally atonal, has recourse to the sonata, the concerto, and the symphony. Both Schönberg and Stravinsky moved outside the tonal environment in which these forms came into being, grew, and developed; why then do they maintain the outer semblance of these forms, whose organic life and vital structural character they have repudiated? Would it not be more logical if, in establishing a new system, each of these composers had created forms as indigenous to the atonal or polytonal techniques as the suite and the sonata are to tonality?

Form is not an artificial or superficial garb that can be imposed on a musical idea. It is an integral part of it and evolves side by side with the growth and expansion of the musical idea. The suite and sonata owe their structural origin to the form-making possibilities and the element of contrast the basic tonic-dominant relationship expresses through the horizontalized triad. Both Schönberg and Stravinsky have rejected the unifying principle that is inherent in the triad and is demonstrated through tonality, but have retained the forms in which its function is the primary motivating force.

The twelve-tone series has been a subject of great controversy. Its proponents believe that it holds many more possibilities for the present-day composer than the older tonal system. For example, Krenek states that "according to authorities on the permutation theory, there are 479,-001,600 different twelve-tone series in existence." [22] Its critics, on the other hand, point to its artificial origin, its mathematical basis, its purely cerebral impulse, and its sterile and chaotic results. Perhaps the most unprejudiced statement from the non-adherents comes from Constant Lambert. He says: "The desire to escape from the tyranny of the key system in music is as understandable as the desire to escape from academic realism in painting; but, whether we like it or not, tonality in music and realism in painting are a norm that is in our blood — departure from them, however successful

[22] *Music Here and Now* (Norton, 1939), p. 170.

and however praiseworthy, is, technically speaking, an abnormality. While a school of normality is a logical and harmless affair, a school of abnormality is a psychological contradiction." [23]

In discussing the abnormal aspects of the atonal techniques, the author is not biased by tradition, convention, classicism, or a desire to retain a musical *status quo*. It is obvious to every open-minded musician that the introduction of new ideas, as well as the expansion and adaptation of the old, is essential to the growth and development of music. It is equally true that the music of the later nineteenth century was of a nature that could not proceed further in the same direction without endangering tonal coherence. No one will deny that both Wagner and Debussy, not to mention Reger, Wolf, Mahler, and Bruckner, had emphasized the chromatic elements to a point where diatonicism was contending with all its strength against the growing supremacy of the chromatic scale.

It is doubtless inevitable that the increasing power of the chromatics should make inroads on structural coherence. This was made clear in certain illustrations from Wagner and Debussy, as well as in some passages from Stravinsky's and Schönberg's early works. The concept of tonality had fostered the use of chromatics as a means of intensifying the structural motion through the added impulse they injected into the prolongations. Later, however, their function in the prolongations began to assume an importance that was reflected in the vagueness of the structural outline, so that the growing power of chromaticism left its impact on tonal stability. Thus chromaticism, which had flourished only through the role it played within tonality, became not only a challenger, but a most destructive antagonist of the system that had sustained it for over two hundred years.

In a summary of the steps leading to the dissolution of tonality, Erwin Stein, an adherent of the atonal school, offers an explanation that not only is pertinent, but presents a point of view reflecting the attitude of a large number of contemporary composers. He says: "The old keys are dead, so far as modern compositions are concerned. The development of harmony during the past century gradually robbed them of their meaning. . . . The numerous meanings to which chords give rise and the possibility of modulating that they provide, as well as such factors as the diminished seventh, which belongs simultaneously to several keys, all these facts were bound to obscure the limits of tonality. Every so-called bold progression

[23] *Music Ho!* (Charles Scribner's Sons, 1935), p. 288.

Schönberg

or innovation contributed to this dissolution. . . . The most important factor was the centralization of power in one tone — the fundamental. From this fundamental one went away, and to this fundamental one returned." [24]

In the final words Stein unconsciously reveals the true cause to which tonality owes its downfall — the accepted definition of tonality as a centralized key from which one moves and to which one returns. It is this misconception of what constitutes organic unity, this misunderstanding of the artistic coherence demonstrated in the works of the great composers of the past, this mésalliance between theory and practice, that are primarily responsible for the breakdown of the tonal system.

Schönberg and possibly many others recognized the inconsistency between the actual definition of tonality and the modulatory adventures permitted by theory. Because of this discrepancy, they believed that tonality had failed. It is evident, however, from Schönberg's analysis of the works of Bach and Beethoven, that it was he who failed — failed to realize that the concept of tonality demonstrated by these composers was not the same concept held by the theorists. He applied to the music the inconsistencies of the theoretical approach instead of molding the approach to the concept revealed in the music. Yet Schönberg is only one of the many who did not recognize the real divergence between theory and practice, the difference between the textbook analysis and what the music itself discloses; he is only one of many who, guided by the false wisdom of the pedants, were more strongly influenced by such sophistry than by what they could learn from the music itself.

TONALITY VERSUS ATONALITY

Throughout these pages, numerous examples have been offered to prove that tonality is the expression of unity achieved through motion within a single horizontalized chord. The music has been subjected to a form of analysis that accounts for every tone, whether diatonic or chromatic, every chord whether of a structural or prolonging nature, as within the motion outlining the basic structure. Passages that are usually regarded as modulations to different keys have been shown to be expansions of a member of the structural progression or members of a harmonic prolongation. In short, every attempt has been made to prove conclusively that in an organic work, every aspect of the treatment must demonstrate

[24] "Neue Formprinzipien," *Von Neuer Musik* (F. J. Marcan-Verlag, Köln, 1925), p. 59.

389

its unified connection with the whole, as an offshoot of the basic structure. If a work is conceived within a given tonality, then it may not extend outside the boundaries defined by that tonality.

From this point of view tonality, through its domination of the motivic, rhythmic, contrapuntal and harmonic elements of a work, is the symbol of unity essential to every form of artistic creation. In place of this, Schönberg has given us the twelve-tone scale in the form of the series. There is only one criterion by which we can evaluate his contribution. In substituting as a concept of unity the tone-complex represented by the twelve-tone series for the harmonic principle embodied in the fundamental-fifth association, has he achieved an equal though different type of coherence from that provided by the horizontalized chord? The first point to be considered is: What fundamental principles does the twelve-tone system discard, and what new principles does it establish in their place?

It denies (1) the existence of a tonal center represented by the fundamental; (2) the concept of unity inherent in the basic fundamental-fifth association; (3) the division of the scale into whole and half tones, the diatonic and chromatic elements with their differentiated functions; (4) the distinction between the contrapuntal and harmonic principles, since the harmonic principle, based on the combination of the first five harmonics into a triad, has been discarded; (5) the contrast between consonance and dissonance, since all twelve tones exercise the same function both horizontally and vertically, and consequently are regarded as organic chord tones.

What new principles has the series evolved to replace those it negates? In discussing the twelve-tone series and the unity it provides, Krenek answers this question. He says: "When key consciousness vanished completely and music became 'atonal,' technical unity could no longer emerge from a solid harmonic groundwork. Quite logically, the attention was focused on the motif relationships. Whereas they had formerly been a superstructure erected above the harmonic groundwork, they now became responsible for the consistency of the whole edifice. . . . Thus the primary function of the series is that of a sort of 'store of motifs' out of which all the individual elements of the compositions are to be developed. By virtue of its ceaseless repetitions throughout the whole composition, however, the series accomplishes more than that; it assures the technical homogeneity of the work by permeating its whole structure, like a red thread which, woven into a fabric, lends its characteristic color shade, without ever becoming conspicuous as such." [25]

It is evident that the type of unity that Krenek claims is inherent in the series is entirely different from the kind that demonstrates tonality. The distinction is not merely, as Schönberg suggests, that "the chromatic scale brings the more distant overtones within the possibility of relationship." [26] The difference in concept is based not on the degrees of relationship among the overtones, but on the degrees of unity these relationships express. In one, the unity arises out of the close association of the first five overtones with their fundamental. In the other, it is based on the relationship of the more remote overtones, whose association, from a mathematical point of view, is more complex. However, even this distinction as to the origin of the association is not the sole factor. In the former, the unity inherent in the relationship has engendered the combination of these tones into a triad, which not only preserves the fundamental connection, but demonstrates it constantly as a principle of structural coherence. In the latter, the more remote overtones have been organized into a group of twelve equal tones whose unifying connection rests on their common origin in one and the same fundamental. These twelve tones are the raw material from which the series has been evolved. The unity inherent in the series is demonstrated by the consistent use of motives as the primordial source from which all other material is derived.

Although in each case it is the association of the tones as defined in the overtone series that gives rise to the concept of unity, in tonality this fundamental relationship has been conceived as a means toward an end rather than as an end in itself. In other words, the association does not represent coherence *per se,* but must constantly prove its function as an active principle demonstrating that every element of a work is an organic part of the basic structure outlined by a single horizontalized chord. In the series, however, the association of the twelve tones has been embodied not in an active structural principle, but in a system that does not attempt to demonstrate the unifying connections of these tones, but accepts them as an established fact. Here the association is the end, not the means of demonstrating an artistic concept.

The reader may argue that there is no difference between a coherence

[25] *Studies in Counterpoint* (G. Schirmer, 1940), introduction.

[26] Schönberg accounts for these twelve tones as derived from the overtones of the three basic fundamentals F–C–G. See *Schoenberg,* edited by Merle Armitage (G. Schirmer, 1937), pp. 270–3.

that allies every prolongation to a basic structure and a coherence that allies every adaptation of the series to the basic row. This is a point well taken, since in both instances the various offshoots grow out of a fundamental idea. The difference, however, lies in the nature of the fundamental idea. The basic structure outlines a motion that not only demonstrates the tonality, but defines the relationship on which the tonality rests through the outlined motion within the tonic chord. The basic row consists of a group of motives in which the arbitrary arrangement of the twelve tones is not motivated by the necessity of demonstrating a structural principle. There is the additional difference between a system that, in recognizing both the harmonic and contrapuntal techniques, determines the status of a tone or a chord by the specific function it serves and a system in which all tones or chords are of equal status and thus possess the same function.

In speaking of the basic functions of tonal material, Joseph Yasser makes this statement: "In the meantime we know they are positively miss-ing in the atonal scale, since it in no way represents what we call a 'closed' organic system but merely a mechanical aggregation of inde-pendent and inwardly isolated units of sound." [27]

Even so firm a believer in the possibilities inherent in the twelve-tone system as Richard Hill recognizes that "Tones, after all, cannot be arbi-trarily related . . . we not only object to lack of functional organization *per se*, but insist upon some means other than absolute pitch by which to orient ourselves in the series of consecutive pitches. . . . In actual practice, Schoenberg uses the row in such ways that no functional relations are engendered; but it nevertheless has inherent within it the capacity for organizing the twelve tones into a functional mode." [28]

These quotations have been used because they are objective consider-ations of a problem that both Yasser and Hill are earnestly attempting to solve, though in different ways. Yasser believes that the twelve-tone scale is an experiment in the direction of the "supra-diatonic scale," a combination of the diatonic and twelve-tone scales. Hill regards the pres-ent series as a necessary stage in the development of the system, but rec-ognizes the lack of a functional basis, which he feels could be supplied by investing the series with the functions of a mode. Both, however, in spite of their widely differing points of view, agree that the system is

[27] *Theory of Evolving Tonality* (American Library of Musicology, 1932), p. 291.
[28] "Schoenberg's Tone Rows and the Tonal System of the Future," *Musical Quar-terly* (January, 1936).

composed of an undifferentiated aggregation of tones lacking all functional organization. In fact, the acceptance of all twelve tones as equal is in itself a contradiction of the varying degrees of relationship that exist among them. It is a purely arbitrary assumption, which the overtone series to which Schönberg refers does not confirm.

Whether these twelve tones can be organized into a system of functional modes, as Hill suggests, so that the lack of unified relationships can be compensated for by an artistic convention that will supply the present need of a constructive principle, is a question that the future alone can answer. The value of these techniques can be judged only by what they already have achieved.

A final consideration of atonal methods necessarily brings up the subject of dissonance and its growing supremacy through the new techniques.

DISSONANCE

The substitution of the twelve-tone system for the tonal concept has deprived dissonance of its natural concomitant — consonance. This is due primarily to the acceptance of all twelve tones as of equal status, to the recognition of all foreign tones as organic chord tones, and to the rejection of the harmonic for the purely contrapuntal approach.

In the older system, the use of both consonance and dissonance, with the differentiated functions they exercised, was not merely a convention, a heritage from the past. It rested on a fundamental law of variation that is not limited to music or any other form of art, but is the essence of life itself, which seeks relief from monotony.

Consonance, originating in the close association that exists among certain tones, was expressed through the combination of those tones in a triad. The horizontalization of the triad became the symbol of structural unity — tonality. Dissonance, achieved in the contrapuntal voice leadings that prolonged the structural motion, created tension and suspense, the richness and variety that stimulated the emotional interest. Consonance and dissonance represented component parts of a system in which the harmonic and contrapuntal principles function both independently and in combination to preserve the coherence of a musical idea while enriching the possibilities for variety and contrast in the treatment.

In rejecting the harmonic in favor of a purely contrapuntal technique, Schönberg reverts to the stylistic idiom of the fifteenth and sixteenth century. He does not, however, adhere to the principles of voice leading enunciated in the works of that period. A study of these compositions reveals that the striking dissonances that do result from the independence of the melodic lines are nevertheless dependent for their existence on consonances that precede and follow. Therefore, even before the harmonic principle had been established, consonance and dissonance had clearly defined functions.

Similarly the works of Bach, to which Schönberg so frequently refers to prove the truth of his own theories, demonstrate that the fundamental principles of voice leading, as they apply to consonance and dissonance, have been retained. It is true that Bach's use of dissonance is extraordinary. Yet it is equally true, as we have seen in an examination of his technique, that these dissonances are the result of contrapuntal devices in the form of passing tones, appoggiaturas, suspensions, retardations, and passing and neighbor chords, all of which acknowledge their dependence on the consonant tones or chords that outline the space within which they occur.

What, then, is the function of dissonance in the twelve-tone series? Krenek answers this question. He says [29] in effect that the nature of an interval is determined by the degree of tension expressed by the chords that precede or follow. If they show a higher tension, it becomes a "mild" dissonance by comparison; inversely, if they show a lower tension, it becomes a "sharp" dissonance. Thus, as Krenek admits: "Atonality has neither rules for a special treatment of dissonances nor does it formulate a harmonic theory comparable with that of tonality." [30]

It is clear from such statements and from Hill's equally frank admissions, that at the present time the atonal system is not based on a structural or functional principle demonstrating a type of coherence for the twelve-tone technique that the harmonic and contrapuntal principles demonstrate in tonality. However, since the new system is in its infancy, it is possible that in the various stages of development through which it may pass, a strong functional principle of its own may emerge.

The reader may question why we have restricted our discussion of Schönberg's later period to a single illustration of his new theoretical approach rather than attempting to analyze various works in which the theories are demonstrated. First of all, some of these works have been analyzed by composers well versed in the technique, whose personal experience is of greater value than any interpretation that could be offered by

[29] *Studies in Counterpoint* (G. Schirmer, 1940), p. 7.   [30] *Ibid.*, p. 19.

the author. In most instances, however, the explanation is based on the same descriptive method that is used to interpret works of a tonal character. It is concerned in one case with naming a chord; in the other, with indicating the motive groups of the series. Both describe the techniques, one in terms of harmony, the other according to counterpoint. Neither, however, demonstrates the function of the chord or motive, nor indicates how the technique attains and preserves the essential elements that symbolize either the tonal or atonal concepts. Secondly, to have shown how Schönberg applied the techniques of inversion, crab, and the inversion of crab to the original form of the series would indicate the concrete means he used, but would not reveal what the devices achieve. In a similar fashion, to point to the use of inversion, augmentation, diminution, and stretto in a Bach fugue, does not clarify the function of these techniques as a means either of outlining or of prolonging the structural motion; it merely accounts for the different contrapuntal devices that have been employed.

Since this method fails to unfold the meaning of these techniques when applied to the tonal system, why should we regard a similar description of them as an adequate explanation of the meaning of a Schönberg work within the twelve-tone system? If the only significance of a work lies in the mechanical devices a composer has used, then the genuine creative urge, of which techniques are only a manifestation, is lacking. If, however, as Schönberg would have us believe, the series is a means of communicating a genuine emotional impulse, then we must find a better method of interpreting its meaning than the present system of analysis provides. We should evolve a method of analysis that not only describes the techniques, but actually explains what is taking place in the music. In view of the fact that the system lacks a functional principle, it is unlikely that any method could offer a concrete analysis of the music, but could only provide a different means of demonstrating the various purposes the primary series serves in the adaptations that follow.

This is undeniably the weak point in the twelve-tone system — that through the acceptance of the equality of the tones it denies them the individual functional rights necessary to the establishment of a structural principle. Whether, as Hill suggests, this principle will be established by means of a functional mode is a matter that the future will decide. At the present time, it is obvious the system has not compensated for its negation of the harmonic and contrapuntal functions by evolving a principle that is as indigenous to the series as the principle of coherence is to tonality.

The foregoing expositions of the weaknesses of the atonal and polytonal systems should not be interpreted as a plea for a return to tonality. As every step in the development of music reflects the changes in the mental and spiritual outlook of its own period, it is inevitable that the twentieth century, with its spiritual, political, economic, and physical conflicts, should leave an equally strong imprint upon contemporary music. It is not the impact of these extra-musical factors on tonality that engenders this discussion. It is rather that the systems in which present-day composers have given expression to these extra-musical factors are so weak and emasculated by strong contrast with the older system they seek to replace.

We believe, with Constant Lambert, that a musical norm exists as part of our biological and psychological heritage. It has nothing to do with conventions, rules, styles, or personal prejudices. It is based on a recognition of unity, in the form of organic oneness, as a principle essential to every form of creative art. This ideal motivates every human aspiration and the democratic way of life. In music, organic oneness has been represented by the tonal concept, which has endured because the very boundaries that it has imposed have offered an artistic challenge to the imagination and technical prowess of composers for over two hundred years. It has established a way of hearing which, based on a fundamental association, is the closest approach to musical unity that we have discovered. It constitutes an artistic principle by which variety in multiple forms can be achieved without sacrificing the clarity of the musical concept.

If we are to reject this way of hearing for a new one, the substitute must offer a type of coherence that may be different, but must nevertheless satisfy our needs. The value of any system depends on what it offers as an aesthetic, intellectual, and emotional stimulus. It depends, not on the assimilative capacity of the ear, but on its own power to express clearly and in comprehensible terms the unfolding of a single musical idea.

In applying the principles of structural coherence to works of the past two hundred and fifty years, we have covered the rise and decline of the tonal era. Although no one composer was responsible either for its beginning or its end, Bach, the first composer to explore its possibilities thoroughly, serves as the starting point of our discussion, as Schönberg, the first to experiment with and systematize the twelve-tone techniques, provides the concluding chapter. They represent the beginning and the end of a great period in the history of music. Each is a challenger of tradition — Bach through his affirmation of tonality and Schönberg through his rejection of it. Both are innovators, but the results only of Bach's contribution can be estimated, since its value has been proved as the foundation of all later developments within the tonal concept.

This book offers no plea for a return to the musical values embodied in the tonal system. That is the concern mainly of composers, who will use whatever system most adequately expresses their musical ideas and artistic convictions. It does, however, advance the belief that if composers reject the older principles of structure and prolongation, they should evolve new ones to replace them that are indigenous to the atonal and genuinely polytonal concepts. Furthermore, it contends that it is essential to understand the meaning of tonality as it is manifested in the music of Bach, Philipp Emanuel Bach, Haydn, and Beethoven, before we accept Schönberg's statement that it has failed; that we must first recognize the principles governing Bach's techniques before we are influenced by Schönberg's analysis of a chorale or by Mlle Boulanger's analogy between Bach's counterpoint and Stravinsky's.

Until we admit that we fully comprehend the techniques of the past and the different functions they fulfill, we are ill equipped to deal with the intricate problems presented by the atonal and the so-called bitonal techniques. Finally let us explode the theory that these systems are an outgrowth or development of tonality, for we must realize that the concepts underlying present-day techniques are totally divorced from the type of coherence demonstrated by tonality. Only in this way can we approach the music of both the past and the present with an open and unprejudiced mind and grant each the individual right to preserve its own integrity.

Such a course not only offers some present-day composers freer and less restricted opportunity to establish the new musical values and formulate the new principles that alone will clarify their systems, but it also opens the way to others who, understanding the true meaning of tonality, believe that it still has a vital part to play in twentieth-century music.

Sources Consulted

BACH, JOHANN SEBASTIAN

Boughton, Rutland: *Bach, The Master.* New York: Harper and Brothers, 1930.

Bruyck, Carl van: *Technische und Ästhetische Analysen des wohltemperirten Klaviers.* Leipzig: Verlag von Breitkopf und Härtel, 1889.

Forkel, Johann Nikolaus: *Johann Sebastian Bach.* Translated by Charles Sanford Terry. London: Constable and Co., Ltd., 1920.

Gray, Cecil: *The Forty-eight Preludes and Fugues of J. S. Bach.* London: Oxford University Press, 1933.

Kurth, Ernst: *Grundlagen des Linearen Kontrapunkts.* Berlin: Max Hesses Verlag, 1922.

Parry, C. Hubert H.: *Johann Sebastian Bach.* New York: G. P. Putnam's Sons, 1909.

Pirro, A. G. E.: *Johann Sebastian Bach.* Translated by Goodrich. New York: G. P. Putnam's Sons, 1909.

Riemann, Hugo: *Analysis of J. S. Bach's Wohltemperirtes Clavier.* Translated by J. S. Shedlock. London: Augener Ltd., 1914.

Schenker, Heinrich: *Der Tonwille.* Heft I, 1921; Heft I, 1922; Heft V, 1923, Wien.

Schenker, Heinrich: *Das Meisterwerk in der Musik.* Wien: Drei Masken Verlag, 1925.

Schweitzer, Albert: *J. S. Bach.* English translation by Ernest Newman. London: A. & C. Black, 1923.

Spitta, Philipp: *The Life of J. S. Bach.* Translated by Clara Bell and J. A. Fuller Maitland. London: Novello and Company, 1899.

Taylor, Stainton de B.: *The Chorale Preludes of J. S. Bach.* London: Oxford University Press, 1942.

Terry, Charles Sanford: *J. S. Bach, A Biography.* London: Oxford University Press, 1928.

Terry, Charles Sanford: *The Music of Bach: An Introduction.* London: Oxford University Press, 1933.

Terry, Charles Sanford: *Bach, The Cantatas and Oratorios.* London: Oxford University Press, 1925.

Terry, Charles Sanford: *The Music of Bach.* London: Oxford University Press, 1933.

Sources Consulted

Terry, Charles Sanford: *Bach: The Historical Approach*. London: Oxford University Press, 1930.

BACH, PHILIPP EMANUEL

Bach, K. P. E.: *Versuch über die wahre Art das Klavier zu spielen*, 1759. Leipzig: C. F. Kahnt, 1925.

Hullah, John: *The Transition Period of Musical History*. London: Longmans, Green & Co., 1876.

Oxford History of Music. Edited by J. A. Fuller-Maitland. Age of Bach and Händel. London: Oxford University Press, 1931.

Schenker, Heinrich: *Ein Beitrag zur Ornamentik*. Universal-Edition, 1908.

Schmid, Ernst Fritz: *Carl Philipp Emanuel Bach und seine Kammermusik*. Kassel Bärenreiter-Verlag, 1931.

Vrieslander, Otto: *Carl Philipp Emanuel Bach als Theoretiker. Von Neuer Musik*, J. F. Marcan-Verlag, Köln, 1925.

HAYDN

Brenet, Michel: *Haydn*. Translated by C. Leonard Leese. London: Oxford University Press, 1926.

Cowen, Frederic: *Haydn*. New York: Stokes, 1912.

Fox, D. G. A.: *Joseph Haydn*. Musical Pilgrim. London: Oxford University Press, 1929.

Geiringer, Karl: *Joseph Haydn*. Potsdam: Akademische Verlagsgesellschaft Athenaion, 1932.

Haddon, J. C.: *Haydn*. London: Oxford University Press, 1926.

Hadow, William H.: *A Croatian Composer*. London: Seeley & Co., 1897.

Mason, Daniel Gregory: *Beethoven and His Forerunners*. New York: Macmillan Co., 1927.

Nef, Karl: *An Outline of the History of Music*. Translated by Carl F. Pfatteicher. New York: Columbia University Press, 1935.

Nohl, Ludwig: *Die Geschichtliche Entwickelung der Kammermusik*. Verlag von Vieweg und Sohn, 1885.

Nohl, Ludwig: *Life of Haydn*. Translated by G. P. Upton. Chicago: Jansen, McClurg & Co., 1883.

Parry, C. Hubert H.: *Style in Musical Art*. London: Macmillan & Co. Ltd., 1911.

Pohl, C. F.: *Joseph Haydn*. Leipzig: Verlag von Breitkopf und Härtel, 1878.

Schenker, Heinrich: *Haydn. Der Tonwille.* Heft III, 1922; Heft IV, 1923; Wien: Flügblatter Verlag.

BEETHOVEN

Beethoven Number, *Musical Quarterly.* New York: G. Schirmer, April, 1927.

Bekker, Paul: *Beethoven.* Translated and adapted by M. M. Bozman. London: J. M. Dent & Sons, Ltd., 1925.

Blom, Eric: *Beethoven's Pianoforte Sonatas.* London: J. M. Dent & Sons, Ltd., 1938.

Evans, Edwin: *Beethoven's Symphonies.* London: William Reeves, Ltd., 1923.

Fiske, Roger: *Beethoven's Last Quartets.* London: Musical Pilgrim, Oxford University Press, 1940.

Gottschald, Ernst: *Beethoven's Pianoforte Sonatas.* Translated by Emily Hill. London: William Reeves, Ltd., 1903.

Grove, George: *Beethoven and his Nine Symphonies.* London: Novello & Co. Ltd., 1896.

Hadow, William H.: *Beethoven's Opus 18 Quartets.* London: Musical Pilgrim, Oxford University Press, 1926.

Hadow, William H.: *Collected Essays.* London: Oxford University Press, 1928.

Halm, August: *Beethoven.* Berlin: M. Hesses Verlag, 1927.

Helm, Theodor: *Beethoven's Streichquartette.* Leipzig: C. F. W. Siegels Musikalienhandlung, 1910.

Kastner, Rudolf: *Beethoven's Sonatas and Artur Schnabel.* Translated by G. Abraham. London: William Reeves, Ltd., 1935.

Lenz, Wilhelm von: *Beethoven et ses trois styles.* Paris: G. Legouix, 1909.

Marliave, Joseph de: *Beethoven's Quartets.* Translated by Hilda Andrews. London: Oxford University Press, 1928.

Marx, Adolf Bernhard: *Anleitung zum Vortrag Beethovenscher Klavierwerke.* Berlin: Verlag von Otto Janke, 1898.

Marx, Adolf Bernhard: *Ludwig van Beethoven, Leben und Schaffen.* Berlin: Verlag von Otto Janke, 1875.

Meyer, Hans: *Linie und Form.* Leipzig: C. F. Kahnt, 1930.

Mies, Paul: *Beethoven's Sketches.* Translated by Doris L. Mackinnon. London: Oxford University Press, 1929.

Sources Consulted

Milne, A. Forbes: *Beethoven's Pianoforte Sonatas I–II*. Musical Pilgrim. Oxford University Press, 1928, 1933.

Nagel, Wilibald: *Beethoven und seine Klaviersonaten*. Langensalze: H. Beyer und Söhne, 1903–05.

Newman, Ernest: *The Unconscious Beethoven*. New York: Alfred A. Knopf, 1927.

Riemann, Hugo: *Beethovens Sämmtliche Klavier Solo sonaten*. Berlin: M. Hesse, 1919–20.

Riezler, Walter: *Beethoven*. Translated by G. D. H. Pidcock. New York: E. P. Dutton, 1938.

Rolland, Romain: *Beethoven the Creator*. New York: Harper and Brothers, 1929.

Schauffler, Robert Haven: *Beethoven, the Man Who Freed Music*. New York: Doubleday, Doran & Co., 1929.

Schenker, Heinrich: *Das Meisterwerk in der Musik*. Band III. München: Drei Masken Verlag, 1930.

Schenker, Heinrich: *Beethovens Neunte Sinfonie*. Wien: Verlag der Universal-Edition, 1912.

Shedlock, John S.: *Beethoven's Pianoforte Sonatas*. London: Augener Ltd., 1918.

Sullivan, J. W. N.: *Beethoven, His Spiritual Development*. New York: Alfred A. Knopf, 1927.

Thayer, Alexander Wheelock: *Life of Beethoven*. New York: Beethoven Association, 1921.

Tovey, Donald Francis: *A Companion to Beethoven's Pianoforte Sonatas*. London: Associated Board of The Royal Schools of Music, 1935.

Turner, Walter J.: *Beethoven, the Search for Reality*. London: E. Benn Ltd., 1927.

Wagner, Richard: *Beethoven*. Translated by Albert R. Parsons. Indianapolis: Benham Bros., 1873.

Weingarten, Felix: *On the Performance of Beethoven's Symphonies*. Translated by Jessie Crosland. Leipzig: Breitkopf und Härtel, 1907.

WAGNER

Barzum, Jacques: *Darwin, Marx, Wagner*. Boston: Little, Brown & Co., 1941.

Bekker, Paul: *Richard Wagner*. Translated by M. M. Bozman. W. W. Norton & Co., 1931.

401

Brink, Louise: *Women Characters in Richard Wagner.* New York: Nervous and Mental Disease Publishing Co., 1924.

Chamberlain, H. S.: *Richard Wagner.* Translated by G. A. Hight. London: J. M. Dent & Sons, Ltd., 1900.

Cleather and Crump: *Ring of the Nibelung.* New York: G. Schirmer, 1903.

Dannreuter, Edward: *Wagner and the Reform of the Opera.* London: Augener & Co., 1904.

Dickenson, A. E. F.: *Musical Design of the Ring.* Musical Pilgrim. Oxford University Press, 1926.

du Moulin-Eckart, Richard: *Cosima Wagner.* Translated by Catherine Alison Phillips. New York: Alfred A. Knopf, 1930.

Glasenapp, C. F.: *Life of Richard Wagner.* Translated by W. A. Ellis. Kegan Paul, Trench, Trubner & Co., Ltd., 1900.

Hight, G. A.: *Richard Wagner.* London: Arrowsmith, 1925.

Kapp, Julius: *The Women in Wagner's Life.* Translated by Hannah Waller. New York: Alfred A. Knopf, 1931.

Kobbé, Gustave: *Wagner's Life and Works.* New York: G. Schirmer, 1896.

Krebhiel, H. E.: *Studies in the Wagnerian Drama.* New York: Harper & Brothers, 1891.

Lavignac, Albert: *Music Dramas of Richard Wagner.* Translated by Esther Singleton. New York: Dodd, Mead & Co., 1902.

Leroy, L. Archier: *Wagner's Music Drama of the Ring.* London: Noel Douglas, 1925.

Letters of Richard Wagner to Anton Pusinelli. Translated by Elbert Lenrow. New York: Alfred A. Knopf, 1932.

Letters of Hans von Bülow. Edited by du Moulin-Eckart. Translated by Hannah Waller. New York: Alfred A. Knopf, 1931.

Lorenz, Alfred: *Das Geheimnis der Form bei Richard Wagner.* Berlin: Max Hesse, 1924.

Mann, Thomas: *Freud, Goethe, Wagner.* New York: Alfred A. Knopf, 1937.

Newman, Ernest: *A Study of Wagner.* New York: G. P. Putnam's Sons, 1899.

Newman, Ernest, *The Life of Richard Wagner.* New York: Alfred A. Knopf, 1933, 1937, 1941.

Newman, Ernest: *Wagner as Man and Artist.* New York: Alfred A. Knopf, 1924.

Sources Consulted

Nietzsche, Friedrich: *Birth of Tragedy*. Translated by William A. Hauss-mann. London: T. N. Foulis Ltd., 1923.

Nietzsche, Friedrich: *The Case of Wagner*. Translated by J. M. Kennedy. London: T. N. Foulis Ltd., 1911.

Nietzsche-Wagner Correspondence. Edited by Elizàbeth Foerster-Nie-tzsche. Translated by Caroline V. Kerr. New York: Boni & Liveright, 1921.

Peterson-Berger, Wilhelm: *The Life Problem in Wagner's Dramas*. New York. Musical Quarterly, October, 1916. G. Schirmer.

Wagner, Richard: *Gesammelte Schriften*. Leipzig: Verlag von C. W. Fretzsch, 1887.

Wagner, Richard: *My Life*. New York: Dodd Mead & Co., 1924.

Wagner, Richard: *Prose Works*. Translated by William Ashton Ellis. Lon-don: Kegan Paul, Trench, Trubner & Co., Ltd., 1895.

Wagner, Richard: *Letters to Mathilde Wesendonck*. Translated by Wil-liam Ashton Ellis. London: H. Grevel, 1911.

DEBUSSY

Bauer, Marion: *Twentieth Century Music*. New York: G. P. Putnam's Sons, 1933.

Boulanger, Nadia: *Debussy: The Preludes*. Houston, Texas: The Rice In-stitute Pamphlet, April, 1926.

Calvorcoressi, M. D.: *Claude Debussy*. Musical Times, London, 1908. Vol. 49, No. 780.

Daly, William H.: *A Study in Modern Music*. Edinburgh: Methuen, Simp-son Ltd., 1908.

Debussy, Claude: *Monsieur Creche*. New York: The Viking Press, 1928.

Dyson, George: *The New Music*. London: Oxford University Press, 1923.

Gatti, Guido: *The Piano Works of Claude Debussy*. New York: Musical Quarterly, 1921, G. Schirmer.

Gilman, Lawrence: *Debussy's Pelléas and Mélisande*. New York: G. Schirmer, 1907.

Gray, Cecil: *A Survey of Contemporary Music*. London: Oxford Univer-sity Press, 1924.

Heyman, Katherine Ruth: *The Relation of Ultra-modern to Archaic Music*. Boston: Small, Maynard & Co., 1921.

Hill, Edward B.: *Modern French Music*. New York: Houghton, Mifflin & Co., 1924.

Challenge to Musical Tradition

Jean-Aubry: *Debussy*. New York: Musical Quarterly, October, 1918. G. Schirmer.

Lenormand, Réne: *A Study of Modern Harmony*. Translated by H. Antcliffe. Boston: B. F. Wood Music Co., 1915.

Lockspeiser, Edward: *Debussy*. London: J. M. Dent & Sons, Ltd., 1936.

Miller, Horace A.: *New Harmonic Devices*. Boston: Oliver Ditson, 1930.

Rosenfeld, Paul: *Musical Portraits*. New York: Harcourt, Brace and Howe, 1920.

Shera, Frank: *Debussy and Ravel*. London: Musical Pilgrim, Oxford University Press, 1938.

Thompson, Oscar: *Debussy, Man and Artist*. New York: Dodd, Mead & Co., 1937.

Vallas, Léon: *Claude Debussy*. Translated by Maire and Grace O'Brien. London: Oxford University Press, 1933.

Vallas, Léon: *Theories of Claude Debussy*. Translated by Maire O'Brien. London: Oxford University Press, 1929.

STRAVINSKY

Babitz, Sol: *Stravinsky's Symphony in C*. New York: Musical Quarterly, January, 1941. G. Schirmer.

Bauer, Marion: *Twentieth Century Music*. New York: G. P. Putnam's Sons, 1933.

Belaiev, Victor: *Igor Stravinsky's "Les Noces."* London: Oxford University Press, 1928.

Blitzstein, Marc: *The Phenomenon of Stravinsky*. New York: Musical Quarterly, July, 1935. G. Schirmer.

Boulanger, Nadia: *Stravinsky*. Houston, Texas: Rice Institute Pamphlet, April, 1926.

Coeuroy, André: *Oedipus and Other Music*. New York: Modern Music, November–December, 1927.

Copland, Aaron: *Our New Music*. New York: Whittlesey House, 1941.

Evans, Edwin: *Stravinsky*. London: Musical Pilgrim, 1933. Oxford University Press.

Ewen, David: *From Bach to Stravinsky*. New York: W. W. Norton, 1933.

Fleischer, Herbert: *Stravinsky*. Russischer Musik Verlag, 1931.

Gray, Cecil: *Survey of Contemporary Music*. London: Oxford University Press, 1927.

Sources Consulted

Kall, Alexis: *Stravinsky in the Chair of Poetry.* New York: Musical Quarterly, July, 1940. G. Schirmer.

Lambert, Constant: *Music Ho!* New York: Charles Scribner's Sons, 1935.

Mersmann, Hans: *Die Moderne Musik.* Akademische Verlagsgesellschaft Athenaion, 1929.

Montague-Nathan, M.: *Contemporary Russian Composers.* London: C. Palmer and Hayward, 1917.

Rosenfeld, Paul: *By Way of Art.* New York: Coward-McCann Inc., 1928.

Rosenfeld, Paul: *Musical Chronicle.* New York: Harcourt, Brace & Co., 1923.

Rosenfeld, Paul: *Musical Portraits.* New York: Harcourt, Brace and Howe, 1920.

Schaeffner, André: *On Stravinsky, Early and Late.* Modern Music, November–December, 1934. New York.

de Schloezer, Boris: *Igor. Stravinsky.* Von Neuer Musik. Köln: F. J. Marcan-Verlag, 1925.

de Schloezer, Boris: *The Enigma of Stravinsky.* Modern Music, November–December, 1932. New York.

Stravinsky, Igor: *Chronicles of My Life.* New York: Simon and Schuster, 1936.

White, Eric Walter: *Stravinsky's Sacrifice to Apollo.* London: L. & V. Woolf, 1930.

SCHÖNBERG

Armitage, Merle: *Arnold Schoenberg.* G. Schirmer, 1937.

Citkowitz, Israel: *Schönberg's Suite for Orchestra.* Modern Music, November–December, 1935. New York.

Engel, Carl: *Discords Mingled.* New York: Alfred A. Knopf, 1931.

Gray, Cecil: *Schönberg.* Music and Letters, London, 1922. Vol. III, No. 1.

Gray, Cecil: *Survey of Contemporary Music.* London: Oxford University Press, 1927.

Hill, Richard S.: *Schoenberg's Tone-Rows and the Tonal System of the Future.* New York: Musical Quarterly, January, 1936. G. Schirmer.

Kilenyi, Edward: *Arnold Schönberg's Harmony.* New York: New Musical Review, Vol. XIV, 1915.

Krenek, Ernst: *Music Here and Now.* New York: W. W. Norton & Co., 1939.

Krenek, Ernst: *Studies in Counterpoint.* New York: G. Schirmer, 1940.

Leichtentritt, Hugo: *Schönberg and Tonality.* New York: *Modern Music,* May–June, 1928. New York.

Linden, R. Cort van den: *Schönberg.* London: Music and Letters, Vol. VII, 1926.

Mersmann, Hans: *Die Moderne Musik.* Akademische Verlagsgesellschaft Athenaion, 1929.

Pannain, Guido: *Modern Composers.* New York: E. P. Dutton, 1933.

Perle, George: *Evolution of the Tone Row.* London: The Music Review, November, 1941.

Reich, Willi: *Schönberg's New Männer Chor.* Modern Music, January–February, 1932. New York.

Schönberg, Arnold: *Harmonielehre.* Wien: Universal-Edition, 1922.

Schoenberg, Arnold: *Models for Beginners in Composition.* New York: G. Schirmer, 1943.

Schönberg, Arnold: *Problems of Harmony.* Modern Music, May–June, 1934. New York.

Stein, Erwin: *Neue Formprinzipien. Von Neuer Musik.* Köln: J. F. Marcan-Verlag, 1925.

Stein, Erwin: *Schönberg's New Structural Form.* Modern Music, June–July, 1930. New York.

Weiss, Adolph: *The Lyceum of Schönberg.* Modern Music, March–April, 1932. New York.

Weissman, Adolf: *Problems of Modern Music.* New York: E. P. Dutton & Co., 1925.

Wellesz, Egon: *Arnold Schönberg.* New York: E. P. Dutton & Co., 1925.

GENERAL SOURCES

Abraham, Gerald: *This Modern Stuff.* London: Search Publications, 1933.

Andrews, Hilda: *Modern Harmony.* London: Oxford University Press, 1934.

Blom, Eric: *Limitations of Music.* London: Macmillan & Co. Ltd., 1928.

Copland, Aaron: *Our New Music.* New York: Whittlesey House, 1941.

Cowell, Henry: *New Musical Resources.* New York: Alfred A. Knopf, 1930.

Ewen, David: *From Bach to Stravinsky.* New York: W. W. Norton, 1933.

Gantvort, Arnold J.: *Familiar Talks on the History of Music.* New York: G. Schirmer, 1913.

Sources Consulted

Grabner, Hermann: *Allgemeine Musiklehre*. Stuttgart: Ernst Klett Verlag, 1930.

Grimm, Carl W.: *Simple Method of Modern Harmony*. Cincinnati: George B. Jennings Co., 1900.

Grove, George: *Dictionary of Music and Musicians*. Philadelphia: Theodore Presser Co., 1927.

Hindemith, Paul: *Craft of Musical Composition*. Associated Music Publishers, 1941–42.

Hull, A. Eaglefield: *Modern Harmony*. London: Augener Ltd., 1914.

International Cyclopedia of Music and Musicians, edited by Oscar Thompson. New York: Dodd, Mead & Co., 1939.

Jeans, James: *Science and Music*. New York: Macmillan Co., 1938.

Jepperson, Knud: *Counterpoint*. New York: Prentice-Hall Inc., 1939.

Jonas, Oswald: *Das Wesen des Musikalischen Kunstwerks*. Wien: Im Saturn-Verlag, 1934.

Kurth, Ernst: *Die Voraussetzungen der theoretischen Harmonik*. Berne: M. Dreschel, 1931.

Láng, Paul: *Music in Western Civilization*. New York: W. W. Norton Co., 1941.

Leichtentritt, Hugo: *Music, History and Ideas*. Cambridge: Harvard University Press, 1938.

Myers, Rollo H.: *Modern Music, Its Aims and Tendencies*. London: Kegan Paul, Trench, Trubner & Co., Ltd., 1923.

Pisk, Paul: *End of the Tonal Era*. Modern Music, March–April, 1926. New York.

Piston, Walter: *Harmonic Analysis*. Boston: E. C. Schirmer Music Co., 1933.

Piston, Walter: *Harmony*. New York: W. W. Norton Co., 1941.

Pole, W.: *The Philosophy of Music*. London: Kegan Paul, Trench, Trubner & Co., Ltd., 1924.

Potter, Arthur G.: *Modern Chords Explained*. London: W. Reeves, 1910.

Pratt, Carroll: *The Meaning of Music*. New York: McGraw-Hill Co., 1931.

Redfield, John: *Music a Science and an Art*. New York: Alfred A. Knopf, 1928.

Schenker, Heinrich: *Neue Musikalische Theorien und Phantasien; Harmonielehre. Kontrapunkt. Der Freie Satz*. Wien: Universal-Edition.

Schoen, Max: *The Effects of Music*. New York: Harcourt, Brace & Co. Inc., 1927.

Scott, Cyril: *The Philosophy of Modernism*. London: Kegan Paul, Trench, Trubner & Co., Ltd., n.d.

Shirlaw, Matthew: *Theory of Harmony*. London: Novello & Co. Ltd., 1917.

Thomson, Virgil: *The State of Music*. New York: William Morrow & Co., 1939.

Trotter, T. Yorke: *Music and Mind*. London: Methuen & Co. Ltd., n.d.

Turner, W. J.: *Orpheus; the Music of the Future*. London: Kegan Paul, Trench, Trubner & Co., Ltd., 1926.

Yasser, Joseph: *A Theory of Evolving Tonality*. American Library of Musicology, 1934.